SAVAGE SISTERS

It was a tough enough assignment to have to travel the rugged, dangerous trail from Lubbock to New Mexico, but Spur had to do it saddled with a wagon-load of nuns and a whiskey priest. To top it off, the Mescalero Apaches were on the warpath. When the promised Army patrol was unavailable at Camp Houston, Spur had to rely on his beautiful half-breed guide and his rifle to get them safely to their destination.

HANG SPUR McCOY

Left for dead by a band of outlaws after trying to save a family of homesteaders, Spur was discovered and taken to the sheriff of Twin Falls County. But instead of praise, Spur was greeted with a loaded six-gun—the townspeople thought he was one of the killers. Before he could defend himself he was almost strung up by a rowdy lynch mob. If Spur survived, he would see to it that each of his executioners suffered a death worse than hanging.

Other books in the SPUR series:

ROCKY MOUNTAIN VAMP
CATHOUSE KITTEN
INDIAN MAID
SAN FRANCISCO STRUMPET
WYOMING WENCH
TEXAS TART
MONTANA MINX
SANTA FE FLOOZY
SALT LAKE LADY
NEVADA HUSSY
NEBRASKA NYMPH
GOLD TRAIN TRAMP
RED ROCK REDHEAD
SALOON GIRL
MISSOURI MADAM
HELENA HELLION
COLORADO CUTIE
TEXAS TEASE
DAKOTA DOXY
SAN DIEGO SIRENS
SPUR ANNIVERSARY SPECIAL:
    PHOENIX FILLY/DODGE CITY DOLL
LARAMIE LOVERS
SPUR DOUBLE EDITION: GOLD
    TRAIN TRAMP/RED ROCK REDHEAD
BODIE BEAUTIES
FRISCO FOXES

SPUR DOUBLE EDITION

SAVAGE SISTERS

HANG SPUR McCOY

Dirk Fletcher

LEISURE BOOKS   NEW YORK CITY

A LEISURE BOOK

Published by

Dorchester Publishing Co., Inc.
276 Fifth Avenue
New York, NY 10001

Printed in the United States of America

SAVAGE
SISTERS

ONE

Spur McCoy lay back on the soft bed in the Hotel Texas and relaxed, an unopened telegram in his hand. He'd been on a jolting, bouncing, hard-seated stagecoach for the last five days getting to Lubbock, Texas and now he was going to take it easy for a few hours. The matchbox sized room was not the fanciest he had ever seen—maybe eight by ten feet with a bed, one chair, a washstand with the usual heavy porcelain bowl and rose painted porcelain pitcher full of water. The dresser had two drawers and a wavy mirror. A kerosene lamp sat on top and a packet of *stinker* matches lay close at hand.

The walls were painted plaster over lath. He could tell by the uneven surface. One of the walls had been covered with flowered wallpaper to brighten up the room. It would have helped if the pattern had matched from one section to the other. It wasn't a palace, but it was home for a couple of days.

McCoy was a big man at six-two and two

hundred pounds. He was tanned a light brown and his windblown brown hair had a reddish cast in certain lights. Mutton chop sideburns met his full, reddish moustache. He stared at the world from slightly jaded green eyes that had seen more than their share of outlaws, raiders and killers.

Now he looked at the telegram again and put it down. No sense in reading it until after supper. It was his new assignment and he wanted to put off knowing what it was for a while. He had hit town on the noon stage, had an hour long bath and then taken a nap on a real bed with springs! Now he should be getting dressed for supper.

Yes! He would dress up for supper. It had been a long time since he had even thought of wearing a tie. It would be more like the family suppers back in the New York City townhouse. That was longer ago than he cared to think about. But he would dress.

Lubbock, Texas was one hell of a long way from New York, and the rich, plush life he had left. But working in the big city business world of his father had not appealed to him.

He sat up and stared at the telegram still sealed in the envelope.

He should open it. The general said his assignment details would be waiting for him when he got to Lubbock. He swung his feet off the bed and dressed. The dark blue suit seemed right. Spur slipped into the pants, tucked in the tails of the ruffled front white shirt and added a black half-inch wide string tie. His belt notched in one hole tighter than usual. Too many days rattling around the prairie and deserts without enough to eat. He needed some good home cooking for a change.

Spur pulled on his suit coat and decided not to wear a vest. It felt good to get in his best suit, for a change. He had heard something about an acting troupe in town. Maybe he could catch their show tonight.

orders ... assignment ... damn ...

The yellow envelope lay there on the bed mocking him. He picked it up and tore it open. The yellow sheet fell out, he unfolded it and read:

SPUR McCOY:
HOTEL TEXAS
LUBBOCK, TEXAS

MEET ON JUNE 28 AT TEXAS RANCH HOUSE HOTEL IN LUB-BOCK WITH MOTHER SUPERIOR M. BENEDICT AND FATHER CLARK. YOU WILL GUIDE AND SHEPHERD THEM AND SIX NUNS, A COVERED WAGON AND VARIOUS RELIGIOUS GOODS, FROM LUBBOCK TO DEVIL WELLS, NEW MEXICO. THE TOWN IS ON THE RIO GRANDE ABOUT 140 MILES SOUTH OF SANTA FE. PICK UP TEN MAN ARMY ESCORT AT CAMP HOUSTON NEAR LUBBOCK. THEY HAVE BEEN NOTIFIED. RE-PORT BY QUICKEST MEANS WHEN ASSIGNMENT COMPLETED.

It was signed by General Wilton D. Halleck, Capitol Investigations, Washington, D.C.

Spur tossed the message on the bed and

snorted. He had to nursemaid seven nuns and a priest through some of the toughest, most hostile, most unforgiving country in the nation? And the damned Apaches were probably prowling again. Mescaleros over this far. Damn, he had tangled with them enough to last a lifetime! The Mescaleros were cunning, crafty and treacherous. They were warriors, looters and killers just for the pure hell of it!

He read the message again. Spur had no idea where it had been sent. There was no telegraph in Lubbock. It had come to the hotel several days ago on one of the regular runs in the stagecoach mail sack, the hotel clerk told him.

Devil Wells! That sounded about right. Somewhere in the middle of the desert, he expected. Seven women! Seven nuns and a priest! Just dandy!

At least he could have a drink before dinner. He found a small bar attached to the hotel and went in for a straight whiskey. He felt it burn all the way to his belly. This was not starting out to be a good evening.

He checked with the barkeep about the actors. He said the traveling troupe of thespians was in town and putting on the last performance that evening in the Lubbock Town Hall. Spur considered ordering another drink. He hadn't seen any good theatre for two years. He would go, alone or with someone, it didn't matter. Then maybe he would get a bottle of the best booze he could find and really tie one on before he met his religious charges.

He looked at the telegram again. Hell, it said June 28 he had to meet them. That was tomorrow! Not even time enough for a three day drunk. At least he could have dinner. He'd decide about the bottle later.

Hotel Texas had a good dining room. Many of the customers were from the town, not travelers. That was always a good sign of fine food. Maybe he could enjoy a delicious meal before he had to make any decisions.

The dining room along the main street side of the hotel was packed. Spur could not see a single free table. A waiter came forward and smiled.

"Sorry, we're a little bit busy right now." He paused, then looked at the far window. "But I see someone leaving. I'll have a table for two in just a moment." The young man hurried away and cleared the table then came back for Spur.

"Yes, right this way." He gave Spur the small, well printed menu. "Oh, since we're so full, would you mind sharing a table if another single person comes in?"

Spur lifted his brows, then smiled. "Only if the person is an attractive young lady."

The waiter grinned and moved away.

McCoy was surprised at the menu. It was quite good, with more than a dozen entrees and numerous side dishes. He felt the hand of an Eastern style management running the dining room. Before he had selected his choice for dinner, someone stopped near his table.

"Begging your pardon sir."

Spur looked up. It was the waiter and someone behind him.

"Sir, you said you would be willing to share your table?"

He stepped aside and the woman behind him

was young, attractive and smiling. She had startling blue eyes and soft, short blonde hair.

Spur stood quickly, grinning.

"Of course, any time. Miss, you're more than welcome. I haven't even ordered yet. Please, may I help you sit down?"

She smiled, her blue pools of eyes dancing.

"You sure you're not waiting for someone? I don't want to impose . . ."

"No, I'm quite alone. I hate to eat by myself. Please, sit down."

She closed her eyes and gave the hint of a nod, then slid gracefully into the chair he held and edged forward to the small table complete with place settings and a white linen tablecloth.

He sat across from her.

"Now, this is a pleasant surprise. My name is Spur McCoy."

She held out her small, white hand that had carefully cared-for nails. "I'm Teresa White. How do you do?"

He took her hand and she shook it strongly then let go.

The waiter opened a white linen napkin and laid it in her lap, then handed her a menu.

"Thank you," she said to the happy waiter.

There was an awkward pause.

Spur cleared his throat and she looked up at him. "I'm delighted you came. Eating alone in a strange town is always a little sad, lonely."

Teresa smiled, then read the menu and her eyes widened.

"Oh! There are so many choices! And all the dishes sound so delicious."

Spur felt himself relaxing. They talked about

the various entrees, and at last he selected the pound and a half steak and she had roast beef with horseradish. As they waited for the meal the waiter brought hot black coffee.

For the first time, Spur noticed that her face seemed softly white, not tanned and brownish like so many frontier women.

"I'm just passing through Lubbock," Spur said. "Are you a resident here?"

She shook her head. "No, some friends and I are going through as well. We'll leave in a day or two."

As the meal ended Spur could not remember what they had talked about. He did remember she had seemed better educated than most women he met on the job. She could play the piano and organ, and originally came from New Orleans.

When they stood, McCoy touched her arm. "There is a troupe of actors in town and I hear they are going to do some Shakespeare. Would you like to go see them with me?"

She hesitated. "No, I couldn't, I . . ." She turned away and he saw confusion on her pretty face. She turned back a moment later. "Well, I love Shakespeare and there are so few chances to see any. I would love to go, but I must get back to my hotel right after the performance."

He frowned.

"Goodness, I hope you don't think I'm being too forward," Teresa said.

"Not at all, no. I see no reason a woman can't do something she wants to. It will be my pleasure to be your escort."

He paid the bill and they walked to the desk.

The clerk told them where the performance was, two blocks down.

"Let's walk," she said.

The traveling troupe was about as Spur had expected. An older man and a woman he guessed was the actor's wife, and a younger man and woman made up the cast. They did scenes from Hamlet, Romeo and Juliet, and Henry the Fifth.

"Just average," Spur whispered during the intermission.

"No, I think they are quite good," Teresa said. "Especially the young Hamlet. He was convincing."

Then it was over and they moved slowly back toward the hotel. She held his arm as they made their way along the boardwalk and across the dust filled streets and soon they were on the second floor of Spur's hotel.

"Oh, I'm sorry," Teresa said. "I wasn't watching where we were. This isn't my hotel."

"You didn't say where you lived. My room is just down the hall. Would you like to stop by for a sip or two of wine?"

"Oh, no, I couldn't," she said quickly, looking up at him with surprise but no real alarm.

He kept walking. At his door he held her arm. "One small glass of wine and I'll rush you back to your hotel. It would be the culmination of a perfect evening with a beautiful lady."

Her smile came slowly, then blossomed. "Well, I don't see what it would hurt. It will round out a simply wonderful evening for me."

Spur unlocked the door and waved her inside. He left the door open a foot and went to the dresser where he had put the bottle of light port —for emergencies. He uncorked it and found two glasses on the washstand.

"Just a little," Teresa said.

He poured each glass half full and handed her one.

"It's a very light port," Spur said. "How do you like it?"

She sipped it, then again. She took a deep breath and her tongue wet her lips. "Yes. Yes, it is good!" She drank again and smiled. "Oh, my! That makes me feel just warm all over!" She sat down suddenly on the bed. "And a little light headed."

Spur sat beside her on the bed. "Are you all right?"

Teresa looked at him, her eyes soft and dreamy. "Oh, yes! I feel fine. It's just . . ." She handed him the glass, closed her eyes and slumped backwards on the bed.

Spur put both glasses on the floor and leaned over her.

"Teresa! Are you not feeling well?"

She smiled but did not open her eyes.

"Feel fine. Just a little warm . . . and, and wondering."

"Would a cold cloth on your forehead help?"

"No." She opened her eyes, caught his hand and kissed it. Then Teresa reached her hand behind his neck and pulled his face down to hers. She kissed him softly, then once again with more force. All at once she scooted away from him and stood up.

"I really do have to go. Mother would kill me if she knew."

Spur stood beside her.

"Do you actually have to go?" He bent and kissed her lips and then the side of her neck and the tip of her ear.

Her arms slid upward and around his neck.

"Spur McCoy, you don't know what that does to me. I absolutely forbid you to kiss me that way again!" But her words came softly and with a longing Spur had not heard in years.

She pulled his head down and he kissed her again. This time her mouth came open for his tongue and he probed deeply, drawing soft moans of pleasure from her. She pushed her hips hard against his, then her breasts pressed firmly to his chest and she held him tightly.

"Darling, marvelous Spur!" she said when their lips parted. "I must leave right now. You know that. I told you that. I can't let you do this to me." But she never let go of him. Her hips began a gentle grinding against his groin and Spur's crotch bulged with his instant erection. She nestled her head against his chest for a moment, then looked up at him, soft blue eyes wanting him.

"Kiss me again before I explode!" she said her voice ragged and breaking with the intensity of her desire.

He kissed her and this time her tongue dug into his open mouth, searching, battling with his tongue and her hips began a slow thrusting and pounding against his now obvious erection.

Spur picked her up and laid her on the bed. She wore a white blouse and light jacket, with a green skirt that brushed the floor. He leaned over looking down at her a moment, then moved to the door and closed it softly, locking it. He turned the key halfway in the lock so no other key could be used. Spur put the straight backed chair under the handle and braced on its rear feet to prevent a forced entry.

Back at the bed she watched him. She pushed the light jacket down her arms and took it off, then lay back on the quilts. Gently he kissed her again and her whole body curled toward him.

She held out her arms and he lay gently on top of her. His hard body crushed her into the mattress and she moaned again with pleasure. Teresa kissed him, then caught his hand and put it over one of her breasts. His hand lay there a moment, feeling the heat of her mound coming through the fabric, then he began soft circular motions and she gasped and smiled.

"Oh, yes, marvelous Spur! Never stop touching me there! Just so wonderful."

He kissed her again, then pushed off her and lifted her up so she sat beside him. Now her breasts pressed against the white blouse and he continued to fondle first one, then both.

He kissed her once more and she nibbled at his lips.

"Teresa. We can stop this any time you want to. If you say the word we will stand up right now and I'll walk you to your hotel . . ."

She smiled and kissed him, then her hand reached out and rubbed the long lump behind his pants fly.

"Wonderful Spur McCoy, it's all right. I'm here because I want to be here. It has been so long. Oh, God, it's been four years! You try to get away now after getting me so worked up this way, and I'll probably shoot you!"

He laughed and she began unbuttoning her blouse. The fasteners went to her chin. He helped and when he was halfway down, his hand slid inside the fabric and found more cloth over her breasts. He caught her mounds and teased her growing, throbbing nipples.

Quickly now she stripped out of the blouse and pulled a chemise off over her head.

Her big breasts swung out, pure white mounds with large pink areolas and her dark nipples throbbing and swolen to a half inch long.

He touched her breasts and she sighed, closed her eyes and reached for his crotch.

"Spur McCoy, I want you! I want you right now!"

TWO

Teresa remained sitting up as Spur lowered his head and kissed her breasts. She squealed in delight and erupted into a long climax that dropped her flat on the bed, her hips slamming upward in a series of jolts and her whole body shaking and vibrating as the tremors shook her again and again.

Spur had moved with her, his mouth covering one breast, chewing on the morsel, sucking the nipple until she at last gave a long sigh and leaned up on her elbows so she could see his mouth on her tit.

"Ooooooh, but that was beautiful, Spur McCoy! I've never been started out that way before. Such a monstrous feeling! So sharp and hard and . . . and wonderful."

"Oh, God!" she said almost as soon as she stopped talking. It was a cry of pain and anger and remorse. She pushed him away and sat at the end of the bed, her head down, her hands clasped in front of her. Teresa still wore her clothing from the waist down. Quiet sobs shook her body now and she turned to him, tears still coming down her cheeks, her eyes red and swollen, nose running.

"Spur McCoy, do you have a cigarette?"

"You smoke?" he asked, surprised. He did not know a woman who smoked in public. He had watched one or two who tried to smoke in private and gave it up. He shook his shirt pocket and came up with a long thin cheroot. The thin, black cigar had been bent in the wrestling match on the bed. He found a match, lit the thin cigar for her and passed it over.

"Never tried a cigar before," she said. "Are they strong?"

Spur said they were.

She puffed on it, then tried to inhale and went into a spate of coughing. She puffed it without inhaling and handed it back to him.

"Thanks. Now for some more of that wine."

They had more port, then she began undressing him. When she had him bare to the waist she played with the hair on his chest, then kissed his nipples, and looked up at him.

"Is that any good? Does it excite you at all?"

"No, it's not something I'm used to."

She rubbed the erection inside his pants.

"But you like that?"

McCoy nodded and stroked her breasts.

"Why does a woman keep her most beautiful part covered up and hidden away?"

"The customs of the people. In Africa breasts are not covered."

"I'm moving down there," Spur said.

She hit him on the shoulder. "Not before you finish the work you've started here."

She stood, and put his hands on her skirt. Spur lifted her back on the bed and hovered over her. He kissed both her breasts, then her mouth and rolled her on top of him. Slowly he pulled her up until her hanging twins dangled over his face.

"I want you really ready before we take off the rest of our clothes." He let her downward until her breasts lowered into his open mouth.

"Yes, yes! You know just what to do!" She purred.

He chewed each tit thoroughly then rolled again until he was on top of her.

Teresa panted now, her eyes wide, her skin flushed. He could feel the raw heat of her desire burning through her thighs against his. He ran his hand down her skirt, found his way under it and came up her leg.

She gasped, then stared at him for several seconds. At last she nodded and lay back, her mouth open, her eyes closed.

Quickly Spur unhooked the skirt and petti-coats and took them off. He started to pull down the knee length panty drawers as well, but her hands held the top of the soft white fabric of the drawers.

He kissed her hands away, then the hot string of kisses continued down from her waist as he pulled the cloth lower and lower.

She gasped again as his lips touched the top of her pubic hair.

As he worked down through the soft blonde crotch growth her hips heaved and Teresa shivered.

"Oh, yes! Oh, yes! Oh, yes!" she whispered to

herself. Her hands rubbed her breasts now, massaging them tenderly, her eyes closed, and she breathed like a blow torch through her mouth.

When Spur came to the soft pink lips he found them swollen, moist. He kissed them and she climaxed. A long low wail came from her mouth and he kissed the soft wetness again. It brought another racking series of spasms as she bounced and jolted and rolled half over before the tremors worked through her.

She lifted up, her eyes half closed, rapture on her face.

"Your turn, your turn," she said and crawled toward him on hands and knees. Eagerly she pulled off his pants and underwear, then sat there staring in amazement at his erection.

"So beautiful!" she shrilled. "Just absolutely wonderful!" She caught his phallus and stroked it, played with his heavy, hairy scrotum, then bent and kissed the purple head.

She kissed it again, then slowly her lips parted, she bent forward and sucked him into her mouth. She pulled half his long shaft down her throat, then began bouncing up and down on it.

Spur caught her shoulders and pushed her away.

"Teresa, that is fantastic, but not for the first time; later." He pushed her down on the bed and hovered over her.

"Yes, Spur McCoy, I want you inside me, right now. Do it before I go out of my mind! Please, now!"

She spread her legs, lifted her knees and Spur went between them, lowered and found the wetness. The natural lubricant lathered him as he drove into her in one strong surge and she squealed in delight.

They made it last for nearly an hour. Each time Spur surged toward his climax, she stopped him, kissed his cheek and began talking.

"Then there was this time in New Orleans when I was just three. My daddy came home and said he lost his job and we were going to have to move. So we moved in with our in-laws, my uncle. He was my dad's brother. It was just a three room house, and the six kids slept in one bedroom and the front room. The adults slept in the other bedrooms.

"They had a big double bed and the first night Dad and his brother decided they might as well share, so they swapped sides of the bed and made love with the other guy's wife. That lasted for about two months, then the women put their feet down and said no more, and so we moved again. Can you imagine that, everybody doing it with everybody else whenever they wanted to? The men loved it, but the women got worried about getting pregnant again."

When she stopped talking Spur lifted her legs to his shoulders and jolted into her. The new angle brought results quickly and he raced to a climax, just as Teresa exploded again and they nearly rolled off the bed before they both collapsed in a heavy sweat on the bed.

Somebody next door pounded the wall.

Teresa laughed.

Spur grinned. "Guess we should be a little more quiet next time."

She looked at him. "Next time?"

"Didn't your first lover tell you that once is never enough?"

Teresa giggled, stroked his chest, then pushed him off her and they lay side by side. "If he ever told me I was too excited to hear him. I was fifteen at the time. Had my tits full grown by then, and all the boys were playing *grab-tit* with me every chance they got. That first time when I lost my virginity was in a garden swing at my other uncle's house. I stayed with his wife while he was on a business trip to Atlanta."

Spur rolled out of bed and got the wine bottle and the two glasses.

They talked and drank wine until the bottle was empty, and made love twice again.

When Spur woke up the next time, it was daylight, and Teresa White had dressed and left. He had no idea when.

McCoy rinsed the old wine taste from his mouth, shaved and got dressed. It was a little after seven A.M. His meeting with the nuns was not until eight.

He had breakfast, walked around two blocks of Lubbock and decided they would be able to find the supplies they needed in town for the trip across the plains and desert to the Rio Grande. If they went. He hoped to talk the priest out of this journey. If they only had ten soldiers as a military escort, it would be a dangerous situation.

At five minutes to eight he walked up the steps to the Texas Ranch House Hotel, and asked the room clerk where he could find Mother Superior Benedict.

The clerk had on heavy glasses and a bow tie. He squinted through the spectacles and pointed.

"Right over there by the front window with the priest. Can't miss them."

Spur looked the way the man pointed. A nun wearing a wimple and long flowing black robes that brushed the floor stood looking out the window. Beside her slouched a slender, short man with thinning brown hair on a high forehead and a priest's white collar. It was time.

Spur walked up to the pair and held out his hand to the priest.

"Father Clark? My name is Spur McCoy."

The priest looked at him curiously for a moment, then a faint smile showed on his sallow face. He sniffed.

"Yes, Mr. McCoy, our guide and protector," the priest said taking the hand limply.

The nun turned and Spur saw the large white collar, the tight white front of the wimple that covered her hair and half her forehead revealing only a round, slightly tanned face with snapping brown eyes, a general nose and a no-nonsense set to her thin mouth.

"Mr. McCoy!" she said, the tone of her voice at once pleasant, friendly and neighborly. Here was a woman who insisted with two words that it would be hard to dislike her.

"We had hoped you would arrive on time from wherever you were. But enough of that, you're here now and we can get down to business." She paused and looked at him.

"Yes, you are certainly big enough for the job. I also would say that you know your way around this part of the country, spend most of your time under the sun and the stars rather than a roof, and that you can use your pistol in that tied down holster."

Father Clark coughed, then wheezed. Spur looked back at him and saw the priest's hands shaking. The churchman scratched his face, and Spur made an effort not to frown.

"Well, now that you two have met," Father Clark said, "I can leave you. I need to get over to the church and make some arrangements with the local parish priest. Mother Benedict is the expert on such moves as this, she has moved her school and teachers three times already."

Spur waved and the sallow faced priest lifted a shaking hand, then lowered it quickly and walked toward the front door. Spur did scowl at his back when the nun could not see him. If he didn't know better he would guess that Father Clark was in a hurry to get a long shot of whiskey to calm down his nerves.

Spur turned back to the Mother Superior who had not missed Spur's interest in the priest.

"Yes, we worry about him, too, Mr. McCoy. Father Clark is not a well man. We try to shield him as much as we can. That's partly why you and I will select what we need for this trip."

Mother Superior Mary Benedict was on the far side of forty, maybe five feet four inches tall and on the heavy side as if to assert her authority. She wore spectacles with wire rims for reading. When not wearing them, they hung on a thin chain around her neck.

"Should we sit down over there in the chairs, Mr. McCoy? I have a list we need to go over."

Spur went with her to the chairs, but before she could go on, he spoke first.

"Mother Superior, have you ever been this far west before?"

"No."

"Yet you want to move out in the wilds of New Mexico with six nuns and a sickly priest to start a new parish or a school?"

"Precisely, young man. The Lord has told us to go to the heathen. We must go and teach. We're a teaching order. We go where we are ordered to by the mother church. Our lives and our daily work as well as our immortal souls, are all in the care of the Lord."

"Mother Superior, have you ever killed a rattlesnake?"

She looked up sharply. "No, of course not. Snakes are God's creatures like all the rest of the animals."

"Out here, Mother Superior, it is far better to kill a rattlesnake than to let the snake kill you. Have you ever shot a firearm?"

"No, well, a long time ago I did." Her forehead creased, her eyes hooded. "Young man, are you deliberately trying to frighten me?"

"Frankly, yes. Between here and the Rio Grande lies some of the most desolate, barren, worthless, primitive, uninhabited, useless land in the entire nation. This is near the end of June. The temperature will be well over a hundred degrees most of the time during the day. That kind of heat hour after hour saps your strength, sucks the moisture out of your body, and can drive a man insane after only a few hours of exposure. This is a rugged trip for trail hardened cavalry soldiers with proven mounts. How are seven nuns going to withstand a long march like this?"

"Mr. McCoy. You have your orders. We have our orders. We do not question the instructions we get. Remember, the Lord is always there helping us. We have faith, and faith can move mountains."

"The mountains are no problem, Mother Superior. What worries me is if your faith will stop a razor sharp arrow fired by a Mescalero Apache who suddenly rises up out of the desert where he has covered himself with sand? Dozens of travelers and settlers get killed out here every year by the Mescaleros. They kill whites and enemy Indians for sport, they make war for amusement, they are vicious and treacherous by nature, by design and because of social customs."

Mother Superior Mary Benedict sat up straighter. "Faith is not supposed to stop arrows, Mr. McCoy. Faith gives us the will to find a *method* to stop the arrows, or better to prevent them ever being released. Faith and commitment and obedience give us the power to use our minds to solve our problems." She watched him for a moment.

"Now, no more questioning of our orders. We WILL be going across this land. We WILL do it successfully. Women and even nuns, or should I

say *especially* nuns, are much stronger and re-
sourceful than you may think. All six of the
sisters are volunteers for this outpost. Two are
former farm girls, two have actually shot firearms. We will overcome all obstacles, Mr.
McCoy."

She waited, giving him a chance to reply.
When he only grimly nodded at her she went on.

"Now, to the project. We have a rough map of
the suggested route. This, of course, will be the
primary responsibility of you and the guide we
hire."

Spur looked at the four times folded piece of
paper. The march led across the high plateau of
Texas, into New Mexico, across the plains there
and then slightly south to the city of Roswell,
New Mexico. That was half way across. From
there it turned north to a pass through the
Rocky Mountains and on west to the Rio
Grande river.

"Most of this territory is a virtual desert,
Mother Superior. It gets from three to seven
inches of rainfall in an entire year! Water holes
normally there are dried up this time of the
year."

"Enough, Mr. McCoy. We will need to know
about this problem, so we can plan around it. All
problems have solutions. Now, one more small
item. Father Clark is not well. He is fragile
and has other problems, but it is our duty
to see him safely across this desert. I am in
charge of the move. The money needed for the
equipment is in my care and responsibility. This
is at the direction of our bishop. Don't be too

quick to judge Father Clark. He is a good man, and a fine priest. As you suggested, he tends to drink now and then, but for that problem too, we will find a solution.''

THREE

Spur McCoy stood, walked to the front window and looked into the street for a stormy pair of minutes. Seven woman and a whiskey priest and General Halleck wanted him to take them across the New Mexican deserts in the middle of the summer? It was suicide! It was ridiculous! They all were out of their minds. He would not go unless they had at least fifty troopers to guard the nuns against the Mescaleros. His mind was made up. He walked back to the upholstered couch where Mother Superior Benedict sat and dropped into the chair he had used before.

"This whole trip is absolutely unthinkable. The risks are too great. The weather will be horrendous, and I'll have seven women and a whiskey priest to take care of. The chances of making it through with only ten troopers as escort are not good. Maybe half of us would be alive when we reached the Rio Grande. Do you want to see three of your nuns dead before they get to the big river?"

"Naturally, Mr. McCoy, I do not wish that.

However, such an estimate is highly suspect since it is only your own. I work closely with a higher authority who has indicated this trip should be made. He will guide and care for and protect us. We will go across, with or without your help. I am perfectly capable of hiring a guard and a wagonmaster, contacting the army for the escort and moving out. So, right now is the time for you to decide. Either you defy your orders from Washington and walk away from here, or you accept the challenge of getting us through with as little trouble and as few injuries and casualties as possible."

Sister Mary Benedict looked sternly at the man before her. Spur could read nothing more in her eyes but determination. She would go by herself if she had to, with the nuns pullling the damn wagon!

"All right, I'll go only because I figure you will do it yourself if I don't. But I'm stipulating that we get twenty troopers as escort at Fort Houston outside of town."

Mother Benedict grinned. "Good, good. If you were French I would kiss you on both cheeks! As it is, a handshake should suffice." She held out her hand, which he saw was somewhat suntanned and he found out it was strong when she gripped his.

"Deal. Now you have some lists? Why don't we start with a wagon. I'd say a good strong Conestoga maybe two or three years old, with wooden bows and a heavy canvas top. We can go to the Wagon Works two blocks down. Should I get a buggy?"

"Goodness no. The good Lord gave me two

strong legs and feet to walk on. I have my funds, and I'm ready to go now." She stood up quickly and they went out to the steps, turned left and at once stepped over a cowboy sleeping peacefully on the boardwalk in front of the hotel. A puddle of vomit near his mouth had attracted a cloud of flies.

"Poor soul," Mother Superior said as she stepped over him. She looked at a pad of paper in her hand.

"You said a Conestoga, right? I'm hoping we can find one with a twelve or a fourteen foot box, one of the bigger freight wagon types if possible. That will give us more room for our supplies and the organ."

"An organ, Mother? We're taking an organ along?"

"Yes, a pedal pump kind. They are relatively new, but we had one donated. Then there is the bell for the new church. It is the heaviest thing we have. So we need a wagon with a carrying capacity of about six thousand to sixty-five hundred pounds."

"And eight oxen to pull it," Spur said. "I'm afraid we won't find a freight wagon that size. A ten or twelve footer will be more likely."

They stepped down off the boardwalk into the dust of the street. Mother Superior lifted her habit as she stepped over fresh horse droppings. A thousand flies scattered as they walked past. She ignored them all, a set, determined smile on her face.

Stepping up to the boardwalk on the far side of the street, the long black skirt snagged on a splintered pine plank and stopped her.

Spur knelt and unhooked the heavy cloth.

"One more thing, Mother Superior. You and your nuns must wear more practical clothes. I would suggest pants and shirts for all of you. These heavy habits will be deathly hot, and they are too bulky and cumbersome for the travel and camp work we'll be doing."

"Impossible. The order dictates quite plainly our habit. We would need a release from the head of the order in Chicago before we could alter our dress."

Spur stopped and scowled. "Sister, I thought you were the smart one here, the practical, efficient person who could manage people and situations and get good things accomplished. You just failed your first test. Have you ever climbed up on a Conestoga front driver's seat in your habit? Ever sat a horse with those bulky multiple skirts on? Have you worn your head and neck covering during hundred and ten degree weather for twenty or thirty days outside?

"To make this trip safely we first must be extremely lucky, then we must be damned smart and take advantage of every possible chance we have, and third, we must be as basic and practical as possible. What does your logical, practical, efficient mind tell you how your people should dress for the trip?"

Mother Superior Benedict smiled, took off her steel rimmed glasses and cleaned them with a soft white handkerchief. When she put the spectacles back on, she nodded.

"Of course, Mr. McCoy, you are right. We will

buy trousers and shirts and alter them to fit before we leave."

"Thank you, Mother Superior."

"I'm not always stubborn, am I? You were right to appeal to my practical nature. That will usually win a tough argument with me—at least for this trip where you are the expert."

They found the Lubbock Wagon Works a half block later. It was a well established firm, and made wagons, mostly for the farmers and ranchers. The owner had a dozen used wagons, but only one Conestoga. It had wooden bows and a heavy canvas top.

Spur examined it, checked the date burned into the front of the box. It had been made six years ago.

Amos, the owner of the firm, saw Spur checking the big wagon and he walked over.

"That Connie is sound as a dollar, Mr. McCoy. Army drove her in here two years ago then she was too big for their regular rigs so they traded me."

Spur checked the box, twelve foot. She had two and a half inch wide steel rimmed wheels, standard three foot eight inchers in front but on back larger four foot ten inch wheels with nearly a three inch steel rim around the wooden spokes and outer wooden circle. He liked the rig at once.

"How much?" Spur asked. "Remember, this is for the church. Should be a good discount."

"In Boston, that Connie would cost you a hundred and twenty dollars new. But out here, and since it's the church and all, I could let her go for say, ninety-five."

"Beat up and six years old," Spur said. "Needs two new spokes in that front wheel, and we'll need a stiff tongue and a gear brake. Might go as high as sixty dollars."

"Hell, man, I paid eighty-five!" Amos stirred a circle in the dust with his toe. "Well, seeing it's the church and all, I'll fix up those things on her and let you steal it from me for seventy-five."

Mother Superior Benedict walked up while they were talking. "Amos, I am surprised at you, trying to make so much profit on a sale to the church. Come down to seventy dollars, fix everything Mr. Spur suggests, throw in two lead ropes twenty feet long and you have a sale."

Amos laughed and agreed.

Spur examined the wagon critically, found one more spoke that was about to break and saw that they fixed everything, then installed the gear brake and made sure that it worked. The stiff tongue would be easier to hitch up. Mother Superior gave Amos forty dollars and would pay the rest on delivery in two hours.

As they left, Amos was smiling, yelling at two of his men to get to work on the old Connie.

Spur and the nun went to the Bedlow Livery Stable next. He picked out two teams of mules that were used to working together, haggled the price down to fifteen dollars each, then bought one more at the same price. While he was there he picked out a saddle horse for himself, bought a saddle and a rope, a boot for a Spencer and talked the livery man into throwing in a pair of saddle bags.

Most liveries in that part of the country had a

tack shop at one side. This one did too, so Spur
and Mother Superior arranged for complete
harness and reins for the two teams. Spur har-
nessed two of the mules and led them to the
wagon works. When the Conestoga was ready,
Spur hitched up the team and met Mother
Superior at the general store. The mules pulled
well and the Conestoga handled like she was
new.

It took them nearly three hours to select, buy
and load the supplies for the trip. Spur and the
merchant worked out the shopping list.

For 310 miles they figured 15 miles a day or
from 20 to 25 days. They took food and supplies
for 30 days just to be safe. They stocked up on
bacon, beans, flour, sugar, coffee, rice, rolled
oats, dried apples, raisins and dried apricots,
three sacks of potatoes, a 50 gallon drum for
drinking water and Spur added three Spencer
7-shot rifles and 500 cartridges.

"Absolutely no firearms!" Mother Superior
said.

The merchant guffawed and then apologized.
"Sister, you just ain't never been on the desert,
and you don't know the Mescaleros. With them
you shoot first if you see them, but mostly you'll
never see them, and when you do, half the time
you're dead anyway so it don't matter. You
going out there to Roswell without rifles is like
lining up them six nuns of yours and shooting
them out there in the public square. Only thing
is, it would be more merciful for you to shoot
them here and now than to let the Mescal's have
them. Begging your pardon, Sister, but you
have no idea what they do to white women

before they kill them."

Mother Superior Benedict stared at the merchant and slowly nodded. "I'm afraid you're right. Yes, let's put in six of the rifles, and a thousand rounds."

Spur McCoy turned so she couldn't see him and grinned.

When they got the food, camping and cooking supplies on board, they drove to the Western Freighters and Spur looked at the organ, the three-foot wide bell, and the stack of boxes that had to go on the wagon.

The freighters helped them load, putting the heavy bell and organ in the middle of the wagon, then packing the boxes and other gear around them. Spur opened boxes and consulted with Mother Superior. They found eight cartons of tracts and literature that they decided the would donate to the local parish. They were still overloaded.

Spur went through the boxes again, found three more the nun said they could leave, then he unloaded the tent and took it back to the store. They just had no room for it.

Spur and Mother Superior picked out two pair of pants and two shirts for each of the nuns. They had approximate sizes, but all would need to be altered to be practical. Sister Ruth could do that, she was a whiz with a needle and thread, Mother Superior said.

It was nearing four o'clock when Spur realized they had not eaten at noon. He checked the wagon again, making sure the food was placed where it would be available, that the camping and cooking gear were on the outside. The water barrel was in back, well wedged into place.

He sent Sister Mary Benedict back to the hotel to rest while he drove to the Wagon Works and bought a spare front wheel, which they wired in place under the center of the wagon box. Front wheels broke more often than rears, and it would be practical to have a spare. Spur admitted he was not the best wheel wright in the world, so he didn't want to be repairing a wheel on the trail.

Spur parked the Conestoga at the side of the hotel and put the mules in the small stable at the rear. Once more he walked to the livery and picked out three saddle horses for the nuns to ride. He found the most gentle animals he could that looked like they could stand the long trail. That meant three more bridles and saddles.

After he settled up the bill for the mounts and gear, he rode his own bay gelding back to the hotel and tied him up outside. Spur had agreed to meet Mother Superior in her hotel lobby and they would go to the small restaurant across the street for supper. She said it would cost half as much as eating at the hotel.

He went to his own hotel room, washed up, combed his hair, then checked his six-gun. It was clean and oiled and ready for the range again.

Spur put on his low crowned brown hat with the string of Mexican silver pieces around it, and headed for the other big hotel. He was not overly anxious to see the rest of his charges for this trip, but there was no way to put it off now.

He found the nuns, all in their habits, clustered around the shorter and stockier

Mother Superior. Father Clark was not with them.

Spur came up at the side of the flock and cleared his throat. One of the nuns looked up and smiled. She had deep brown eyes and a softly white face.

"Mother . . ." she said.

Mother Benedict turned and saw Spur and smiled.

"Sisters, look around here and be thankful. This is the gentleman who is going to help us get across this unfriendly land to the Rio Grande."

Spur watched them turn and look at him. He saw six round faces bound tightly by the cowl like head covering, making them look like peas in a pod.

"Mr. McCoy, I'll introduce you to each Sister. We won't expect you to remember names just yet. Over here we have Sister Mary Cecilia, then Sister Mary Francis, Sister Mary Joseph, Sister Mary Ruth, Sister Mary Maria and Sister Mary Teresa."

The last nun turned when her name was called and stared at him. A tentative smile edged around her mouth, and Spur thought he was going to drop straight through a crack in the floor. The same darting soft blue eyes, the crinkling nose and the sensuous mouth. She was the Teresa he had tumbled with in bed last night! He had made love with a nun!

Her eyes were laughing at him, enjoying his surprise and his discomfort.

Each of the nuns had nodded and said a few words to him, and now it was Sister Teresa's turn.

"Mr. McCoy. I'm sure you are the man to get us across the desert. It will be a hard job, but I know you'll be able to do it."

To the rest of them it was idle chatter, but to Spur the loaded words hit him like two kicks to the crotch.

Somehow he collected himself enough to thank them all and suggest they go have supper. They went across the street and down a block to a small family restaurant. Mother Superior had arranged it. They sat together at a long table in the back of the room and all had the same food, vegetable soup, crackers and cheese sandwiches. They drank milk.

The meal was over quickly and Spur found himself next to Sister Teresa as they walked back to the hotel.

"Lovely last night," she whispered back as he stepped to the side to let the others go up the hotel steps.

"That's a challenge!" she said softly as he held the door for her as the last nun walked inside.

Spur spoke to Mother Superior for a moment in the lobby.

"Tonight I'm looking for the best guide I can find. Nobody is going to be wild to take this kind of job. What do you have in your budget for wages?"

"What is a fair price?" she asked.

"Fifty dollars."

"No more. Our funds are limited." She sighed. "I'm sorry, Mr. McCoy, I did not mean to be sharp with you, but I am starting to be concerned about money."

"I'll do the best I can."

He went first to the sheriff, but the lawman had no ideas about scouts or guides across to the Rio Grande.

"Been talk about the Mescaleros getting nasty again," the sheriff said. His name was Prescott, and he looked like he could handle the big Colt on his thigh.

"The Mescaleros are always nasty when they aren't being vicious or treacherous," Spur said. He left his name and hotel room number in case the sheriff heard of anyone looking.

He tried the bars. The first two proved to provide fairly cold beer but no scouts.

In the third one a young halfbreed said he knew the land, but if the Mescaleros ever captured him, they would use him as a human sacrifice to their gods. He was staying as far away from Mescalero territory as possible.

The fourth bar and gambling hall he found a grizzled man in his forties who said he would make the trip to Roswell but no farther.

"Cost you two hundred to get to Roswell," the man said. He was half drunk, but his eyes shone with a horse trader's gleam.

"Can't even offer you a hundred," Spur said.

"You do and you got a guide," the man said. "Billbrough is the name. You want me, just put in a word with the bar man here. He can find me. I've lived all through that area, but the damn Mescals are going in for more raiding than they have in years. A caution, my new friend. Whether you hire me or not be sure that you watch your ass out there."

FOUR

Spur McCoy checked in the last drinking parlor in the town of Lubbock slightly before midnight. This one had boards laid across saw-horses for the bar, sawdust on the floor and no ice for the beer.

Two men at the bar said they would be glad to scout the trail and lead the wagon over to the Rio Grande. Both were over sixty-five, toothless, wasted by long years in the outdoors, and Spur was sure that neither one could sit a horse.

He found no other candidates for the job, left his half a warm beer on the board top, and talked with the apron.

The man was thin and wheezing. His nose ran and his thinning hair showed brown splotches on his head. He wiped his nose on his sleeve and shook his head.

"No chance to get a scout for that trip now. Too damn many Mescals out there lifting scalps. Last week we lost two wagons trying to run across."

Spur thanked him and headed outside. He kicked at the boardwalk as he moved back to his hotel. Tomorrow he would make the circuit again, and talk to the store owners. The livery stable man might have an idea. Yeah, tomorrow.

McCoy was tired when he unlocked his hotel room door and pushed it open. He scratched a match and lit the lamp, then shoved the door closed with his foot.

Just after the door latched he heard a deadly click as a six-gun hammer cocked ready for fire. His back was to the sound, both hands still near the lamp.

"Can I turn around, or are you going to shoot me in the back?" the Secret Service man asked his unseen opponent.

"Turn around slowly, hands way up," the voice said. It was a woman.

He turned gradually, making sure she would not shoot. His head moved faster and he saw her sitting in a chair next to the window, the ugly black muzzle of a .44 angled over the back of the chair and centered on his chest.

She was dark, with long black hair, but her face looked part Indian to go with her more obvious Mexican heritage. A Breed. He had never seen her before.

Spur stopped turning and smiled. "So, you're not here to rob me, or kill me. What do you want?"

"Just to see the surprised look on your face when that hammer clicked back," she said quickly, then laughed. She let the hammer down softly on the weapon and it vanished. "You can put your hands down now. You're tall."

"Yes, and you're short. My name is Spur McCoy, but you must know that. Who are you?"

"You ask a lot of damn questions, don't you?"

"Bad habit of mine."

She left the chair and he saw she wore man's pants that fit tightly across her sleek young body. She was barely five feet tall, slender but with a white blouse that punched outward. The Breed had black bangs hanging across her forehead. Now she sat on the edge of the bed closer to the lamp. Her brown eyes were wide set, cheekbones high leaving little hollows in her cheeks. Her mouth was small and cupid curved. It was a pretty face. He guessed she was eighteen, maybe nineteen.

He saw the .44 in her right sided holster.

"You always pack so much firepower?"

"When I'm in town. Most folks here don't like me."

"Just because you have a mixed racial heritage?"

"You noticed."

"I always notice pretty girls who sneak into my room at midnight and hold a gun on me."

She laughed. "I think I'm going to like you, Spur McCoy. My name is Chiquita. You are looking for a guide to take your Catholic missionaries over to the Rio Grande."

"That's true, and so far I've been looking without much success."

"I'll do it. I know the country better than anyone in the area except the Mescaleros. I am half Mescalero and spent ten years out there. I know the water holes, the trails, the traps and the blind canyons. There is no one in town who can get you through Mescalero country as safely as I can."

"Besides all that, you're modest," he said smiling.

"No, I'm good. I also think like a Mescalero does, so I can avoid them, go where they are not."

"Are they raiding again?"

"More than ever. They stopped two wagons a week ago. Nobody came back. The burned out hulks are still out there. I could have led those people safely across."

Spur frowned as he watched her. She was small, but a white hot determination burned from her dark eyes. Also she was half Mescal. That could be tremendously important.

"If you lead the roundeyes, you are not on good terms with your people."

"No, for several reasons. They do not consider me a part of their tribe. I am *Woman in Two Camps,* and accepted in neither. So I live as I can."

"How much for the trip?"

"I should charge you two hundred, but I know that drunk roundeye said he would go for a hundred to Roswell. That's only half way. I will go to Roswell for eighty dollars in gold. I do not trust the Yankee paper money."

"That's three months wages for a cowhand. Clerk in a store works two months for that much gold."

"But neither of them has to dodge the Apache arrows or bullets. Many Mescaleros have rifles now and they have learned to shoot well. They raid wagons for more rifles and for bullets. I know where they hide, where they wait, where they hunt and how they move. I am your life-savor for the nuns. You know what Mescalero raiders do to white women. Think what would happen to the Catholic nuns."

"I know, I've been there." He watched her. She showed him a stern Indian stare, her bargaining look.

"I'll recommend you to the boss tomorrow. Can you be at the Texas Ranch House Hotel tomorrow at ten o'clock? I'll introduce you to Mother Superior Benedict."

Chiquita smiled. "A nun giving you orders. You must like that."

"Depends on the orders."

She moved toward the door and suddenly a four-inch knife materialized in her right hand and she tapped it on his chest.

"Don't get any funny ideas, gringo. If you touch my body, I will cut your heart out." She slipped past him and opened the door. "Of course another time, another place, who knows? Tomorrow at ten, I'll be there." She stepped out the door and closed it behind her.

McCoy watched the space for a moment. The door did not reopen. He went over and locked it, then sat down on the bed. It had been a long, tough day. A whiskey priest, a nun who scoffed at her vow of chastity, and now a pretty little Breed with a Mescalero mind and a Mexican hot temper who was going to be his guide and scout.

It was turning out to be one hell of an unlikely group of people to make a dangerous trip through the Apache Mescaleros who were riled up and raiding everything that moved through their traditional territory.

Maybe he could get thirty army troopers for escort duty, this being a church group and with seven women. Maybe.

Spur got undressed and into bed. Tonight was for catching up on his sleep. He didn't get much last night.

The next morning Spur slept in until almost eight o'clock, an unheard of time for him. He ate a leisurely breakfast downstairs, then made sure the two mules in the small stable behind the hotel had hay and a bite of oats. He sat on the steps outside the Ranch House Hotel in his blue jeans, blue striped shirt and a black leather vest. He tipped the brown, low crowned hat back on his head and soaked up some early morning sun. It would be a blistering ninety degrees today in the shade. He had been in that kind of heat before.

He could ride out to Camp Houston and check on the military, but an early visit would make no difference. When they came to pick up the escort it would be ready or not or doubled or halved according to the unpredictable orders of the Division of Texas Army Headquarters. He pulled his hat down over his eyes and relaxed.

Ten minutes before the set meeting time, someone flipped his hat off his head. He came up, his hand hovering over his six-gun tied down on his right hip.

"Take it careful, hombre," a small voice said. "You are as safe as if you were in your own bed."

Chiquita sat down beside him. She had on the

same dark brown pants but now a brown blouse that was not quite as tight as the white one. It still revealed where Chiquita had put in a lot of her growth, rather than height.

"Are you through staring so we can meet the nuns?" Chiquita said, her voice layered with impatience.

"Might just as well, it's time." Spur stood, stretched, waved toward the door and walked behind the small woman. He noticed that a low crowned black, wide brimmed hat hung down her back on a black cord. She wore boots, not moccasins.

When Spur pushed open the door to the hotel, the desk clerk looked up, his face darkened and he started toward Chiquita.

Spur McCoy lifted one hand and pointed his finger at the man, who glanced nervously at him as Spur touched Chiquita's shoulder and moved her to the front window where Mother Superior Benedict stood. The clerk scowled and retreated, throwing angry looks at Spur.

The Mother Superior saw them coming, she turned and smiled, and Spur felt something pass between the two women before either spoke.

"Mother Superior, this is Chiquita," Spur said when they stopped in front of her.

The nun spoke quickly in fluent Spanish that Spur had trouble following. It was a pleased, cordial greeting, and she reached out one hand and clasped the smaller browner one.

Chiquita replied in Spanish.

Then the Breed switched to English.

"Mother, I would like to be your scout through the Mescalero country. I am half

Mescal myself and know their ways. Mr. McCoy has approved and my price is $70. I hope that is not too much."

There was no bargaining, Mother Superior Benedict nodded quickly. "Yes, that is agreeable. Can you start first thing in the morning?"

"Of course."

"Next order of business is to have Chiquita look over our rig and our gear," Spur said. He looked at her. "You might have some suggestions."

"Yes, good. Let's go now."

"You can meet the sisters later," Mother Benedict said.

"Five-thirty start in the morning?" Chiquita asked.

The other two agreed and Spur and Chiquita left for the small stable behind the hotel. The night stable man had watched the wagon for them, and nothing was missing.

Chiquita spent an hour going over each item in the loaded rig and when she was done she called to McCoy.

"We need another twenty gallon keg of water, and a two gallon cask of whiskey. If we get in trouble we throw out the cask of whiskey and within two hours every Mescalero brave on the raid will be falling down drunk!"

Spur laughed.

"It has worked before. Whiskey is like a poison to the Mescaleros. Oh, we should take some dried beef, twenty pounds. It will last for months."

Spur agreed and they went to the store for the supplies, brought them back and loaded them on board. They hid the whiskey so Mother Superior would not see it, and especially so that Father Clark could not find it.

When they were done they sat on a stack of blankets near the back of the covered wagon.

"Any good job interview should include some background," Spur said.

"Finally you ask." She stared at him with a frank, open expression. "I will tell you, I am not ashamed of my parents. My mother was captured by the Mescaleros on a raid of a small Mexican village across the border. She was so pretty the capturing brave kept her as his second wife.

"A second wife is important to most Mescalero braves. The women do all the work, and a second wife can make things easier for the first wife. Also my father had only two daughters, and he wanted a son. My younger brother fulfilled his dreams and he let us go back to the Mexican village. But he kept his son and raised him as a Mescalero."

"But the Mexican villagers drove you and your mother out, right?"

She looked at him quickly. "You know a lot about my country, my people. Yes, they said my mother was not fit to live among them. They hate the Mescals. Since I was a Breed, they despised me ten times as much as they did her. I have known much hatred and now I am a squaw in three camps, and can live in peace in none of them."

"Times change, people change."

"But I will not live long enough for that. The hatred killed my mother when I was still ten.

Two gringo nuns found me in a street begging and took me in. They raised me. It was a small village in Texas near the border, away from the Mescaleros country. I have known many wonderful nuns . . . and a few whiskey priests."

"We have one on this trip."

"I heard." She lifted her black brows. "I also hear that he spends his days in the chapel praying, and his nights slapping around the whores in a bordello."

FIVE

Father Wilbur Clark sat up in the strange bed
and glanced around the unfamiliar room. Jesus!
This place looked like a whorehouse! He had
been amusing himself lately by swearing in his
thoughts. It had produced hours of euphoric
pleasures for him.

He inventoried the bedroom with his eyes. It
was fancy, with a real brass bed frame and
elaborate head and feet. The walls were papered
in a bright flower pattern, with border strip four
inches wide circling the room a foot below the
ceiling which was papered with a softer, more
relaxed print.

The one window was draped luxuriously with
two lined curtains that hung to the floor and
were swagged back on each side with luxuriant
pink ropes that ended in showy tassles. A soft
white thin material covered the window which
was hidden by a pull down blind.

The cream colored blind had been painted with
a scene of a pleasant mountain meadow.
Definitely a woman's room.

It still looked like a whorehouse. The closet was jammed with fancy clothes and on a dressing table he saw all sorts of creams and lotions and colors for applying rouge and makeup to the face.

It not only looked like a room in a whorehouse, it was, and not just a crib, the room that belonged to the madam herself.

Someone snored softly beside him.

Father Clark looked down at the henna red haired woman. Her face was flat and plain, her nose too large and lips too tight. Now her mouth hung open inducing the snore. He reached over and pushed up her chin holding her mouth closed. The snoring stopped. He figured she was about forty years old.

She lay on top of the sheet as naked as he was. Her small breasts were now flattened against her chest. In her sleep she curled one hand between her legs and moaned softly in pleasure.

He looked to the other side and saw the younger woman awake beside him. She was softly blonde, even to the blonde thatch over her golden triangle. Her breasts were two hand size, and still looked large enough when she lay on her back. She was no more than twenty. She said her name was Lily.

She winked at him. "Ready to spend another five dollars?" she said, her pretty face grinning, strange blue eyes quick and ready.

"What about my discount?"

"You used that up last night," she said, her voice only a whisper. "Better idea. Bet you five you can't stick yours in old Gert there without waking her up."

Wilbur Clark laughed softly. "That's like taking candy from a whore, a Lily whore. Watch me."

He softly touched Gert's breasts, then petted them, using a little more pressure all the time until he was kneading them firmly bringing small gasps of pleasure from the sleeping woman.

Then he moved one hand to her legs and massaged her inner thighs until she moaned softly and moved her hand, then edged her legs apart slowly. His hand rubbed the black fur over her prize until she moaned again, then his fingers found her slot and teased it a moment, then toyed with the already wet and juicy labia.

Clark noticed that Lily moved closer to him, now she had her hands at his crotch working her delicate magic on his shaft which was almost erect. She bent and licked his throbbing tool and grinned.

"I think you're ready," she said.

Gert moved her hips slowly around and around now as his fingers kept up a steady stroking of her labia and a casual touch of her clitoris.

Clark eased Gert's legs apart more, lifted her knees and settled between them, then slowly he touched her red, swollen lips with his shaft and slid it forward.

Gert sighed and thrust her hips upward, then she yelped softly as he lanced past the first tight muscle and slid gently into her until their pelvic bones touched.

He grinned at Lily.

"You owe me five dollars, younger whore,"

Clark said.

Lily shook her head. "Gert has been awake since the first time you touched her tits. It's a game we play with old bastards like you."

"Lily, I'm not going to pay you a dime," Clark said. He watched Gert and she didn't move. "That proves she's sleeping!" he whispered. "You owe me five bucks, right now!"

Lily rolled off the bed. "Finish what you got started, old man, then we'll talk."

Clark looked back at the woman under him and snorted, then he pumped hard a dozen times, exploded inside her and came away. Gert still lay where she had been.

"I was awake all the time, Padre," Gert said, bursting out with a raucous laugh. She sat up. "You two were whispering so loud it would wake up anybody. I knew the first time you touched my tits, so you owe her the five dollars."

Father Clark slapped Gert on one washed out, painted cheek, knocking her backwards on the bed.

"Bitch! Damned whore! I didn't come in here to get swindled by a pair of trollops! I paid enough last night to last me the rest of the day. That was the deal. Thirty dollars for the two of you for twenty-four hours."

"The deal is off when you get rough," Gert said. "If I call Amos he'll throw you butt bare right out the second story window, collar or no."

Clark slapped her again and she tried to roll away from him. He dove on top of her pinning her to the bed. Lily jumped on his back, her fingernails making long scratches down his shoulders and back. Then she beat on him with her small fists.

"Get away from her! Let Gert go!" She turned and found a heavy porcelain pitcher on the dressing table and swung it at Clark. He dodged and the pitcher hit Gert on the side of the head. She slammed backwards on the bed, unconscious.

"You killed her!" Clark roared. "You slut! You murderer! You killed poor Gert!"

Lily dropped the pitcher, staring at the still form on the bed, then she fell beside her on her stomach, weeping hysterically.

Clark watched her a minute, then moved behind her, lifted her hips off the bed and began stroking her soft buttocks.

"No!" Lily said. "No!"

Clark spanked her six times as she squealed.

"Lily, old Gert isn't dead, you just knocked her out. Remember you're both bought and paid for until noon today. You got to do damn well what I tell you, woman."

"Then Gert is not dead, not hurt bad?"

"Hell no, you just grazed her with the pitcher. Now get on your hands and knees and hang them beauties into my face. Like to get half smothered with them, unless I eat my way free."

"She's going to be all right?" Lily demanded.

"Yeah, yeah. Just knocked her senseless. She'll be coming around as horny as ever in a few minutes. Now hang them tits of yours for me to chew on!"

She went down on all fours and he crawled under her, licking and chewing.

Lily shrugged. "You're ready to pop again.

How long had it been since you'd done a woman?"

"Fucking near a year. Kept me in a cell, a monastic cell, only they had the key. All because I drank a little and they caught me fucking this fourteen year old one day when she came in with some questions. I answered her big question!"

He pushed Lily away and knelt behind her.

"Oh, no, please, not there!"

"Why not, you been had there before."

"It hurts. Really, I'm not made quite the way most women are, and it really hurts."

"That's too bad, I want your asshole, now."

He tried to mount her and she yelled and crawled across the bed. Clark went after her. As he did, Gert lifted up with the heavy porcelain pitcher and swung it at Clark. She missed his head and slammed it into his shoulder.

He growled and sat up on the bed, holding his shoulder. Then he slid off the bed and found his pants. He took out a knife and opened a four-inch blade.

"Time we start playing the game for keeps!"

Lily saw the knife and ran for the door. He jumped in front of her and swung the knife toward her breasts. She sagged backward and fell on the bed.

Gert slid off the bed and as Clark advanced on Lily, Gert opened the door and screamed for Amos, then ran naked down the hall screaming his name.

Clark let her go. He hovered over the naked girl on the bed.

"You have not been nice to me, Lily. I bought and paid for you and you were not nice. So I'll have to give you a lesson—one slashed breast."

The knife darted out, sliced a two inch gash in her right breast. Blood sprung up and flowed a red river.

Lily screamed, then put her hand over her breast to slow the bleeding. She scurried off the far side of the bed, but then was in the corner of the room.

"Lily, you have been a bad girl. You have sinned in the sight of man and God, and you must be punished. I am the right hand of the Lord. I am his mighty sword that strikes down all evil doers. I am a warrior of the Lord!"

He sprang forward, the knife arcing through the air toward Lily's throat. She fell backwards screaming.

Clark stopped and stared at her naked body on the floor. She was so lovely, such a marvelous sex machine! But she could not be spared. She had to die. He was the warrior of the Lord! It would be like last time. She would pay for her sins, and his own debt would be paid as well.

He moved forward.

Lily crowded backward, sitting on the floor, edging toward the wall. Looking for something to protect herself with. There was nothing, not even a pillow. The chair! She pushed it at him and he swept it aside.

"Lily, you have sinned," he said solemnly. "You have sinned before the most holy God!" He knelt in front of her. Lily pressed against the wall. Clark held the knife out so she could see streaks of her own blood on it.

Blood ran down her breast to her stomach.

"Lily, you must die for your sins!"

He lifted the knife and began to swing it toward her.

"May God have mercy on your soul!"

A big black fist slammed into the side of Father Clark's head before the knife reached Lily. Amos's blow pounded Clark to the side and against the bed. His head hit the oak sideboard and he slumped unconscious to the floor.

Lily trembled in shock. She blubbered in anguished hysteria, and Gert rushed in with water and a towel, bandages and a bottle of whiskey.

"Drink," she said. Lily took a shot of the booze, then Gert wiped the blood away from her breast. She sloshed the whiskey over her slash and Lily passed out from the pain.

Amos gathered up Father Clark's clothes, hoisted him over his shoulder and carried the priest down the back stairs. He knew what to do. He walked down two blocks then to the alley door of the county jail. He knocked twice on the door and a few moments later had deposited Father Clark with his clothes in a back cell.

The deputy sheriff listened to the story and shook his head. Someone would be coming to get him out. But first the priest had to sober up and pay for the damages to both property and to the dance hall girl, Lily, who was extremely popular in town, especially with the sheriff.

SIX

Spur McCoy edged his mount up to the side of
the Conestoga and looked over at Mother
Superior Benedict. Her habit was gone. She
wore overalls and a too large shirt over them.
Now Spur could see that her hair was a gentle
brown, cut short and combed back. There was a
distinct white band around her forehead below
her hairline where the habit had covered her.

Mother Benedict took a pocket watch from
her overalls and looked at it, then glanced up at
Spur.

"He's not coming, is he?" Spur asked. The
nun shook her head and frowned.

"As you can imagine, this has happened
before. I'm afraid you'll have to go find him."

"May not be hard. Heard there was a fight
earlier this morning in a . . . saloon. Wait for
me."

Spur kicked his horse and it moved down the
street toward the sheriff's office. That was
always the best place to start. He had enjoyed
watching the sun come up that morning as they

57

put the final touches on the Conestoga and the nuns got used to their overalls and blue jeans. The shirts were much too large for most of them, and a little small for others, still they served their purpose.

Chiquita had been everywhere, checking the shoes on the mules and the horses. That was one reason they were held up. She sent one riding horse back for a new shoe to replace the one that was about to come off.

They had been ready to roll an hour late at 6:30 A.M., only the priest was not to be found.

Mother Benedict had left a note on his door the night before telling him to be packed and in the lobby at five that morning. She said the note was still on his door this morning and he was not in his room.

Chiquita told Spur the priest had been at the Two Dollar saloon the night before with two whores. He might still be there.

When Spur stopped in front of the Lubbock County Sheriff's Office, he was just in time to meet the sheriff coming to work. Inside the sheriff nodded to Spur.

"What can I do for you?" the lawman asked.

"Missing a spare priest. Could he be a guest of the county?"

The all night deputy came in from the cells.

"He sure as hell is, Sheriff. Came in about two hours ago drunk as a skunk and passed out. Amos brought him naked as a jay bird. I think he finally got himself dressed."

"What kind of charges?" Spur asked.

"He cut up Miss Lily over at the Two Dollar. Lot of folks around town gonna be unhappy about that. Cut one . . . breast."

"It bad, Ira?"

"Don't reckon. Doc said he pulled the cut together and tied it up. Probably be only a thin scar. About two inches long he said."

The sheriff turned to Spur.

"You gonna pay the fine?"

"I guess I'll have to."

"Going rate is ten dollars an inch, plus ten dollars court costs. Thirty dollars."

"Any discount for the clergy?" Spur asked. All three men laughed and Spur gave the sheriff a twenty and a ten dollar bill.

"Roll him out," the sheriff said. "This whiskey priest of yours is a sick man. Better take care of him. If you don't one of these days he's gonna kill a girl, and then he'll hang for sure. His collar won't stop that trap from springing or that hangman's knot from breaking his neck."

"Sheriff, I think you're right," Spur said.

Five minutes later Father Wilbur Clark came through the door squinting. He was both hung over and wrung out. His collar was not straight and his black attire rumpled and dirty.

Outside, Spur pointed the direction, and walked beside him a ways.

"Clark, let's you and me get something all talked out. I tried to get Mother Superior Benedict to leave you here to rot, but she insisted you come. A promise she made your bishop. Frankly, I don't think you'll make it across the country we have to travel. One thing I want you to understand. To me you're no priest, I'll call you by your last name only. On this trip I'm the boss, you do exactly what I tell you to do because there will probably be somebody's life hanging in the balance. Now, do we understand each other?"

For a moment Father Clark frowned at Spur.

"Sir, I answer only to my bishop, not to you. I'll act as I please, do as I please. I am in command of this group, if you don't like that, then I sug . . ."

Spur slammed a right cross into the priestly jaw. The blow knocked him into the dust.

The priest sat up, felt his jaw, and spat at Spur.

"Now, Clark, do we understand each other?"

"Absolutely," Father Clark said. "And you may expect that the first chance I have I will discredit you and send you packing. If that doesn't work, I'll tie you up and castrate you. Enjoy the trip, McCoy, but you better always be watching over your shoulder and sleeping light."

Spur was tempted to use the rope on his saddle and drag the priest back to the Conestoga, but he decided it would make it more difficult to deal with the ladies on the wagon. He rode behind the man as they walked the five hundred yards to the covered wagon.

Chiquita had three of the nuns on horseback. Two were farm girls who had ridden before. The nuns were to ride on each side of the wagon and look out for holes and problems. Chiquita saw Spur load the priest on the wagon, then she took off west out of town, heading for Roswell, New Mexico.

Mother Superior Benedict had driven teams

before. She had a little trouble with the double team, but soon learned how to hold the reins. The mules were steady, and slightly faster than oxen would have been. Both teams had worked together before and soon they settled into a steady pace that carried the big wagon across the three thousand foot high plateau of western Texas.

Spur had not spoken with Sister Mary Teresa that morning. Both had projects to finish. Now he was glad she was inside the wagon. The army post, Camp Houston, was four miles west of town. They should reach it in an hour. Getting the mules settled down and into the routine would mean slow progress the first day or two.

As the big Conestoga rolled along, he checked the rig. The wheels were sounding right and Mother Benedict understood how to work the brake.

He spotted a small tear in the canvas top that he would have sewn up as soon as they stopped. Sisters Francis, Joseph and Maria were enjoying their horseback riding. That too would get old quickly.

Spur trotted up to where Chiquita sat on her horse watching the country. She heard him coming but did not turn.

"Any problems?" he asked.

She shook her head. "Not this close to town and the Army. I can see their smoke ahead, just over that slight rise."

"Yes, good idea," Spur said. "I'll ride forward and check out our escort, and try to get it doubled. Would you object to that?"

"Tripled might be better. If we get hit by

Mescalero, it means I have not done my job. I don't want to fight our way through. It's much safer to slip past the Indians than it is to fight them."

"I agree, but troops are specified on my orders." He touched his hat brim in a salute. "I'll try to meet you with the escort before you reach the fort."

Spur touched the bay with his toes and she moved ahead sharply. The army. It had been a lot of years since he had seen a full time soldier. He carried a card detailing his current rank as that of Lt. Colonel, unassigned and on temporary duty. He would use the card if he needed it.

The army being what it was, he probably would have to use it. He rode the remaining three miles to the camp quickly, and came past a small stream with trees nearby. It would be a good place to camp if it were not so early in the morning.
morning.

The army camp was not a fort. There were a scattering of fifteen or twenty buildings, all made of native stone and mortar with flat roofs, a minimum of windows and those with heavy shutters that could be closed and locked in place from the inside.

There were six long buildings for the enlisted men's barracks, five officers' houses, and a large mess hall and kitchen that probably also served as a meeting center. Spur saw the guidon of the 3rd Calvary fluttering by the gate, a formal affair that had no fence nor fort on either side of it.

What was the 3rd doing up here? Last he remembered they were stationed several hundred miles south at Fort Davis. He shrugged and rode up to the sentry.

"Colonel McCoy to see your commander, Corporal."

The corporal saluted and called for the sergeant of the guard.

A moment later a proper greeting occurred as the sergeant rode out, saluted formally and led Spur to the commandant's quarters. It was the largest of the stone buildings. There wasn't a bush, flower or tree anywhere in the camp. The sergeant knocked on the door, opened it and stepped inside.

McCoy followed. The building was a residence with an *office* room up front. A large American flag with thirty-eight stars in the corner covered half the rear wall. The inside of the room had been plastered and painted. It was army through and through. A brass spittoon sat to the side ready for use by both the men in front and behind a large desk.

The officer behind the desk rose and smiled. He was short, stocky, and held major's oak leaves on his shoulders. His uniform was clean, pressed and precise. A thin moustache adorned his upper lip and he stared over half glasses.

"Sir, may I present Colonel McCoy," the sergeant said. "Colonel McCoy, this is Major Donaldson, Camp Houston commander."

Major Donaldson saluted. Spur returned the salute, and the sergeant left by the front door. The officers sat down.

"Major, I hope you knew I was coming. My orders were in Lubbock, and I assume you also received yours from Washington."

"Yes, yes I did." He opened a box and held it

out. "Cigar, Colonel McCoy?"

Spur took one, it was short and thicker than he liked. He knew it would be mild without the usual bite of his favorite black twisted cigars. They went through the ritual of snipping off the end of the stogies and lighting them.

Major Donaldson leaned back and blew out a mouthful of smoke.

"Sir, my orders originally called for me to furnish you with a detachment of ten mounted men to serve as an escort to Roswell and on to the Rio Grande. I was prepared to do so. Then yesterday a rider came through from San Antonio. That's the U.S. Army's Department of Texas headquarters, as you know.

"Colonel Zackery there has instructed me to cease at once furnishing or providing any kind of escort service through Apache country, especially the Mescalero lands and the Chiricahua country."

Spur leaned forward, eyes hooded, his face showing surprise and anger. "There must be some mistake, Major Donaldson. Were not my orders signed by Major General Wilton D. Halleck?"

Donaldson stood and walked around the room.

"Yes, Colonel, they were, and he outranks my boss Colonel Zackery. However we have a problem of timing. The date on the telegram detailing my orders concerning you and the escort, that was forwarded by mail, was over three weeks ago. My orders from San Antonio are dated six days ago. The rider came in late last night."

"Ten men and a non-com, Major. Surely you can spare us that many men."

"Specific orders to the contrary, Colonel. As

you know, orders that come through regular Army channels always take precedent over casual orders and requests. What would you do in my place, Colonel?"

"I would indicate to my superiors that the current order did not arrive until after the ten men left to safeguard my party. You do know that I have seven nuns and a priest who insist on making the trip?"

Major Donaldson nodded.

"They threatened to go without me, if I refused to take them. I can't believe that you would let us cross without an escort. Weren't two wagon loads of civilians massacred last week out there?"

"Yes, our burial detail had to function after the raid. Six men, seven women and four children, all dead."

"Major, we've both been in the Army long enough to know that there are ways around and through any order."

"Colonel, I didn't tell you all of my communication from my headquarters. Word has been received of a general uprising of the Apache renegades now in the Mescalero and Chiricahua tribal zones. This post is to brace itself for a possible external attack, and to send out patrols on a daily basis reaching up to twenty miles into hostile territory to show the flag and to watch for any Indian movements."

"Almost a state of war."

"Still a state of war with the Indians, Colonel."

"But we can pass through, without your aid?"

"I was surprised the orders did not indicate

that we should stop all traveling between here and Roswell. That order might come at any time. I suggest you turn around and wait in Lubbock."

"That's what I told the ladies, but you don't know Mother Superior Mary Benedict."

The major sat down and Spur stood and paced. He was checkmated at every turn. He knew the army. Major Donaldson was right, he had to obey his immediate superior. Halleck's orders did not go through channels, and were secondary. He turned toward the door.

"Major, my compliments to your colonel. We'll be pushing on for Roswell. I hope we don't cause any extra work for your burial detail."

He went out the door without waiting for a reply. His horse was tied outside. Spur mounted up and rode. He would ask once more that they return. He would try to get Chiquita on his side.

A half hour later he pulled up with Chiquita, where Mother Benedict had stopped the mules. The three outriders came in and they talked. Spur presented the situation bluntly.

"So that means no army escort. Not one soldier will ride shotgun for us. It leaves us no option, we have to turn around and wait out the order in Lubbock. I'll send a letter to the nearest telegraph office and try to get authorization through the San Antonio Army headquarters."

"And how long will that take?" Mother Benedict asked.

"Two, maybe three weeks. If we had a telegraph in town it would be a matter of two or three days."

The Mother Superior looked at Chiquita. "You told me you're half Mescalero. Do you know your people well enough so that we can sneak through, get past them without having to fight them?"

"Most of them, Mother. Nobody, not even another Apache can sneak past all the Mescaleros. That means a wagon can't do it either. We can go around or in back of most of them."

"But one band of ten Mescalero braves would turn us into live targets. We would be little more than hunting practice for them," Spur said.

"Maybe, maybe not," Chiquita countered.

The three stared at one another.

Spur snapped his reins and wished he could swear for five minutes. He looked at Chiquita, then at the nun. "Mother Superior, you are responsible for eight lives, eight Catholic church worker lives. From a practical standpoint, I don't see how you can vote to go across. I'm casting my vote against making the trip."

The white strip over Mother Superior's tanned face was already showing a pink tinge. She frowned and rubbed her forehead, then closed her eyes and clasped the cross that hung just inside her blue shirt. She sighed.

"I vote to cross, to continue," Mother Superior Benedict said.

She and Spur looked at Chiquita.

"I am half Mescalero. I know the country. I know the good spirits. Look!" She pointed upward and they stared into the blue sky and saw a swooping split wing hawk, gliding around and around on a rising current of air.

"When the crooked nosed hawk rises on the wind, all will be well. It is Mescalero. I say that we go forward."

"Damn!" Spur said. He turned his bay,

slapped her flanks with the reins and galloped two hundred yards into the country, stopped and stared at the sky. He turned the reddish brown mare around and walked her back to the wagon. Spur got off his horse and pulled a shovel from where it had been fastened on the side of the Conestoga box for ready use.

He showed it to the women.

"Do you know what this is?" he shouted. Before they could answer he dug a spadful of earth and flung it away from them.

"This is a shovel, and if you insist on making the trip against my recommendation, and against that of Major Donaldson of the United States Army, then this shovel will be used often. To bury our dead before we get to Roswell!"

Spur marched back to the wagon, secured the shovel where it had been before and walked to his bay.

He mounted and glared at both women.

Both returned his stare calmly.

"We continue," Mother Superior said.

"We continue," Chiquita echoed.

The middle-aged nun on the wagon seat briskly slapped the reins on the mules' backs and the Conestoga rolled forward.

Chiquita, smiling at Spur, swung her horse around and moved in front of the wagon, taking the lead.

Spur McCoy, mother hen to eight little chicks and one dragon, scowled and watched the wagon moving westward.

When it was about fifty yards away, he took off his hat, wiped the sweat from his forehead, then reset the low crowned Stetson, still scowling, and rode after them.

SEVEN

Spur caught up with the Conestoga and two nuns riding next to the rig. He turned a stern face toward the Mother Superior. He tipped his hat and then rode in closer.

"Mother Benedict, remember what the store-keeper said about your nuns? That it would be kinder to line them up in the city and shoot them. Remember that, the man was serious. We are moving into a life and death situation. How well we can do what we must do, will determine how many of us are alive to ride into Roswell."

"The Lord will protect us, and we'll do everything we can to protect ourselves," she said.

"Good. On our noontime stop there will be required rifle instructions for everyone, including Clark and you. Be sure your whiskey priest is sober enough to learn something about these Spencer repeating rifles." Before the nun could respond Spur wheeled his horse and galloped forward toward the slight figure on the roan gelding a quarter of a mile along a slight downslope.

When he came up to Chiquita, she had dismounted and was sitting on the ground, her legs folded, her arms outthrust as she stared at the cloudless sky.

He dropped from the horse and waited.

She remained in that position for another two minutes, then turned and stared at him.

"I know, Chiquita, the Indian spirits are everywhere. Go to it, anything might help. Right now I'd take a Shaman if I could find one and use him as scout."

"You are right, roundeye. The Indian spirits are all around us, in the rivers, the trees, the broad plateaus, the parched mountains. They are in every animal from the ant to the buffalo and in this seven dog I ride. I would not expect a roundeye to understand or even appreciate.

"The spirits bring us either success or failure, make the game run near us for a kill, heal the sick, guarantee fertility. The spirits watch over the welfare of all Mescaleros, everywhere."

"Even a Breed?"

"Especially, because I also have a St. Christopher's medal with me."

"You know this is a fool's mission. It could become a total disaster, a tragedy."

"Not with Chiquita as your guide. Remember, I, too, am Mescalero!"

"A Mescalero arrow or .52 caliber rifle slug will slam into your flesh just as easily as into one of the roundeye Catholics back there. Do you realize you have seven women and a drunkard in that wagon? They know nothing of the high desert, nothing of how to defend themselves. And none of them have ever raised a hand in violence. Not very good troops."

"But Mother Superior is determined, that makes up for a lot." She pointed ahead to the west. "See the thin line of green? A small river. One of the last we will see for some time. We must refill our water barrels there. We need to make fifteen miles today."

"I'd guess you will swing to the south so we miss most of the better hunting grounds of the Mescaleros?"

"How did you . . ." She looked up and she nodded. "You must know more of the Mescalero and this country than I thought. You've been here before."

"And survived, which could be more than I'll do this time. The deeper we get into Mescalero country, the more we must consider moving at night and sleeping during the day. Do you agree?"

"The third day will be our last travel in the sunlight." A new appreciation for him showed in her eyes. "This roundeye may be useful yet on our dangerous journey," she said, a small smile showing. Then she rose, leaped on the back of her horse and rode ahead.

Spur wheeled and walked his mount toward the wagon. He tied his bay on a lead rope and swung up to the back of the wagon. Two sisters were altering pants. One of them was Teresa. She smiled and now he could see her short blonde hair again.

"Sisters, I need to get a box and do some work with it. Is there room?"

Sister Mary Ruth said she wanted to ride up front with Mother.

Spur found what he was hunting and sat down on another box and took out the Spencer rifle tubular magazines. He began loading seven of the big .52 caliber rounds into each of the tubes.

"What are those?" Teresa asked.

"Magazine tubes for the rifles," he said, looking up. Then he couldn't help staring at her. He glanced around. "Do you know how surprised I was when I saw you?"

Sister Teresa laughed softly. "I have some idea. I haven't been a nun very long. I . . . I just had to break out of the order for a few hours."

"You certainly did that." Spur went back to loading the tubes. If they got hit by Mescaleros they would have a supply of the loaded tubes ready to go. He wanted ten tubes for each rifle, but they didn't have that many back at the store. He remembered buying four of the boxes with ten tubes in each box.

"Can I help?" Teresa asked.

He showed her how to load the shells, pushing each one in the tube against the pressure of the spring. She caught on at once and soon was loading them as quickly as he did.

"You'll get a chance to use these this noon," he said. "We're having basic rifle training. I have a gut feeling we're all going to need to know how to shoot the Spencers before this trip is over."

"I don't know anything about guns," Teresa said.

"You will before nightfall."

She let her hand brush his leg and he looked at her sharply. She pulled the hand back and continued loading the rounds.

"Seemed like a good idea," she said and smiled again.

They were over half done. Spur eased to the tailgate and jumped out. He walked along behind the tailgate watching her.

"Finish up on these, would you please? I have to check up ahead and see if there's a place to stop for dinner."

Spur felt a relief when he stepped into his saddle and rode. Teresa could be a problem, but not if he didn't let her. She was looking for more loving, but it was impossible. Not even Father Clark would hump a nun in a situation like this. Spur snorted and changed his mind. Clark would try for any female within reach, and he was sure the Mother Superior had warned all her nuns about him.

He rode forward a quarter of a mile in front of the wagon. The trail, such as it was, showed faint and often became non-existent. It made little difference since west was the direction, and the flat land with only a few streams, could be crossed at almost any point. Now and then they saw wheel tracks pounded into the earth when it had been much softer than it was now.

McCoy could not see the scout, Chiquita. He wondered where she was. He paused for a moment on the big bay mare and scanned the land ahead. He'd heard that on a level place you could see only seven miles in any direction. Beyond that the curvature of the earth sent your line of sight out into space.

Nowhere in the next seven miles could he see the line of green that he and Chiquita had spotted before from the small rise. Fortunes of travel. They would stop within an hour wherever they happened to be. They did not need a stream, although the animals would want water by nightfall. They would have to wait until mid afternoon at least and the small stream and the splotch of green he had seen.

Spur rode back to the wagon, tied his mount and climbed up on the front bench. The white stripe across Mother Benedict's forehead had turned from bright pink to boisterous red.

He took off his hat and eased it on the nun's head.

"I'm burning?"

"Yes. We forgot to buy you hats. Sunbonnets would be a help. Can one of your ladies sew up some?"

"Yes, we'll use cloth from one of the habits. That's a fine idea, Mr. McCoy."

He took the reins while Mother Benedict swiveled around and climbed in through the front of the covered wagon and called to the sisters in back.

An hour later they stopped on the raw prairie of the high plateau of Western Texas. Sister Maria had been designated as cook and she fried up bacon and eggs as a treat. They would use them up today and tomorrow before they spoiled.

Spur got out the seven Spencers and checked them over. He found a large rock about thirty yards away that he used as a target and loaded each of the Spencers then shot a round through each weapon.

Three of the nuns watched him.

"Ladies, now is as good a time as any." He

positioned the three ten yards from the wagon facing outward and had them sit on the ground. He stood in front of them with a Spencer.

"Ladies, this is a Spencer repeating rifle. It will fire seven times without reloading. It fires a .52 caliber slug from a number fifty-six spencer rim fire cartridge. The barrel is round and thirty inches long and rifled with three broad grooves. The rifling makes the bullet spin so it travels straight once it leaves the barrel."

He moved his hand to the rear sight. "This is the sliding rear sight, and up here is the blade front sight. The total length of this weapon is forty-seven inches and it weighs a little more than ten pounds."

He unlocked the magazine and drew it out of the butt of the rifle. "The rounds in this tube load through the base plate, then lock in place. When it's empty you open it, take out the used tubes and put in a loaded one. The spent brass fly out of the breach of the weapon. Have any of you fired a rifle before?"

One had, Sister Mary Francis. Spur handed her a Spencer.

"Sister, lift your knees to rest your elbows on, then sight it on that rock out there and fire."

She took the rifle and looked up, surprised. "It's so heavy!"

"You'll get used to it. Try a shot."

She lifted the rifle, braced her elbows on her knees and fired. Dust spurted up twenty yards beyond the rock. The two other nuns laughed. The kick of the heavy round slammed the rifle into her shoulder.

"Try it again."

This time the round hit twenty feet in front of them. Spur frowned, then went to the wagon and brought back a wooden box.

"Rest the rifle on this and try it again."

She did. This time she hit the rock. He had her fire until the seven shots were gone. Then he talked her through taking out the empty tube and putting in a new one.

One by one he trained the nuns in how to use the Spencer.

They took a break for a trail dinner, the bacon and fried eggs and some baked bread they had brought from the town's small bakery. Any bread after that would have to be fresh baked biscuits.

As the ammo tubes emptied, Sister Teresa refilled them.

Spur thanked her. "Yes, we should keep the forty tubes filled at all times. We never know when we might need them." He showed everyone where the tubes would be stored. The rifles were at several locations around the wagon for quick use. Four loaded tubes were with each Spencer.

At first Mother Superior Benedict backed away from the weapons training.

Spur spoke softly to her. "Sister, you got us into this mess, and you might have to help hold off a few dozen Mescaleros. I suggest you learn how to shoot extremely well. Your very life may depend on it. This would be a ridiculous, senseless way to die, proving nothing, certainly not a fitting ending to your service to your church."

She watched Spur for a moment. Then took the Spencer, hefted it a moment and standing up put all seven of the rounds in the center of the rock.

The nuns cheered.

"I was raised on a farm before I went into the order," she said.

Father Clark came late to the meal. He took one bite of the fried eggs, rushed to one side and threw up. Mother Benedict vanished inside the wagon and a few moments later Spur saw her pouring what was left of a pint of whiskey into the dirt. She threw the bottle as far as she could.

They did not take the usual two hour dinner break of a normal wagon train. Instead they pushed forward. By three that afternoon they could see the green band of trees near the stream and by four-thirty they pulled in and stopped in the shade.

Chiquita told Spur this was the best place to camp for five miles ahead. They had covered almost twelve miles.

"We'll camp here tonight," Spur told them. Then he found Sister Cecilia, the other farm girl, and helped her unhitch the mules. She was a tall woman, about thirty and could handle the hitching and harnessing. They pulled off the harness and tethered the mules in some knee high grass after giving them a good long drink.

When all the horses were also cared for, they began to gather wood for a small cooking fire. Three of the nuns took off shoes and stockings, rolled up their pant legs a few inches and dangled their feet in the cool, clear water of the stream. It was no more than a foot deep and perhaps fifteen feet wide. After the day's dry, hot ride it was a practical oasis.

Supper came just as it began to get dark.
Sister Mary Ruth had put a five gallon crock full
of beans to soak. She would cook them at breakfast and again at noon. Supper was beef jerky
and bread, with plenty of dried apricots and hot
coffee.

Spur had seen Chiquita ride off just after they
stopped. She came back at full dark, had some
food and talked to Spur.

"I found some signs up river. Two or three
Mescaleros were here hunting, rabbits probably.
They made a small kill and left two days ago,
moving west and north. We should not be bothered by them. That was the only sign I saw of
any of my people."

"That phrase worries me a little, Chiquita.
You said *my people*. Will that make a difference
if the Mescaleros attack us? Can you shoot
down your people?"

"Spur McCoy. Know that I am Mexican by
choice, Indian by accident. I have chosen the
roundeye way of life, not the Mescalero. The
Apache, and especially the Mescalero, raid and
kill for pleasure. War is the Apache's vocation,
they glory in it. The Mescaleros are honest but
cruel, treacherous killers who torture their
captives. I was raised by nuns in a softer, more
human atmosphere.

"Yes, Mr. McCoy. I can and I will defend my
charges, and my own life with every skill and
power that I have. They are *my people* only by
chance, not by choice."

"Good, which guard duty do you want, dark
or midnight, or midnight to five A.M.?"

"The early morning hours are most

dangerous, I'll take them," she said. Chiquita finished her food. "I'll be by the golden cottonwood, wake me at twelve."

She took her blanket to the cottonwood and was soon sleeping.

After the meal the small camp quieted. The nuns were bone weary after the first day. Father Clark appeared for only a short time to eat, then went back to the wagon. Spur knew that by tomorrow he would be bone dry, desperately sober, hung over and hurting. Then Spur would start turning up the pressure on Clark, and get him functioning and helping them. As much as McCoy disliked the idea, Clark would have to help them in a tight situation. He would need some rifle training first.

Spur saw Mother Superior bed down her charges. They were on the ground in blankets, with their feet to the fire. They slept in twos, close together, touching for security. Then Mother Superior went back to the front of the wagon where she had built a small nest of her own.

McCoy established a perimeter guard trail, and walked it one way and then the other. He hunkered down next to a clump of brush and listened. There was almost no sound. A night hawk called now and then. He heard the beating of the wings of a big owl which quieted when the huge bird soared from one tree to another. The sound of nothing beat at his ears, creating a soft rushing.

His evaluation of the day was quick and simple.

So far, so good.

It was what lay ahead that worried him. The deeper they plunged into Mescalero country, the more apt they were to run into a band of Mescaleros or to be seen by a hunting party or a wandering scout.

Then the fun would begin. Then people would start dying. An attack by Mescaleros would not be a massive horse charge. The Mescaleros seldom used horses. They were more apt to eat a horse if they could catch one, rather than ride it. They could run all day through the high desert, and usually outdistance a man on horseback.

A Mescalero brave moved through the land like a wolf or coyote, taking advantage of cover and the terrain.

If they attacked it would be suddenly, with deadly surprise. When they were out maneuvered, or out gunned, they simply melted away into the plains or plateaus or hills and were not seen again.

That was the Mescalero way, the killing way, the ages old way of death.

Ever vigilant was the key. Now there was little danger. The Mescaleros almost never fought or attacked at night. If they had spotted the lone wagon, they would rest now and ready a welcome for them shortly after daylight.

At midnight he woke Chiquita with a touch on her shoulder. Before he could pull back his hand a sharp knife lay against it and round black eyes stared up at him.

"Don't ever touch me!" she said sharply. "A word or two will wake me. Stay out of reach of my blade."

"Good morning to you, too, Chiquita. Nothing

is stirring. Time for me to get some sleep." Spur moved away, not watching her rise or to see where she went. She would do it right, she was a hired scout, and she was Mescalero.

He rolled up in his blankets, looked over at the six sleeping nuns and wondered which one was Teresa. He snorted, turned over and went to sleep.

EIGHT

The missionaries were all sore, stiff and complaining in the morning. Father Clark answered the breakfast call and looked half dead. His hangover was still pounding at him. He growled at the nuns until Mother Superior Benedict had a quiet word with him. Then he took his bacon and cooked dried prunes and sat by himself on the ground, eating and glaring at everyone.

Spur helped Sister Cecilia with the harness for the mules. She remembered her farm days and learned quickly. She would be able to do it by herself from now on.

They hit the trail at slightly before six A.M. while the touches of light were breaking apart the solid black of the east behind them.

The three nuns who had not ridden the horses the first day got to ride today. They were far from expert, but could ride well enough to stay up with the plodding mules. Teresa was the best rider of the group.

Chiquita talked briefly with Spur over her breakfast.

"Yes, here we swing more to the south, as you guessed. We go around two water holes, but we will have more than enough water for two days. At that time we will come to Agua Caliente. There are some warm springs there but the water is not sulpur so it is fit to drink. Few Mescaleros travel that far south this time of year to hunt."

"Nothing for the stock to drink after this morning?" Spur asked.

"Late in the day there should be a small stream that has not yet dried up for the summer."

"Our animals hope so."

"I may not be back until noon. Southwest until midday and we should be right. I'll find you." She put down her tin plate and fork.

"Hey, so far so good," Spur said. "What are our chances of getting through unseen?"

"About a hundred to one." She shook her pretty face sending the braid bouncing behind her. Dark eyes shaded even deeper purple black. "No, worse than that. No chance at all. The Mescals are hunting meat. Do you know how long a tribe of twenty-five can live off one mule?"

"Best hunting this time of year is the seven-dog and whatever roundeyes happen to be along for the walk. How did the Mescaleros ever call the horse seven-dog?"

"We used to use big dogs to pull sleds and made packs for them. They could carry about sixty pounds. When the horse came along the Mescaleros decided a horse could carry seven times as much as a dog, so . . . seven-dog."

"Makes sense."

She looked at him sternly. "We are going to have much trouble before this trip is over. But it may be well that you are along. You are not the worst roundeye I have ever met." She let the smallest trace of a smile touch her serious face, then she stood in an easy move and ran to her horse. A moment later she had mounted and was gone. There was not even a canteen on her saddle.

Spur dug into the supplies and found the canteens, and made sure each of the riding horses had a filled water bottle hung over the pommel. A precaution.

The little band moved slowly across the prairie of the great plateau. They were still in Texas since it was sixty-five miles as the crow flies to get to the New Mexican line. With the wandering route any wagon must take, it would probably be five days before they reached the state line.

In places the spring grass had not yet turned brown. It rose in undulating waves across the wide expanses of land, looking sometimes more like a sea than a landmass. In places the soil had given up the last of the spring moisture and the grass was a rich golden color, turning a square mile at a time into a prospector's fantasy.

The Conestoga rolled on. Spur was glad he had settled on the sturdy wagon. So far they had experienced no trouble with it and the mules were pulling a relatively light load for the four of them. He hoped that would mean no mechanical problems with the rig.

As they angled southwest they followed a

gentle depression that began a valley here but was never more than ten or twelve feet below the rest of the land's contour. The small wet weather stream had long since evaporated into the sand, but here and there they saw a damp spot. They were nothing worthy of the word spring that could be used.

Half a mile farther down Mother Superior made her first driving mistake. She elected to go through one such wet area, rather than drive fifty yards around it.

The mules sank in past their hocks into the dampness and the front wheels dropped in a foot deep, but the mules, now on firm footing beyond the sink, pulled the front wheels through. The wider rimmed rear wheels would have no trouble in the soft mud, Spur hoped. He was on the verge of shouting at Mother Benedict to whip the mules for more power.

Too late. The rear wheels with the most weight on them quickly sank to the axle and the mules pawed the ground. The big Conestoga was securely stuck in the mud in the middle of a semi desert.

"Everybody out!" Spur bellowed. The nuns scrambled out, then slowly the priest exited.

Spur stared at the sink. It was barely six feet wide. Already the front wheels were on dry ground. He hated the idea of unloading the whole wagon and levering it out. Instead he called to the nuns riding the horses. Using ropes they hitched the four riding horses to the singletree the first team was fronted by.

The ropes went around the singletree and then around the saddle horn of each mount.

Spur looked over all the knots, then at the women.

"When I give the signal, we all ride ahead and pull that wagon right out of the mud. Everyone ready?"

Heads nodded. Behind, Mother Superior Benedict took off her sunbonnet and wiped her brow. Then she said she was prepared.

"Ready . . . Go!" Spur shouted.

The four mules and four horses strained against the leather and the ropes. Slowly the rear wheels began to move, an inch, then a foot, then one of the mules slipped and fell in the traces and all progress stopped.

Spur dismounted and went back to the mule. He urged the animal to stand, then stroked his ears and the side of his neck. A final pat on the mule calmed it and Spur went back to his saddle.

"Progress, we're making progress. Let's do it again. Ready . . . Go!"

This time the wagon refused to move for a moment, then it inched ahead, slowed and then in one burst slid forward and rolled out of the muck to the dry land.

Everyone cheered.

They paused for five minutes while Spur checked out the wagon. The undercarriage was mudded, but it would dry, the mud harden and fall off within a few miles.

Mother Superior had stepped to the ground to look over the rig as well. She glanced at Spur now and smiled.

"I know. Next time if I have any question about the footing, I should drive around it. I'll remember. But you get to drive when we have to ford the first river we come to."

"That won't be much of a problem. We might touch the headwaters of the Sulphur Draw stream, but up here it won't be more than a creek. Then we'll see how much water the Pecos has in it."

They rolled again. By noontime Spur figured with the early start and lack of trouble that they had covered a little over eight miles.

Chiquita had not returned. They stopped on a slight rise so she could find them and ate biscuits and baked beans for lunch. The beans were not quite done, but could be eaten. They would be cooked for as long as the noon break lasted, then cooked the final time at the supper stop. They were laced with the ever present bacon.

The way the bacon was smoked and cured it would last even in the heat for three to four weeks, and quickly became the meat staple. Some wagons carried along a chicken coop, to produce eggs and a cow for milk. Larger units herded a dozen steers along the route, killing one a week to provide meat for fifty to a hundred people for two days before it turned rancid. Salt pork also was a staple for wagoners, but for a two week trip, Spur had elected not to bring any.

Chiquita came back just as they were packing up. Ruth provided her with a tin plate of food and a large cup of coffee and biscuits.

She brought with her two large jackrabbits she had shot, but not with her rifle. On her saddle hung a newly made bow and two arrows.

"A Mescalero is not worthy of the name if she can't make a bow and arrow in the hunting grounds," she told them. "We are now deep enough into Mescalero country so we should not fire our weapons unless we must. A rifle shot can be heard out here for twenty miles if the wind is right."

She gave the rabbits to Sister Cecilia who deftly butchered and skinned them and put the slender carcasses in a big pot filled with salt water. They both would be roasted for supper.

Soon they were moving again. Chiquita told Spur there was another small stream half a day's ride ahead. They could get to it by driving the wagon until nearly dark.

"Any more sign?"

"No, not here, they must be staying to the north. Our luck may be holding."

Spur laughed and pointed at her. "Or our spirits are with us on this trip."

"Do not make fun of something you don't understand," Chiquita said sharply. "You are a roundeye."

"Which means I can't understand anything Indian?" Spur asked quickly. "I know when a person has been rejected by both her cultures that it must hurt terribly. I know that a woman needs more than a horse and a .44 and a job so she can make an honest living. I know a lot about you, Chiquita."

Her black eyes watched his for several seconds. Neither of them looked away. At last her face curved into a real smile. "I hope you do know me, gringo. Then you will know what I am going to do when we have a fight with the

Mescals. You will know my tactics and I yours. It will help us defeat the Mescals and that way we both will live longer." She rode rapidly away for a hundred yards, then came back letting her horse walk.

"There is a soft place ahead we must cross, no way around it. A seep of some sort and probably the last one. See how the land becomes more dry with every mile? Caution Mother to be careful at the wet spot."

"We'll get through."

"I'm going to probe to the north, see what I can find. I'll leave the horse on a lead rope behind the wagon. This is Mascalero work, the seven-dog would only get in my way and attract attention. A wolf or a coyote is harder to see than a horse." She rode to the wagon, tied the horse and trotted away to the north, her newly made bow and three arrows in her left hand, where any good Mescalero hunter would carry them.

Spur McCoy watched her go. If there were any Mescals within five miles of their route, she would spot them, stay unseen and return to warn him.

He sat on his mount and dug out a crooked black cheroot and lit it with a stinker match. The smoke was bitter and biting and he blew it out. At least he had chosen the scout well for this ill conceived and ill advised trip. If they made it to Roswell, New Mexico, they would owe it mostly to the skill and knowledge of that small Mexican-Indian Breed jogging into the distance. Today she wore tan pants and a tan blouse almost the same color.

Even at a hundred yards he had trouble finding her as she blended into the combination of prairie grass and more and more bare patches of thin sandy soil.

Spur told Mother Benedict about the soft spot ahead, then rode forward to find it. Teresa rode a way with him, but he sent her back.

"Teresa, you know we can't ride off alone," Spur said with a sudden anger. "Our first job is to get across to Roswell."

"My first job is to show you how well I can make love. You'll see." She turned, her sunbonnet shading her face, and rode back to the wagon.

Spur found the soft place and waited. It was an almost stream that oozed and puddled for five miles across a traversing gradual slope. He walked his bay into it and she sank in to her hocks but then the ground seemed to hold. He worked across the twenty yard width of the soggy ground but found no real problem until near the far side. There it turned into a real sink which could probably swallow up the mules and wagon and not leave a trace.

He moved to the left and tried again. After another half hour of trial and error he found the end of the sink, and marked a safe route across with sticks.

When the wagon arrived, Father Clark rode one of the horses. He had been on a mount before. He saw the sticks, guided Mother Benedict along the path and led her safely through to the other side.

The nuns in the wagon cheered, and the other two nuns on horseback followed the wagon through the same path.

Father Clark rode up to Spur and scowled at him.

"I know we have to put up with each other for a few more days out here. I also know that you don't like me. I'm not telling anyone you are my favorite cowboy either. Don't worry, I can ride and shoot. I was in the army during the war, the Gray, naturally. When we're in Roswell, we will have a settling of accounts."

"We may," Spur said. "If you're a priest again by then, you won't have any trouble from me."

"So? You may still very well have some trouble from me." Father Clark stared past a long, slightly reddish nose at Spur, said nothing more and swung back toward the wagon.

The sun came down hotter than it had been the first day. Spur pulled the kerchief around his neck up to cover half of his face as they rode forward. Sweat ran down his hair and dripped on his neck.

He slashed away the moisture under his hat brim and resettled the Stetson. It was going to be over ninety degrees that day.

Spur was half asleep in his saddle when he heard a scream behind him thirty yards. He came alert at once, spun the bay around, his hand on his .45.

The big wagon sat at an odd angle. The mules had stopped, and Spur saw that the left front Conestoga wheel had dropped into a hole and splintered three spokes.

There was not a chance they were going to make the next water before dark now. He rode back to the wagon, remembering the joys of changing a wagon wheel on a heavily loaded rig —especially with only one other man to help him.

NINE

Spur, Father Clark, and all the nuns had been working hard for almost an hour. The mules had been unhitched and the wagon tongue removed, then several wooden boxes had been brought from the wagon to form a fulcrum. The boxes had been placed just outside of the wagon box near the front end of the rig.

Spur and Father Clark carried the wagon tongue to the fulcrum, placed the heavy end of it on the box and then tilted it downward until it would slip under the wagon frame.

Spur pushed it under the wagon box a foot and waved his arms.

"All right, the hard work is done. Let's rest a minute." He slumped on the box, panting. The temperature was still climbing. He figured it was nearing a hundred degrees. "Do you ladies have that wire loosened up on the spare wheel?" he asked.

A variety of answers came back. He heaved to his feet and went around the box to check the wheel wired to the undercarriage of the wagon.

It was loosened. He moved the nuns back, snipped one wire with the side cutter pliers and let that side of the wheel down to the ground, then cut the other side. He slid the wheel out and positioned it next to the wagon.

"Now comes the part that takes lots of brain power. We all jump on the wagon tongue and hope we weigh enough to lift the wagon up with our basic machine lever here. Hang on to the tongue, sit on it, lay on it. Anything to boost up the axle so we can push some more wooden boxes under it. Let's give it a try."

He caught the tongue that was slanting six feet into the air and pulled it down so the nuns could grab it. Then they jumped on it bringing it lower and lower and the wagon box higher.

Spur let go and hurried to the front of the wagon. Father Clark had pushed a second box under the axle. They needed another foot. Spur found three timbers, four by fours and placed them on top of the wooden box under the axle, then put the last one on top of those and it was high enough.

The nuns let the wagon tongue down slowly and the wooden boxes under the wagon held.

"Now, all we have to do is pull this wheel off, throw it away and put on the new one," Spur said. "Then pray that we don't break another one."

With the pressure off the wheel it came free in a few minutes and the new one was rolled on and pinned into place. They hoisted the wagon box once more with the lever so the men could take out the blocking under the axle and let the box down slowly. The wheel hit the ground and held.

A tired cheer went up.

Another half hour and the boxes had been stowed back in the wagon, the tongue put back in place and the mules hitched up. They would be too late to get to the patch of greenery before dark that they could see some four or five miles ahead.

Spur pushed them along, but called a halt a half hour before dusk. They had brought firewood with them from the last stop as a precaution. They needed it. There were no trees not even any brush here. The tall grass had given way to stunted growth and a small bush now and again. They were coming more into a desert area of lower rainfall.

Chiquita walked into the camp just as it grew dark. She looked tired. She at once took over roasting the two rabbits over an open fire. She let the flames burn down to glowing coals and lowered a spit until the meat was two inches from the heat, then turned them slowly.

Soon fat sizzled in the coals and the meat cooked. It was the best meal they had eaten since leaving Lubbock. Roast rabbit, well done baked beans, biscuits and dried apples for desert and plenty of strong, black coffee.

Spur talked to Chiquita as they ate.

"Find any friends?" he asked.

"No signs at all. No more game, either. There should be no Mescals hunting this area because there's nothing here to hunt. The raiders should be working the regular route across to Roswell. We should be about ten miles south of that."

"Good. Let's hope your spirit friends, and my Irish luck stays with us. I'll take both watches tonight. You need some sleep."

"No. I do my job. You take the first watch as usual. I'm going to sleep over on that side." She pointed to the north just off the firelight. Spur took his tin plate and cup back to the pot of hot water and washed them, got a second cup of coffee and walked around the tethered horses and the six mules.

For a moment he wondered if they should have brought extra harness for the spare mules? It would have come in handy to pull the wagon out of the sink. Without the harness for the mules he had to rely on the saddle horses.

McCoy dismissed it and concentrated on walking around the little camp. The wagon shielded the fire so it showed only to the south. Couldn't be too careful. Only one more day of traveling in the daytime? Night movement with a wagon would be slow and dangerous. He would have another talk with Chiquita about it.

He watched the camp fire burn down. Sleeping had been no problem for any of them. The nuns were used to working, but this was a different kind of labor. There had been far fewer problems with Father Clark than Spur had figured. Perhaps he only went on occasional flings with the whores and John Barleycorn. Perhaps.

The fire went out. He saw the six sleeping forms near the embers. Mother Superior and the priest still shared different ends of the wagon at night. Chiquita was a small curled ball between the fire and the horses and mules.

Spur stood and looked out as a half moon rode into the sky. Not a cloud. The stars sparkled and winked at him.

Not a sound. No wind, no birds calling out here.

Then a solitary coyote howled in the distance. He listened. An answering call came from the other way. Then a third and a fourth. For ten minutes there was a chorus of coyotes serenading to each other. It was some crude form of communication, and probably part of the mating rituals. The calls were higher pitched but not as complex as those of wolves.

A pack of wolves howling up a chorus could run chills along a grown man's spine. The calls of the coyotes seemed more of a serenade than of signalling any danger. Coyotes were afraid of humans. The only one he had ever see even try to attack a human was a large male that had rabies. The animal had been actually foaming at the mouth before he was shot dead in a small town in Kansas.

Spur watched the Big Dipper climb in the sky. It was on its nightly journey of making nearly a complete circle around the North Star. By watching the position of the Big Dipper any cowhand worth his beans and bacon knew what time it was to within ten minutes.

When the Big Dipper told Spur it was one A.M., he went and called softly to Chiquita. She came awake at once, the knife already in her hand. She looked at the sky.

"Why did you let me sleep an extra hour?"

"Because I'm bigger than you are, and I'm tougher than you are, but most important, because I'm your boss. Any questions?"

She smiled, checked her .44 and folded her blankets.

"Quiet?"

"Yes."

"Anything?"

"Not even a nightbird. We did have some coyotes serenading us, but they are either paired up for the night or sleeping."

She shot him a quick look, then waved in the thin moonlight and walked toward the wagon and a drink of coffee from the pot that still sat on the now cold coals.

Spur took his blankets from the back of the wagon and lay down in a slight depression twenty yards from the fire. He stared at the stars for a moment, then turned on his side and cushioned his head with his arms. His eyes had begun to get heavy when he was aware of someone near him. He tensed, his hand holding the .45 under the blankets.

"Be quiet, Spur McCoy and I won't scream," a soft woman's voice said.

He opened his eyes and saw Teresa's beautiful face staring at him from her blanket beside him.

"I thought we might share our covers . . . so we could stay warmer," Teresa said. She folded back the heavy cloth and in the moonlight he saw her white body, naked against the darkness.

"Teresa!" he whispered. "I told you . . ."

Then she had pushed on top of him and pressed her mouth over his. The kiss had begun as an attack to quiet him, but soon the intensity wavered and it became softer, more pliable, more seductive, and then it was a plea, a whimper of desire that Spur could not ignore.

Spur was angry at first, but as the kiss continued and he felt her body against his, he remembered how she set him on fire back in Lubbock, and he opened his mouth for her tongue to slant into him.

A moment later he had pulled the blanket over her and his hands found her breasts. Teresa was panting as she unfastened the buttons on his pants.

"Don't even take them off!" She whispered. "I want it rough and sudden and hard! Take me right now before I even get ready! Be rough with me this time."

She rolled on her back and pulled him over her. His weapon was cocked and ready and she lifted her parted knees and he lanced into her waiting slot with a suddenness that left her gasping for air, moaning in delight with touches of pain. Then she wrapped her legs around his waist as he lifted a little off her chest and pounded into her.

For the moment pure lust commanded him. Spur McCoy was a sexual animal craving satisfaction. He hammered at her and she rose to meet each powering thrust. Her breasts heaved and her face worked as she surged into a climax of her own.

Spur barely noticed. Again and again he slammed his hips against hers until his pelvic bone hurt with each plunge. Then the trigger opened the valves and closed others and his seed blasted deeply into her and he heaved and panted again, then for a long moment he lay, locked inside of her.

"Wonderful, sweetheart!" she cooed into his ear in a whisper. "We have all night. Cecilia is my sleep partner. She never wakes up, and she snores. We're safe.''

He lay there a moment more, then slid away and lay beside her.

"Don't worry about my being a nun. I'm really not a nun. My father made me join the order. I'm still a novice. My father caught me in bed at home with two boys. Evidently he watched a while before he came crashing in. He said I had to join the convent or a brothel. As soon as we get to Roswell I'm renouncing my vows and staying there.''

"I'm a little relieved to hear that, Teresa. But we have to be quiet, Chiquita could be watching us.''

"Too bad,'' Teresa whispered. "Let her find her own man.'' She reached under the blanket to his crotch.

They both laughed softly, put their heads under the blanket and talked, then made love again. Spur got her into her clothes and back to her spot by the fire a little after two A.M. He guessed that Chiquita knew of the movement. Spur was not worried about it. He was more concerned with getting some sleep so he could function rationally tomorrow. The deeper they penetrated Mescalero country the more the danger.

He turned on his side again and closed his eyes. Before he could drift off to sleep he heard a scuffle away from the wagon, then a man's scream of pain, and an angry eruption of Spanish that could come only from Chiquita.

Spur was on his feet, running, his .45 in his hand. Twenty steps from the wagon he saw

Chiquita kneeling, the moonlight glinting off her knife.

The blade lay against Father Clark's throat. Spur saw dark stains of fresh blood on the steel. Chiquita's brown blouse was torn open, hanging by threads, exposing her two full breasts in the moonlight.

Clark held his left arm with his right hand. Blood seeped between his fingers and there was a look of terror on the priest's face.

"He dies," Chiquita said simply.

Mother Superior Benedict hurried up. She wore a long white nightgown and took in the scene in a second. She spoke rapidly in Spanish.

Spur caught most of it. She said yes, Father Clark deserved to die for attacking her. But he was still a priest, a servant of God. Only God can punish him. God has before and he will again. Chiquita must put away the knife.

"Give me the knife, Chiquita," Spur said softly kneeling beside her.

She looked at him, her face distorted by fury, hatred and remembered pain.

"My Mescalero name in Pohati, it means knife woman who never forgets. This man is not my husband, he attacked me. He must die. It is the Mescalero way!" She moved the sharp blade until it touched the priest's throat, her eyes glinting with a fury and hatred that Spur had never seen before in any woman, Mexican, Indian or white.

TEN

Chiquita increased the pressure with the biting sharp knife against the priest's throat until a trace of blood showed.

"This man must die, it is the Mescalero way!" she said.

"It is not the Spanish way," Spur said gently. "The Mexican people are known for their fairness, for order and justice. Would your mother have said the same words you have?"

The knife pressure eased. She glanced at him, then back at the priest.

"He jumped me in the dark like a coward. Then he threw me to the ground, tore off my shirt, he touched me in my most private places. I got one hand loose and sliced his wrist. If I had not been able to do that he would have violated me. This rapist must die!"

"Your mother would not have said that, Chiquita," Spur said. "She was Mexican and proud. She suffered much for you. Wouldn't she want you to follow her way and her teachings about this situation?"

"He attacked me, like he was an animal! We Mescaleros put to death our rabid dogs. He is a rabid dog! He must die before he spreads the sickness. I will kill him."

"He will face justice, but not this way," Spur said sharply. "It can't be Mescalero justice. They abandoned you, they rejected you, they threw you out of their village and their tribe. You have no loyalty to the tribe or to its laws."

"He ripped open my shirt! He pawed me and kissed me! His hands violated me!"

Spur reached slowly toward her hand still holding the blade.

Father Clark's eyes were wide with fear, then he went limp. Unconscious, Spur figured. He put his hand over her fingers that held the blade. For a moment her hand tried to move the weapon, to slash Clark's throat. Then her arm and hand relaxed, let go of the blade and Spur caught it.

He lifted the small woman, and Mother Superior Benedict was there, her arms around the girl, talking quietly to her in Spanish and English as they walked back toward the wagon. Clark sat up at once. He had been faking.

"Suppose I should thank you, McCoy."

"I don't ask a rattlesnake for thanks when I don't kill it."

"That is some woman! Did you see the size of those . . ."

Before Clark could finish the sentence, Spur backhanded him across the mouth and he slammed backward to the ground. A line of blood came from the side of his mouth.

"I'll remember that, McCoy. One of these

nights when I'm not a priest, I'll settle with you."

"Not when you're tied up to a wagon wheel, because that's where you're going to be for the rest of the night, and every night we're on the trial."

"You wouldn't do that!"

"Watch me!"

Spur grabbed the man by his arm and towed him to the wagon. Clark held back but he did not fight, he knew he would have no chance against the larger man. To Spur, Clark was no longer a priest, he had lost any respect, rights and privileges he might have once commanded from Spur. Now Clark was simply a man, and not a good one.

Spur used rawhide, tied one end securely to Clark's wrist and forced him to sit beside the rear wagon wheel. He tied one hand at shoulder height to each side of the wheel. Clark began groaning and whining. Spur wanted to back-hand him but he never hit a man tied up. Instead he threatened to dump a bucket full of dishwater on him, and Clark quieted.

When morning came, Chiquita had the cooking fire going and coffee ready. She hurried everyone, prodding them to finish their chores and get moving.

Spur sat down beside her, avoiding Teresa.

"Chiquita. Do you think we're far enough south of the Mescals so we can still travel during the daylight hours from now on?"

The half Mescalero sipped her coffee and looked at him over the rim of the cup from her deep, dark eyes. "I've been hoping so, Spur

McCoy. After today's scouting I'll tell you. We can move nearly twice as far by traveling during the day, which means we cut down our stay in Mescal territory by half. On the other hand we are twenty times as likely to be spotted by the hostiles during the day."

"If we stay over a daytime, we'll need cover, a good sized creek and lots of trees. We should be stocking firewood as we go along."

She nodded.

Spur watched her, not sure how to continue. At last he struggled with the words.

"About last night. Do you want to ride in the wagon today?"

"No. He didn't hurt me. I should have been quicker and killed him before you came. I'll do my job as usual. You don't have to worry about me. Worry about Clark."

"You don't have to be concerned about him. He's going to be tied up each night."

Chiquita looked up at Spur in a curious way that he could not read. She wore the same tight brown pants but a different shirt, this one a darker brown shade. It would blend well into the more desert like country they approached. She turned, walked to her horse and rode away. He had not seen her speak to anyone except Mother Benedict and himself.

The sisters were whispering about what had happened last night. They seemed indignant but not surprised about Clark. Some of them stared at him in open worry and anger. Spur went over and cut Clark loose from the wheel, told him to eat quickly they were about to roll.

The priest glared at Spur then rubbed his

wrists where they had been tied and did as he was told.

Two hours after they left the camp site, Chiquita rode back and signaled to Spur. He met her and they rode side by side.

"We were too quick to judge the Mescals," she said. "Less than a half hour ahead there is an old Mescalera squaw sitting in the trail. She is ancient, toothless, hairless, wasted away. She sits beside a cactus plant with three blossoms on it waiting."

"Waiting to die," Spur continued. "It is the way of the Mescaleros. Can we go around her?"

"Not without wasting a lot of time. It would cost us almost five miles."

"We'll go ahead. You talk to the missionaries. Explain about the old one."

Chiquita shook her head. "I am your scout, not their teacher. You tell them if they need to be told. I need to scout along the trail the rest of her family clan left. There were eight to ten of them, with one seven-dog dragging a travois. Don't worry, they won't see me. The old woman said she has been waiting to die for two days. The rest of the Mescals could be twenty miles to the north by now."

The scout kicked her horse and the roan gelding darted forward.

Spur took off his hat and slapped the dust out of it against his jeans pants leg. It was going to be hot again today, in the nineties somewhere. He wiped a line of sweat off his forehead, then rode over and talked with Mother Benedict. He told her there was something he needed to speak to them all about. She called in the horseback riders and brought up the three nuns from the back of the wagon. They watched Spur as he rode along beside the wagon.

"Up ahead, we're going to see an Indian. She is a Mescalero and old. You may wonder what she's doing sitting beside the trail. In many of the plains and southwest Indian tribes, life is extremely hard. Existence and enough to eat day by day are the primary goals.

"This means that every member of the tribe or family group has specific and important jobs to do. The hunters bring in game, the root gatherers dig for edible roots and tubers, the berry pickers and fruit pickers do their jobs. If one person fails to do the work, the whole tribe suffers.

"The old squaw up ahead has decided that she can no longer hold up her end of the productive life. She can't benefit the tribe any longer. She is a liability, a drain on the very existence of the other tribal members.

"So she has one final talk with her family, then sits down by the trail to die."

There were excited whispers and talk among the girls.

"Like I tell you sisters, if you don't work, you don't eat," Mother Superior Benedict said. "Only these people mean it and live by that code."

"We can help her when we get there!" Sister Mary Joseph said.

The nuns all chimed in with offers of aid. Spur held up his hand.

"No. Absolutely not. When we come up to her,

none of you is to touch her, nor try to speak to her. It would be the most kindness to the woman if you did not even look at her. She is waiting to die. It is a religious experience for these people, the last one, and they insist that it be done right."

"We just go on by?" Mother Benedict asked. "We can't even give her a sip of water?"

"No, nothing. We won't even stop the wagon."

"That's cruel, inhuman!" one of the nuns said.

"Life is cruel, unfair, and often difficult. She would be shamed in the sight of the Indian spirits if she accepted help. We will look, but not stare, we will ride past without speaking, or helping her in any way."

"How long has she been there?" Sister Teresa asked.

"Chiquita being Mescal could talk to her. The old woman said it was her second or third day. This could be her last. She had prayed all night to the spirits to take her soul today."

"How awful!" a sister said.

Someone began to cry.

Spur shook his head. "No! This is not a sad time. It is the ultimate day for this woman. Tonight she will be with the spirits. Her soul will be released of its earthly pains and ills, and she will be free."

Spur turned and rode away to the front. He saw the Indian woman beside the trail where it slanted down a gentle incline to a crossing of a deep crevase that had been cut by hundreds of years of cloudbursts hitting the desert, boiling down small ravines, then gathering here and digging a deep ditch as it all ran off quickly.

He waited a hundred yards off for the wagon, then led the mules past the woman. No one spoke. The harness jangled, the wagon creaked and groaned as it rolled past on well greased wheels. The Indian squaw did not look at them. She was covered with three or four layers of clothing and one Navajo woven rug of many colors.

One of the nuns began to cry, then a second and a third. Sister Maria turned and stared at the huddled figure, but did not speak.

A few minutes later they were past and the nuns buzzed with chatter.

Mother Superior Benedict quieted them with a glance. "If only we could be as dedicated, as unswerving, as devoted to our beliefs as she is to hers." Mother Benedict sighed, looked at the nuns. "Sisters, there will be no communicating for the next hour except in emergencies. Let us meditate on the unusual strength of the old Indian woman, and learn from it."

Chiquita met them at the noon stop. She had spotted no Mescaleros after riding up their trail of the travois for five miles. She was convinced the family unit was moving back to the more favorable country to the north, after having been perhaps as far south as Mexico.

"No other traces of Mescals?"

"None."

"Then we shall drive by day tomorrow," Spur said.

Chiquita nodded her agreement and picked at

the bones of a rabbit which had been salted down.

Father Clark had found his hidden whiskey bottle and was silently drunk in the wagon. He would eat nothing.

They rolled again. Sister Cecilia had been alternating the teams of mules. They each worked two days then had one day off. They were holding up well.

That morning they had passed through the small stream seen the day before. All of the animals had been watered well, and their water keg and barrel refilled. They gathered all of the dry dead wood they could find and tied it in bundles and bound them to the sides of the wagon box.

Now, far ahead they saw smoke. They had not seen any smoke since they left the edge of Lubbock. Chiquita went forward at once to investigate.

She came back quickly and asked Spur to ride ahead with her.

"Three small houses and the start of a cattle operation. No sense trying it way out here. Not enough grass. Not enough water. Too many Mescaleros."

"The settlers, are they hurt?" Spur asked.

"None of them hurt anymore. The Mescaleros killed everyone, took whatever they wanted and fled north. It may have been the old squaw's family. There was a travois, heavily loaded."

They rode faster then, and pulled up at the edge of the first house. Spur saw a man with his head half hacked off and his belly sliced open.

Near a well lay the body of a naked woman her legs still spread where she had been tied down and raped.

Spur loosened his .45 in the leather.

"Let's go in and see if anyone is still alive."

ELEVEN

Spur swung down from his bay and stared at the two bodies. He knew there would be more. Three small ranchers had evidently tried to defy the odds and started ranching far out from anyone else. Land was probably not theirs, squatters. Evidently they had settled too far into the Mescaleros traditional lands.

His six-gun was out as he ran to the first house and looked inside. A six year old boy sprawled on his stomach on the living room floor. A large pool of blood had seeped from where his face once had been. A woman lay beside a kitchen table in the next room, her clothes gone, her crotch bloody, one breast cut off.

It went on and on. Spur holstered his weapon. There was no one to fear here anymore. The pain, the torture, the rape, the killing was over.

In the third house in the small compound he found only two bodies. So far he had counted four men and six women. Multiple marriages?

115

Ten children had been cut down before they had a chance to live.

He kicked a wall in the last house and leaned against it a moment. So much death.

The sound went past him at first. Just another small remembered noise in a place where there had been joy and laughter only two days before. The small sound came again, and he caught it, turned and went to the next room.

A house cat?

Now it was a cry. A baby's cry!

He rushed through the rooms, searching in every place where a baby could be hidden. He had heard the cry first in the small kitchen. There was nowhere to hide a baby, not in there. Maybe. He began pulling out drawers. One was a sugar bin, the next for home milled flour . . .

Two soft blue eyes stared up at him. The face twisted into a scowl and quickly cried.

Spur picked the blanket covered baby from the flour and brushed it off. He met Chiquita in the yard, the baby crying now with anger and hunger.

Chiquita let a small smile cross her face, then she took the baby, lay it on an outside table and unwrapped it. She cleaned the small white female body, found some towels and tore them into diapers for the infant, then wrapped her in a clean, dry blanket.

The well had not been polluted, so Spur drew water and they let the baby, perhaps a month old, sip at the water and suck it from their fingers.

Soon the small girl quieted and slept.

"I should bury them," Spur said looking at the bodies in the yard.

"A strange and pagan custom," Chiquita said. "Why put their bodies under the ground where their spirits will be trapped forever? They are better this way."

"Twenty-three are dead," Spur said. He had satisfied his curiosity about the men-women ratio. He had found a Book of Mormon in one of the houses.

"They were Latter Day Saints," Spur said. "I have no idea what they were doing way out here."

Spur held the child while Chiquita walked around the houses again and the three corrals. She came back after fifteen minutes of examining the grounds.

"Ten to twelve Mescalero braves on foot," she said. "They drove away nearly thirty head of beef and four horses." She hesitated. "They also took with them five white women, three full grown and two younger ones."

Spur slammed his fist into the table.

"They left here a little over a day ago. That's why the child is still alive."

"Let's get back to the wagon," Spur said. "We'll make a detour around this place."

"I agree. We slant more to the south. The family group that raided these houses has enough cattle to last them for years, if they would settle down in a valley somewhere. But they won't. They will kill too many beef too quickly. Some of the steers will wander off and die in the desert. Some will be stolen by other

Mescals. Natural hunters and raiders like the Mescals make rotten cowboys."

They rode back to the wagon which was still half a mile away. Spur carried the small bundle.

Traces of smoke could still be seen from the buildings as Chiquita angled the wagon more to the south. Two of the nuns had ridden to meet Spur and when they saw the baby, they squealed in delight.

The wagon stopped as the nuns gathered round the small one. They sobered as Spur told them she was the only survivor at the houses.

Mother Superior looked at her nuns.

"Sister Mary Joseph, you had three younger sisters at home. You will be responsible for our small visitor. We have no milk, no baby bottle. You will take over the place where I had been sleeping for the nursery. We'll talk about feeding her. What should we call her?"

A dozen names echoed around the wagon.

"Blossom," Chiquita said. "She is a small flowering blossom on this barren land. The last blossom of a whole settlement."

It was decided.

Sister Joseph took the bundle, moved into the front of the wagon and began preparing food for the small one, now named Blossom. The food all had to be liquid. She soaked dried fruits, made thin gravies with flour, made sugar water and fashioned a sugar tit on a small jar and a piece of white cloth the liquid could seep through.

It would work.

Chiquita rode up beside Spur and stared at him until he glanced at her.

"It is the time of the Great Battle?" Spur asked.

"You've heard of that?"

"Most people who try to live in this area know about it, fear it."

She waved one hand as if wiping out a sand painting. "No, I've heard nothing about the Great Battle around here. There has been little talk lately of driving the Mexicans and the Americans out of the historic Apache lands. The old men talk little of it. Some of the younger braves have never heard the story. Most realize there are too many roundeyes now, it is impossible."

"Then all this sudden raiding? Why does the army think the Mescaleros are getting ready to go on the warpath?"

"Ask the army. All roundeyes forget the Apache and especially the Mescaleros are raiders by nature. We make war for sport, we Mescals live by raiding, not by hunting or digging in the ground or growing strange animals."

"Like the steer."

"And the horse and the pig, yes."

"And those twenty-three souls back there lying dead in the hot sun?"

"A chance, a surprise target, an easy kill not to be passed by."

"A chance at life, or a chance at death. At least one of them has the possibility of living through it," Spur said.

"Blossom will live, she is a strong baby or she would have died already. She will live."

"Let's talk about moving ahead. We're now well south of most of the Mescalero areas. What's your suggestion about traveling during the day?"

"Yes, move in the light."

"I agree. We'll start pushing harder, daylight to dusk, try for twenty miles a day. Today included."

Chiquita looked up with a new appreciation showing in her eyes. Quickly she hid it, turned. "I'll check ahead for the best spot to stop." She glanced up at the burning sun. "We have five more hours before dusk." She touched the roan gelding's flanks with her boot heels and galloped away toward the southwest.

Spur told the missionaries about the new plans. He also said that he and Chiquita had decided that the raiders on the ranches were part of the same family group of Mescaleros who had left the old squaw to die.

"So we'll push farther and faster during the day," Spur told the sisters. "If we can move twenty miles a day instead of fifteen, we can be in Roswell three or four days quicker. But more important, we can cross the danger zone here that much faster."

The nuns were holding up better than he had expected. Most of them were used to hard work, and the riding and camp work was like a vacation to them. Their sunbonnets were showing signs of wear, and they tried to wash their spare pants and shirts whenever they came to a stream.

Spur left his bay and walked around the wagon. The spare mule team plodded along

behind the Conestoga. The wheels were getting
a little dry on axle grease. He would take care of
that chore tonight. Spur spent five minutes
walking beside the mules, checking the harness,
the doubletrees and the traces and driving lines.
He found no problems.

He tied the bay on a lead line beside the mules
and jumped up to the driver's bench in front.

"Spell you a while with the reins, driver?"

Mother Benedict smiled.

"Yes, and I can play with Blossom. She's such
a cute little baby!"

"First, we need to talk."

She looked up quickly. "About Father Clark."

"Yes. Back in Lubbock there was the spec-
tacle of the whore house, and then assault and
battery and jail. Now we have attempted rape.
Another thirty seconds and Chiquita would
have killed him."

"Yes, I know that, Mr. McCoy. So did Father
Clark. I don't expect any more trouble from
him."

"When we get to Roswell, I think we should
turn him over to the sheriff with charges."

"Oh, my, we could never do that. The church
takes care of its own whenever possible. That's
partly why the bishop sent Father Clark out
here."

"Do we have to wait until he kills a girl?"

"By all the saints in heaven, Mr. McCoy, I
pray that we don't have that happen. He used to
be such a fine priest, such an outstanding
pastor."

"Mother Benedict. Priest or no priest, if he
tries anything like this again, I'll turn him in an

and swear out the complaint as soon as we get to
Roswell. You might tell him this if it happens to
be convenient, even if it isn't convenient."

"That I will, Mr. McCoy. Now let me play
with our small one."

Spur turned the two teams a little more to the
west to bypass some breaks showing ahead in
the plains. It could mean some relief from the
high plateau of a low range of hills or perhaps a
large river.

Three hours later, Chiquita returned, and
Spur turned the driving over to Sister Cecilia
who had a delicate touch with the eight pieces of
leather in her hands.

Chiquita waited for him to mount and ride to
her.

"Three more miles ahead," she said. "It's a
good sized sink and plenty of water for the
animals. Maybe even time for a quick bath."

"Bad for the skin," Spur said.

She grinned. "You're teasing. Sometimes it's
hard to tell." She pointed. "Just to the left of
those breaks. It's about twenty feet below the
rest of the prairie and makes a perfect wind-
break."

"Any sign?"

"None. We may be lucky. I'll ride ahead and
get a fire started."

"You can have a bath, too," Spur said.

She whipped the horse away from him, turned
and smiled over her shoulder, then was gone.

Father Clark came out of his sanctuary. He
was almost sober. He took one of the horses and
rode. Spur watched him for a while, but he was
simply plodding along with the wagon, his head

down as if in thought, sitting the saddle well. He must have some reason for riding the horse, but Spur could not figure it out. Unless he wanted to establish a riding pattern late in the afternoon. Then when they were within a few miles of Roswell he could ride, slip away and head for town without them and make his escape from the law.

With a man like Wilbur Clark, anything was possible, Spur thought.

An hour later the mules stopped and danced a strange jig. Spur had been a hundred yards ahead, and now he came charging back on his bay mare to see what the problem was.

The rifle shot caught him by surprise. He listened to it echoing in the distance and hoped there was not a Mescalero within ten miles of them.

He saw Mother Benedict stand up on the front of the wagon, the rifle in her hands.

Even before he arrived he saw what had been the problem. A rattlesnake lay between the mules. It had been surprised and the sharp hooves had sliced off six inches of its tail and its rattlers. The rattles popped and crackled as the muscles in the severed section made the dismembered part dance as they spasmed.

The snake had tried to coil and strike, but the natural instinct of coiling was wrong somehow, and the strikes at the mule's dancing legs had been short and inaccurate.

The dead snake lay between the lead team, its head blown half off by the big .52 caliber Spencer round.

Spur moved the teams and kicked the dead

snake away to the side and the mules settled down. He looked at the seat in front of the canvas.

"Glad you're on our side. Not a lot of rattlers out here yet. Wonder where that one came from?"

"Sunning himself. By the time I saw him the lead team was stomping all over the creature."

Spur waved them forward.

An hour later they eased down an incline into the hollow and found the water and gush of green trees in the two acre oasis.

Camping, cooking and the other routines of the end of the day were second nature to them by now. Each of the nuns did her job with surprising skill and good humor. Spur admitted he had never been on such a pleasant wagon trip. If it wasn't for Clark it would be ideal.

Sister Ruth set up her small reflector oven and baked biscuits for them, made bacon gravy without the aid of milk and added fried potatoes and onions for night's meal. They refilled the water kegs and as dusk settled down four of the sisters went to the left and took quick baths in the surprisingly cool water.

Spur, Clark and Mother Benedict sat around the fire until the nuns came back chattering and cool after their bath. As soon as it became dark, Spur began walking his guard duty, then settled down near the mules and horses and listened to the new night sounds.

Several species of birds used the oasis as a sanctuary, and they talked to each other at night. He heard the hooting of a big owl somewhere far below them, and the wail of a solitary coyote. Then nothing.

The Big Dipper wheeled around the North Star. Night feeding rabbits scampered nearby.

He started to stand to make another circuit.

"Don't move," Chiquita said six feet from him. He knew her voice at once.

She slid to the ground beside him.

"McCoy, I think it's time we had a long, quiet talk." She picked up his hand it put it over her breasts. She put one hand behind his neck and pulled his head down to hers and kissed him hard on the lips.

When it ended she pressed against him. "Spur McCoy, I've seen you watching me, and I've been watching you. I want you, right now. I want you to take off my clothes and show me that you're as good a lover as I think you are."

TWELVE

Spur's hand slowly kneaded her breast through the shirt. He leaned back so he could see her clearly in the moonlight.

"What was all that knife work, that 'touch me and I slice your face off' business?"

She smiled. "For some reason men think I'm easy to get in bed. Maybe it's my big titties. So I am fierce, hard, and they stay away." She smiled again and kissed him. When she pulled back she continued. "They stay away until I invite them to come play. Is that not a good idea?"

She unbuttoned her blouse. "All of the nuns are sleeping, including your little friend Teresa. I will show you I am better at making love than she is."

"You noticed."

"Of course, I was on guard." She let the blouse fall away from her shoulders and turned her breasts to him. They were fuller than he had thought, heavy, with pink aerolas and large pink

127

nipples. He bent and kissed one, then the other one.

She shivered for a few moments, then watched him. "Yes, gringo, bite me and chew on them."

Her hands worked down his chest unbuttoning his shirt, then loosening his belt and working on the fasteners of his fly. Spur felt the heat surging from her breasts. It was as if they were on fire and he had to put them out with his mouth. He licked them and nibbled on the pink morsels, then sucked one deeply into his mouth.

Chiquita gasped, suddenly, her face clouded, then she relaxed and smiled. She pulled away and stood.

"Come down this way," she whispered. "Sometimes I make noise when I am loving."

They walked fifty yards to the far end of the sink, and settled down on soft green grass. Slowly she stripped off his boots and pants, then his underwear.

"Oh, my, yes, gringo, I like your big friend." She nestled at his crotch, kissing his erection, then pulling it into her mouth and pumping back and forth until he touched her head and she came away and kissed him.

"You liked my mouth on you?" she asked.

"Yes." He ran his hands down her sleek sides to her pants, then brushed fingers across her belly to her crotch and rubbed at her through the cloth. He touched the buttons but she held his hand.

She pushed him to his back and moved lower until her breasts were at his phallus. She held her breasts together around him and looked up.

"Tit fuck me," she said.

Spur grinned and slowly began thrusting his big member, stabbing upward and sliding past her two big breasts which Chiquita held together around him. After a dozen strokes she giggled like a school girl and rolled away from him.

She caught his hand and moved it to her fly. Slowly he undid the buttons, and edged the trousers down. She helped him. Under the pants she wore a pure silk undergarment. He had never seen anything like it. It was much shorter than the usual drawers of cotton that most women wore. It gathered at her waist and came down halfway on each leg, but was soft, silky and so smooth.

He pushed his hand under the top and downward past the soft cloth along satiny flank and belly to a nest of dark fur.

Chiquita shivered and whimpered. He looked at her. She lay rigid on the grass, staring straight upward at the sky. He stopped his hand, bent and kissed her lips gently. He pulled back his hand and kissed her again, then put his arms around her and held her gently.

"Chiquita, little flower. You have never made love with a man, have you?"

"Of course, many times." She said it sharply, but there was no foundation of truth in her tone.

He kissed her again. "Did a man take you by force once, several years ago and it hurt terribly?"

Slowly she nodded.

"And ever since you've been wanting and

wondering and hoping it would be good when it could be done in love, but you were also much afraid?"

Again she nodded. She turned her face toward him and cried softly. When the tears were gone, she wiped her eyes and watched his face.

"You won't laugh at me?"

"Never."

"I was about sixteen, and in Lubbock, just after I had left the nuns. This man was drunk and grabbed me off the sidewalk and pushed me into a dark alley. He held one hand over my mouth and tore off my clothes. He was rough and it hurt for two weeks. That's why I cut men who come near me. I learned well."

He kissed her eyes, and then her nose, and at last her lips.

"Chiquita, making love with someone should be soft and gentle, with each person trying to make the other pleased and happy and satisfied. It's easiest to make love with a person you really love." He leaned back and held her close, her small body tightly against his. She was shivering again.

"I think we better get our clothes back on."

"No! I'm so close. And I . . . I like you, Spur McCoy. Isn't like enough? I mean . . . I want to know what it's like to do it and not hurt and not be angry and scared. I want you to help me make love the right way, Spur McCoy!"

"Damn!"

"Did I say something wrong?"

"Why now, Chiquita?"

"You saw what happened back at those ranches. We . . .we could be in the same kind of situation, at any time. I . . . I want to know how good making love can be. Is it like I have heard? I don't want to remember only the pain, the anger, and the shame."

"It would be so much better in Roswell, safely snuggled in a big bed with the lights on and some fine wine and cheese . . ."

"Now, please, Spur."

He kissed her softly, then harder and the flames in him rose up and he wanted to show her how gentle a man could be. He touched the silk undergarment again and her hand helped him. Slowly they pulled off the shimmering silk and put it to one side.

She shivered and he kissed her lips, then both her breasts, then his hand touched the soft fur and she gasped.

"Chiquita, making love is the most beautiful thing two people can ever do together. It is magic, it is wonder, it is the joining together of two people in a feast of desire, and respect and love and beauty. Making love develops the most powerful feelings that most people ever have."

As he talked quietly his hand stroked the fur, working lower and lower. His fingers probed gently through the black hairs and brushed against the soft, moist labia.

"Oh! Oh, Spur! Touch me there again!"

He did. She murmured deep in her throat, reached and pressed his hand again to her outer lips. She began nibbling at his ear.

Softly he moved his fingers, stroking the moist lips, then lifting higher and finding the magic node and strummed it twice.

She frowned, then looked at him.

He hit it five, six, seven times and Chiquita gasped and then shivered and moaned in the start of a climax that shook her like a willow in a tornado. She trembled and jolted as the vibrations coursed through her. She found his mouth and kissed him as the tremors faded and passed.

For a moment she didn't move, then she grabbed his face with both hands.

"That was marvelous! Nothing like that happened to me last time. Why?"

He kissed her cheek and smiled. "Because you were terrified, you were being assaulted, raped. Now you are relaxed, receptive, wanting to understand."

She nodded, serious. Then grinned. "Now show me the rest."

His hand caressed her labia, then he probed with a finger and she gasped. Spur eased her knees apart and knelt between them. He entered her slowly, gently and she was ready and wanting him.

When they were locked together she smiled. "This is almost as good as the other."

Spur could not hold back any longer and he jolted suddenly, erupting into her and she pounded back against him in a natural movement that surprised and pleased her. As he finished his climax she soared into a second one of her own, and again trembled and moaned as the spasms lanced through her again and again.

They both gasped trying to get enough air into their lungs. They lay side by side, staring at the stars. Impulsively she leaned over and kissed him.

"Thank you, Spur McCoy. Tomorrow night

we'll have to wait until later for my second lesson." She sat up and scrambled into her clothes. He dressed as she did and when they both were fully clothed again, she leaned over and kissed his cheek.

"You were right, I did have a bath this afternoon." She laughed softly and they walked back toward the wagons. The Big Dipper's open cup was almost due west of the North Star. By four A.M. it would be directly below the North Star so the star could fall into the cup if it came loose in the sky.

She looked up at the Big Dipper. "Your watch is almost over. Are you going to be brave and take the rest of the night?"

"Might as well, I couldn't sleep much now, anyway," he said.

She touched her lips to his cheek. "Not a chance. I do my share, and it's my watch until dawn." She hestitated. "But I guarantee you one thing. The next time I break into your hotel room, I'll use your bed for something better than just sitting on." She grinned, and ran to put her blankets near the wagon, then began circling the small camp.

Spur walked to the wagon, picked up his blankets and found a stretch of grass away from the horses. He had checked and Clark was tied securely inside the wagon. It might be an unneeded precaution, but the madman would be tied up every night until he was safely inside a jail cell.

McCoy thought about Chiquita for a moment, smiled at the memory of the past hour and faded into sleep.

The cry of a baby woke Spur a half hour before dawn. Most of the camp was up and moving around. Three of the nuns were trying to feed the baby. Sister Joseph came and provided the right cloth tipped bottle of sugar water and Blossom settled down for a quick meal and another nap.

The rest of the travelers came awake and another day on the trail began. Spur had only coffee and a biscuit and some jam for breakfast. He applied more axle grease to the hubs of the four wheels, and knew he could soon have to take one wheel off to completely regrease it. But for now it could wait.

They were rolling by the time Mother Benedict's pocket watch said five-thirty. They were determined to get in a good twenty miles that day.

Father Clark moved from his bed to the front seat on the wagon and took over the driving chores. Mother Superior watched him for an hour, then decided she could trust the job to him and went into the wagon with the baby. It had been years since she had a baby so young all to herself. If they kept Blossom she would be spoiled absolutely rotten.

Spur rode ahead to check the trail and found Chiquita waiting for him a half mile across the high plateau. He had lost track of the days, but guessed they were in New Mexico now. There might be a survey marker somewhere, but most boundaries in the west were indistinct and not that important with land valued at five cents an acre.

Chiquita rode over by the side and leaned in to

be kissed. He touched her lips and she clung for a moment, then sat down in her saddle.

"No sign that has anything to do with Mescaleros."

They rode half a mile without speaking, then Spur touched her shoulder.

"How was your mother captured?"

Chiquita watched him a moment, then her face softened, and she pretended to throw cornmeal to the four points of the compass.

"Did you know that in some Indian tribes, when a person dies, the name is never mentioned again? The idea is that the person's soul can not be in two places at once, and the constant repetition of the name keeps the spirit bound to the earth.

"I think we're safe now, my mother has been dead for nearly five years. We lived far to the south in Texas near the border, and the Mescaleros living in Mexico often swarmed across raiding the smaller villages. The Indians waited until the men went to the fields to work the land, then they swept in and took any horses and cattle they could find, and now and then caught a young woman to take back as a special prize.

"Mother was in the last house in the village toward the border and as they drove a dozen horses past they charged through the house, found her, bound her hands and feet and threw her over a horse and carried her away.

"She was the property of the brave who caught her, and he married her as his second squaw. Only a few weeks later this branch of the Mescaleros picked up and moved four hundred miles north into central New Mexico, to the more traditional lands of the Mescals. They settled in the mountains and for a few years time stood still for them and life was as it had been fifty years before. They hunted, they raided other tribes, and now and then they attacked a roundeye who wandered too close to their lodges.

"I was born exactly a year after Mother's capture, given an Indian name, and grew up learning both Spanish and the strange mixture of Spanish and the Apache dialect. When I was five, Mother and I tried to run away, but they caught us. Mother had her nose pierced by a hot nail as punishment. She kept the scar for as long as she lived.

"Then a year later she made so much trouble for my father, that he left us beside the trail one day with the clear understanding that we should not come back to his tipi. Mother carried me and we both walked and at last came to a ranch house where they took us in. Eventually we got back to Mother's village. But they threw us out of there, too."

"Because she had been captured by the Indians?"

"Yes, and because of me. Obviously Mother had *relations* with the savages. So we wandered. A few years later mother died and I was on my own, really on my own. I begged on the streets for a while. I existed. The nuns found me. Here I am."

"You mentioned a brother once."

"Yes, I never knew much about him. He's a Breed as well, but he stayed with the tribe. He's

out there somewhere." She frowned. "Every
Mescal I see I'll be thinking that he could be my
brother."

"He will kill you if he gets the chance," Spur
said. "You can't let the thought of him interfere. . . ."

"I know!" She looked at him and there were
tears sliding down her pretty face. "I know, but
I can do it. I will forget that I might have a
brother out there somewhere. My brother the
Mescalero Apache! If he attacks us, I will kill
him without a moment's hesitation."

Chiquita looked at him from tear filled eyes.

"I must," she said, "I must!"

THIRTEEN

Spur kissed away a tear as it ran down Chiquita's cheek and hugged her around her shoulders as they both sat on their horses.

"Just forget about maybe having a brother out there," Spur told her. "There is a thousand to one chance that he's not even in this part of the country. For the next two weeks, you've got to forget all about even having a brother."

He lifted her chin with his hand so she looked into his eyes.

"Agreed?" Spur asked.

"Yes, agreed." She wiped at her eyes, then moved away from him a few feet. "I'm all right. Don't fret about me." She took a deep breath and shivered, then straightened her shoulders. "About last night. . . I don't know how to talk about it. I don't know the right words . . . Just wonderful!" Her eyes were bright now with memories, and her smile came back, warm and honest and open. A man could do a lot worse picking a woman.

"I know what you felt, Chiquita. I felt it too. Yes, wonderful says it."

"Good." She looked to the west, the rolling high plateau meandered forward. "There's a small little bluff of some kind out there about five or six miles. I'm going to get on it and find out what I can see to the west and north. Something still bothers me about the Mescals. They must be here somewhere. If I'm missing them, and they know we're here, coming through . . ." She left it unfinished. They both knew what would happen. "I'll be back for lunch." She smiled. "Does making love always leave you so hungry? I'm so starved that I could eat a cactus blossom!"

Spur laughed and watched her respond, then she waved and rode off to the west. Spur pulled his reddish brown mare around and headed back to the wagon.

For the next two days they rolled along over the dirt and sand and dry washes and slight rise and falls of the prairie.

They found no signs of Mescaleros, they saw no game, they found no new water. The small drum was empty, the larger barrel was getting low. Everyone was warned to go easy on water. At places there were miles and miles of only the scantiest of vegetation, a few grasses, some small sagebrush bushes, but no trees, no streams and no brush.

The seventh day of the trip, Spur and Chiquita held a conference, and decided to swing back north toward a water hole she knew of. It should still contain water this early in the year, and they could get there before it ran out. If Indians were there they would have to risk it.

Father Clark had been a model of priestly behavior during the last two days. He was polite, sober, even held morning mass one day. He drove the wagon half the time now, but Spur still tied him securely at night. He submitted with little complaint.

But he was planning, Wilbur Clark never had been a man to let someone get the best of him. Now as he drove the wagon he watched the nuns. He enjoyed seeing them in the pants and shirts. Two of the shirts were too small for the women and outlined their breasts dramatically.

He remembered an early parish he had in Louisiana where he had dug a peephole through the wall of the nuns' bathroom. Glorious! He had seen more naked female bodies that six months than before or since. He picked out the one with the least inhibitions, and worked on her slowly, and a month later went to bed with her. It had been with her permission. She loved to be loved. After that they made love every three nights for almost three months. Then she became pregnant and she ran away before it showed.

He had hastily asked to be moved to another parish where the girl could not find him.

Yes! Women! His vow of chastity had long been an empty shell. He needed a woman again, it had been too long. Two nuns rode by on the horses, and he decided. Sister Mary Francis. She had a cute little ass in those pants, and she definitely had the biggest tits of any of the nuns.

She would be the one.

He guessed that she was twenty-two or three. Had a face he could stand, but oh, her body! His hand wrapped the reins around the brake handle for a minute and he pushed his right hand into his pocket. The bottom had been ripped loose and he wormed his hand to his crotch. Just watching the nuns gave him a boner. He squirmed to let it straighten out and then sighed. He would work on her for two or three days. No, there was no secret place, no spot where they could be alone.

It would have to be a one time conquest, perhaps when she was alone getting water, or gathering wood. Yes, tonight when they stopped, after supper, but before he was tied up. Yes, that would be the timing. If only they could find some woods.

He kept his hand in his pocket massaging slowly as he thought back over his conquests. At first he had been surprised how easy it had been. When he was only two years out of seminary and serving in a large church as a fourth pastor, he had caught two nuns in a lesbian tryst.

He had lectured both of them for fifteen minutes, requiring them to remain unclothed while he reminded them of their vows, and the unnaturalness of their behavior. Then he told the older one to dress and to leave. He told her he would keep her secret if she were extremely pious and hardworking. She agreed, dressed and left.

The younger nun was much prettier, and slender with good breasts. He sat beside her and

told her what she had done was wrong, that it
was much more interesting if a man did the
same things. She was trapped, knowing she
could not deny him for fear of being exposed to
the Mother Superior.

He had made love three times to the woman
that afternoon, and the next week he arranged
that three of them could be alone in a locked
room and he had been royally entertained.

He had learned quickly that there was always
a chance for female companionship close at
hand. If not in church circles, then certainly in
the bawdy houses and fancy women rooms of
the town. Whores seemed to delight in servicing
a priest!

That night just after the supper stop, Sister
Mary Francis wandered along a dry streambed
hunting branches or drift wood she could claim
for the fire. It was a half hour to dusk.

Father Clark slid away from the wagon,
angled the other way behind a slight rise and ran
hard around it to come up behind Sister Francis.
She had bent over to pick up some wood and
Father Clark growled in his throat the way the
pants outlined her buttocks. He slid up quietly,
then put one hand around her from behind
covering her mouth. His other hand grabbed one
of her breasts.

"Sister Francis, don't be afraid," he said
gently. She tried to turn to look at him. "You
know me, Sister, Father Clark. I won't hurt you.
No matter what you've heard, I've never made
love to a woman who didn't agree."

His hand began to fondle and rub her breast.
His erection jolted up full and hard and he

pressed it against her side. Her eyes were wild, still frightened.

"Francis, have you ever made love? Ever slept with a man and had his big cock pushed up inside your soft, wet pussy?"

Her eyes flared and Sister Francis shook her head.

"Really? I'm surprised. Such a pretty girl. Would you like to right now, quickly before anyone misses us?"

Her eyes clouded and again she shook her head.

"It would be a thrilling experience," he said. Father Clark unbuttoned her shirt front with one hand, keeping the other over her mouth. His hand went inside her shirt and under the thin chemise onto her bare breasts.

"Oh, tits!" he said gently. "Wonderful, marvelous tits!" He spread her shirt and lifted the chemise so he could see them. Not as large as he had thought, but a good double handful. He squeezed them, and played with the nipples until they hardened.

"Francis, just you and me. Nobody else will ever know." She stared the other way. He tried to press her to the ground but she was stronger than he figured. His free hand went between her legs and rubbed until she pulled her legs together.

"Come on, Francis. It will be wonderful, it will be so good you'll want to do it every night." His hand ripped off her blouse and then the chemise so she stood naked to the waist. His head bent to her breasts where he licked and then chewed on one delicious mound.

Sister Francis had been moving her face under his hand, until at last she had it in the right spot. She opened her mouth and bit one of his fingers. Blood spurted, Father Clark howled in pain and anger. He jerked his hand from her mouth and Mary Francis screamed so loud the Mescaleros in Mexico could have heard her.

Clark pulled back his hand and slapped her. She reeled away a step and he doubled up his fist and punched her in the face with a roundhouse right he had used in the army. Mary Francis jolted to one side, lost her balance and fell, her head striking a foot high boulder jutting from the sand of the dry stream bed.

She rolled to one side and lay still.

Spur McCoy had run fastest. He slammed a .45 slug between Clark's legs.

"Don't move even an inch, or I'll blow your brains out!" Spur called from fifty feet up the hill. Clark hesitated as if to decide what to do, then slowly he raised his hands.

"She fell down. She was airing out her shirt, I guess when I came back from my walk . . ."

Spur interrupted the words with another .45 shot, aiming precisely and thundering the big slug into Clark's upper left arm. The force of the blow knocked him down and blasted him two yards to the rear.

The other nuns had run up. Mother Superior took one look at the scene and hurried to Sister Francis. She cradled her head in her lap, pulling the tan shirt over the unconscious nun's breasts.

Spur kept his weapon trained on Clark where he whined in the dirt.

"Bad?" he asked. "I got here just as he

punched her and her head hit that rock."

Mother Superior Benedict stared hotly at Father Clark for a moment. "Yes, Mr. McCoy, it is bad. Her head must have hit the rock extremely hard. She's unconscious, her breathing is light and ragged. Help me get her shirt on."

Spur held the white shoulders as Mother Benedict worked Francis's arms into the sleeves, then buttoned her shirt.

McCoy picked her up and they went back toward the wagon. He turned to Clark.

"You can stay right there and rot as far as I'm concerned," Spur said. "After this, you have no excuse to go on living."

Mother Superior motioned to one of the nuns who went to the priest and bound up his still bleeding arm.

"Our Lord Jesus judges and God punishes, Mr. McCoy. They are not our responsibilities, or rights."

"Begging your pardon, Mother Benedict. But with scum like that one, I do quite a bit of judging and punishing."

"He's still a priest in God's service."

They lay Sister Francis on the soft blankets spread in the back of the wagon. Mother Benedict sat beside her, cradling her head on her lap. Tears touched the older eyes and wetness dripped onto the young woman below.

Spur touched Sister Francis's throat for a pulse. It came weakly, and not regular. Her breathing was also shallow. He scowled and stepped back from the wagon.

Clark and the two nuns had walked to the

camp. The nuns rushed to the end of the wagon to ask about Sister M. Francis.

Spur found a half-inch rope and tied a hangman's noose. He fitted it around Clark's neck and cinched it up.

"Clark, if I had a handy tree you would be a dead man in about fifteen minutes."

"Shoot me, it's quicker."

"Not a chance. I'd want to watch you struggle and kick, see your eyes bulge out and your breath come in smaller and smaller gasps. I wouldn't let the noose break your neck, that's too fast. It would strangle you slowly, making you suffer for as long as possible."

"You wouldn't do that to a human being," Clark said.

"No, but for you the term does not apply. In the morning I'll find an ant hill. We'll leave you spread eagled over the side of the hill. That way you'll be of some value. The ants will eat on your corpse for six months or more. Them and the buzzards."

Spur used the loose end of the rope and tied Clark's hands behind him.

"You can't kill me, there are witnesses. You'd hang for it yourself."

Spur spun around, his hand flared out and slapped Clark across the face, making him stumble three steps away.

"Don't ever say *can't* to me again, you shitface! I'm a United States lawman, I give ORDERS to the U.S. Marshalls. I can gun you down, write out a one paragraph report and that will be the last of it. What's more important, it would be the last of you!"

Spur pointed to the wagon wheel. Clark sat down in front of it and Spur tied him securely to the spokes, leaving his arms behind him.

McCoy went to the back of the wagon. Mother Superior had been crying again.

"How can something like this happen, Mr. McCoy? This poor girl was minding her own business, doing more than she had to to help with the trip, and now . . . now . . ."

Spur touched the limp wrist, then moved his hand to her throat and felt for a pulse. The beat was so weak that it was almost not there.

"I know her parents. I promised to take care of her. Her mother told her not to come way out here in the wilderness. But Mary Francis wanted to come. She said she was needed. She had prepared to teach, now was her chance."

The other sisters were putting cold cloths on her forehead. The ugly wound was just over her ear. Blood had oozed and ran down her neck. They kept it wiped up and a compress covered the wound now.

Someone lit a lantern and hung it on the high hook down from the heavy wooden box.

"Mr. McCoy! What can we do? I don't know what might help!" Mother Benedict let tears seep out of her eyes as she held the girl in her lap.

"Keep her head up, use the cold cloths," Spur said. "That's all I can suggest. Not even a trained physician could do much more. It is out of our hands."

Spur looked out of the wagon at Clark. He was still in place.

Mother Benedict gave a startled little cry. She

caught the young face and watched it, felt for a pulse.

Spur was beside her in a rush. He could find no pulse. He pinched her nostrils closed for several seconds, but there was no reaction. McCoy reached over and slowly closed the lifeless eyelids to cover the staring eyes.

"She's gone, Mother Benedict."

Spur McCoy turned and marched to the front wheel and stared down at the killer who sat there.

"I'm going to kill you, Clark. I don't know how yet, but I'll decide by morning. I'm going to execute you for the murder of Sister Mary Francis!"

FOURTEEN

Spur's hand hovered over his holstered .45 for several seconds, his fingers twitching, his whole body rigid with fury, as he stared at Father Clark. Then he gritted his teeth and turned slowly. He took two strides to the side of the wagon and pulled off the spade fastened there. For a moment he hefted it, wondering if he could cut off Clark's head with one strong thrust of the spade at the man's neck if it were held to the ground.

He might find out tomorrow.

Mother Superior Benedict slid down from the back of the wagon and hurried up to Spur.

"Mr. McCoy. We simply must not take any harsh action against Father Clark. He is still a priest, a vessel of God, a holy man. We have no authority over him. I know you feel strongly about Sister Francis's death. In a way it was an accident. He had no intention of harming her."

"Just raping her." Spur stared at the nun, his eyes still glowing with his anger. "According to the law a death occurring in the commission of a felony is murder. He's guilty." Spur rubbed his mouth with the back of his hand. "I just want to see justice done, Mother. One way or another that man is going to pay with his life. That's a promise."

Spur turned and carried the shovel out of the low dry stream bed. Six feet above the narrow water course he found a level place. It would take a tremendous amount of water to touch it here. He began to dig.

For an hour he struggled in the half light of the moon. He threw dirt, squared up the hole, digging deeper. Spur pulled off his shirt and his browned torso glistened with sweat in the coolness of the night air.

He went down four feet for the narrow grave, then jumped out and looked at it.

One life gone.

One life ended so quickly, so uselessly.

One killer still breathing.

It was not right.

Mother Benedict walked up and watched him a moment. Her fingers were working on her rosary. He saw her lips moving in the moonlight.

"Mr. McCoy, I know you wouldn't approve so we did it already. We carried Sister Francis to where Father Clark was tied so he could give her the last rites. This was extremely important. We put her habit on her, so she can be buried in it."

"With first light, Mother Benedict. Just so Clark has nothing to do with it."

She bobbed her head, as if she had assumed that.

"Thank you, Spur McCoy, for digging the

grave. It would have been hard for us. You're a good man."

She left, walking the thirty yards back to the wagon. Spur slammed the spade down into the mound of dirt wishing Clark had been under it.

Clark had to die. Seldom had Spur seen a man who deserved it more than this one. The fact that he was a priest carried no weight with McCoy whatsoever. He killed, he must die. Simple justice.

Chiquita had hovered in the background after the attempted rape and the injury and then death played out. The violence was all too familiar to her. She had rebelled against it before, and she would again. Now she came to Spur and touched his arm.

He whirled, surprised.

"It's me!" she said quickly knowing he could not tell at once who it was in the partial moonlight.

"Yes. It is quiet out there?"

"So far. We have been lucky, threading a needle between the Mescalero hunters and a few travelers."

"We need another week of luck."

"You may be asking for too much." She pointed to Clark. "What happens to him?"

"If I had a tree tall enough, I'd hang him."

"You're a vigilante?"

"No, a lawman, a U.S. lawman with jurisdiction. He could always die while trying to escape."

Chiquita smiled but Spur saw only the hardness. "Or the Mescaleros could sneak into camp at night and kill only Clark," she said softly.

"No, that job is mine, one way or the other, his hide is all mine."

The next morning they buried Sister Mary Francis. Mother Superior read a simple ceremony. Spur carried her into the grave, lay her out with her hands folded on her chest and holding wild flowers. He leaped out of the hole and stood by, as uncomfortable as he always was at funerals. When the service was over, he sent the women away, and slowly shoved the dirt and rocks back into the grave. He did not look at Sister Francis's starkly white face as the earth slowly covered it.

Spur put a cross on the top of the rocks he had piled over the grave. No animals could get to it, and only a cloudburst would let water reach it. The cross was made of metal and was only six inches high. It had been given by Mother Superior. The metal cross would outlast all of them.

When the grave was filled and topped, the nuns went back and prayed at the spot, then they got the wagon rolling toward Roswell.

The little sleep Spur had before dawn helped temper his fury at Clark. A judge and jury would be best, but there simply were no such niceties out here in the wilderness. He had talked with Mother Benedict and at last agreed to let Clark live until they came to the first civilized town, Roswell. There Clark would be turned over to the town lawmen and charged with murder. They would pause there for the trial.

Spur had insisted that Clark be tied in the wagon hand and foot, that he be untied only to relieve himself and Spur would oversee those short trips.

Clark glared at Spur, but had enough sense left not to roil the big man again.

All morning they plodded westward. Spur had been on cattle drives, where ten to twelve miles was a good day. But there you constantly had work to keep you busy. Here there was nothing to do but think and plan and let the dreary hours drag by.

After a half hour stop for a quick nooner, they moved on and Spur left Chiquita with the wagon and ranged ahead on his bay to check the lay of the land. They came to the spring they had searched for midway through the afternoon. It was still running and the water was pure and sweet.

It took them an hour to fill both of their barrels with water, then they moved again.

Chiquita took the lead, and less than a mile from the spring, Spur heard four rifle shots from ahead. He grabbed three loaded tubes of rounds for the Spencer and raced ahead.

Chiquita met him a quarter of a mile out.

"Two Mescaleros," she said. "They made sure that I saw them. It was a test, to see if the wagon people were armed and if they would fight."

"They know now."

She took a drink from her canteen. "They stood on the brow of a small ridge, skylining themselves so I couldn't miss them. I put two shots into the dirt in front of them, then two over their heads."

"They'll be back," Spur said.

"Yes, with plenty of help."

"How many?"

"The Mescaleros are scattered all over three states. They have trouble getting together for fiestas and celebrations, let alone for fighting. This would be a small loot affair. I would guess they would test us again with ten or twelve braves."

"Can we handle them?"

"If they all have rifles, we have a big problem."

They rode back to the wagon, told everyone what had happened, and got them ready. It was nearly four in the afternoon.

"They won't be back today," Chiquita said. "Mescaleros never fight at night, so we should be safe until tomorrow morning."

. They stopped at five that afternoon in another shallow wash to get as far out of sight as possible. There was no advantage in secrecy now, Spur decided. He made each of the nuns shoot her rifle fourteen times, and change the loaded tube of rounds herself. His troops would not win any prizes for marksmanship, but they could throw out a lot of lead at anyone who attacked them.

Spur decided they would not unload the wagon to form a barricade to fight behind tonight. He wanted higher ground where he could at least see the enemy coming.

They moved before daylight, rolling through the pre-dawn darkness, into the scratchy light and then welcomed the sun's first full rays. Chiquita had directed the wagon along the spine of a low, rounded ridge. They could see five miles to the north and almost that far to the south.

Spur frowned and looked north again. The flash came again. The polished metal of a rifle receiver or un-blued barrel had glanced the sunlight his way. The Mescaleros were coming. Nobody had told them about sun flashes off rifles.

The nuns untied Clark and Spur made him help them unload a dozen heavy wooden boxes from the wagon and form them around the outside of the wheels. It created a miniature fort, with firing ports between the boxes. They had it high enough so it covered them when they sat down. They lined up the rifles around the square, and put loaded tubes of cartridges beside each weapon.

Chiquita and Spur took the watch. It was slightly after eight thirty when Chiquita spotted them.

"Four on my side, about three hundred yards out," Chiquita said.

"I can't see any to the south," Spur said. "Show me where the four are, the check this side." Spur found the hostiles, and the Breed looked the other direction.

"We'll let them get in to two hundred yards before we open fire," Spur said. "That means they have nothing to hide behind except sand out there."

Father Clark caught the Spencer Spur threw at him. He looked like he knew how to use a rifle.

"Shoot them out there, Clark, not us," McCoy said.

The priest nodded, hefted the rifle, then

sighted through the opening.

Sister Ruth had tears in her eyes. "I don't know if I can kill anybody!" she said.

"Sister Ruth, you just shoot high if you want to. The idea is to let them know we have a lot of rifles. Chiquita and I will try to cut down on their population."

"Now," Chiquita said. Spur leveled the Spencer repeating rifle through the niche between two boxes of Bibles and sighted in on a shadow in the sand where there should not be one. He fired, then watched the target. The round was a bit right. He corrected and fired twice and saw a sand colored form lift up, scream and fall to one side. Two rifles from the north fired at the wagon. Spur heard one round go through the canvas top, and another hit one of the wooden boxes and stopped.

Chiquita's rifle spoke twice behind him, Spur scanned the area and saw two more Mescaleros.

"You may fire now, ladies," Spur said. Three of you shoot to the front and three to the back. Let's do it."

He spotted another shadow on the open stretch nearly two hundred yards out and fired again. The shadow became a man who rolled to the left and out of sight into a small furrow.

Spur saw no more targets.

"Hold your fire to the north," he said. One more rifle was fired before the nuns stopped.

From the south a dozen rounds slammed into the boxes and the wagon. Spur felt the mules and horses were safe. The Mescals wanted the animals alive so they could ride or drive them back to their camp to use as food. A dead horse would have to be carried. Nobody carried a seven-dog.

"How many more?" Spur asked.

Chiquita fired and looked back. "One less. Four, maybe five. I've found two with rifles. One of them just went silent."

Spur moved to her side, spotted movement and put three bullets into the area as fast as he could lever new rounds into the Spencer. The movement stopped.

"Hold it," Spur said. The nuns on the south side stopped firing. "We may have discouraged them."

Chiquita agreed. "But they will be back. They need more braves, so one will run hard and fast to a neighboring camp or hunting area and bring them back. Six mules and five horses would feed their families for six months. This is not a prize they will give up as easily."

It was quiet then, deathly quiet as they waited. One of the nuns sat staring at the north, her lips moving without sound. Another sobbed behind one of the boxes.

Chiquita watched both sides for a few minutes, then crawled over to Spur.

"They're gone. Everyone has pulled back. That way we won't know where they are coming from next time. We should stay right here, no sense in trying to outrun them, it's too far."

Sister Teresa sat by the wheel loading tubes with cartridges for the rifles.

None of them had been hit. Father Clark sat beside the box staring to the north.

Chiquita took two extra tubes for her rifle and edged past one of the boxes.

"I'm going out there and check on the bodies. They left two dead they couldn't get to. I have to know if one of them is my brother—or my father. His name was Black Eagle, and he could still be an important chief with the Mescalero. I haven't heard anything about him since I came back this way."

"I'll come with you," Spur said.

She shook her head. "No, I go the Mescalero way. I don't want them to know I'm checking the bodies. I'll be back before you know it. I just have to be sure I didn't kill . . . That I didn't kill my brother, or my father."

FIFTEEN

The Indian was larger than most of the Mescaleros. He waved his rifle and the eight braves
with him broke off the fight and faded into the
rolling country to the north.

He glared at the braves and screeched at
them.

"How could we fail? It was only one wagon.
We are Mescaleros!" He stared at each brave
until the man looked away. His name was Black
Eagle, a subchief in the Mescalero tribes and
leader of twenty families thirty miles to the
north near a year round spring in a small green
valley.

Hunting had been poor this year. Their lodges
were empty, there was little food put away for
the hard winter. The horses and mules that this
roundeye party had would be enough to last
them through the coldest year.

"We will not fail again. They are moving west.
We will get to the place of the coyote and wait
for them. Three of our braves will not be coming
with us. We will wait for the wagon to move,

then two of you will go back and help our brothers to their final resting place on the highest hill in the area, so their spirits may fly into the heavens."

Black Eagle flexed his bronzed shoulders. There was a bullet wound on his upper arm. He bent, picked up a handful of sand and slowly poured it over the wound until it was filled. The bleeding stopped.

The subchief had a high forehead, black hair now showing traces of gray that had been tied in a loose twist down his back. His face was square and strong. The eagle is the king of the sky. So he must be as strong to lead his people. If he had not taken the Mexican woman into his lodge he would today be chief of all Mescaleros. She had shamed him, until he put her and her girl child out of his lodge and divorced them.

He wore only a loin cloth made of deer skin, and heavy moccasins worthy of long runs and hard battles. His lean, powerful body had a dozen scars on it from battles.

Black Eagle gave a curt hand signal and the small band of eight braves moved west. They had only three rifles. One had been lost in the attack. They would send a brave back to check for it when the wagon left, but chances are the roundeyes would look for it and take it with them.

This wagon was unusual. It was almost as if they were Mescaleros, or thought like Mescaleros. They protected themselves well and had many rifles. That was another big reason to capture this wagon. Six or seven more rifles from the roundeyes and many rounds of ammunition, would make Black Eagle the most feared subchief in the nation!

The raiding party had no horses. They walked or more likely trotted where they were going. They would set a pace that covered a mile in ten minutes, and they could maintain that rate for six hours without stopping. Such a six mile an hour pace was fifty percent faster than the usual four mile an hour that a horse or a mule traveled.

Most Mescalero braves could run forty miles and come up ready to fight.

The Mescalero raiding party with Black Eagle leading it, quickly outdistanced the plodding mules of the target wagon. Both headed west. Black Eagle moved steadily to his next attack point. This time he would pick the time and the place, he would have the advantage and surprise. He and his men would be victorious and win the horses and much more.

He could almost taste the sweet meat of the riding horses now after it roasted over an open fire!

Chiquita returned to the wagon after a twenty minute patrol. Spur gave her a drink and lifted his brows in question.

"We killed three of them, and they took one away. They'll be back for the others."

She handed Spur an old Sharps rifle.

"They are one rifle short, but will plan on getting it back. Knowing the Mescals, the leader has pulled his braves off and will attack us again where he wants to. They'll set up some sort of ambush and wait for us to walk into it."

"So we move on, now."

"Yes, and if we see anything that looks like it could foster a trap, we go around it, five miles out of our way if we have to. A detour is better than dead. The Mescalero is in no hurry. They know they have a hundred miles to jab at us, to look for an ambush spot, to find a weakness."

Spur pushed away from the shade of the wagon. The sun was still warm. He told the nuns it was time to pack up and move on. Even Clark helped, but quickly Spur tied him up inside the wagon, this time tied him to the big bell.

A half hour later the wagon was loaded. Spur showed the three riders how to tie a rifle onto the saddle, even though there was no rifle boot. He wanted them all to have a weapon close at hand.

Mother Benedict drove.

Spur moved out two hundred yards ahead of the wagon looking for problems, and Chiquita rode a half mile to three quarters of a mile ahead checking for any long range troubles and laying out a general route west.

Chiquita came back to Spur as it moved toward dusk.

"We better keep traveling," he said. "They won't attack us at night. We can drive until midnight, then take a break and look for a place to defend."

"That might not work, Spur. The Mescals are already ahead of us. The subchief or whoever leads the raid is looking for an ambush point. It won't help us to move by night." She nodded. "Believe me, Spur. I'm thinking like a Mescal raider. We can make only ten miles at night. The raiders can cover that distance in an hour and a half. They will know where we are. If we go 30 miles in 24 hours they can catch us in five hours of running."

"So there is no chance we can outdistance them?"

"Not unless we leave the wagon and everyone gets on horses and mules and we ride day and night."

"No chance."

"Let's drive until dark and make a quick camp. We're safe enough in the darkness."

Spur took the first watch as usual, and just after eleven o'clock he saw someone moving toward him from the blankets around the fire.

"Teresa, what are you doing out here?"

"Guess," she said. She wore the man's shirt that covered her to just below her waist. Now she opened it showing him she had on nothing under it. Her arms went around him and he felt her soft body pressed tightly against his.

"Teresa, we can't."

"We can. I'm not a nun, I never was a nun. I was forced into being a novice, remember?" She pushed one hand between their hips and found his crotch. A hard pole was already growing behind his fly. "You want to, I can tell."

"Oh, damn!"

"Right over here in moonlight. I'll spread out my shirt."

"You are terrible, Teresa!"

"And you love me being terrible." She reached up, put her arms around his neck and kissed him. "It gets lots better than that!" she whispered.

They sat on the ground, watched the stars for

a minute then she slipped out of the shirt.

"God, but you are beautiful in the moonlight!"

His hands moved to her breasts.

"You just like my breasts, my tits. You get all excited by tits, don't you?"

He bent and kissed them, then nibbled on the pink nipples. She waited for him to be satisfied there, then pushed him gently to his back and unbuttoned his fly.

"Tonight it's my party, I get to do what I want to." She opened his fly and reached inside. He had to help her get his erection free and jutting from his pants.

"I want to do you all the way, until you spurt it right in my mouth! I've been dreaming about this all week."

She moved lower until she hovered over his upright phallus, then dropped down on it. She pulled him into her mouth and then began to massage his scrotum.

"Oh, yes!" Spur said softly, then felt her head bobbing up and down on him and he moaned in delight.

Spur knew he couldn't hold out long. He caught her breasts with both hands and rubbed them.

She seemed to pull more of his big tool into her mouth and he felt it hit the back of her throat.

There was no way Spur could hold back then, the surges came and he tightened every muscle in his body as his hips jolted upward. Teresa made small sounds and stayed with him as he pumped six times and then relaxed.

A moment later she leaned over his face and kissed him and he kissed her back.

"That was great!" McCoy said.

"I hoped you would like it."

"Give me ten minutes and I'll repay the compliment."

They watched the stars. He stroked her breasts and they talked about what she would do when they got to Roswell.

"I'll go to the priest there, and explain it all, and ask him to release me from my vows because I'm not worthy. That's about the only thing that works."

He slid his hand between her legs and she laughed softly.

"First we have to get there. We have those Mescaleros out there somewhere."

"I don't want to worry about them. Right now is more fun, and what we're going to do. You rested up?"

"Insatiable, that's you. Never enough, you always want more."

"Depends on the man. I wouldn't let that priest touch my fingertips!"

"We agree on that." His hand moved upward until his fingers found a brushy jungle.

"Oh, yes, you're finding the way. Don't get lost."

He pushed her over on her back on her shirt and watched her in the moonlight.

"You are so beautiful, and so sexy, and so much fun to make love to. I hope you find a fine man who is rich and good to you. That probably won't be in Roswell, but it's a start."

He strummed her clit until she yelped and then climaxed in a flurry of tremors and contractions and spasms that turned her face into a mask of pleasure. When it passed she reached up and kissed him.

"Inside, now!"

He pushed into her and even when she put her legs around his back he found it took him longer to come to his own climax.

"You are getting tired," she said. "Teenage boys are remarkable. I saw one ejaculate six times once in an hour. It was a bet. He said I had to help, so I did. He just touched me. He was never inside me. That guy was amazing."

When Spur at last climaxed he finished it quickly and came away from her.

"I thought I heard something out there," he said sharply. He buttoned his pants and slid away into the night. Teresa put her shirt on and moved quietly back toward the wagon. He came to her before she got there.

"It was just a rabbit feeding," Spur said. "Damn good thing. A Mescal would have had both our scalps on his belt."

"They don't wear belts," Teresa said.

"You noticed."

He kissed her softly, pointed to her blankets and she hurried to them, waved and snuggled down to sleep.

Spur kept the rest of his rounds. The horses and mules were quiet, the big dipper swung around to the left making its circle around the North Star. He woke Chiquita at one A.M.

She came alert, put her knife away and glared at him.

"I hope you were satisfied."

"What do you mean?"

"Fucking that nun. How are you any better than Father Clark?"

"She came to me. Anyway, she isn't a nun. She hasn't taken her final vows. She's a novice. She's quitting the order as soon as we get to Roswell."

"Ha!"

Chiquita backed away from him. "Don't worry, I'll do my job. I was just surprised." She laughed quietly. "I guess I'll just have to prove to you I can do anything she can."

Chiquita grinned at him in the moonlight and faded into the darkness as she began making her rounds.

SIXTEEN

Everyone snapped and snarled the next morning, or it seemed that way to Spur. The whole group was on edge, nervous, worried. Mother Superior Benedict tried to calm everyone down, but it seemed only to make matters more touchy.

Breakfast was over quickly and they rolled. Spur had a talk with the Mother Superior about Clark. The man could shoot, they might need his trained hand. But he could also shoot Spur in the back and make a break for Roswell.

Spur decided to meet the problem head on. He untied the man from the big bell, let him rub out his wrists and then put him on one of the riding horses. Spur tossed him a Spencer, fully loaded and gave him three filled reload tubes.

"Clark. Way I figure it is a man has a right to defend himself against the Mescaleros. Your collar won't do a bit of good with them. If they take us, you'll be just another roundeye scalp on a lance drying in the sun."

Spur waited but Clark said nothing.

"Way I figure it too, is that you don't like me

171

none too well. The feeling is mutual. Problem is
the Mescals hate both of us. When it comes
down to the killing time, I'm counting on you
shooting at the other guys, and not at me. Am I
wrong?"

"You'll have to wait and see, won't you,
McCoy," Clark said, a slow grin shading his
face.

"Not by a damn sight, Clark! I get your word
right here and right now, that you'll shoot that
weapon only at the Mescals. You go back on
your word I got five, six witnesses. They'll see
that you are put away for good, whether I'm
around or not. You read me true, whiskey
priest?"

"Yes, yes. You have my word. Mother
Benedict is all the witness you need. Where do
you want me to patrol?"

"Hang on the south side of the wagon. They
came from the north before. Figure the sneaky
Mescals will hit us from the south this time.
Stay close to the wagon. I'll be out front or
slightly north. Mescals like to pull ambushes.
I've seen them dig a hole and cover themselves
with sand. Man can be six feet from them and
never see them until they come up shooting.
These savages are professional raiders, looters,
warriors."

"I get the picture. I was a captain at
Shenandoah, cavalry." He touched his fingers to
his brow in a salute and rode twenty yards to the
south of the wagon.

"You're a gambler, Mr. McCoy," Mother
Benedict said. She bobbed her head, her face
serious. "But this time I think it is a safe

gamble. The man will try his hardest. He's been sober for two days now."

Spur swung up on his bay and rode. He went out a quarter of a mile and saw Chiquita on her roan gelding another half mile along the sweep of a gentle downgrade.

In the distance there were some breaks, a low bluff or ridgeline that was higher than anything for miles around. He studied it. The mass seemed to be ten, twelve miles long and at an angle across their route.

He rode forward until he caught Chiquita's attention, then she came to meet him.

She too had been looking at the bluff-like barrier.

"What do you think?" Spur asked.

"It's a long one, and it looks too steep to drive the wagon up and over. We go around it or find a way through it."

"Any water courses heading that way?" Spur asked.

She sent him a glance of appreciation. "You could be a scout yourself. Probably have been. A mile to the north there is what looks to be like a dent in the ridgeline. There could be a break there where these gushers boil through in the rainy season."

"Let's have a look," he said.

They both knew the wagon was safe. It was in the open with three riders around it, all with repeating rifles. And there was no good way to ambush it where it was.

They galloped a quarter of a mile, slowed to a gentle trot and soon came to a place where they could see that there plainly was a cut through the bluff. A now dry water course meandered across the high plateau's prairie and ended at the sliced out section through the soft mound. It had been no match for the raging waters that finally broke through and then year by year kept widening the cut.

The wagon was a mile and a half behind, heading at the wrong angle for this new course.

"You go back and give Mother Superior our new route," Spur said. "I want to check out that gap. As you are thinking, that would be a great spot to ambush a single wagon. Get everyone in the gap and close both ends."

"Are you sure?"

"Yes. If I run into your Mescals, I'll hit them with three quick shots so you'll know, then I'll try to save my hide. They won't keep their position if we know they are there."

"True. The Mescals are masters at running away when outnumbered or outgunned to live to fight another day." She smiled at him, pulled her roan around and galloped toward the wagon.

Spur moved slowly toward his objective. It was still four miles ahead. With luck the wagon would get there about noon. He had over five hours to do his recon. He rode out of sight of the gap to the south, then masked behind the more rolling plains, he came to within a quarter mile of the cut still out of sight. Spur ground tied his animal, then looped the reins around a low growing, sturdy bush and slid the three tubes of reloads for the Spencer inside his shirt. He moved off like an Apache at a ground eating trot toward the ridgeline.

He would come in from the other side of the

bluffs, work up to the top and see what he could
see below. It took him another half hour to get
into position. Then he edged to the top of the
sandstone barrier and looked down into the
other side, the approach the wagon would take.

Sand, rocks, the eroded sides of the cut which
he saw now were almost fifty feet apart at the
base where the dry water course angled through.
Plenty of room for a wagon to get through. The
water had created a smooth highway for them.

Sand, easy to dig, easy to cover up a
Mescalero. He sectioned the sides of the
approaches to the cut and stared at it in a yard
by yard inspection. When he found nothing he
took a new grid line, working across the
approaches systematically so he would miss
nothing.

When he had finished the horizonal grids, he
fashioned vertical ones and checked the area
again.

Nothing.

No depressions, no wagon wheel tracks. No
straws sticking out of the sand. He snorted. He
could see nothing that small from this distance.
Would the Mescals bury themselves in place and
wait five or six hours to spring their trap?

Absolutely!

He went down the reverse slope out of sight of
anyone on the other side, then moved up to the
lip of the cut and looked down into the water
course between the smoothly worn sides.

No one there.

Again he worked his search grids, but could
see nothing out of place.

They had to be here. It was the best ambush

position for ten miles any any direction. If he
were an Apache he would certainly use it.

Rocks.

There were no big boulders or rocks anyone
could hide behind. No jagged rock falls inside
the cut or on the outside.

Strategy. They had no horses to they could
not wait until the wagon was in the cut and then
storm it from both ends. They had to be in place.
He worked his way back to the lip of the ridge
and nestled into the hot sand on the reverse
slope. When he saw the wagon coming he could
move up two feet and be in an ideal spot for
supporting fire if it were needed. If the wagon
rolled through without any ambush, he would
borrow one of the horses and ride back and pick
up his bay.

Wait. There was nothing to do but wait.

How did the Mescals do it? If they were down
there covered with a layer of sand, it had to be
twenty degrees hotter than Spur was.

The morning sun warmed, then became
downright hot. Spur pushed up a foot and edged
his head without hat over the ridgeline and
looked to the east. He could see the top of the
white wagon canvas rolling over the prairie.
Another hour, maybe an hour and a half.

He had noticed some holes along the down
slope of the bluff. Now he saw movement and
eight feet down he spotted a triangular head
slide out of a hole and deady eyes blink in the
bright sun. The rattler paused for a moment,
then slithered forward, and angled down the hill.

The snake was four feet long, with ten or

twelve rattle buttons on its tail. Spur watched it
go, made sure it was moving well down the hill,
then studied the other holes he could see. None
were any closer to him. He divided his attention
between the holes now, and the bobbing, rolling
sight of the covered wagon.

The outriders had pulled in within twenty-five
yards of the Conestoga. One rode on each side,
and one behind. Chiquita was no more than fifty
yards ahead of the mules.

They moved forward. The wagon was less
than half a mile from the cut. Chiquita rode
forward half that distance and looked at the cut,
then at both sides and at the flared, level
approach to the passage through the dry sand.
To her nothing looked out of place. It didn't to
Spur either and that was what bothered him the
most.

The wagon rolled closer.

Of course! The ambushers would not be
directly in the water course, they would be to
the side of it so they would not be trampled by
the mules! Again he studied the sides of the dry
river. This area on both sides was not as smooth.
It had lumps and some rock fall, but none larger
than a bucket.

A chilling thought came to him. He had not
checked out the far side of the top of the bluff!
Across the fifty feet to the other half of the
sandstone barrier there could be half a
Mescalero tribe and he couldn't see them. Spur
studied the slant of the sandstone again down
the reverse slope. Evidently it dropped off lower
because he could see only the front edge.

He laid out the three tubes of rounds, checked the Spencer again and eased up to the top of the ridge.

Chiquita sat on her horse twenty yards from where the wagon would hit the sand and move into the final approach to the cut. She was maybe fifty yards from the pass through the bluff. The wagon came slowly twenty yards behind her.

If it happened, they would wait for the wagon to be nearly to the mouth, then shoot a lead mule to stop it and pick off the surprised defenders.

Chiquita had kept the three outriders all behind the wagon now, back by fifty yards. Yes! The wagon could be all the way through before the last riders were even at the cut. Good strategy to spread out the people.

He watched silently as the wagon moved closer. Sweat dripped off his nose and his chin. He edged the blued barrel of the ten-pound .52 caliber rifle over the edge pointing down.

Nothing moved on the cliff or the slopes below. With six men on both sides of the cut he could hold off a company of infantry regulars.

Chiquita carried her rifle in one hand across her saddle. She stared at the slopes a moment, then spurred the gelding and it jolted foward. She rode hard into the start of the cut, then on through it.

Nothing happened.

Spur wiped sweat off his forehead before it got in his eyes. He scanned both sides of the route again. His side! If the Mescals were there they would be on his side with the braves on the ridge on the other side for crossfire! He scanned the slope below him.

It seemed to happen in frozen motion. Below as he watched, a patch of the sand and rocks erupted and a Mescalero brave lifted up, swinging his rifle to aim it toward Mother Superior.

Spur slammed the Spencer muzzle downward and blasted two shots so fast the Mescal never had a chance to fire. The Indian flopped back to the ground and never moved.

The moment the first shot sounded, Mother Benedict lashed at the mules with the long reins, screaming at them, slapping them to move forward faster.

Two more Mescals near the first one lifted from the sand below and fired, but their shots were hurried. The first clipped Mother Superior's right arm, the second went through the top of the wagon. Spur shot one of the Indians through the head, brought his rifle around to bear on the other one when a shot from the mouth of the cut hit the brave, knocking him backwards into the dust.

One more enemy rifle blasted from the top of the cliff across the way. Spur moved his sights that way and saw three Mescaleros standing on the ridge line. A shot from behind the wagon cut down the brave with the rifle, and the other two released arrows, then dropped out of sight.

The mules had responded slowly to the whipping, but now surged ahead into a trot, and slanted the Conestoga into the cut and out of sight. Spur put three more rounds over the ridge line across from him to discourage any more arrows from that quarter. Below he saw the three horseback riders come into the cut and through it at a gallop.

Father Clark brought up the rear pounding off shots as he rode aimed at the cliff top where the Indians had been.

Spur looked below. Three Mescals lay where they had fallen. The rifles were more important than the braves now. McCoy slid over the top of the ridge and scrambled down the other side. An arrow slapped the rocks just behind him. He turned and sent two rounds at the ridge line, then he was down.

He caught up the first rifle, pryed the second one from dead fingers and fired a round point blank into the third Mescalero who suddenly came alive, and reached for his rifle. The Indian slammed backward into the ground as half the top of his skull blasted into the reddish stone, turning it pure red.

Spur carried the three weapons like cord wood as he jogged to the south toward his horse. He was soon out of arrow range but there was still a rifle on the far cliff.

He saw a rifle bullet plow up dirt in front of him and then heard the sound of the shot. They did not have repeaters. He ran again, angled lower on the side of the bluff and then into the flatness of the rolling plain. One more shot came, but it was not a marksman behind the weapon.

Spur hurried with his forty pounds of rifles, and ten minutes later found his bay mare where he had left her. He mounted, put two rifles in the boot and carried one over each shoulder by the slings, then rode straight for the bluff. It was not so high nor steep that a good horse could not walk up it.

His bay made the job look easy, and a half hour later he caught up with the wagon where it had stopped a mile from the cut, and a mile from the Mescaleros.

Teresa had bound up Mother Superior's arm.

"The bullet went all the way through, Mr. McCoy. Don't look so worried," Mother Benedict said. "I was the only casualty. Chiquita thinks we were lucky, and that you were in exactly the right place."

Chiquita came up and suggested they move on. They did. Spur found out that Father Clark had been the one to cut down the rifleman on the ridge.

"Old habits die hard, Captain," Spur told him.

Father Clark looked up and nodded. "Sometimes they don't die at all. All of the soldiering." He turned away and then rode back, handed Spur the rifle and two reload tubes. "You better keep these." He wheeled the horse and moved to his position behind the wagon as rear guard.

Spur and Chiquita rode a hundred yards ahead of the Conestoga.

"How did you know where they would be?" she asked.

"Basic military science," Spur said. She looked up puzzled.

"I just tried to think what I would do, how I would trap the enemy in the same place. I figured it out almost too late."

"But not really too late. They should have had us dead. You saved all of us."

"Our equipment saved us. If they had put six repeating rifles on both sides of the cut, we all would be dead."

"Whichever way, I'll take it," she said. "They will try again. Even though they may only have one rifle now. They have lost six braves. They will come at us with more men and more rifles the next time. We should have two days before they can get a force to hit us."

"That puts us two days closer to Roswell, but still about three days away," Spur said.

SEVENTEEN

As Chiquita predicted, the next two days on the trail went well and without any attacks by the Mescaleros. The route slanted slightly north to compensate for their south swing, and angled for Roswell. Spur had no idea how far away they were now. Chiquita said on the second day after the Indian attack that there were two, perhaps three good days of riding yet before they saw Roswell.

Little Blossom was thriving on her combination of soup and sugar water. She needed milk, but another few days would not harm her growth. The nuns fussed over Blossom like she was a choice toy, a favored duty. She would be spoiled totally within three months, Spur decided.

The third day after the attack began as the others, a quick breakfast of the last of the bacon, some hardtack mixed in and then biscuits and coffee.

They were on the trail shortly after sunup. Spur rode up to Father Clark, who had asked to ride rear guard. The Secret Service agent looked at the whiskey priest. He was still sober.

Spur handed him a Spencer barrel first.

"You should have one of these. Chiquita says the Indians could be back for a visit today or tomorrow."

Father Clark held the barrel of the Spencer. "You think you can trust me?"

"Have so far. You can use that rifle, that's the important thing. You don't want to be scalped anymore than I do. You know I also can use a rifle, so why cut down your odds of getting killed by the hostiles by blowing my head off? You're an intelligent man, Clark. So am I, Harvard class of fifty-eight. Let's just say we have an armed truce until we get out of here. Then if you want to play a game of hide and seek in the desert with me, with the Spencers as referee, I'll play."

Clark grinned. "I'm not that dumb, McCoy. I've seen you shoot. I'll go with the detail and take my chances when we get to Roswell. Oh, I thought about charging off when we're a day away. Figured you'd come hell-bent and ventilate my hide with about seven rounds from your Spencer. I play the odds. If we get through, I'll keep on playing them. Right now the odds are stay with the detail and throw out lots of lead."

Spur pushed his hat back and lit a thin, black, twisted cheroot as he stared at Clark. "You were probably a damn good soldier, Clark. Don't see where you went wrong."

He reined the bay around. "Keep a sharp lookout to the rear. Remember they will be running, and the little bastards can't hide when they're jogging along." He kicked the bay and rode to the front, then on to where Chiquita rode the point.

There was no real trail. Here and there they saw wagon tracks, but the country was so open that one line across the prairie was as good as the next. West was the direction, and now slightly north of west to bring up Roswell.

Here and there they found grass on the rocky barren soil. A few sparse shrubs and sages grew in patches. He saw Chiquita stop and then ride to her left, due south. She went fifty yards, then swung down from her mount.

Spur charged that way at a gallop.

When he got there, he found Chiquita giving a whiskered old man a drink of water. He had the look of a prospector, but there was no gold out here.

Spur dismounted. The man sat in a small depression and had been trying to get a fire going. He had used the last of his matches without success. There was no mule or donkey. He had only a dirty pillowcase near where he had stopped.

The man was almost dead from heat prostration and exposure. They wet his lips with water. He licked them. They let him suck on a wet cloth for five minutes, then gave him a small sip of water. When he could talk he touched Chiquita's hand.

"Thanks," he said slowly. His tongue still swollen.

"I'll get the wagon over here," Spur said.

A half hour later the oldtimer was in the back

of the wagon. Sister Ruth let him sip water slowly. He was sunburned and had lost a lot of water from his body. Gradually Spur got his story. He had been prospecting, then his mule died after drinking some bad water, and he ran out of food.

"Would have been all right if I'd stayed with the mule. Could have eaten off her for two days before she went rancid. But I figured I could walk all night and be nigh on to Roswell by morning. Turned out I was wrong. You say we're still more than two days from that little town?"

Spur left him talking with the nuns and went back to the point. Chiquita had seen no evidence of the Mescaleros.

"We won't walk into an ambush spot this time," she said. "There seems to be nothing out here but plains."

"So what is their strategy to handle this terrain?" Spur asked.

"They will hit us while we're moving. So we don't have time to set up a barricade like we did last time. For this attack they will have more rifles, more men."

"Then to counter them we turn the inside of the wagon into our fort. We put the boxes around the sides and cut holes in the canvas to shoot through." He pulled his mount around. "I'll get busy on that, you be careful."

He rode hard back to the wagon and began moving boxes, putting the wooden ones on their sides and cutting firing slots in the heavy canvas.

The old prospector's name was Edgar. He watched the procedure for a few minutes.

"I take it, young feller, that we're looking to be visited by the Mescals."

"They'll be back, they owe us, and they want our horses and mules for food."

"Figures. Got an extra Spencer like I seen around here?"

Spur gave him one and put him to refilling empty reload tubes.

"Handy dandy little gun," Edgar said. "This the one the Rebels said the Yankees loaded in the morning and fired all day."

Spur kept working. A half hour later he had room for four people inside the wagon fully protected behind the boxes. Each had a firing slot to shoot from and a foot square hole in the canvas to see through.

Edgar approved and took over one of the firing slots.

"Bring on them damn Apaches!" Edgar said. "Been wanting to even up with them ever since they got away with my mule and my traveling kit last year. Only thing they didn't get was my scalp."

Spur checked the outriders. None had seen anything. Teresa was on a horse just behind the wagon. He rode knee to knee with her a moment.

"The other night was delicious, you ready to try me again?" she asked.

"First the redskins, then the pretty, naked lady. But in Roswell. Too damn dangerous out here right now to take our clothes off." He left her grinning and rode back to see Chiquita.

Just before noon the Mescaleros attacked. Ten of them had been hiding behind small bushes and in the sand to the north. They lifted up and fired four rifles and bows and arrows in a sudden move that caught the travelers by surprise.

"Into the wagon!" Spur bellowed. Already he heard return fire. Father Clark had seen the start and from his drag spot had begun firing almost at once. Chiquita rode back from her place three hundred yards ahead of the wagon. Before she got to the wagon, another ten braves rose up to the south and began firing.

Sister Maria had been riding flanker to the south. The first volley from three more rifles blew Maria from her saddle. Her horse reared, then raced away from the shots.

Spur had talked with Mother Benedict and Sister Ruth the other driver about this situation. The plan was to whip the mules and run forward as quickly as possible. This would make the Indians move as the wagon rolled, get them out of their hiding places.

Now Mother Benedict lashed the reins at the mules who walked faster, but would not break into a trot.

It didn't matter. A moment later two rifle bullets slammed into the lead right mule's head and it went down in the traces, dead in ten seconds and the wagon came to a halt.

Spur leaned behind his bay and fired over her back as he raced for the wagon. He fired at the braves on the south side. There was no chance to try to get Sister Maria. He felt a rifle round slice over his head, and ducked lower. A moment later he was at the wagon and he tied his bay there, then squirmed behind a wheel and began firing at the brown on brown patches in front of

him to the south. He saw one brave move, and
Spur sighted in and squeezed off the round.

The big Spencer round dug into the Mescalero
and tore through his heart, dumping him into
his happy hunting ground forever. Fire from the
wagon came rapidly now. Spur could tell that all
four of the firing slots were in use. Clark had
gone down behind his horse somewhere to the
rear, and soon his Spencer spoke with authority.

The first of the Mescalero barrage was over.
Spur guessed they were short on rifle rounds.
He saw them begin to creep forward through the
uneven ground and sparse vegetation. McCoy
tracked one Indian moving forward, sighted in
and the next time the Indian slithered forward
on his stomach, Spur put a round through the
top of his head.

Two down.

Mother Benedict had leaned into the wagon
when the mule went down, caught up her
Spencer and got to a firing position. She was not
thinking of her vows or of the church, she was
simply trying to stay alive. She fired at the
brown shapes fifty to sixty yards ahead of her to
the north. They moved silently forward. She
fired again and again. She reloaded the tube and
fired at the forms. At last she hit one. She didn't
weep, she wasn't sorry for the savage. He was
trying to kill her! She went on firing with a
renewed vengeance.

Teresa had seen the first attack and rode to
the wagon safely. She was inside reloading
tubes with shells and trying to keep Blossom
from crying.

Chiquita saw quickly that she could never get

to the wagon. She swung to the side and to the rear of the hostiles on the south. She got down from her mount, tied him to a sage and took the three tubes of shells and worked silently forward. A small hummock only six feet above the plain, gave her an observation point.

She saw the Mescaleros now in front of her and only seventy-five yards away. They had closed to fifty yards of the wagon. She lay down, cleared some grass so she had a perfect field of fire, and sighted in on the first Mescalero. She fired, moved to the second one and fired. By the time her seven shot tube of rounds was empty, three of the Mescals were dead or wounded so seriously they couldn't fight. Two of the Indians raced toward her. She slid in a second tube and brought down one of them at thirty yards and the other dove into the sand and rolled away.

On the far side, Father Clark had the same idea. He was outside the attack zone, and swung to the north where he saw the savages. He counted twelve, then sat on his horse and fired seven rounds at them, killing at least one. The others turned, spotted him and four of them moved toward him.

He rode straight at them, firing as he went. He killed three before one of their rifle rounds caught him in the shoulder and blasted him from the saddle. He grabbed his two full tubes of shells and rolled behind a rock. The hostiles were out there somewhere. He would take as many of them with him as he could!

Besides that, he could put a large hole in their trap. If he managed to blast enough of the hostiles up here, Spur could cut that dead mule out of the traces and get the wagon moving. Yes! He had to do that.

He felt his shoulder and his hand came away bloody. But he could still lift his left arm. It couldn't be that bad. He would make the bastards pay!

A Mescalero lunged at him from nowhere. Clark's Spencer came up with precision as he triggered the weapon, the round splashing through the redskin's throat, changing his flight path and dumping him into the stones and dirt six feet away.

There would be more. He lifted up and fired four times at the Mescaleros shooting at the wagon. One screamed and rolled over. Two more dodged back from their vantage point to take cover.

"Now!" he screamed toward the wagon. "Get that wagon out of here!"

Clark was not sure if anyone heard him. He would call again, each time he had a chance. It could work. For a moment he thought of the line from Charles Dickens, "It is a far, far better thing I do, then I have ever . . ." Two Mescaleros interrupted him. He shot one, slammed the butt of the Spencer into the skull of the second, killing him.

Father Clark chuckled softly to himself and aimed the long Spencer at the savages out there trying to kill his friends.

"Get that wagon out of here now!" he screamed again.

Under the wagon, Spur McCoy heard the words. Clark was right. If they stayed there the hostiles could pick them off one by one. The level of firing had slowed from the south where Clark was. Spur drew his four-inch hunting knife that was sharp enough to shave with and worked his way slowly under the wagon to the front, then under the tongue and between the stamping mules.

He should be able to get to the traces and the harness connectors and cut the dead animal free. If the Mescals saw him he would be a new target.

Spur moved slowly, hoping not to attract the enemy's notice. One mule saw him and stomped to the side as far as the harness would let it move. Spur talked to them, chattered with the three skitterish animals, trying to calm them.

After five minutes he was at the dead animal. He slashed the leather straps, cut them cleanly and unhitched the straps on the doubletree. Just two more leathers and they could leave.

He lunged forward, sliced the last of the harness, stood and ran around the lead mule and back to the wagon wheel. Spur leaped on the seat, whacked the mules with the reins and got them moving.

"Let's get out of here!" Spur bellowed. "Keep firing as long as you can see them. They'll be running after us."

Mother Benedict leaned out from the covered section and reached for the reins. Spur vaulted off the slowly moving rig, found his bay walking along behind the wagon and shouted for everyone to move out.

Edgar looked out the end of the wagon at Spur as he mounted, ducking a rifle round. Spur rode up to the wagon and waved at Edgar.

"Hey, we running away from the fun? I was just getting my shooting eye back."

"Shoot all you want to, Edgar, they'll be coming after us for several miles."

Spur turned and looked where Sister Maria lay. There was no chance to go back for her, not even to see if she were alive or dead. But he knew she was dead by the way she lay, sprawled with her head to one side at an unnatural angle. Spur sent a pair of shots at the Indians, and kicked the bay into a gallop heading west.

EIGHTEEN

Sporadic gunfire followed the wagon as it bounced and rattled along at more than its normal speed. Spur and Chiquita rode the rear guard, firing whenever they saw a Mescal run close enough so they could get a good shot at him.

Gradually the wagon and the horses tired out the running Indians and they fell behind.

The Breed rode up beside Spur as they checked their back trail again.

"You know why we got out of their trap, don't you, McCoy?"

"Yes. Because of what Father Clark did."

"Yes. He rode directly into their north side ambushers. I saw him riding and firing until he was knocked off his horse."

"He kept them busy enough so we had time to cut the mule free and get moving out of the trap."

"The church will make a hero of him," Chiquita said. She lifted the Spencer and sent two shots into a brown smear at the side of a

195

small bush three hundred years away that could have been a Mescalero.

They turned and rode hard for two hundred yards, then paused and looked to the rear again.

"It was Father Clark's final atonement. He knew he was in the worst trouble of his life."

Spur agreed with a nod. "I said he would die for his sins, and he sure did. I didn't think he would pick the time and the place for it to happen."

"What about Sister Maria?" Chiquita asked.

"Dead. No other answer. She was killed instantly when they shot her in that opening volley. I saw the way she fell. Her neck was broken as well. Anyway, now that we've left the area . . ." He did not continue.

"I better tell Mother Benedict," Spur said at last. He rode ahead to the wagon, suggested they slow the mules to normal speed and then he told Mother Benedict about Sister Maria and what happened.

The sturdy nun listened to his description of how the sister died.

"We knew she was not here, but we hoped that somehow . . ." Mother Benedict wiped a tear away. "There is no chance for a Christian burial, for the last rites . . . Oh, Father Clark, too." Her face contorted and she turned away. "Dear Lord in Heaven, that is three of our party!"

"Mother Benedict, we're going to make damn sure that there are no more killed on this trip." Spur wheeled rode to the back of the wagon.

"Edgar!" he called.

The old prospector wormed out from between

the boxes.

"Yes sir, you called?"

"Ever driven a team of four . . . well, three now."

"Does the Big Dipper swing around the North Star? Course I have. Suggest we take that other lead mule off. Won't do no good, cause nothing but trouble."

"Good, Edgar. You take over the driving chores."

Back up front, Spur told Mother Benedict he wanted her to be with the remaining nuns. No one else would ride horses. She had four nuns left out of six. They left the boxes the way they were inside the wagon for protection. Mother Benedict had to tell the others about Father Clark and Sister Maria.

Spur helped unhitch the third mule and roped her behind the other two on a lead line.

The wagon rolled along.

McCoy rode up to Chiquita and asked her to pull back within a hundred yards of the wagon.

"I'm going to swing down our back trail a ways and see how our Mescal friends are doing. Will they keep following us now? We hurt them badly?"

"Depends how hungry they are. My guess is that they will give it up and go back to their lodges. They are not used to losing so many men on a raid. Especially one that produces nothing but widows. But, you be careful back there."

Spur touched his hat brim and rode. He had three full tubes of rounds for the Spencer. That gave him twenty-eight shots. He drifted a quarter of a mile to the left as he worked back the trail. Every quarter mile he paused and studied the terrain. There was no way that even a Mescalero could hide as he jogged forward. Spur checked the land for a mile across, but could see no movement.

Once he thought he had a Mescal, but it turned out to be a coyote running from one small bush to the next as it worked away from the hated man smell.

When he was about three miles back, Spur turned and rode toward the wagon. The Mescals had turned back, or were circling them wide to hit them once more. Spur McCoy did not know which.

The last attack had come about ten in the morning. Spur looked up at the sun and saw that it was nearing three in the afternoon. They had missed their noon break.

By the time Spur rode back to the wagon, Mother Benedict was driving again, with her bandaged arm showing some signs of bleeding. Edgar rode the one saddle horse they had left. He met Spur a hundred yards out.

"Troops are wondering about a rest. We need to change the mules too. Have to do it every half day with just two to pull."

"Do it," Spur said. "Stop it anywhere. I'll go get Chiquita."

Sister Ruth gave them strips of jerky to chew on and dried fruit for their meal. She made coffee. It was a somber group. The four nuns clustered together. Spur and Sister Cecilia unhitched the mules and rotated two fresh ones into the traces.

They had stopped less than half an hour when

everyone was back on the wagon ready to go.

Edgar slid into the driver's seat and they rolled.

The country they passed was much the same as it had been, high and dry, a plateau that stretched for what looked like a thousand miles Westward.

Spur made one more two mile circle to the rear, but raised no Mescal fire and saw no movement. He was not convinced that the raiders had given up yet. They had one dead mule and two horses if they could catch them. That might be enough to show for their work and their losses.

They camped the night in a small depression that could almost qualify as a valley. The water course through it was dry, and there was no water anywhere.

Chiquita said this was new territory to her. The Mescals she moved with never came this close to Roswell when she was with them. There could be more water during the next day and a half to two days and there might not be. She decided they should go on short water rations just to be sure.

Water could be used only for cooking, drinking, and a small drink for the animals.

Edgar shook his head when they asked him about water. He couldn't remember even coming through this part of the country, but he must have.

"Consarn it, ladies, this just beats the consarnits out of me! Wish I could be more help."

Spur stood the first watch as usual, and was

joined by Edgar.

"Consarn it, looks like I should be helping a little. You folks saved my old worthless hide, that's for consarn sure!"

They talked softly, listened and watched.

"Them Mescals is twenty miles the other way by now," Edgar said. "They got themselves one dead mule to butcher and cut up, and two scalps, and two live horses to haul the meat on. Land sakes, they probably were butchering that mule five minutes after we hightailed out of there. Then they sent two or three of their braves chasing us just to get rid of us. Course they'll hide out somewhere and cook the liver and brains most likely."

"I really hope that you're right, Edgar. But I'm not counting anything for sure until we're safe and sound inside some hotel in Roswell."

They woke Chiquita at two and she scolded them, but she had appreciated the extra two hours of sleep. "Now you two get some sleep," she said.

Spur slept little thinking about the three who had died in the trip. He had warned them, but still it riled him that they had been lost when he was leading the escort. At last he rolled over and went to sleep.

Chiquita's toe nudged him awake. It was daylight. They were almost packed and ready to go.

"You're not the only one who can let a person get some extra rest," she said. She sat down beside him with a tin plate of fried potatoes and onions with the last strips of bacon and fresh biscuits for him. The coffee was scalding hot, black and there was plenty left.

The wagon rolled at six A.M.

Chiquita rode to the front to scout the trail.

Spur rode to the rear to check out the back trail in one long loop.

Edgar rode beside the wagon trying to watch all four ways at once.

Edgar and Chiquita decided the Mescals were well on their way back to their lodges, but Spur was not so sure. He held out for vigilance, and made two three-mile loops on their back trail before noon.

They cut a small river about eleven in the morning, and paused to let all of the stock drink their fill. Upstream they found a good place and refilled their water barrels. The women washed their faces and arms and waded in the cool water and splashed, enjoying the relief from the perpetual heat. They sounded like excited, happy children.

If anything it was hotter now than it had been the past ten or eleven days. Everyone had lost track of how long they had been on the trail.

They had cooked oatmeal for their noon dinner. It had been peppered with cut up pieces of dried fruit that soaked up and became delicious as they cooked. There was no milk, but plenty of sugar, and Ruth had made sure the oatmeal was a little watery.

A new feeling swept through the eight adult travelers. It was a sense that they were going to make it. They had decided that the worst was over and they could walk on into Roswell now if they had to!

Edgar shouted an hour after they rolled, and pointed to the west.

"Dadblamed bluff over there! Remember seeing that the first day on my ride out. We can't be much over a day from Roswell! Know that danged bluff anywhere!"

Chiquita heard him and rode toward it. She came back two hours later. She had ridden to the top of it and through a light haze had seen green splotches ahead and what looked like about a hundred cooking stove smokes. There could be only one answer to the question.

"It must be Roswell out there about ten miles!" she said.

Everyone cheered. Two of the sisters started to cry and Spur McCoy heaved a small sigh. But he was not going to let down his guard just yet.

They camped that night in the shadow of the big bluff, found another small stream and Mother Superior and the nuns all had quick baths in the cool water.

That night when Spur woke Chiquita at twelve o'clock, she touched his arm.

"Wait a minute," she said. She reached up and kissed him. "I want you to know that if I had a mind to, I could show you all sorts of interesting Indian ways to make love. But right now is not the time. We have to get what's left of our charges safely into Roswell. Perhaps you'll have a hotel room, and I will come visit you."

She slid away from him without waiting for a reply. Spur smiled and waved at her in the dark, then found his blanket and tried to go to sleep.

Tomorrow, Roswell, New Mexico Territory!

NINETEEN

The wagon arrived in Roswell the next afternoon just before three in the afternoon. They drove straight to the small Catholic church and Mother Superior Benedict took charge. She had the nuns all dressed in their regular habits and once again they did look like nuns.

She paid Chiquita the agreed to fee and suggested that she keep one of the Spencer rifles as well. They shook hands and the small guide rode her horse back toward Main street.

Spur shook hands with the five ladies and rode away, heading for the livery stable, then a hotel and a long hot bath and all the thick steaks he could eat.

The nuns would remain at the church until they had new orders from their bishop. They would need a new priest and replacement nuns for those lost. It was the end of their journey for a few months at least.

Edgar had dropped off the wagon when they passed the first saloon. He said he still had a few dollars and his credit was good all over town.

Spur found the sheriff's office and reported the deaths of the three citizens on the trail all attributed to Mescalero raiding attempts.

The sheriff was a short, fat man who did not wear a gun. He lit a cigar and snorted.

"Damn lucky to get through, I'd say. The Mescals have been raising all kinds of hell out this way. Army cut off any more escorts as I guess you found out. Well, I'll record the deaths for the books. A Catholic priest and two nuns, you said? Sounds like a risky trip. You have a scout?"

"Chiquita, a Mescal Breed."

The sheriff grinned. "No damn wonder you made it through. That little lady thinks Mescal out there. No damn wonder. She's the best scout in half a dozen states."

"What about mail. Any going through to Denver?"

"Not out of here. We might get something over toward Phoenix and maybe Sante Fe if the stage ever gets back to running. You in a rush to send a letter?"

Spur grinned. "Not really. What's the best hotel in town, one with a bathtub and lots of hot water?"

The man said the Westerner, and Spur walked out, stretched and then wandered around until he found the hotel.

He finished his bath in the special room at the end of the second floor of the hotel and went back to his room wearing a robe and carrying his thick towel. The door to his room was open a thin crack. His guns were inside. He tried to look inside, but he could see nothing. Someone started up the steps and he moved quickly, stepping inside and closing the door.

Chiquita sat on the bed. She had taken off her tan shirt and now lowered her arms and lifted her chest and smiled at him.

"Hey, stranger. You looking for a good guide? One that knows the territory and how to get from one place to the other? I could even show you where the bed is."

Spur dropped his towel and key and walked over to the bed and sat in front of her.

"I'm used to the best guides in the West. I wouldn't want to be disappointed."

"We've got the rest of the afternoon, and then dinner in that fancy dining room downstairs, and then all night. If you're disappointed after that, Mr. McCoy. I guarantee I'll do it again and again and again, until I can satisfy you."

Spur bent and kissed her gently pouting lips.

"Anyone ever tell you that you look a little like an Indian?"

"Not lately."

"One request," he said, slipping out of the robe.

"Yeah, roundeye?"

"I want to unbraid that long black hair and help you have another bath. I go crazy in a bathtub."

Chiquita giggled.

"You just got yourself a guide."

Three hours later they sat in the hotel dining room. Spur had a two pound T-bone steak with four vegetables, a cold beer, a quart mug filled with coffee and asked what was for desert.

Briefly he thought of Major General Wilton
D. Halleck back there in Washington, D.C. He
would be waiting to hear. But from Roswell,
New Mexico Territory the mail might not go out
for a week or more, maybe two weeks.

He had time. First he had to rest up, and get
his strength back with some good food, taste a
bit of fine brandy and some of the local whiskey.

Naturally he had to stock up on his supply of
thin, black cheroots.

He would send off a letter tomorrow or the
next day, or the next. Chiquita would get bored
with town life after maybe only a week. Then he
would figure out how he was going to get back
to civilization. Santa Fe probably, and then a
stage coach ride or a horse to Sand Creek and
Fort Wallace in Missouri. He could catch a train
there and send a telegram.

"Dessert's here," Chiquita said.

Spur looked down. She had ordered a whole
lemon cream custard pie with egg white
frosting.

Spur McCoy knew he was going to die, but
what better way than eating yourself into a
stupor?

He had his first bite then glanced up and saw
a beautiful girl come into the dining room
looking around. She saw him and her face
brightened.

The girl was Teresa, in civilian dress. She was
not a nun anymore and she walked straight for
his table. It was going to be one hell of a week!

HANG
SPUR McCOY

1

A rifle slug smashed into the boulder Spur McCoy huddled behind, hitting only six inches above his head, shattering the lead and tearing sharp granite shards off the rock and spewing them behind him. The shot came so close McCoy could smell the burned black powder. He jerked his head down at once and moved to the far side of the horse-sized upthrust of natural rock protection.

Spur leaned out and fired the Spencer repeating rifle as quickly as he could, levering the second round in, only half aiming as he sent the thundering .52 caliber chunks of hot lead toward the outhouse thirty yards to the rear of the small ranch cabin a hundred yards below him in the farthest end of the small valley.

Spur McCoy was a big man with sandy brown hair, a full brown mustache and mutton chop sideburns. He was one of the few United States Secret Service Agents in the West and roamed half the nation on assignments straight from Washington, D.C. usually via the telegraph key. But this was one job he had stumbled into on his own.

The man Spur had shot at behind the facility decided he'd been exposed too much and for too long. He ran for the house, firing a shot from his rifle toward Spur as he ran. Spur leavered around the rock, aimed, followed, then led the runner and fired. It was like gunning a duck on the wing or at a bouncing mule deer running across your path.

The lead was exactly right. The .52 caliber slug bored through the left side of the gunman, churned through muscle, tissue and small bones, smashing a rib and continuing in six pieces straight into the gunman's heart. The attacker stumbled and fell, his rifle skittering ahead of him, his hands thrown out in fatal protest. His chest hit in the reddish brown dirt first, then his head flopped forward and his face gouged a two foot trail in the dust before his body came to a stop.

As soon as he saw the hit, Spur turned his sights on the small cabin. It was typical of the kind of domiciles homesteaders threw up to meet the terms of *improving* the land. That meant first a house, and then a barn or corral, and of course a herd of steers or milk cows, or some evidence that tilling the soil had been undertaken. Here in this southern Idaho valley not far south of the Snake river, it was cattle.

Spur was berating himself for getting caught in such an awkward situation in the first place. He had been on his way to Twin Falls, Idaho, in the southern part of the state, after coming most of the way from Pocatello on the stage. At a stage overnight stop he had been told of massive Indian gatherings ten miles to the north. He fought the idea, but at last his conscience won. He was probably the only federal lawman within a thousand miles, and if there was a large number of Indians grouping for some kind of attack . . .

He had rented a horse and investigated, then discovered only a family meeting of fifteen Shoshoni Indians from the same tribe. They were branches of the same family and had been separated for almost a year. It was a reunion. They were so friendly and peaceful, that it took Spur two days to pay his respects and get back on his way toward Twin Falls.

The "massive" gathering of Shoshoni had congregated to harvest a particularly tasty variety of wild onions, which they harvested and dried for use later in the winter. They also gathered acorns and pine nuts for their winter lodges. The Shoshoni were just as well known as "the grass people," since they were not hunters or agricultural, but roamed wherever they might find food and buffalo.

Another bullet whined away from the rock Spur lay behind. He moved to the other side and peered over a mound of decomposing granite.

A small yard in front of the house held a well, a hitching post and the sprawled body of a man Spur guessed was the owner of the homestead. Spur had seen two men charge into the house and heard shots, but now all was quiet.

A horse whickered from behind the house. He heard leather creaking in the silent mountain air.

They were moving out!

Spur jumped up and ran downhill until he could see around the side of the cabin. The third man swung up on his horse. Spur jerked up the Spencer and sent two rounds at them, but the quickly aimed shots missed. He saw puffs of smoke where the rifles below him returned fire.

Something hit him hard in the right leg. His last shot went into the air as he spun backward and tumbled into the dirt. The pain came in gushing waves as he looked down at his leg. Already his pants leg was red with blood. He lay down the Spencer and watched the three horsemen charge away from him, bent low in the saddle to make the smallest targets possible.

McCoy felt sweat pop out on his forehead. The waves of pain plowed through him as he tried to sit up. He made it only by pushing with his right hand. His whole lower pants leg was red-wet with blood.

He had to stop the flow. He pulled his knife and slit the pants leg from the knee down. The ugly gash pulsed blood out of his leg with every heartbeat. Spur pulled off his neckerchief and wrapped it around the wound, then tugged the cloth as tight as he could.

A vicious, thundering hammering slammed into his head, then everything faded into gray and splotches of black as the knife edges of pain sliced patterns through his brain. He blinked and shook his head until it cleared. He had seldom felt pain so pervasive.

How could he lose so much blood so fast? His vision returned to near normal. There was no possibility that he could get to the well for water, not unless he hopped, or dragged his wounded right leg. But he had to try or he would die where he lay. He tucked the ends of the kerchief under the last wrapping and decided the makeshift bandage would stay in place. He had to get moving. If he stayed there he would be some hungry buzzard's breakfast.

McCoy gritted his teeth, picked up the Spencer and slid forward a foot toward the well. He pushed with his left foot, letting his right leg drag. Sweat ran into his eyes. The sun beamed down in all its noontime splendor and heat.

Ten minutes later he had moved thirty feet. Behind him he could see where his leg made a trail in the red shot soil. Here and there were splotches of blood.

His eyes clouded again, and this time it took him longer to clear his vision. Another half hour and he would be in the shade of the little well house.

If he made it.

How had he lost so much blood so quickly? The bullet must have hit an artery.

For a moment he thought he heard hoofbeats through the ground. He put both hands flat on the ground and listened. A bird called somewhere in the woods a quarter of a mile north. Then he felt the vibrations, horses were coming.

Quickly he picked up the Spencer and levered a fresh round in. If the killers were coming back, he should be able to get one more of them before they finished him. Two for one, not too bad.

The shapes on horseback wavered through the heat at first. They did not seem to be attacking. Four of them at least, he decided. Another cloud covered his eyes and he had to rub them to bring back the light.

At last he spotted the riders again, four, riding fast. They had guns out now, but no one was shooting. As they came closer he thought he noticed something on one man's shirt. Then he saw it again. The sun glinted off a silver star. Yes, a marshall or a sheriff. Good, he might just make it yet.

Then the cloud closed in around him, the sky darkened, and Spur McCoy fell forward his head resting on his arm, as unconsciousness overwhelmed him.

Cold.

Something cold.

He felt it again. This time it came suddenly and he snorted, gasped and his eyes jolted open. His face was wet. Someone had thrown water in his face. He tried to sit up.

Hands held him down. He was out of the sun. Spur frowned, then looked up at the closest face. His vision was clear. He saw the badge on a slightly out of focus chest, then a full moustache on a stubble-cheeked face with large brown eyes that were now bloodshot and weary.

"Come on, damnit! You've had enough sleep." The sheriff slapped Spur's cheeks gently. "Wake up, man. We've got the blood stopped. I want to know who the hell you are."

Spur saw it was the man with the badge talking. He faded out of focus, then came back sharp and clear. Spur frowned and blinked.

"Drink?" Spur asked, his voice low, uncertain.

The same big man held Spur's shoulders and gave him water from a tin cup. With the water Spur gained strength and sat up. Three other men were in the fuzzy background on the cabin's rough porch.

Spur saw the word "Sheriff" on the silver badge.

"Name is Spur McCoy, Sheriff. Going to Twin Falls on business."

"Or you just come from there," a nasty voice said from the shadows. Spur could not see the man who spoke.

"Give him his say," the sheriff snapped. He looked at Spur. "I'm Sheriff Sloan of Twin Falls County. I'm the law here."

"Howdy. I was south into the mountains a ways and coming back toward the stage road when I heard some shots. When I got over here I saw these four guys had surrounded the cabin and were shooting up a small war. One man was already dead out by the well."

"You was one of the killers, wasn't you, asshole?" The slurred, angry words came from a man who leaned down into Spur's face. He had thin features and wore an expression of abject hatred. His small, tight mouth never smiled.

"No, I wasn't with them," Spur said. "I was fighting them."

"He's about the right size," a new, older voice said from behind Spur. "Horse is the right color, and his hat even matches. We found his Spencer 7-shot rifle, too. Hell, that's more than enough for me."

Sheriff Sloan sat back on his heels. "Get this straight, you three. This is a duly constituted posse, not a damn lynch party. You're working under me. You will take all of your orders from me. Any disagreement with my orders and you're in your saddle heading back to town. I'll do the questioning, make the decisions and give the orders. That all clear?"

Sloan stood and looked at each of the three. He was nearly six feet tall, solidly built and carried his six-gun tied low on his leg as if he knew how to use it. Brownish gray hair spilled out from under a battered brown hat. His brown eyes studied them. Spur knew the lawman was ready for instant action. His hand hovered near the weapon as he waited for their responses. One man grunted assent. The bearded one shrugged. Agreement came from the other man Spur could not see.

"Tell the rest of your story, McCoy," Sheriff Sloan said. "Ain't saying I believe you, but ain't saying I don't neither."

Spur told him what happened, from his first hearing the shots to his attempt to stop the three riders from leaving when he was shot. After Spur had finished, one of the men walked up to the sheriff and whispered to him.

It was Spur's first real look at the man. He was short, about five feet six, and heavy at over a hundred and eighty pounds. The fat man watched Spur.

"Like we figured, Sheriff. The woman inside has been stripped naked and raped and cut up some, then half her head was shot off. Two kids in there, both stabbed to death and their throats slashed. So the whole family is deader than a day old buzzard feast." He glared at Spur. "Leastwise we got one of the bastards who done it!"

"Not a chance," Spur said. "I can prove who I am and what I am, and . . ." He stopped. He couldn't prove a thing! In that last river crossing his mount had slipped and fallen and he went into the water. His wallet with half his cash and his new identification card from Washington D.C. had been swept downstream. There was no telegraph for two hundred miles. He could not prove who he was without waiting for a week to ten days for a letter!

"So prove it," the thin faced, black eyed man said. "I say he can't prove nothing. We got all the damn evidence that we need to convict!"

"For once I agree with you, Long. We take him back to Twin Falls to stand trial for the deaths of Ned Bailey, his wife and kids, as well as the rest of all this."

Spur knew he had to talk his way out of this mess. His six-gun was gone from his holster. The Spencer leaned against the cabin out of reach. The sheriff seemed like a fair man, maybe he had a chance.

"Sheriff, I'm a lawman, a federal lawman. Get me

to a telegraph and I can prove it. I'm on my way to
Twin Falls on government business."

"Sure, and I'm fucking President Grant!" The fat
man shouted, his voice rising into a howling laugh.

"All I ask is a way to prove who I am," Spur said.
"I'll gladly go to Twin Falls with you and you can
send a letter to the nearest telegraph station and
have them get my identity from Washington, D.C."

"Sounds reasonable," Sheriff Sloan said. "You
just might be who you say. Course, then you might
be one of the four killers we've been chasing since we
left Twin Falls yesterday afternoon. The four held
up a saloon owner, robbed him of five hundred
dollars, then killed him when he went for his gun.
We chased them out of town and lost them last
night. They stayed at a small farm. By the time we
got there this morning, they had raped the mother
and daughter and killed the farmer."

"I've never been in Twin Falls before," Spur said.

"Mite hard to prove that," Sheriff Sloan said.
"You do fit the general description, even your horse,
hat and rifle match the killers. You could have come
here, got yourself shot up and the other three left
you behind so you wouldn't slow them down. I seen
that happen before."

"Three horses rode out, check the prints," Spur
said. "So where does that fifth man come from, the
one dead by the outhouse?"

"Yeah, you got a point. Tolerable point. But like I
said, he could have been a hired hand. Guess we
should get you patched up a little better so you can
ride back to town."

"No need for that, Sheriff," the bearded man said.
He had drawn his hogsleg and cocked the hammer.
"This Jasper ain't traveling much more than a
hundred feet to that oak tree over there. Easy

Sheriff! Just lay your iron on the porch right there.
We decided, the three of us. No sense dragging this
killer all the way back to town. We'll have a little
necktie party right here, on that oak. Save the
county the cost of a trial and a hangman."

Sheriff Sloan turned slowly and looked at the
other two men. "This one is crazy, we all know that.
But, Hoffer, you're no fool. You know this evidence
is circumstantial. Might not be true at all. You ain't
going along with a wild man like Gabe Young, are
you?"

"We decided, Sheriff," Hoffer said. "Hell, Abe,
ease up a little. Ain't no damn leather off your
saddle. Just a little old fashioned justice. An eye for
an eye. We got him dead to rights!"

The sheriff scowled. "Boots, you going along with
these idiots? Against the law to do this, Boots.
You're usually a good, reliable man. Could get you
in one hell of a lot of trouble if you go through with a
lynching."

Boots shuffled his feet. He was twenty-eight, tall,
gangling, with soft blond hair and a narrow face. He
grinned with a lopsided tilt.

"Hell, Sheriff, we just having a little fun. Worked
damn hard all week. Man's got to have a little fun."

"Damn, Boots, you still drunk? When in hell you
going to sober up? You said you wouldn't drink
until we got back." The sheriff stood there, hands on
his hips.

"Now, Sheriff, don't you fret," Gabe Young said
waving his six-gun. We deputies! We just upholding
the law. Found us a murderer and we sentenced him.
Now we gonna put him on his horse and watch the
bastard stretch hemp! Nothing you can do about it,
except watch. Move away from your six-gun and sit
down. We got to tie you up till the fun is all over."

"But you can watch, Sheriff," Hoffer said. "Wouldn't deny you the enjoyment of watching a good hanging."

"Yeah, Sheriff," Long said. "Hanging is a right fun time for everybody." He laughed. "Hell it's fun for almost everybody." He kicked Spur in the kidney and laughed when he doubled up and rolled off the porch into the hot dust.

2

Gabe Young grabbed Spur by the shoulder and pulled him to his feet. As soon as he stood up some-one tied his hands behind him. Until that moment, Spur was sure he could get away from the four men. The sheriff would be a help. But the quickness of the hand tie ruined his chances.

He would have to kick the one with the gun.

Young moved back out of range of Spur's sudden flailing foot.

"You'll have to do better than that, McCoy!" Young shouted. He laughed softly. "Not a chance in hell that you're going to get out of this. So just take it easy, you murdering bastard! We want to do this right, snuff out your worthless life with a two foot drop! Yeah, this is getting better all the time!"

"You hang him, you know I'll come after you, Young," Sheriff Sloan said. "You're the instigator. You take a prisoner from me and I'll hunt you down and shoot your balls off just for fun and then you'll die so slow you'll be begging me . . ."

Young slammed the side of his six gun against Sheriff Sloan's head, toppling him into the dirt off the porch.

"Shut up, old man! Just shut up!"

"You sure this is the guy you saw busting out of the saloon?" Hoffer asked Young softly.

"Hell yes! I said so didn't I? You getting chicken feet here, Hoffer?"

"No. I just want to be sure you saw this one."

Boots came up and stared at Spur.

"Sure looks mean enough to kill them," Boots said, his drunk grin fading a little. He looked at Spur again, then nodded and went to his saddle for a rope. He came back with his lariat, a stiff throwing rope not much more than three-eighths of an inch in diameter but strong enough to stop a nine hundred pound steer.

"Need a bigger rope," Young said.

"Don't got one," Boots said.

Young spat on the ground, eyed the rope again. "Hail, it'll have to do. Tie a good hangman's knot with thirteen loops, and make sure it's done right."

"Don't know how," Boots said.

"Christ! I have to do it all?" Young shrilled.

He took the rope and tried to tie a hangman's knot. Three times he wound the rope and made the loop. It never came out right.

Hoffer watched him but threw up his hands when Young offered him the rope. At last they went to the sheriff.

"Old man," Gabe Young said. "You tie us a hangman's knot or I'm gonna shoot you in the leg. You savvy?"

"If I don't, even then make a noose for you?"

"We'll turn this Jasper loose and let him run for it

while we use him for target practice. Take your pick."

Sheriff Sloan waited for Hoffer to untie him, then took the rope. Young stood six feet in front of him with his six-gun aimed at the unarmed sheriff's chest.

"The hanging would be more humane, I guess," Sheriff Sloan said. He quickly fashioned a hangman's noose with thirteen loops around it and gave it to Young.

Young put his arm through the noose and pulled the free end. The rope slid through and tightened around his arm. Young grunted and motioned for the other two to move Spur toward the oak at the side of the small corral.

"McCoy!" the sheriff called. The trio stopped and turned. "Look, I'm sorry. This got out of hand. Any in-laws I can notify? Anything I can do?"

"Looks like you've done enough," Spur said nodding at the noose.

"I'll track these guys down," Sloan said. "Last thing I do I'll get them for you."

"Helps me a hell of a lot when I'm dead," Spur said.

The men pushed him toward the tree. Spur watched the sheriff a minute longer. He whispered some words, but Spur could not read his lips. The only word he caught was "noose." He turned and looked at the instrument of death that Boots carried. It was a small version of the hangman's noose since the rope was thin, but he could see nothing unusual. What did the sheriff mean?

"Bring his horse," Young said. "And take off the saddle. That's the way it's done."

Spur watched every move. There was simply no

chance. He could run, but they would chase him down and bring him back. He might get in one lucky kick but that still left two of them, and they all carried guns. Young was the one to go for, but he stayed well out of range. It took Young three tries to get the noose end of the rope thrown over the oak branch that jutted from the oak tree fifteen feet off the ground.

They dropped the noose down to the right height, then had to tie two lariats together, so the rope could be tied around a low branch on the tree.

It took all three of them to boost Spur onto the back of his horse. He sat facing backwards on the horse and Hoffer held the reins in front. There was no chance to surge away and ride out of danger. He would have tried it even backwards, but there was not a chance.

Spur looked at the swinging noose and felt sweat on his forehead. That was death staring at him. That loop of rope would strangle him if it didn't break his neck.

Hoffer rode up and slipped the noose over his head and pulled it snug. Spur could still breathe.

"Take up the slack," Hoffer directed Long. "The damned rope will stretch enough to give him a jolt when he hits bottom."

Spur looked and saw Boots holding his horse. Still no chance.

Hoffer rode away and Spur could feel the pressure on his neck as the horse under him shifted positions. Boots kept her from moving much.

Long and Hoffer rode up beside Spur. Both were grinning.

"McCoy, you bastard, you raping, murdering son of a bitch!" Young said. "Your life of crime is

almost over. Anything you want to say to the
assembled throng?" Long giggled.

Spur stared at him a minute.

"You'll have to live with this, all three of you. I'm
a United States lawman, and did not hurt anyone in
this county. I only just arrived . . ."

Long hit him across the face with the back of his
hand.

"Hell, I never did like long speeches." He took out
a six inch sheath knife and nodded at Hoffer who sat
his mount on the other side of Spur's horse. Hoffer
took out a knife and grinned at Spur.

"Don't rightly care if you're a federal lawman or
not," Hoffer said. "Might even be a mite relieved if
you are, come to think. But what the hell, a hanging
is a hanging. I love to go to hangings."

Spur watched both men, then looked at the way
the rope looped over the limb and was tied off. It
was a good job. He would not reach the ground.

He knew he would not live forever, but this
seemed like a useless, senseless way to die. His life
did not flash in front of him. Rather he concentrated
on memorizing the faces of the three lynchers. If he
ever had the chance he would haunt them as long as
they lived!

Spur McCoy looked at Long. He could see the
nature of the man. He was all bad, always had been,
always would be until somebody killed him. There
was a brief moment of recognition as Long accepted
the fact that Spur was a lawman and that they had a
certain kinship in living on the very edge of disaster
and euphoria, never knowing which one would come
next, but knowing that therein lay the thrill of
living. The not knowing made every day a new
challenge and a new thrill.

Then the spark died in Long's eyes.

"So long, asshole," he said and nodded at Hoffer.

Both men thrust their knives foward, slashing at the hindquarters of the horse. The mount bellowed in pain and rage, dug in her back hooves and her powerful rear quarters drove her forward.

Spur McCoy jolted off the horse and dropped to the end of the rope. The hemp stretched, and held.

3

Spur's mind was clear, sharp as he heard the mount bellow in rage and surge forward. He felt his body dragged off the horse's rump, felt the rope tighten around his neck more gradually than he had expected.

Then came the searing burning on his neck as he dropped to the end of the slack and the rope tore away flesh. His head rolled to the left and he felt the heavy knot on the right side of his neck.

For just an instant he realized his neck was not broken, but there was still strangulation that would kill him just as dead if not quite so quickly. The six or eight seconds seemed like an eternity. He saw the green of the tree overhead, knew his body was swinging on the rope. He remembered that the sheriff had tied the knot, had he done something to give Spur a chance? The sky was blue, he saw that. He heard a low laugh from one of the lynchers. A moment later it was too much effort to keep his eyes open.

Then it all faded and wavered, came back for a second, then it was gone in a blinding rush as the black clouds closed around him and Spur McCoy knew nothing else.

Gabe Long shrilled a long laugh. "Keeeeereist! Look at that! His damn neck must be broke, and his eyes are bulging. Will his tongue stick out? Never seen me many hangings, leastways, not up close like this. Keeeeeeeeeeeeriest! Look at that!"

Boots stared at the man hanging by his neck. The last of his alcohol fog evaporated and he looked at the hanged man, then at the three of them and closed his eyes. He'd been a part of it! Damn! How drunk had he been? And for how long? There would be hell to pay for this. He just hoped that he wouldn't have to move to another state. Not another time. Goddamnit, he was swearing off the booze . . . again.

Josh Hoffer watched the body swaying back and forth, then saw it turn slowly until it had made an entire circuit. Hell, the guy had to be dead by now. Hoffer had never seen a hanging before and he wasn't overjoyed by this one. It sure was a new experience!

"Let's get the hell out of here!" Hoffer said. He looked at Young who stood at arms length from the body. McCoy's boots hung two feet off the ground. "I'm going," Hoffer said. He walked back to where his horse was tied. Then he remembered the sheriff. He hurried over to him, untied his hands but kept the lawman's six-gun.

"Don't want you doing nothing foolish, now, Sheriff. You get yourself up on your horse and we're riding out of here."

By the time they were mounted up, Boots and Young had joined them. Young wanted to use the corpse for target practice, but the others ignored him and they rode out.

They had watched the body twitch for two or three minutes. When they were half a mile away, the sheriff turned.

"You can shoot me in the back if you want, but I'm going to go back and cut him down. He deserves a decent burial, at least." The sheriff turned and rode away. When he realized the trio was not going to interfere or shoot him down, he rode harder and came up to the oak tree in a rush. He looked behind him and saw the trio of riders vanish over the ridge, then rode up to McCoy and slashed the lariat in half, letting the man's body crumple into the dirt.

Sheriff Sloan dropped off his horse and loosened the noose around McCoy's neck and stared hard at him.

Spur McCoy coughed.

Sloan grinned and sat beside him, taking the noose away, staring at the ugly rope burn on McCoy's neck.

The sheriff bent and listened to McCoy's heart beat through his chest. He laughed softly.

"Yeah, McCoy, don't know if you can hear me or not, but you should pull through. Tying that hangman's knot was our only chance. I did the Murphy knot. It puts most of the pressure on the side of the head, and if it's tied right, is guaranteed not to break the man's neck and not even strangle him.

"Sure it cuts off the blood supply to part of the brain, but not all of it. That's the secret. You look damn dead, but you really ain't."

McCoy coughed again. The sheriff cut the rope off his hands and wiped his face with a wet kerchief.

He listened. The man was breathing deep and regularly. Sheriff Sloan slapped Spur's face lightly, then harder. There was no response. He took his canteen off his saddle and sloshed water over the secret agent's face and he snorted, shook his head and groaned.

"That's better, McCoy. Come on, snap out of it. You're not half dead yet. Want you to walk down to the porch so I can get you back to normal."

McCoy groaned again, lifted one hand to his face and then his eyes fluttered, opened, closed against the sun and Sloan shaded his eyes. This time they came open and turned toward the sheriff.

"Right, McCoy, you're still alive. Not many men get hanged and live to tell about it. Saw it happen once before. You won't be able to talk for a while, maybe not for a day or two. Don't worry about it, voice should come back. Might be a little different sounding though." He shrugged. "Hell anything is better than dead."

He got Spur a drink of water from the well. Spur tried to drink, spit out the first try, then sipped a small bit at a time and got some down.

The sheriff helped Spur sit up, then to stand. They walked slowly down to the cabin and sat on the porch. It took almost twenty minutes to move the hundred yards.

Sheriff Sloan lolled on the porch as if he didn't have a thing in the world to do.

"Damn glad they asked me to tie the knot for them. I was hoping they couldn't tie a real hangman's knot. Not many people can, and it's against the law when you come right down to it. So I tied them Murphy's knot. I was trying to tell you not to worry so much when they led you away, but not much I could do. I didn't want them to look too close at the noose. Whole idea is to fix it so the rope will pull through, but it binds against itself so the pressure isn't as great and course with that little rope, that knot itself isn't big enough to break a man's neck. So you worry about strangling and cutting off blood to the brain."

Sloan looked at Spur. "Time. Time is what we have lots of now. Don't want to move too fast. Them three will think I'm back here doing the burying on five or six bodies, so it should take some time. It's a good long day's ride back to Twin Falls from here. We'll let them get back and situated. Then when you feel like it, we can move."

Spur looked up waved his hand to get the sheriff's attention, then tried to say something. The croak that came out surprised Spur more than Sheriff Sloan.

"Yep, sounds about right. You're bound to do that for a day or two. Good sign, though, McCoy. Shows that the voice box is still there and functioning. Now all we have to do is let mother nature fine tune the instrument."

The sheriff went for more water from the well, gave Spur another small drink, then checked the leg wound. He went into the death house and came back with a bed sheet and a tablet and two pencils.

"Figure you might want to give me some more details about yourself and your job out here," Sloan said. He passed the tablet to Spur who took a pencil and began writing.

"Yes, thanks. I am a Secret Service Agent. You probably never heard of me, but you can check me out by wiring to General Wilton D. Halleck, in care of Capital Investigations, Washington, D.C."

The sheriff read it and nodded.

"Don't see as how I have any real need to do that. I size up folks quick like. You say you're a lawman for the Federal people, that's good enough for me.

Why you coming to Twin Falls? We only got about a thousand people in the whole town, maybe fifteen hundred in Twin Falls county."

"Can't tell you yet, Sheriff. If I need your help I'll give you all the details . . . later."

"Fine. Like I say I figure people out quick." He stood. "I better get at my gardening, or I'll never get finished." He went to the barn, found a shovel and came back.

An hour later the sheriff had dug two shallow graves and buried the two men. He went up near the oak tree and dug again, then carried the blanket wrapped body of the woman and then the two children up and lay them in the same grave. He was done well before dark.

Spur had been up and walking. He carried his head at a strange angle because his neck felt better that way. When the sheriff came back, he looked in the house again and found some ointment and made some bandages from the sheet, then treated Spur's neck and his leg. He wrapped both with yards of the white three-inch strips of sheet, then tore up some more and rolled them up and stuffed them in his saddle bags.

The sheriff found fresh bread in the house, some nearly melted butter and a jar of preserves. Behind the barn he located the milk cow and they had bread and jam and fresh, warm milk for supper.

Twice more Spur had tried to talk, but his voice croaked and wheezed. The third time the words were understandable, but still tinged with strange creaks and whistles.

"By morning you'll be feeling better," the sheriff said. "You need a good night's rest, then with some breakfast in our bellies, we'll strike out for Twin Falls."

* * *

By noon the next day, Spur's voice had almost returned to normal. It had a deeper sound now, more resonant, and the sheriff said it might stay that way forever, or it could slip back to the tone it had previously.

They stopped at the family where the farmer had been killed and were given a late dinner. The women were quiet, polite but reserved. Spur did not blame them. Spur put down enough beef stew and vegetables and chunks of good wheat bread to feed three men. He was feeling better. He spoke only when he had to, and did not trust his voice.

They rode late into the afternoon, then it turned dusk and they could see the kerosene lamps glowing ahead in Twin Falls.

"Sheriff, tell me about those three men," Spur said.

"Whatever they done is my responsibility," Sloan said. "Wish I could charge them with murder, but that would be hard to do, you walking around and all. I can charge them with *attempted* murder, but our judges don't hold much with that kind of legal maneuvering."

"They think they killed me," Spur said slowly. "I just might be able to scare them to death. Tell me about them."

"Thought you had an assignment here?"

"Do, but it can wait a day or two. Tell me."

"Boots Dallman is the blond guy. Surprised he went along with it, but then figured out he was still drunk. Never got him to go on a posse before. Probably wouldn't have gone if he wasn't pied right up to the gills that afternoon. I needed him, needed at least four against four.

"Dallman is a family man, wife and two kids.

Lives outside of town to the south about five miles on a little spread. Homestead I think. He works sometimes for the Box B ranch, a big outfit. Boots is a good man. He just got carried away, then was in over his head. Gabe Young had him scared shitless out there."

"I had the same feeling," Spur said, the whistles lessening. "What about Young?"

"Been in trouble in half of the state, mostly between here and Boise. Drifter, gambler, gun for hire sometimes. A killer who doesn't care who goes down. I only took him because he can use those guns of his. I had to have some firepower. He's maybe twenty-five or six years old. Figure he'll never make thirty.

"Other man is Joshua Hoffer, nearing fifty now. A merchant in town but not exactly a lily-white character. He is not a pillar in the church or the community. Has a good General Mercantile, and you can find things you need there they don't even stock in Boise."

"Bloodthirsty little bastard," Spur said, the croak coming back into his voice.

"True, this time. Generally he's harmless." The sheriff watched Spur as they rode toward the outskirts of the town.

"Lawman or no, I'm going to be watching you. There are no legal charges I can bring against the three that will stick."

"Fair enough, Sheriff."

"So don't go off half cocked. I'd hate to have to hang you for murder."

"Sheriff, I'd hate to have to hang for murder. Way I look at it, if one or two of these guys has an *accident* it would be mighty hard to prove that it was murder."

They stopped a block from the only hotel in town, it was a three story affair over a saloon. One door led into the hotel, the other door to the drinking, gaming, fancy-lady establishment.

"McCoy, you had a rough time, but you've alive. It's better than being dead. I helped keep you alive. Don't make me move against you."

"Sheriff, you ever been hanged?"

The big man on the black horse shook his head slowly.

"Then don't be telling me what I can and can't do, not until you've walked at least a mile in the boots of a man who has been!"

4

Sheriff Abe Sloan laughed softly to himself.

"I know you're right, McCoy. But I still don't want to hang you. You bury any of the three of them in my county, and I'll put you on trial for murder. Don't believe that I won't."

The two men stared at each other for a minute, understanding the other's point of view, feeling a strange camaraderie that set them apart from normal mortals. At last they both smiled, nodded, then they continued their ride into town.

The sheriff took Spur up the back stairs of the hotel and put him in a room, then went downstairs and registered him.

When he came back he gave Spur the key. "Looks like the county owes you one night's lodging," Sloan said. "Best damn bed in the place." He hesitated. "You, ah . . . You need anything else?"

"Just some supper, maybe a bath and then a good night's sleep. Thanks for that Murphy knot. I owe you a rather large favor one of these days."

"That you do. I'll stop by Doc Rawson's place and have him come up and look you over. He'll cuss and fume and rant about my sloppy doctoring, but he was the one who trained me two years ago. I had been losing shot up suspects. He showed me how to stop the bleeding at least."

Sloan paused at the door, his big, rough hands turning his hat by the brim. When he completed one full turn, he glanced up.

"McCoy, you need anything, you just give a call. I'm damn glad you're still alive." Sheriff Sloan put on his hat and hurried out the door and down the hall.

Spur watched him go. He would be as careful as he could about not *burying anybody* in Twin Falls county. Outside the county line might be another matter. He liked the big, rough and ready sheriff. He was the kind most towns in the West needed: tough enough to handle the job, but smart enough to know when to be gentle. Most towns couldn't find the right kind of man.

A half hour later Doc Rawson came and stared at Spur a moment, then sat on the bed and rubbed his face. The medic was small and wiry, wore a black suit, carried a black bag and had dried blood stains on his shirt sleeves. He swore as he unwrapped the bloody bandage from Spur's neck.

"Rope burn?" Doc Rawson said.

Spur nodded. "I'd be grateful if you didn't let it get around about me or about the little scrape I got into that produced that rope problem," Spur said.

"Abraham told me about the same thing . . . the sheriff." He touched the wound and the side of Spur's head. The fingers hurt where he pressed on his head.

"Bruise up there. You actually were hung?"

"That's not a thing a man brags about, Doc."

"At least not in this world. Was it a Murphy's knot?"

"That's what Sheriff Sloan called it. He did the tying."

"Then hurried like hell back and cut you down before you strangled! That old son of a bitch!" Spur could feel the admiration and respect come through the doctor's words. He probed with a pair of pliers looking things, pulled free some stuck cloth and nodded.

"Hell, we'll have you up and around in a week or so." He applied something to the neck wound and Spur reacted. "Hurts, like hell, don't it? My old mother used to say if it didn't hurt, it wasn't helping any. Any rate it's a hell of a lot better than the alternative . . . dead."

He clipped off some curled up skin, trimmed another place and then asked Spur to talk. He did.

"Your voice has come back quickly. Don't use it too much in the next few days. No loud hollering, hog calling, or bellowing at fancy women."

Spur grinned.

"Thought I would hit something familiar sooner or later. Understand you could use a telegraph?"

"Right."

"I use the one down at Salt Junction, in Utah now and then. Made arrangements with the operator down there. I send in my message by mail direct to him. It's just north of the Great Salt Lake. Have to send it by mail to Pocatello on the stage. That's six days. Then six days coming back. Figure two weeks. That help you any?"

"I hope not. My plans call for me being on that stage myself before that long. But thanks."

The doctor looked at his leg, swore again, doused the wound with alcohol and brought a surprised shriek of pain from Spur.

"If it don't hurt . . ." the humorist medic said. Then he went to work and dug out the slug which for some reason had not gone all the way through. Spur gritted his teeth and pounded the bed once with his hand. The pain was twice as bad as the alcohol on the raw flesh, and it lasted longer.

"Missed most of the bone," Doc said. "But sure did cut up some of your leg. Gonna hurt like hell for two days. Advise you to try some Southern Comfort or Old Crow whiskey as a pain killer. Course I want you to stay off it for a week. By then you'll be in shape to get back to work. Whatever that might be."

Spur paid him twenty dollars for the surgery and house call. Doc Rawson looked at the twenty dollar bill and smiled.

"If I had more patients like you, Spur McCoy I could retire rich in five years. Usually I only charge two dollars to deliver a baby, fifty cents for a house call. Trouble is most nobody has any money to pay. I do get chickens, and garden vegetables and fruit in season, though."

Spur thanked him, promised he'd be to his office every two days so he could check the bandages, and closed the door. Spur looked at himself in the wavy mirror over the wash basin. He scrubbed his face, chest and arms, combed his hair and found he could hold his head straight if he tried. He put a red kerchief over the white bandage, slipped into a clean shirt and went down to the dining room for the last lean, rare steak from the kitchen. By the time he got back to his room it was almost nine o'clock. He had just taken off his shirt when someone knocked on the door.

He frowned, picked up his Colt .45 and thumbed back the hammer. He held the six-gun behind the door as he opened it a crack.

One pretty blue eye and a narrow slice of pouting red mouth looked back at him. Spur edged the door open farther and saw the whole girl. She was barely five feet tall, had silver blonde hair piled high up on her head and wore too much rouge and lipstick to be an honest woman.

"Abe Sloan has a message for you," she said, her blue eyes dancing, looking him up and down and not showing disappointment.

"A message?"

"I can't deliver it out here in the hall."

"Oh, come in." He held the door open, then left it a foot from being closed.

"My name is Clarice, that's French. My name means little brilliant one." She smiled and closed the door, then leaned against it.

"You had a message," Spur said smiling now.

"Yes. Mr. Sloan says he knows that you have been hurt, and that you may need something to take your mind off the pain, and that he welcomes you to Twin Falls and wishes you success on your assignment here."

"That's very kind of Sheriff Sloan . . . ."

"He said you might be difficult. I used to dance, did you know that? I was pretty good. But my costume kept falling off, so pretty soon I built that into my act, and changed jobs and before long, all of my clothes were falling off and I was a smashing success."

She took his hand, sat him on the bed and then

humming a scratchy tune, began to dance for him.

He stood. "Clarice, there is really no reason . . ."

She stopped dancing and stamped her small foot. As she did the strap that held up the top of her dress came loose, fell from her shoulder and dropped so low it revealed one large breast with a brown areola and red nipple.

"Just sit back down and please don't interrupt again," Clarice said. She continued dancing, ignoring the broken strap and the exposed breast. The dance picked up in speed and in the small room there was little space. She did a series of quick steps and the other side of her dress dropped down to her waist revealing the other breast.

Clarice clapped her hands and hummed the tune. Three steps later she did a small jump and the dress she once wore slid over her slender hips and dropped to the floor. She wore only thin, pink panties that barely covered her crotch.

Clarice turned and pranced toward him.

"This is not one of those dances where you can't touch the performers. In fact touching is encouraged. Kissing is expected, fondling is demanded."

She sat beside him.

"Think I could take your mind off your troubles tonight?"

"Clarice, I'm sure you could, tonight or any night. But I am really tired, and I do hurt."

She shushed him and put her hands on his shoulders and pushed him down on the bed, lying on top of him. She was careful not to touch his neck or his hurt leg.

"I'm a specialist on tired, and I'm not too heavy to smash you down. I'll do all the work, all you have to do is have fun and enjoy."

"Just pure sex?"

"Just fun fucking!" Her face came toward his. She lowered herself more and more until her lips touched his and pulled away.

"Kissing?"

"Some do, some don't," he said.

She laughed and kissed him. "I do." She kissed him again, her tongue exploring his open mouth. When the kiss ended, she smiled.

"You have an insistent third leg growing down there." Clarice smiled and lay on his chest for a moment. "I am sorry you were hurt. I'm not sure how or why, it doesn't matter. I just want to kiss it and make it feel better."

"Somehow I think you'll do just that," Spur said.

"Good! First, let me get your boots off, and then these pants. I'm really anxious to get a look at your good parts."

She undressed him slowly, carefully, not allowing any pain to his leg. When he was naked, she stood over him and beckoned.

"Into the next room. There's a connecting door. Everything has been arranged."

She opened the door and inside the next room he saw that it was twice as large as the one he had been in. There was a large bed, two soft chairs, and a steaming portable bathtub and three extra pails of hot water.

"I want you clean and smelling like a whole pine forest! I love the pine forests. And we'll be careful not to get your bandages wet. The sheriff warned me about that."

She smiled at him, her soft silver blonde hair loose now and falling half way down her neck.

"Come on, slow poke. You first in the tub. Step in and sit down with one foot, and we'll put your bandaged leg up on the side."

He stepped in on his good leg and sat down, yowling at the hotness of the water. Clarice laughed and dumped in half a bucket of cold, then began washing him, lathering him with two large cakes of pine-scented soap. She washed his face and his shoulders, all the time careful not to get the neck bandage wet. Then she worked lower and found a strange swelling just under the water.

She bent lower and pushed one of her breasts into Spur's mouth and he chewed on it.

Quickly then she stood, stripped down the pink, silk panties and moved toward him. Gently she sat down facing him, lowering herself on his stiff penis until she had enveloped all of him. Then she shrieked in victory and began bouncing up and down on him.

Spur felt himself building quickly to a climax and before he wanted to, he exploded and jolted her upward with each thrust, then sank back below the water as she leaned forward and brushed his lips with hers.

"Sweetheart, that was nice, but too common. We're just getting started. Do you know of the one hundred and thirty-seven traditional Japancoo positions for having sex, six of them are in a bathtub? I bet you didn't know that."

She lifted away from him and went on bathing him, scrubbing all except his injured calf, and when she was through, there was not a spot of water on either bandage.

Spur touched her breasts and she looked at him.

"You didn't get your turn."

"I don't get a turn, I'm working. You know that."

"With me you still get a turn."

"Later. Right now we need to get you out of that

tub and rubbed dry and stuffed under those silk sheets on the best bed in town. I've never been in this room before. The owner reserves it for extremely important people. Then again he isn't against making a few extra dollars. Why is the sheriff going to all this trouble for you?"

"I was hoping, Clarice, that you could tell me."

"Not a clue. I'm not paid to think, and most people say I'm not very smart but that I have a cute little ass and a pussy that just won't ever get tired of getting filled full. So what do I know?"

"You know plenty, and your dumb act is a cover-up for the real you. I just wished that I had the time to uncover you."

Clarice laughed. She spun around naked in front of him and he saw how her breasts swung out delightfully.

"Spur McCoy, I'm about as uncovered as a girl can get. Do you like what you see?"

"What I see and what I hear."

She led him to the bed and folded down the silk sheets. Spur could not remember silk sheets but back there sometime in New York he was sure his mother had them just for show, and on the guest room bed.

He slid between them and held them up for her. She snuggled against him and sniffed.

"You're a pine tree!"

He tucked the silk sheet around her. "Have you heard about anything crooked going on by the sheriff?"

"No. He's pure as the driven snow. I mean it. I offered it to him a dozen times, and he says no, but thanks. He's got a wife and he wouldn't cheat on her, not ever. He's tough, and he can shoot. I saw him kill two robbers once in a saloon. Just as cool and cold as hell! Next day he helped deliver a baby when Doc was out of town."

He lay there a moment, then moved his hand over one of her breasts and massaged it gently.

"I bet you know how to go around the world. I'm tired, but with you directing my tour, I bet we can get at least all the way across Europe and around to India somewhere."

Clarice laughed "You're going to China or I don't know my business. First we have to do New York. You ever been to New York?"

"I was born and grew up there," Spur said.

Clarice showed him a New York he had never suspected.

Well before India, Spur McCoy went down for the count. He never answered the bell for the seventh bare knuckled contest and Clarice declared herself the winner. She snuggled down in the silk sheets dreaming she was a princess, and went to sleep with one arm across Spur McCoy's broad chest.

5

Clarice sat on the bed, hugging her knees to her bare breasts and watched Spur McCoy.

"You're a pretty man," she said. "What a fine body you have." She giggled. "And you certainly do know how to use it! You almost filled me up and made me want to stop, almost but not quite. I don't ever remember that happening before."

McCoy pulled on a pair of town pants, soft brown ones with a crease down the front.

"Oh, Sheriff Sloan said to tell you, case you was interested, that Gabe Young hit town, changed horses, bought a bottle and lit out down the stage road toward Boise. That was about half an hour after he got into town."

Spur sat down beside her, reached in and kissed one bouncing breast, then the other one.

"Thanks, you saved me half a day." He pulled off the town pants and switched to denims, then put on a blue shirt and a brown leather vest. He tugged his boots on over two pair of soft cotton socks.

"You're going after him?" she asked.

Spur nodded.

"Damn! That means I got to go back to work."

Spur was turning his head slowly from one side to the other. It was stiff and sore, burned like Hades, but there wasn't anything he could do about that. He knew he couldn't afford to get in a situation where his injuries would slow him down. It could be a deadly problem.

Clarice stood on the bed. She was naked. She leaned over and put her arms around Spur's shoulders and looked him right in the eye.

"You come back, nice man. Last night was something special for me. It wasn't work at all. You keep your body from getting cut up or shot any more!"

Spur kissed her and smiled.

"Do my best. I better get moving. Leaving my gear here. You're welcome to stay. Not just sure when I'll be back."

Spur slung his saddle bags over his shoulder, hoisted his Spencer and went out the door. He had a cold trail to follow, so he better get moving.

At the livery he picked up his horse where the sheriff had taken it, paid for the keep and needed help in saddling the big black. She was sturdy and deep chested, and could outlast three mules. Ten minutes later he was on the stage road northwest.

He had never been to Boise, capital of the Territory of Idaho.

Spur asked about Gabe Young and the livery man knew him. Said Gabe was a sharp man when it came to horse trading. Talked the livery man out of a white stallion he'd been saving. Traded him a half blown sorrel and twenty dollars for him. Livery man said Young wanted the horse because it matched his high crowned white hat.

Spur rode. His neck pained him more than he thought possible, a continual dull ache and sharp pains shooting into his head. He stopped at the first farm house near the main road.

The woman who came to the door eyed him suspiciously. She said she'd seen the man on the white horse. He rode past the previous day sometime. Didn't stop. Spur thanked her and pushed on.

It was almost noon when he turned down a half mile lane toward a small ranch. Just as he got to the well house fifty feet from the side door of the small frame residence, a shotgun boomed birdshot over his head.

"Far enough!" A man's voice bellowed. "State your name and your business, or move down the road!"

"Spur McCoy is my name and I'm tracking an outlaw who rode past here on a white horse."

"You a lawman?"

"Yes. Any help you can give me would be appreciated."

"Oh, sorry. Step down and come in for some victuals. Wife is just ready to set up dinner."

A man came from the side door of the house carrying an old Greener double barreled shotgun. He still had one live round.

Spur got down slowly and kept his hands well away from his holster.

"You chasing Gabe Young, I'd figure," the rancher said. He wore overalls, and long johns but no shirt, even though it was June. "Bastard was here. Offered the sonofabitch a bed for the night and he took it. Sometime during the night he broke the lock on my eldest daughter's room and raped her. She's still all broke up about it. Don't know if she'll ever be the same. She was really a fine girl, promised to a guy over a section. Now the wedding is off, of course."

"You should ride into town and file a complaint with Sheriff Sloan. He will be interested."

"Might just do that." The man paused, wiped a rough hand over his sun-weathered face. "Yep, I might just do that. Won't help my daughter any, though." He stared at the barn for a minute, then waved Spur foward.

"Come in, come in. Meet the family. We're having fried chicken and biscuits and gravy for dinner. Hope you're hungry. Wife makes the best pot of coffee this side of Denver."

An hour later Spur was on his way. The hand drawn map he had picked up at the Mercantile before he left Twin Falls, showed the route to Boise was 145 miles. The stage road followed the Snake River downstream much of the way. He went across a ferry run by a family called Glenn. They had been moving people across the river at that point for years. People called it Glenn's Ferry.

The trail led more northerly then. Spur tried to maintain forty miles a day. Somehow he missed the stage, but it was just as well, since he had to check with ranchers and small settlements to make sure that Young had passed through.

He had, and seemed to leave a trail a dozen axe handles wide. Either he had no fear or a death wish hoping someone would find him.

The fourth day Spur's leg began to bleed. He made it into town just after noon and hobbled into a doctor's office. The medic looked at the leg and laughed.

"You come in from Twin Falls and old Doc Rawson wrapped up that leg, I'd bet a dollar!"

"Right, but no bet. Why did it start bleeding again?"

"You probably pushed it too fast. You young guys always seem to be in a rush for some reason."

The medic treated Spur's leg, taking a dozen stitches with some heavy black thread and told him to come back in a week for a checkup.

Then Spur took off his neckerchief.

"Better take a look at this, too."

When the medic had the bandage off he swore.

"Never seen but one like that before. Must have been a small rope to gouge into your flesh that deep. Damn! You could get infection in there easy. You should be in bed somewhere."

"No time, Doc. Put some of that salve or something on it. Doc Rawson didn't seem too worried."

"Naturally, it ain't his neck!"

The doctor fussed and worked for fifteen minutes, then bandaged up the ugly wound.

"Like I said, you should be in bed resting. Give your body a chance to heal itself."

"Soon as I have time, Doc." Spur gave the man a ten dollar eagle gold coin. "Appreciate it if you don't tell anybody about my neck. Little piece of business I need to do in town."

"Guy who hung you is here?"

"Didn't say that, Doc. So don't you."

Out on the street, Spur talked with a friendly barkeep. He knew Gabe Young.

"The man is a scoundrel and a worthless no-good. Lives with a woman up the street a ways. Small yellow house with a white picket fence on the corner. You can't miss it if you try."

"Thanks, I better get up there. I owe Young some money and I want to pay him before he comes looking for me. He can get nasty that way."

Spur finished his beer and went out the door. It was four blocks to the yellow house on the corner with a white picket fence. Spur watched it for a minute, and saw three men go up the walk and into the house. All three looked like hard cases.

Spur sat down next to a big maple tree and watched the house. A half hour later the same three men came out with Gabe Young leading them. They walked downtown.

McCoy followed them from well back. None of them wore guns. They were armed when they went into the small house. Curious. In the small downtown area they separated. Two of them went into the Boise Home Bank. The other pair leaned against the outside, watching the people going by, looking at wagons and riders. One stood near the front door and a second by the door on the side street.

Were the four planning a bank robbery? Seemed like it. Spur started moving foward, then stopped. No guns. They were just looking over the place, working out what they had to do.

The two men came out of the bank one after the other and all four went down the street along the side door. They were walking one possible escape route. These guys must be experienced at bank robbery. They certainly were planning it out.

At the far corner they split, each going different directions. Spur walked back to the hotel dining room. It was closed until five that afternoon. He climbed to the third floor and put his key in the door lock. Someone came up behind him quickly and he turned, his hand on his six-gun.

"Don't move your hand, sir, or I'll shoot," a woman in front of him said. She was wearing brown, had brown hair and a stern face and held a .25 caliber six-gun aimed at him as if she knew how to use it.

"I don't shoot many women," Spur said relaxing, but she kept the gun covering him.

"Open your door and back in slowly all the way to the window," she said.

Spur shrugged. He had never seen the woman. She was young, attractive more than pretty, with a ripe, full figure.

"Just back up and don't talk," she said.

Spur backed into the room to the window. She came in, closed the door and kept the key.

"Take your weapon out and lay it on the floor, carefully."

He did.

"Now, slide it over to me on the floor with your foot."

Spur obeyed.

"Now that I'm harmless you can put away the hogsleg."

She smiled faintly, but little humor showed in her face. Gray eyes studied him.

"You've been asking a lot of questions about Gabe, Gabe Young. Why?"

"I owe him some money."

"Liar. Nobody owes Gabe money. He makes them pay quickly. Why are you asking questions about him? Why were you watching our house, and following him?"

"He's wanted in Twin Falls for murder. I'm a bounty hunter."

"More lies. You're no bounty man. I lived with one for two years before somebody killed him. You don't have the edge, the anger, the stomach for the job. Why?''

"He is wanted in Twin Falls for attempted murder.''

"That charge won't get to trial in Idaho. Why are you hounding him? I know everything Gabe's ever done.''

"Two days ago he raped a sixteen year old girl just outside of Twin Falls.''

"That's possible. He uses lots of women, but he's always gentle and thoughtful with me.''

She put the pistol down and sat on the side of the bed. "You don't know Gabe like I do. His father was a drunk. Never provided, gambled, worked only when he had to, and beat Gabe from the time he was big enough to make a fist. Taught him to fight back. He's been fighting ever since.

"When he was thirteen his mother taught him all about sex, she raped him every night his father wasn't home, five or six times a week. He soon hated her.

"When he was fourteen he was big enough and strong enough to lie in wait for his father. He clubbed him half to death, went inside and cut up his mother's breasts, then ran away from home. He's told me he hates women because of his mother, and he hates men for what his father did to him for so many years.''

"Blaming others won't help him.''

"I've tried to help. A minister tried. Two judges tried, then sentenced him. He broke out of jail. He's had three names in the past two years.''

"Now he's going to rob the bank, the Boise Home bank. He was checking it over today.''

"He's an expert at robbing banks. He has never been caught. That's how we live from day to day, on other people's money.''

She brushed brown hair back from her eyes. "I wish I could stop him, but I can't. I'm tied to him now. If I tried to leave him he would kill me."

Slowly Spur took the kerchief from his neck. Edges of the wound showed around the bandage.

"Ever see what happens to a man when he gets hung, Mrs. Young?"

"I'm not married to Gabe. No, I never have. Were you . . . Gabe lynched you, and you lived?"

"Yes. I have a wound that will leave a scar for the rest of my life."

"That's another reason I have to help you." She stood and took off her light jacket, then began unbuttoning her calico dress that pinched in at her waist and swept the floor.

"I will do anything for you, Spur McCoy, if you will ride away and leave Gabe alone." The buttons came open and the fabric parted revealing a white camisole over her full breasts.

"I am not a loose woman, Mr. McCoy. It takes all of my strength to do this, but I will, for my man. Do you understand?"

"Yes, but I will make no deals with you about Gabe."

She let the dress top fall to her hips, then lifted off the frilly camisole. Her big breasts bounced and jiggled from her motions. Already their red nipples were enlarged with hot blood. Her pink areolas were large and tempting.

She walked toward him, smiling, her breasts jiggling.

"I can be very good for you, Spur. I can satisfy you, make you feel wonderful. I'll do anything you want to. You can put it in me wherever you want!"

She stood in front of him and massaged his crotch.

"I can never have children. God cursed me when

Gabe burned down a church and stole the collection. He cursed me and Gabe cursed me and I have to help him however I can. I still love him, and I always will. So if you harm Gabe, you're hurting me too, don't you understand?"

Spur cupped her breasts and kissed each, then he pushed her away. She was furious, tried again, grabbed him around his chest and ground her crotch against his. Gently Spur unlocked her hands and moved away from her.

She screamed, her voice full of hatred and fury. She turned lunged for the .25 caliber revolver she had left on the bed. She caught it and turned, but Spur slapped it away just as she fired. The bullet smashed the dresser mirror. Spur grabbed the gun and pushed her down on the bed.

"Get dressed and get out of here!" he said harshly. "You sound as sick as your man is!"

She sobbed on the bed a moment, then sat up, slowly pulled on her camisole and then lifted her dress and put it on and buttoned it.

"I'll keep the hardware. Now get out of here and don't come back. If you want to help your man, get him out of town before he tries to rob the bank."

Spur walked behind her until she had left by the side door. He watched her moving down the street until she was out of sight. Then he went back to the hotel clerk, told him he had some trouble in room 303 but wanted to continue to be registered there. He wanted to rent a second room where he would sleep, but did not want it to show on the books. For a two dollar gold piece the clerk decided he could break the rules just this once.

6

Gabe Young had been drinking most of the afternoon and evening. He was bored with drink and with gambling. He searched for Alice and caught her wrist.

"Upstairs, whore!" he bellowed.

Half the men in the room guffawed.

Alice tried to slap him but he caught her hand, then let go of it, grabbed a fistful of breast and tugged her forward.

"At least he knows what to hold onto!" Alice shrieked trying to make something positive out of her humiliation. She had always demanded to be treated as a lady, even when she was playing the role of a dance hall girl/upstairs whore.

Young let go of her breast, picked her up and slung her over his shoulder like a sack of wheat and carried her up the open stairs and down the hall to the biggest room. It was the *Three Dollar Bed*. He dropped her on the mattress and Alice rolled to the other side and held out her hand.

"Three dollars, big spender," she said. "Cash on the butt before the fucking."

Young laughed, fished out a five dollar gold piece and gave it to her. She slid it into a small purse in the top dresser drawer and began to unbutton her dress.

"I'll do it!" Young growled. He grabbed her, tied her hands behind her back. Then he used a kerchief and tied it around her mouth in a gag so she could little more than mumble words.

"Now, we'll get rid of them fancy-smancy clothes," Long said. He preened his full black beard and stared at her a minute from his black eyes. The ever present toothpick in his mouth pointed upward and he drew a sheath knife from leather at his waist. The blade was six inches long, honed so sharp he could shave with it. Now he used it to tease Alice's chin.

She gurgled something. Young slapped her face.

"Goddamn woman!" he bellowed. "You're all alike. You push and demand and order us, and just because you're smaller than us and soft and pretty you make us do it!"

He sat on the bed and nodded. His eyes glazed and he seemed to be in another world. Then he nodded again and opened his fly. His penis came out, stiff and hard.

"Yes. Yes, I'll do it for you, Mommie. We just did it last night. Do I have to again?"

He listened to some unspoken words, then his head bobbed and he gently opened the buttons down her bodice and spread back the cloth so Alice's breasts popped out.

His hands massaged them gently, tenderly, his head nodding as he listened to a voice Alice could not hear. He bent and nuzzled her breasts, then licked them and sucked one into his mouth. He chewed on it for a moment, then came away.

"Yes, Mommie. I can. Don't . . . don't hit me!"

With the knife he slit the side of the dress from the bodice opening to the bottom of the skirt and spread it back. Then the knife cut through more fabric until the knee-length drawers were cut off Alice and she lay there naked before him.

Gabe's eyes went blank for a moment as he stared at Alice.

"You want to be on top again, Mommie? No, no. We did it that way last night. Oh, darn! darn! darn! All right."

He lay down beside Alice, rolled her over on top of him and she watched intently to see what he wanted her to do. When it became obvious, she helped him enter her and then she lowered on his shaft.

"Oh, yes, that is nice!" Alice tried to say through the gag around her mouth. She was aware at once that he never heard her. His eyes were blank again, like black holes, as he listened to a different voice from his foggy memory. She had no real understanding of what was happening. But she had heard about Gabe Young. The girls said not to do anything to make him mad. He had hurt a girl one night.

Now she performed as well as she could and when he climaxed she started to lift off him but Gabe stopped her.

"I'm bigger now, Mommie. Lots stronger. And with this knife I have you can't slap me around the way you used to. Some day I'll make you sorry for all this, Mommie. Maybe even today!"

He pushed her off him to the side of the bed, sat up and caught hold of the sharp knife again.

"I might make you pay for it right now, Mommie

dearest!''

He held the knife under her chin, then moved it to her right breast. He lowered the sharp blade and traced an inch long scratch on the white flesh.

Alice wailed, but only a high keening came out of her bound mouth.

Gabe Young smiled. He touched the line of blood with his finger and then tasted it. His smile broadened and he used the knife again, slicing her left breast from side to side over the top, letting the blade bite into her flesh a quarter of an inch.

Blood erupted from the six inch cut.

Gabe Young laughed.

Alice's forehead beaded with sweat. She arched her back with the pain and tried to scream but the gag stopped it. She tried to roll away, but one of his strong arms pinned her belly to the bed.

"I bet you're sorry now, Mommie! Sorry you did all those dirty things to me when I was only ten years old. I couldn't even get it hard yet and you were playing with me. You didn't care, you just wanted my tongue up your pussy."

Gabe growled and sliced her right breast again so it had a half moon cut across the top. He sat back on his feet on the bed. He was still fully clothed. Only his fly hung open.

Tears melted into his eyes and dripped down. He sobbed.

"Why did you make me do all those things, Mommie? I never tried to be bad. But you said I was and I'd get a licking. You made me take down my pants and bend over your knee, but somehow you never got around to paddling me. Not when papa was gone. You knew it was bad, Mommie!"

Alice watched the knife cut her right breast and

her eyes rolled up and a low sound came from her throat as she passed out.

Gabe never noticed.

"Remember how Papa hit you that time when he caught you, and he pushed the broom handle right up between your legs? You screamed and screamed, but I think you really loved it. I don't have a broom handle, Mommie, but I have my knife. Would you like that, too?"

He spread her legs and moved the knife over her vagina and gently inserted the sharp blade. The flesh was not ready and had no chance to stretch. Blood streamed down the blade and on his hand. He roared in anger and jammed the knife up her sex slot to the hilt, then pulled it out and wiped off all the blood on the blade on her skirt still on the bed.

"Goddamned women!" He stared at the unconscious girl, then slapped her awake. "No! You are not going to faint on me again, Mommie. You did that. I threw a bucket of water on you the last time. You stay awake and watch. Everything! I am going to pay you back for everything you did to me during those four years! You just watch!"

The blade touched her skin again, drawing a blood line from her right breast down to her pubic hair. He traced another line from her left breast to the same point, but this one deeper so it bled a long dark drip line of blood.

Alice wailed through the cloth, then fainted again. Gabe never noticed.

Ten minutes later the ritual was over. Gabe was splattered with blood. Alice lay on the bed with a hundred faint blood lines on her torso, arms and legs, her face was unmarked.

Her breath came in gasps and wheezes now, but

Alice was still alive. She had not regained consciousness.

"One more lesson, Mommie. Don't ever try to rape me again. I'm a big boy now and I won't let you. If I want to play poke-poke it will be when I want to with who I want. Not you. You're too old and ugly! Just so you'll remember . . . ."

Gabe Young lifted the blade and stabbed Alice in the chest. The knife missed her heart but slid between ribs and sliced through her right breast.

He pulled the knife out and stabbed her again and again. When he got to fifty, Gabe stopped, wiped off the blade and stared down at the mutilated form on the bed. He stood, looked at the blood on his clothes, washed some of it off with water from the china bowl, then stared at the body.

He put the knife away, buttoned his fly, then wrapped Alice up in the blanket that had been under her on the bed, and carried her to the window that opened on the back alley. Without hesitation he dropped her out the window, checked the room, put on his hat and walked down the back steps to the alley.

It took him almost two hours to ride with his heavy package to the bank of the Snake River. He threw Alice and the blanket into the water and watched the swift current sweep her downstream.

A soft laugh came from Gabe.

"Nobody will ever find you, Mommie. Nobody!"

He rode back to the small town of Twin Falls, stopped at a different saloon, and drank until he could barely stand up. Then he staggered down the street on his way home. Gabe made it just inside the front door of the yellow house with the white picket fence around it before he passed out.

7

Spur McCoy found Gabe Young that afternoon in
the bar where he was drinking. Spur drifted in with
his hat on low and got a beer and sat at a back table
and watched Young without letting him get a good
look at Spur. Young was not skitterish.

Because of Young's heavy drinking, Spur decided
there was little chance that the robbery could take
place that evening. The next day or the next night,
whichever one Young preferred. When Young took
the dance hall girl upstairs to the cribs, Spur left
and went back to the second room he had rented at
the hotel.

The room was situated so he could see both the
side and front doors to the Boise Home Bank.
Damned convenient. He watched the doors until
nearly midnight, then he took hour long naps and
woke up precisely on the hour to check for any
activity. By four A.M. he decided the robbery was to
be the following day or night.

It was nearly ten A.M. before Spur got up, had

263

breakfast and walked down where he could see the small yellow painted house inside the white picket fence. There was no activity.

Just after one o'clock in the afternoon, Gabe came out blinking at the sun, and dragged himself three blocks to the hardware store. He was inside for fifteen minutes and came out with a small cardboard box and carried it home.

Spur walked into the same store and found the owner.

"Hey, Gabe Young sent me back. He said he figures he got just half enough. He didn't even tell me what it was, just said he wanted half as much more."

The owner was in his thirties, with a sharp face, long nose and bulging eyes. He frowned.

"Do tell. He must have a powerful bunch of stumps to blow out. I just sold him half a case of dynamite sticks."

"Pears he needs another quarter case then," Spur said. "He gave me plenty of money to pay for them."

Ten minutes later, Spur walked out of the store with twelve sticks of dynamite and fuse and detonator caps in a heavy paper sack. He could always use a few sticks of powder as small bombs. One thing for certain: if Gabe Young was going to use dynamite on the bank vault, it would occur when the vault was closed, at night. It would be a night hit on the Home Bank.

Spur went back to his second hotel room where he cleaned and oiled his .45 Colt and the Spencer. When both were in top shape, he gathered all his gear in his saddle bag and brought his horse around and tied her up behind the hotel.

Ten minutes before the bank was due to close at

three P.M., Spur walked in and got change for a twenty dollar gold piece. Then he asked the teller if he could use the bank's privy out back. The favor was granted, and the employee showed Spur to the door that led through the back offices. Spur thanked the clerk and held the door handle from latching and locking when it closed behind him. When he figured the clerk was back in the front of the bank, Spur pulled the back door open.

The clerk was gone. Spur found a small storage closet near the back of the bank, sat down in the corner and pulled a stack of boxes up to hide behind. Then he waited.

Five minutes later someone came to the room, took something out and left. He heard movement in the bank until nearly five o'clock, when everyone left. When he had heard no movement for ten minutes, he checked in front. The bank vault was closed and locked, the stations closed and everyone gone.

Spur checked his .45 again, as well as the hideout derringer with the two loads of birdshot. Then he settled down to wait.

When his pocket Waterbury showed that it was nine o'clock, Spur moved back to his hiding spot and waited again. He left the door to the storage room open so he could hear better.

It was just 9:30 when he heard a sledgehammer slam into the back door handle. It took only one blow, slamming the inside handle off and smashing the locking mechanism in one shot. Someone pushed the door open.

The men walked through the bank, found no one and settled down to fixing the dynamite on the vault. It was one of the old type, with a small reach-in door. Most banks would hardly call it a safe, but here it was all they had. The dynamite would be sufficient to blow it up and shatter all the windows in this end of town.

Spur had no thought of letting them set off the charge. He got out of his hiding spot and waited for one of the men to come into the back. When one did Spur clubbed him with his Colt, grabbed him as he fell and tied and gagged him. McCoy relieved him of his .44 and jammed it into his belt.

That left three.

Spur pulled out one of the three sticks of dynamite he had brought with him and fitted the fuse into the detonating cap pushed into the side of the powder. He cut the fuse to six inches and studied it. This fuse was supposed to burn a foot a minute, but the hardware man had said to allow some extra length because it had been burning faster than that.

Spur cut off two more inches of the fuse. Maybe fifteen seconds. He went to the door that led into the main part of the bank and found all three men in the vault room. That was where the vault would go if and when they got one. Spur lit the fuse from a stinker match, held it two seconds, then underhanded it through the door to the vault room.

The fuse sputtered beautifully as he threw it.

When it landed he heard a scream and one man bolted out the door. Spur tripped him, then kicked him in the side as he went down.

The blast from the one stick of powder was much less than Spur had anticipated. It did not blow out the front plate glass windows. He heard some groans from the far room. Spur crept up on the door and looked inside. One man lay draped over the bomb he was about to plant on the safe. His head had cracked open like an overripe melon where it slammed against the safe.

Gabe Young sat across the room, shaking his head, dazed and shaken by the blast.

Spur ran into the room and propelled Gabe out, took his six-gun and sat him down in a chair. He was still too confused to move.

The Secret Agent checked the front window. No one seemed concerned about the bank. The explosion had been muffled by the building.

Spur went back to Gabe, took rawhide from his pocket and tied the man's hands behind his back. Then he tied his ankles together.

By then Gabe was shaking his head, blinking.

"Dynamite . . . what the hell happened?"

"You just landed in hell, Gabe. How do you like it so far?"

Gabe squinted in the faint light. Two kerosene lamps burned as night lights to discourage robbers. Now Spur used the lamps to his advantage.

"Remember me, Gabe," Spur said, moving down close to him so he could see his face.

"Hell no. What blew up?"

"Not your big bomb, just one stick I sent in for your inspection."

"Who the hell are you?"

"I thought you might remember. Four days ago, down by Twin Falls, you were in a posse. You lynched somebody."

"Yeah, so?"

"You hung me, you bastard!"

"Not a chance, that guy was dead."

"Guess again, bastard. It was a trick knot the sheriff tied for you."

Gabe stared at him, then laughed without humor. "Hell, yes. I remember your ugly face. Sure as hell should have used you for target practice as well as hanging you."

"Is that your reaction? You lynch an innocent man and all you can say is you should have shot him, too?"

"That's enough. Because Will is gonna blast you about now!"

Spur dropped and rolled to the side. He heard the shot just after he moved. It missed. His Colt came up stuttering hot lead. Two rounds cut through the man called Will who stood in the doorway to the back room. One sliced into his heart, the other caught him just under the chin and splattered half his head against the wall.

Spur rolled to his feet and ran to the back room. The first man he had tied was still there.

"Your games are over, Gabe. This one is not only for me, it's for the women you've hurt over the years. Like that sixteen year old on the ranch just out of Twin Falls where you stayed the night.

"Hell, she wanted . . ."

Spur slammed his fist into Gabe's mouth choking off the words. The man jolted off the chair to the floor.

McCoy opened his shirt and unwound a twenty foot length of half inch rope he had wrapped around his body. He slowly, methodically, tied a hangman's noose in one end.

"This is the way it's done, Young. You can show all your buddies in hell how to do it."

"What the hell?"

"You're going to hang, Young. You're going to have the pleasure of thinking about dying, then the rapture of feeling that rope tighten around your neck and strangling you for a few seconds before your neck breaks as you hit the bottom of the rope.

"You'll never hang another man, Young. You're a dead man. Any more jokes?"

Young wouldn't talk after that. Spur found an overhead beam in the bank and threw the rope over it. He pushed over a desk and a small table and lifted Young up until he stood on the top one. Spur put Young's head into the noose, then tightened the slack and snugged the knot up to the outlaw's right side of his chin.

"Any last words, killer?" Spur asked.

Young glared at him. Shook his head.

"The short, dirty life of Gabe Young."

Young snorted. "Get on with it."

Spur knew he should take the man to the sheriff, let justice take its course. He was supposed to be supporting, upholding, defending, making the system of criminal laws work.

Damnit, not this time! Not until his neck was healed. He'd turned too many killers over to judges and juries and seen them walk out of prison two or three years later. Then he had to do the whole job over again when another innocent man fell at the hands of the ex-convicts.

Not this time!

Goddamnit, not this time!

With a vicious jolt from his shoulder, he powered the desk and small table backward.

Gabe Young fell off the table, plummeted two feet down, then hit the bottom of the rope and the knots held.

Spur heard a crack, like the breaking of an inch thick stick of wood. He looked up and saw Gabe's neck slanted to the side at an unnatural angle. His neck was broken.

Gabe's feet twitched. Spur looked in surprise at how long the man's involuntary muscles kept trying to function, even after his heart had stopped beating and his lungs stopped pumping oxygen.

Spur looked at Gabe's face. His eyes bulged out, and his tongue lolled out of his mouth.

Rest In Peace?

Absolutely not! "Burn in Hell, you bastard!" Spur McCoy thought as he checked the dead man by the back room door, then the live one and slipped out the back door. The bank employees would find a grisly mess in the morning, but at least their bank was safe, and Gabe Young was burning in hell.

Spur closed the door of the bank and walked two blocks to the hotel. His horse was ready and waiting where he had left her. He mounted and rode out. This time there would be no problem. He would ride to the first stagecoach stop about ten miles out of Boise and buy a ticket to Twin Falls. He still had two more men to track down so he could make sure that justice was done. He would make sure, because he would be judge, jury and executioner!

8

During the four days and nights of the stage ride back to Twin Falls, Spur McCoy had plenty of time to consider his situation.

He had been on his way to Twin Falls to investigate a case of counterfeiting when he wound up on the end of that rope. Someone was turning out nearly perfect twenty dollar bills. The dead giveaway was that each bill had the same serious number. Only a dozen or so had been turned in, mostly by banks that caught the serial number. The Twin Falls bank had taken the loss rather than arouse the whole community. Some of the bills had been spotted in Boise.

Most of them, however, had surfaced in Twin Falls, and that was the place where Spur was to make his contact.

He had only a name, Van Buren, man or woman he didn't know. He was to meet the person after he registered at the Pocatello hotel under his real name. This was his first trip to Idaho so there shouldn't be many people who knew him or what he did.

Spur had pushed all this into the background with the killing surge that filled him after his lynching. He was still a haunted man, still blood lusting for the corpses of the other two men who hung him. He shivered just remembering what he felt when that horse surged out from under him and he sensed the rope tightening as he fell toward the end of the slack . . .

He looked out the window and shuddered remembering. It was over. He had to forget. But he couldn't forget, he never would. Spur took a deep breath and smiled at the woman across from him in the big Concord stagecoach. There were only three passengers. The third was a drummer, a salesman for something. He hadn't tried to push his wares and Spur was just as happy. His leg and neck both began to hurt the second day. The third day he bought a bottle of whiskey from the man who ran the coach stop and provided them beds and food.

The last two days into Twin Falls Spur spent in a soft alcoholic glow, but it killed the pain so he stopped groaning.

All the time he kept reminding himself he had to work on the counterfeiting. He knew where the other two hangmen were. He could get them anytime. All he had to do was make sure that the merchant, Josh Hoffer, didn't recognize him before Spur was ready.

When the stage rolled in, Spur talked the driver into letting him off at Doc Rawson's little home office. He did and Spur grabbed his saddlebags, untied the lead rope on his horse and limped into the medic's office.

A pregnant woman sat in the waiting room. She blushed the moment Spur came in and turned toward the wall. Most women hid their pregnancies in public as long as they could. Then they stayed home for the last few months.

When Doc got to Spur he snorted and swore for a minute.

"Damn fool, you could be dead by now. You didn't help your leg any. You want me to have to cut it off at the knee?"

That got Spur's attention. "Fix it, Doc. I got business."

"Bet you have. The undertaker can always use another two dollars. Christ! Why won't you people understand how serious something like this can be?"

"I been on a stage for four days."

"Good. Now I want you to stay off the leg for at least two more days. Get a hotel room and sleep. Here." He held out a glass of water he had mixed with two teaspoons of medicine.

"Drink this, and I'll be back and change the bandages."

Spur had the medicine drained before he realized what it was. Laudanum. A tincture of opium. In an hour he wouldn't care who he was or where he was. Already he could feel the pain receding and his head becoming light. Hell, so he'd take off two days and eat and sleep.

When Doc Rawson came back a half hour later, Spur hardly reacted when he pulled the stuck on bandages off his neck. The wound had healed little in the six days. It should be farther along. The medic put on more salve and bandaged it. At least there were no ugly red lines of infection.

By the time Doc was finished Spur could hardly walk. The sawbones closed his office and brought around his buggy.

Ten minutes later he had Spur deposited on a bed in a room on the first floor of the Pocatello hotel. Doc registered him as Harry Smith and paid for two nights lodging from Spur's new wallet. Doc was surprised at the amount of cash Spur carried.

"See that he gets two meals a day brought to his room," Doc told the room clerk. "I'll be past once a day to check on him and give him more medicine."

When the doctor left, a small, dark haired woman talked to the clerk.

"Has Mr. McCoy checked in yet?" she asked.

"Not recently, Ma'am," the clerk said. "You can look at the register if you want to."

"No, that won't be necessary." She frowned, then lifted arched brows. "I'll be back after the stage comes in tomorrow."

Two days later, Spur woke up in the morning with a bad taste in his mouth, a pounding headache and feeling as though he had been wading through a sewer.

He got up and dressed in city clothes, shaved off what looked like three days growth of beard, and made his way slowly down to the dining room. There wasn't enough breakfast in the place for him. He had two orders of eggs, bacon and flapjacks, two big cups of coffee and a helping of canned peaches.

The food killed his headache and made him feel partly human.

The Laudanum! Doc put him on it to keep him corralled! The stuff could get to be a habit. He'd seen it happen before, start out as medicine and soon the victim graduated into pure opium.

At the desk he asked if there were any messages for Spur McCoy, and the clerk lifted his brows.

"You've been registered under another name, here it is, Harry Smith."

"Good name. I've known lots of Harry Smiths. Change it to Spur McCoy and I'll pay you for three more nights."

"Someone has been asking for you," the clerk said.

"Good. Next time tell the person I'm here."

Spur was still a little shaky. His leg felt better, but he had trouble turning his head. He went to Doc Rawson's office to thank him, and see if the bandage needed changing. It did.

Back at the hotel the clerk signalled to him and handed him an envelope. Inside the feminine hand asked him to meet her in front of the bakery at 9:30 A.M. She would be in a black, closed buggy.

Spur checked the hotel's Seth Thomas. It was nearly that time now. He walked the two blocks to the bakery, and found the exercise made both his leg and neck feel better. He saw the black closed buggy and walked up to it. The store side door opened and he pulled it wider and looked in.

A small, attractive woman with dark hair nodded at him.

"Please get in quickly. I can't be seen with you."

He stepped in and she drove the rig down the street and into the residential area three blocks away.

"Mr. McCoy. My name is Mrs. Kane Turner. Eugenia Turner. I contacted the government some time ago. I assume you're here about the counterfeiting?"

He held out his hand. "Yes, Ma'am. I am McCoy,

Secret Service Agent working with the United States Treasury. Counterfeiting is one of our major responsibilities. The director asked me to thank you for your concern."

"I'm more worried about my husband than the general economy of the country, Mr. McCoy. I'm afraid he is mixed up with some unsavory characters here in town, and that they are counterfeiting twenty dollar bills. He has been spending a lot of evenings downtown lately. Once I deliberately followed him and he went to the newspaper office of all places."

"Mrs. Turner. You realize this could get your husband in a lot of trouble. If he is counterfeiting it could mean he would have to go to prison for at least ten years."

"Yes, I know." She looked up him with big brown eyes. For a moment they were troubled. "I would rather give him up for ten years than have him killed. I think he is in real danger with these men."

She reached in her reticule and took out an envelope.

"Look inside, Mr. McCoy."

He did and found three twenty dollar bills. When he spread them out he found that each had the same serial number.

"Counterfeit," he said.

"Yes. At home Mr. Turner hid a box of them. I counted them one day. Each stack has a hundred in it, and there are fifty stacks. That's a hundred thousand dollars!"

"And all worthless, Mrs. Turner."

"Unless he spends it, passes it." Tears seeped out of her eyes. She brushed them away. She looked so small and so hurt and so alone, that Spur wanted to reach over and take her in his arms and comfort her. He touched her shoulder and she swayed toward him a moment, then moved back.

"Mr. McCoy, I have thought a lot about this. I am not used to dealing with tragedy or lawbreaking. I don't know if I should have told you this or not."

"Yes, you did the right thing. Even though he is your husband, he is breaking the law. Thousands of people could be hurt by what he is doing. I'm tremendously impressed by what you have done, and proud of you, Eugenia Turner."

She looked up and tried to smile. "Mr. McCoy, thank you. It's good to know that someone agrees with me. If I hear anything or if I can help you, I'll contact you by leaving a message in your box at the hotel. Now I better take you back to town so I can get back home."

"Thanks for what you're doing, Mrs. Turner. What you are doing is the right thing, believe me."

She let him off near the hotel, then drove away. He walked at once to the small office of the newspaper, THE TWIN FALLS GAZETTE, and went inside.

The familiar smell came at once: the musty slightly sulphur scent of the stacks of newsprint mixed with the acid black smell of the printer's ink. It was an odor Spur would never forget, and one you could find nowhere but in a newspaper office.

A small, thin man with a green visor and wearing eye glasses looked up from a desk behind a waist high counter that ran across the width of the room.

"Yes? You're new in town. Doc was treating you for a bad leg and a neck injury."

Spur chuckled. "Never try to keep anything from a news man. I also am in the trade, or rather nearly. I arrange the sale of newspapers, my speciality. And right now I have a buyer for your paper, your plant, your circulation, advertisers and of course for your good will."

"Hadn't thought of selling. Doing very nicely here now. Town is growing. I expect to be the biggest city in Idaho by the time we get statehood. In the best spot for it. Pocatello will grow and so will Boise because it's the capital, but Twin Falls! We have everything right here!"

"This is known as driving up the price. My name is Spur McCoy, of St. Louis."

The small man stood. He wore a black suit with vest and a string black tie. He held out his hand across the counter.

"Good to meet you. I'm H. Larson Wintergarden, publisher, editor, accountant, pressman, circulation, janitor and general handyman."

"Sounds like a big staff. Understand you have some good equipment. Could I buy the two-bit tour?"

A half hour later Spur knew more about the small plant than he needed to. The important part was the press. This one horse newspaper had one of the best presses made. It was an Issac Adams bed-and-platen press for job work. It had an iron frame, not wooden, with a fixed platen immovably set in the frame. The form was put on an iron bed and this bed raised against the fixed platen. Spur was no expert in presses, but he knew the Issac Adams. The press figured in over two thirds of counterfeiting done on paper currency in the U.S.

He had listened to the merits of the press when Wintergarden extrolled them, but sluffed them off, pretending he was more interested in the flat bed newsprint press.

After the tour, the newsman sat in his chair, and lit a large, fat cigar.

"I'm not really interested in selling, Mr. McCoy, but say I was. What kind of an offer would you make?"

"My standard offer, twice your last year's gross. A flat $3,000."

Wintergarden laughed.

"That is for the newspaper," Spur hurried on. "I don't want your expensive Adams. Why in the world did you get such a high priced press for a small town like this? There is no way that you can make enough to pay for it in five years here in Twin Falls."

Wintergarden hedged. He flicked off the ashes and tried to pass it off.

"Oh, the Adams. Sure, she's a fine press, but I do a big business in job work. Get some in from Pocatello on the stage. I plan on going in heavily into job printing, so I had a chance to pick up this Adams for a song. Printer went bankrupt and I got it for ten cents on the dollar."

"Well, no matter," Spur said. "I still wouldn't need it. You think over my offer. I'll be around another few days until Doc says I can travel. You let me know. I'll be at the Pocatello Hotel."

"I'll do that. Right nice of you to stop by."

Spur went out the front door into the still morning sunshine. The press was the best ever made for precise job work, especially when paper went through the press the second time to put on the second color. He was making progress quicker than he figured. The lawyer and the printer. Who else did they need? Mrs. Turner had said "those men", so there must be more.

It was time to check in with the sheriff.

Sheriff Abraham Lincoln Sloan smiled when he saw Spur limp into his office.

"McCoy. Wondered where you went. You look worse now than when I dropped you off at Doc Rawson's a week ago."

"Feel a mite worse, too. We need to have a confidential talk. You have a few minutes?"

Sheriff Sloan led Spur into his office that had a door, and closed it.

"Sheriff Sloan, I'm here on a counterfeiting problem. We've found twenty dollar bills circulating that are worthless. All signs point to them coming from here in Twin Falls . . ."

"Damn. I was hoping they were just passed here by somebody from Boise or Cheyenne or Denver. What can I do?"

"Keep it quiet for now, and tell me what you know about H. Lawson Wintergarden, printer."

"Figures. He came to town two years ago, started the newspaper from scratch. Worked damn hard. First week he was here he came in and told me that he had been in some trouble back east, but he paid the price and he was free and clear of any legal problems. He just wanted to get it off his chest, I think. He also said then if anybody tried to blackmail him, they wouldn't be able to."

"Given you any trouble since?"

"None. I work with him so he can report arrests and court cases. It's been coming out just fine."

Spur told him about the expensive job press and how they had been used before for counterfeiting.

"Damn, you got any more bills?"

Spur showed him the three Mrs. Turner had given him.

"That ties it! What we going to do?"

"I just wanted to know the background on the printer. There have to be more people involved. Finding them is my job."

"Let me know if I can help." The sheriff stood and walked to the case holding six rifles. He picked one up and then put it back.

"Oh, got a flyer in yesterday from Boise. Seems they had a bank robbery. At least an attempted bank robbery. Went bad for the robbers. One of them got shot dead, a second one knocked out and tied up. Third one got smashed up by a dynamite blast in the vault room. The fourth one was hanged to a beam right there in the bank. Seem strange to you, McCoy?"

"Must have been some vigilante group that caught them," Spur said.

"Must have been. The guy who was hanged was your old necktie party friend, Gabe Young."

"Well, what do you know about that! Looks like I won't have to track him down then, don't it?"

"Looks that way." The sheriff paused. "Not my jurisdiction, of course. But I would hope that you could prove you were here in Twin Falls that day Young was hanged, if you ever had to."

"Like you said, Sheriff, it isn't your jurisdiction."

"Mmmmmm. Thought you might say something like that. Do I need to warn you about the other two, Hoffer and Dallman? There wasn't any charges I could bring against them. Now if you had died correct and proper, I could have . . ."

"Could have . . . yeah," Spur said. "As for me, I got some counterfeiters to worry about. Oh, did Wintergarden say where he was from? What state, what town? Like to know what he served time for if it's possible. Also if Wintergarden is his real name."

"No way I can find out, unless I ask him."

"Yeah, figured. Thanks for the help, Sheriff, and for telling me about Young. Man was on the road to hell for a long time. His luck finally ran out."

9

Spur McCoy went to the livery stable from the sheriff's office. He saddled his mare and got directions to the Boots Dallman homestead. It was only about five miles out of town.

On the way Spur decided he should find out more about Dallman. Right now he was riding blind after the man. He wanted to know what made the man function.

The place was a typical homestead, 160 acres of land that held part of a valley and some hills to the south. The frame house was small but could be expanded with each child if necessary. As he rode down the lane from a scratch trail, Spur saw about thirty cattle grazing behind barbed wire. Beyond them was a plowed field and a second field of wheat growing emerald green on the near side. Farming and cattle. It never had worked yet.

Spur rode up to the brown painted house with white trim and tied his mount at the hitching rail.

The screen door banged and a woman stood just

outside of the house thirty feet away. She carried a
single barreled shotgun and watched him.

"Far enough," she said.

"Afternoon, Mrs. Dallman. I was hoping to find
Boots at home, but seeings as how you have the
scattergun, I'd say he isn't here. Right?"

"Right. What do you want with Boots?"

"Just a small matter we need to talk about. I've
got some of the new British beef cattle breeding
stock, and I thought he might like to take a look at
them."

The shotgun lowered a few inches.

"Boots is working at the Box B. Won't be home
until after supper time. They doing a roundup over
there for a week or so more."

"When does he get time to do all the work around
here?"

"We manage. I do lots of it."

"Your name is Martha?" Spur asked.

"Yes. You didn't say your name."

"Bainbridge, the B Bar B. About twenty miles
upstream. Came into town so I took the chance I
could find him."

"Sorry I can't invite you in. Boots don't hold with
any visitors when he isn't here. Too many renegades
and rawhiders around again." The shotgun now
aimed at the ground.

From twenty feet away he could see that Martha
Dallman was about twenty-five, still pretty, not yet
ground down by the hard work and unrelenting toll
of the elements on a farm. She had a good figure and
was tall for a woman, five feet six maybe.

She put the shotgun over her shoulder and
shrugged.

"Sorry about the silly gun. Boots says I got to. I

did scare off some wild grubstake rider one day who decided he could take what he wanted."

"Pays to be careful, even in these days. You tell Boots I was by, Bainbridge. I'll try and see him next time I'm in town or I'll write him a letter. You pick up mail in town?"

"Sure, at the Mercantile. He's the postmaster."

"Fine, Mrs. Dallman. It's been pleasant talking to you. Hope to see you and Boots again one of these days."

He mounted up, tipped his hat and walked the mare back down the lane. As he left he surveyed the house, the barn, a corncrib and big chicken house. There was a hog pen at the rear of the barn.

Boots Dallman had the look of a farmer. Everything was neat, tools put away, the buildings in good repair, and the house painted.

This was no fly-by-night drunk who charged into a lynching. He even gave his pretty wife instructions about the use of a shotgun and how to handle strangers. Boots Dallman did not fit into the usual pattern of a wild-eyed, hell-bent anything-for-fun lynching participant.

As Spur rode back to town, he tried to remember what Boots did in the lynching. He did not know or would not tie the hangman's knot. Boots was not one of the pair who jabbed the mare to surge her out from under Spur. The man had been there, in the background. But he had not spoken out, he had not opposed the lynching.

When the sheriff talked to him that day, he had said something about Boots being drunk, still drunk. That he had been drunk for two days? Possible. Still he had been a participant. Again Spur felt the overwhelming panic and agony as the rope tightened around his neck and he knew he was about to enter eternity. No! All three had to hang!

Back at the livery he asked the swamper what store Josh ran.

"Got to be Josh Hoffer. He runs the Hoffer Mercantile, just across from the bank." Spur thanked him and walked down to the bank corner.

The Mercantile was the biggest and looked like the best store in town. It boasted of having anything you wanted. "Better stock than any store in Boise!"

To Spur, that sounded like a good way to go broke. Maybe Hoffer was independently wealthy and just used the store as a hobby.

Spur made sure his blue neckerchief covered the bandage on his throat, then he pulled his low crowned brown hat down over his eyes and walked into the store. He moved away from the counter and watched the man wrapping up someone's purchase.

It was Hoffer all right, short and dumpy and wheezing as he walked. There were three or four others in the store, so Hoffer was busy with them. The store was interesting. It had a lot of merchandise that Spur might expect to see in St. Louis or Chicago stores, but not in the wilds of Idaho. How could Hoffer afford to keep a stock like this, including fancy china and leaded glass?

The store had hardware and software, and women's wear all in one. He had a full line of groceries, tools, farm equipment, even rolls of barbed wire, which the cattlemen hated and the farmers said was the only way they could keep them roaming cattle from eating up their crops.

Spur made sure Hoffer did not see his face. He studied the place for five minutes, then slipped out the front door. There was no hurry about Hoffer. His part in the hanging would forever be sharp and clear. He wasn't the idea man, but he came through as a follower who enjoyed watching a man stretch a rope. There was no rush taking care of Hoffer. At least Spur knew he had touched all three bases now. He could concentrate for a day or two on the counterfeit problem.

Spur got to the bank just before it closed. He asked to see the bank president and showed him a twenty dollar bill, one of the counterfeits. The bank man was in his fifties, balding, with eyeglasses that perched on his nose without earpieces.

"Someone told me this bill was no good," Spur said. "Looks good to me. What do you think?"

The bank man looked at it a moment.

"It's genuine. I can spot a bad bill by the feel of the paper. This one is fine. I'll be glad to give you change for it if you like." Spur almost let him, serve the pompous bastard right. But Spur put the bill back in his wallet.

"No, no. I like to have one big bill with me. Takes up less room than all those ones and fives. Thank you, sir." Spur left the bank with his question still unanswered. There were three banks in the little town. Was this one a part of the conspiracy? On the other hand, maybe the bank president really didn't know real money from the good counterfeit. It was a problem Spur was going to have to solve before long.

It was near quitting time when Spur walked past the printing office and newspaper. There appeared to be no one there. A note on the door explained.

"Town Council meeting tonight. I'll be there if anyone has any important business that must be transacted." It was signed H. L. Wintergarden. Spur watched the place from beside a friendly maple tree up the street. An hour later he gave up. No one had come or gone from the front or the side door of the newspaper and printing plant. If any more fake money was going to be printed it was not going to be tonight. Spur guessed that no one in town except Wintergarden could possibly run the printing press.

Spur decided to wash up before he went to the Pocatello Hotel dining room. He came to his hotel room on the first floor and used his key and stepped inside. For a moment he thought he was in the wrong room.

A woman stood before the dresser mirror combing her long, dark hair.

"Good, I hoped you would come soon," she said. When she turned he saw that she was Eugenia Turner, wife of the lawyer.

She put down the comb and smiled at him. He had not seen her standing before. She was barely five feet and an inch tall. Her wide set brown eyes smiled at him.

"You wonder how I got in. I stood in the hall and people kept staring at me, so I simply used one of the keys from my home. These old door locks are not very good. There are only two basic types, so here I am. I hope you don't mind."

Spur took off his hat and dropped it on the bed.

"Not at all. The fact is, I wanted to talk to you. Do you think any of the bankers know about these bills?"

She frowned slightly, then slowly shook her head. "One of them might, Al Jones is extremely smart and quick. He could have spotted them if more than one came to his attention. The other two are not really bankers, just men who had some money and decided they would open banks."

She turned and her hair flowed with her in a black swirl.

"Kane went downtown tonight again. I almost wish he were going to see a woman, but I know it isn't that. Were they working at the printing office?"

"No, I checked it before I came here. There's a city council meeting or something like that."

"Oh, yes, that's right. Kane goes to those, too. I was hoping you might have caught Kane printing money."

"Do you want me to open the door? I mean it isn't quite proper for you here, in my room and all . . ."

"I really don't think you need to worry about that." She walked toward him, smiling. Her dress was tight, showing her breasts, her small tight waist and the flare of her hips before the material fell to the floor.

"I've never been one to worry to much about conventions, and idle talk." She watched him, then let her obvious stare wander deliciously down his body. She paused at his crotch, looked back at him quickly and smiled.

"You certainly are a big man. I've always liked big men. They seem so sure of themselves, so in control. Perhaps sometimes we could . . . " She broke it off and walked to the window.

"Mr. McCoy, I lied to you the other day. I hope that my husband gets caught. I'll do all I can to help you. He's guilty. The fact is I don't like my husband very much. He lied to me before we were married. He has lied to me consistently since. He married me for my money and no other reason."

She lifted her chin and stared at him. "Does my telling you this surprise you, Mr. McCoy?"

"I am surprised by very little these days, Mrs. Turner."

"Then maybe I can shock you. Kane Turner has not slept in my bed for six months. He has not made love to me for almost a year. Does that shock you?"

"No, but it does surprise me. You are an extremely beautiful woman."

She walked to him, reached up to be kissed and Spur bent and kissed her partly open mouth. She pushed hard against him, her whole body melting against his.

She held the kiss a long time, then broke it off slowly. She pushed back from him, caught his hand and held it over her breast. She said nothing more. Her eyes were closed as she felt his hand massage her breast tenderly.

Eugenia sighed softly, opened her eyes and pulled up his hand and kissed it.

"Mr. McCoy, perhaps sometime . . . I mean when you're not busy, I might come back here and . . ." She sighed again, caught up a reticule from the dresser and stood in the soft lamplight.

Spur put his hand on the doorknob and bent, kissing her on the cheek.

"Mrs. Turner, you are a delightful person, and I'm always ready to help comfort you in any way I can."

She smiled, reached up and kissed his lips. She came away slowly. "I hope we can figure out some way you can comfort me, Mr. McCoy." She stopped and looked at him. "You have the most wonderful smile!" She reached in and kissed his shirt over his chest, opened the door and went out without looking back.

10

Josh Hoffer closed his store and stared around. Damn but it was a great little store! He had items here you would have to go at least all the way to Denver or Frisco to find! Yeah, and he was going to have more!

He paid no attention to his wife nagging him about the stock. She said he had houseware items that would not sell in New York City to the rich folks. He was wasting money. But he could not resist a fine piece of china, or delicate glasswork. He was an artist and always would be, despite his current role of playing the bumpkin mercantile owner. A man had to reach out and grasp what he could, but his dreams were there and no one had a right to interfere with them.

His left hand rubbed the mole on his left cheek without his realizing it. The habit had become ingrained lately.

For just a minute Hoffer thought of all the money he had in that cardboard box under the floorboards behind the counter.

"Three hundred thousand fucking dollars!" Hoffer said it aloud, softly almost with reverence. Money was tremendously important to him. Money opened the whole wide world to a person. You could do what you wanted, travel where you wanted to go, have all the best of the fancy women, buy the finest whiskey and food anywhere in the world!

Hoffer wiped a bead of sweat off his forehead. He always sweat when he thought what he was going to do with his money. If it all had been passed and *changed* he would make up his mind in a second.

Yes, the store would go. He would sell out for what he could get and travel. He was almost certain of that. He would simply vanish one day, leaving a few debts and his wife in the house on the side street!

Hoffer chuckled. What a surprise that would be for that old woman! Then he could find some sweet young thing about sixteen and teach her what he wanted her to know . . . and how to fuck the way he liked. Oh yeah!

Hoffer checked his watch. It was two minutes after six. He went to the alley door of his store and lifted the bar he had across the door. At once it came open and Kane Turner stood there.

"I don't like to be kept waiting, Hoffer, not by anybody."

Hoffer shivered in anger. His lips went white and he folded his arms, as his face turned red.

"You high falluting bastard! Don't get prissy and nasty with me or I'll cut you off at the pockets. Never did like you. I have to work with you but I sure as shit don't have to LIKE you!"

"Easy, easy old man, you'll have an attack,"

Turner said. He slipped in the door and pushed the bar back in place. "Sorry, I didn't mean to get you riled up. Just thinking about this money makes me edgy. You said you had a plan to pass a lot of it."

"True." Hoffer took a deep breath. His face began returning to normal and he rubbed the mole. "Yeah, I got a plan. Didn't mean to blow up that way."

"Where is it?"

"Put away."

"Don't you take it out and look at it? I leaf through those stacks almost every night! All that money is fascinating, even if it is phony."

"I know it's safe, that's enough for me right now," Hoffer said. "Come into my office."

They went across the storage area of the store to a small office that had been built into the side of the big room. It had a rolltop desk, a dozen big boxes and two chairs. Hoffer took out a bottle of whiskey and splashed two fingers into two water glasses. He sipped his, and put it down.

Hoffer looked up at Turner. Even sitting down he had to look up at the bastard! He was tall, over five feet ten, and wore a suit of gray wool that must be hot, but he never had seen Turner sweat.

Josh scrubbed one hand back over his thinning brown hair and stared at Turner through slitted, close set green eyes.

"San Francisco," he said.

"What?" Turner asked. "What about San Francisco?"

"That's where we pass the money. We take our *used* bills out there and pass them at the stores, getting at least fifteen dollars change for anything we buy."

"That will take lots of time and we only make

seventy-five percent of the face value."

Hoffer laughed. "You're new to this game, aren't you, Turner? Any counterfeiter worth his plates knows that if he can get fifteen to twenty percent of the face value he's a rich man. The only problem here is the slowness and the exposure. We could work maybe three or four days, then we'd have to leave because by that time the phony bills would get to the banks and somebody would spot the counterfeiting. The secret is to buy something for a dollar or two, use a twenty, then pocket the change and throw away the item. Even haggle over the price."

"We might pass twenty-five bills a day that way," Turner said. "That's only five hundred dollars a day, and if we made seventy-five percent that would only be something over four hundred dollars a day."

"That's the average wage for a working man these days for all year, Turner. How much did you make last year as a lawyer?"

"Yes, I see your point. But four days would be a thousand and five hundred, maybe. Then we would have to leave. Isn't there a better way?"

"Not for immediate cash."

"How about buying a big item like a house in San Francisco, pay say a thousand dollars for it with bogus money. Then sell it to someone else and get real money!"

"That is ridiculously stupid, Turner! You're supposed to be a lawyer! Buying a house in San Francisco would take legal signatures, identification. And the first time the banker looked at those new twenties with the same serial numbers you'd be in a federal prison for twenty years."

"Is the way we're doing it here any better, any safer?"

"With these hicks and these dumb as grass bankers, it really doesn't matter. The bills are almost perfect. I'm at artist, I tell you! Not even the banker flicked an eye when I gave him a twenty last week. He snapped it once and gave me a double eagle. I told him I needed a pocket piece!"

"Josh took out a basket and put it beside him. From the desk drawer he pulled out a packet of a hundred twenty-dollar bills and began crumpling them up one at a time and dropping them in the basket.

"What the hell are you doing?" Turner asked.

"Not even a banker will question a couple of used twenty-dollar bills. These are going to look well used when I get through with them. First I crumple them up, then I sprinkle some dust and sand over them and mix them up. A few sprays of fine water mist and then I stir them again. By the time they dry and I take them out and smooth them into a stack again, it will be two inches high instead of an inch."

"I'll have to do that with some of mine."

"Turner, remember, don't pass more than two a week."

Josh took four of the new bills and put them in his wallet between good bills, then put the wallet back in his pocket.

"They pick up the smell of leather that way, and the other bills," Josh said. "Anything that works."

"You seen that new man in town?" Turner asked. "He's been sniffing around. I saw him come out of the print shop."

"Haven't noticed anybody."

"He's big, over six feet, looks like he could be mean as hell if he got pushed around."

"We can't worry about every stranger in town."

Turner sighed. "Yeah, guess you're right. I am more concerned about our real estate campaign. How long can we convince these people to keep the counterfeit cash out of the banks?"

"You're the lawyer, you figure it out," Josh said. "I can't do every damn thing in this operation. Christ! I got together with Wintergarden and we brought in the damn press. I've done damn near everything."

"Easy, Josh, just settle down. We can work it all out. So far I've bought six buildings on my side of the street. I gave them a hundred dollars down, all partly *used* bills the way you fixed them. The rest of it is on promissory notes on each parcel, set up on yearly payments, one fourth each year for the next four years."

Josh tipped the glass of sipping whiskey again, pursed his lips and looked over at his visitor. "That's about the way you figured it would work. What's the problem? We process enough of the fake bills so we can pay in real money each of the payments. No bank problems." Josh hiccuped and took another shot of whiskey.

"I've bought five properties along on this side. I set mine up on monthly payments, for two years. So I need to launder just enough of the fake bills each month to make the payments. No big bundle of the bogus money goes to the bank this way. Even so, the Federal people are going to get a report of the funny money before long. So we have to be pristine pure by that time."

"In another three months we will own the whole damn town!" Turner said. He slicked back heavy black hair and chuckled. "Right now we buy the business, then rent the building back to the merchant. When we have most of the town, we'll charge any rent we want to, or close up the firms there and open our own. We can even change the name of the town if we want to. Turnerville might be nice!"

Josh kept wadding up the twenty dollar bills and dropping them in the basket.

".You still in line to be mayor in the election next week?"

"Absolutely. And I am prepared to represent my constituents to the best of my ability."

"Bullshit?" Josh said and they both laughed. "You represent our own interests or I'll have you thrown out of office." Both men laughed again and the atmopshere eased.

"So we have the city council in our pocket," Turner said. "You'll be elected again next year, and we can outvote anyone they put up against us around here."

Josh finished crumpling the bills. Now he stirred them around, sprinkled on sand and dust, then sprinkled drips of water on them from his hand. He put the basket to one side to let the bills dry.

"How in hell did you recognize Wintergarden," Turner asked.

"Wasn't hard. I spent almost two years with him back in Illinois where we both worked for the state. His term was up a year before mine so I figured I'd never see him again. Printers and plate makers always kind of get together in prison, just to outbrag each other if nothing else. He had heard of my work in Chicago. I knew he was a top pressman, so we figured if we ever got out we might work together."

"Then you lost track of him?"

"Until he came in to town here to run the newspaper. It's a cover-up he's used before. But he had
changed his looks. He used to be chunky, real
chubby. And he never wore glasses before, and he
always wore his black hair full, almost Indian long.
Now he's a blond, with a short, short haircut, and
thin as a pine tree. I don't know how he does it."

"But he didn't jump at your offer?"

"Not right away. Denied who he was. He had
changed his name, too. But I tricked him into ad-
mitting his past. From then on it was easy. He
needed the money to prop up his little stinking
newspaper. We sure as shit won't get any bad
publicity in his paper about the city council, or what
we do!"

"And he gets enough money on the side to keep
his little paper operating," Turner said. He stared at
Hoffer who had begun straightening out the money.

"You wad up two thousand dollars every night?"
Turner asked.

"Only on good nights," Hoffer said. He pointed a
finger at Turner and his voice dropped into a serious
tone. "You keep that wife of yours under control.
We don't want her finding that money and going on
a buying tear in the stores."

"Don't worry. She's trying to get pregnant. Right
now that takes up most of her time." He grinned.
"That's why I'm so worn out these days."

"Keep her barefoot, in a nightgown and pregnant,
and you won't have any trouble with her." Josh put
the two thousand dollars back in the bottom drawer,
locked it and stood.

"Now I've got to get home. I'm hungry as hell and
I know I'm going to have steak tonight."

They went out the back door, said goodbye and

Hoffer watched the lawyer walk out the long way along the alley.

He never really liked that son of a bitch, but Hoffer knew they needed him, at least for another few months. Then Kane Turner was going to have a serious, and undoubtedly a fatal accident!

11

When Spur woke up the next morning, he had changed his mind. The more he thought about Boots Dallman's wife, Martha, the more worried he became. She would tell Boots about him. She was that kind of woman who would do what her man told her, and fight like hell to protect him. She had been afraid of Spur, he sensed that.

Dallman would know there were no ranchers in the area with new English breeding stock. She would desribe Spur right down to the neckerchief around his throat and Dallman would be off and running.

His only hope was that Dallman had worked so late the night before he couldn't ride home. Or, if he got home he was so tired he did not connect the stranger at his ranch with the man he tried to hang.

Either way it was a poor gamble.

Spur had breakfast as soon as the dining room opened at six A.M. and rode for the Box B ranch which he found out was only three miles from town,

301

but the opposite way from Dallman's. It was worth a try.

For two miles he rode along a dirt road that had barbed wire fences on both sides. The fences protected field crops from the wandering beef cattle, which still dominated this section of the land around Twin Falls. That was despite the long drive it took every summer to get them to a railroad siding where they could be loaded for shipment east.

Spur found a ranch hand just inside the big gate of the Box B.

"Hell, they never come back last night. Up in the breaks there to the south about five miles out, I'd say. Been branding young stuff and castrating the young bulls into steers."

"Is Boots with them?"

"Hell, yes. He's one of our top ropers. He's an expert at getting that loop around a steer's back two feet for a two horse catch."

Spur got directions and rode south. Before long he saw burned out campfires where the crew had worked at branding and gathering the herd. Then two miles off he saw three cowboys sashaying a dozen cattle toward a small valley. He got there about the same time the critters did.

A man left the trio of horsemen and rode to meet Spur. The man sat tall in the saddle, ramrod holding up his spine, and it spoke of a total military background. Cavalry no doubt.

The man was in his forties, tanned, wore a moustache and had blue eyes that squinted in perpetual defense against the bright sun. His hands were large and looked able. He rode with his right hand hanging at his side near a six-gun that leathered there.

"Morning," the stranger said.

"Yes, good morning. I'm looking for an old friend of mine, Boots Dallman. Hear he's riding with you now."

Spur saw the man's whole body relax, but his hand stayed in place.

"Right, he's here. My name is Bennet. I run this spread. Sure as hell hope you're not going to sell Boots any more barbwire." The man grinned. "We kid him about sodbusting whenever we get the chance. Fact is he's a damn good farmer, and good with cattle too. Guess that's a smart combination the way the fence is going up around here."

"Progress, they say," Spur responded. "Any idea where I could find Boots?"

"Still gathering the strays this morning before we get the iron hot. I sent him and some men out south a little more. Should be cleaning out the second valley down that way with two more hands. Welcome to go take a look. Even welcome to help bring whatever you find back this way. Oh, I never got your name?"

"Brighten, Mack Brighten from out in Montana a ways."

"Well, good to meet you. Hope you find Boots. We really think a lot of that young man. He used to be one of my foremen."

Bennet touched his hat and rode back to the milling group of some fifty head of mixed cattle where they were held in a nervous group by six riders.

Spur found Boots riding sweep on a clutch of ten cows and half a dozen calves. The agent let the group ride past a patch of trees on the side of the valley, then Spur rode out and confronted Boots.

At first the man did not recognize McCoy.

"Boots Dallman?" Spur asked. He drew his Colt

.45 smoothly and had Dallman covered before he separated Spur from the morning sun behind him.

"Yeah, I'm Dallman. What's the iron for? Do I know you?"

"You saw me a few times." Spur rode to the side out of the direct path of the sun. "You might know me better with my hat off and with a rope around my neck!"

Dallman scowled and squinted.

"What is this, playing tricks time!"

"No trick, Dallman."

"My God! It's impossible! They hung you. You stopped twitching and we rode off! Either you're some kind of ghost or you didn't die."

"Ever see a ghost kill a man, Dallman?"

"Hey! No! I'm glad you're alive. Haven't had any sleep for a week worrying about that. I was drunk. The sheriff can tell you that. I didn't help them hang you!"

"Squirm, Dallman. I like to watch a man squirm who wouldn't even lift his voice to help me. You sat there on your horse and didn't say a word. Not one fucking word to help me!"

"I was scared! That Gabe Young is a madman. He would have shot me dead if I'd tried to save you."

"You don't have to be afraid of Young anymore. I hung him two days ago in Boise."

"You . . . you hung him?"

"Right, just the same way he hung me. Only he was robbing a bank at the time. It's going to be different with you. Probably hang you from that big beam in your barn. Your wife will have to watch of course."

"No! You've got no right!"

"Right? You're talking about rights after you lynched me and thought you watched me die? You knew I was goin' to die, still you didn't say a word. Dallman you have exactly no rights, no appeal, and no way to escape. You try to run and I grab your wife and kids. You try to bushwhack me and I'll come after you and slice your heart out. What would you do to the men who lynched you and left you for dead?"

Dallman's body sagged. His head lowered. When he looked up there were tears in his eyes. "I was drunk and weak and when I sobered up enough to know what was happening, you were already in the noose. Nothing I could have done then would have stopped them."

"You could have killed them both."

"I . . . I've never killed a man in my life. I was too young for the war. Since then . . ."

"You a Mormon or something?"

"No, I'm just not a violent man."

"Except when you're drunk and you lynch innocent people."

Boots looked away.

"Don't hurt Martha. I don't want you anywhere near my place. Do to me whatever you want, but don't hurt Martha or the boys. That's all I ask."

"I've got no argument with them. Dallman, let me tell you what it feels like to be hung, so you can think about it. I'm in no rush. You're not the kind of man who is going to hit the trail. And I don't think you'd draw on me if I turned my back. But you need to suffer. You can start thinking how it's going to feel to be hung, feel that rope burning your neck and cutting off your air, then the screaming agony as you hit the end of the rope and the knot that's supposed to break your neck doesn't and so you either die slowly of strangulation or brain damage when the blood is cut off."

Dallman motioned to the cattle now well ahead.

"I better get back to work."

"Worried about your job right up to the end, are you Dallman? I'm going to hang you, Dallman, you know that now, don't you. You probably should tell your wife about it. She has a right to know why her man is dead. Why he's hanging in the barn twitching away the last spasms of his life."

"I might tell her."

"The rope burning your throat isn't the worst part, Boots. The roughest time is when you feel your eyes bulge out and you can't see anything. You know your eyes are open, but they don't work anymore. Then your breath cuts off and your neck aches with the strain of the knot. That's nothing of the agony you're coming to, Dallman. Wait until the blackness comes. That's the frightening part.

"The sky goes black and then you can TASTE the blackness! You see shapes in the black void and you know that death is sitting there right beside you, ready to take over your body, AND THERE ISN'T A DAMN THING YOU CAN DO ABOUT IT! That is desperation, that is raw gut wrenching fear. Because you know that this is all there is to life. The religious fear of death syndrome you learned as a child was only childish prattlings by adults. Now you know the truth of death and you don't want to give up those few seconds of life you have left. But you will. Eternity, an eternity of dreamless sleep beckons you, and then claims you . . .

"Then you will be dead, Boots Dallman. You will cease to exist except as a memory, and perhaps a photograph or two."

Spur looked at Boots. The crotch of his pants was stained with a dark wetness.

"Happy dreams, Boots. The next time you see me,

I'll be an avenging angel arriving to hang you . . . just the way you let them hang me!"

Dallman stared at him. Shifted on his saddle and looked away. He slowly shook his head.

"You haven't even asked me why I wasn't dead after the hanging. You deserve to know that. It was the hangman's knot the sheriff tied. He did a Murphy's knot and none of you knew the difference. The Murphy does not break your neck, does not strangle the person but puts enough pressure on the carotid arteries going to the brain to make you LOOK dead."

Spur rode around the cowboy who had slumped lower in the saddle.

"Dallman, you do whatever you want to, but don't forget to tell your wife goodbye. You have no idea how long it will be before I come back with a good strong rope, and a well tied hangman's knot to drop you into eternity!"

Spur stared at the cowboy, then turned and rode away. As he expected, Boots Dallman did not try to shoot him in the back.

12

As he rode back toward town from the Box B ranch, Spur McCoy began thinking about home, New York City. He hadn't been back there in years. The best part of his life had been working with the Secret Service.

Not that his home life had been hard or difficult. On the other hand it had been too easy. His father was a wealthy merchant and importer in the city, and they had three houses: a smart, efficient town house on Park Avenue, a country place out on Long Island, and a hide-a-way place of about fifteen rooms in Connecticut.

Spur's father expected him to take over the family businesses, and Spur was tempted. Wealth and all of the beautiful things it could buy, and the freedom it gave you pulled at him.

He went to Harvard and graduated half way up in his class, then came back to New York and worked in one of his father's importing houses for two years.

The Civil War was on the horizon and Spur took a

commission in the Infantry. After two years of fighting he had advanced to the rank of captain. Then he was called by a longtime family friend and senior United States senator from New York, Arthur B. Walton. The senator needed an aide, somebody who knew what was going on in the war, and who could talk back to the generals and their wild demands. He enjoyed the work.

Then in 1865, soon after the act passed, Charles Spur McCoy was appointed as one of the first U.S. Secret Service Agents. Since the Secret Service was the only federal law enforcement agency of any kind at the time, it handled a wide range of problems, most far removed from the group's original task of preventing currency counterfeiting.

Spur served six months in the new Washington Secret Service office, then was transferred to head the base in St. Louis and handle all action west of the Mississippi. He was chosen from ten men because he was the one who could ride a horse best, and he had won the service pistol marksmanship contest. William P. Wood, the Agency director, evidently thought both attributes would come in handy out in the wilds of the West. He had been right.

Spur's thoughts moved on to the case at hand and Boots Dallman. The man certainly did not fit the Gabe Young mold. He was contrite, he probably had never been in trouble before and he said he was drunk. Any man was allowed one character flaw—unless it killed someone.

Being drunk for two days certainly was no excuse, but it was at least a mitigating circumstance. Spur would make up his mind about Dallman later.

Now he was headed for the lawyer in the case, the

husband of the delicious Eugenia Turner. Spur
decided on the direct approach.

A half hour later Spur slapped the trail dust off
his jeans and leather vest and walked up to the
second floor office of Kane Turner. The sign on the
door said: "Attorney at Law. Specializing in wills,
civil and criminal law." That about covered the
field.

He pushed open the door and went in. The room
was twelve feet square, with a window looking down
on a side street, a desk near the far wall and a chair
for a guest. Two bookcases overflowed with law
books, and a long table at one side was half filled
with stacks of papers.

It was the first time Spur had met the man. He
was two inches shy of six feet with dark black hair
and wore a dark blue suit. Green eyes looked up at
Spur. There was a moment of indecision, then a flash
of recognition, and Turner stood slowly.

"Yes, good morning. I'm Kane Turner, attorney.
Can I be of some help to you?"

"Sure hope so, Mr. Turner. I'm Spur McCoy, just
in town a few days, and I'm thinking of settling
down. I'll need a building I can use for a new
gambling palace, a real classy, first rate place. It's
gonna be better than anything in town now."

"A building. Well. I do know a little about the
property here in town. Just how big a place do you
want?" Turner waved him to a chair and they both
sat down.

"Might consider one of the saloons if it's the right
size. Need something on the ground floor, say fifty,
sixty feet square, with back rooms and an upstairs I
could use for cribs."

"That would be a large establishment," Turner

said. "I'll need to do some checking."

"Not giving you an order," Spur said. "Just looking around for somebody to do the legal work."

"Good. I'm the only real lawyer in town. I read for the law under Judge Anderson in Boise, so I am conversant with all the Idaho Territorial regulations and codes."

"Well, in that case, I might pick you to do my legal work."

They both laughed.

"I can assure you, Mr. McCoy, that I know the town as well as anyone here. I'll make some inquiries and have a report for you tomorrow about this time. If that would be soon enough."

"Suits me. I don't trust the looks of the three banks in town and I sure don't like keeping cash in a carpetbag. So the sooner the better." Spur glanced out the window.

"Looks of this town I'd think three or four thousand would buy what I want. What do you think?"

"Yes, prices are a little down right now with the way things been going. I'd say for four thousand we could get what you need. I have a place in mind . . . if the man will sell."

Spur rose, his dislike for the lawyer increasing. "Fine, tomorrow. I'll stop by after dinner."

They said goodbye and Spur went out to the steps and down to the dusty street. There was something about the man Spur did not like. The fact he was in on the counterfeiting had nothing to do with it.

The Secret Service agent shrugged, decided he was hungry and went back to the Pocatello Hotel dining room and had two portions of beef stew and applesauce for desert.

He went on to his room to change into a clean

shirt. This time the door was locked. He used his key and went in. Eugenia Turner lay on his bed, fully clothed. She heard him come in and sat up, sleep heavy in her eyes. She blinked and smiled.

"Sorry, guess I dozed off waiting for you. You don't spend much time in your room."

"I am a working man," he said.

She wore a white jacket and a silly little hat. Her dress was of some fine material that looked like a high fashion outfit. The black shoes were high button affairs.

"I brought you something," she said, smiling up at him. She opened her reticule and took out a sheaf of U.S. paper money and handed it to him.

They were twenties, banded with a piece of pink paper. He figured there were a hundred of them.

"That's two thousand dollars worth," she said smiling. "I like giving money away."

"Thanks, I always take a gift of two thousand in bogus money." He broke the band and leafed through the notes. Every one had the same serial number. The workmanship was excellent as the others had been. They probably all came from the same engraved plates. The work was done by an expert. He had the press, the pressman, and the lawyer. All he needed was the engraver. The man was an artist, and Spur bet this was not his first work at making counterfeit plates.

"Will that help you?"

"It takes a hundred of them out of possible circulation, so that is a help. I'd like the rest of them sometime, when your husband won't miss them."

"That would be hard. He looks at them every night."

"Oh." There was a pause that stretched out. He had no idea what else she might have on her mind, but he didn't want to suggest that the talk between them was over.

Eugenia smiled and put her reticule to one side. "It's a little warm in here," she said. Then she slipped out of the jacket, folded it carefully and put it on the bed. The dress under the jacket was for formal occasions. It was cut low with the edges of both her white breasts showing and the deepline of cleavage between them.

Spur grinned. "I like the dress," he said.

"I hoped that you would. A lady likes to be appreciated." She looked away and lifted her glance to the ceiling. "Oh, Lordy, I shouldn't have said that."

"Why not? It's true, and I am more than pleased to tell you you are a stunning woman, beautiful."

"Thank you. I usually don't go looking for compliments." She glanced at him. "I am a little confused."

"Why?"

"I don't know. I dressed up and fixed up just to come here and see you. The money was just an excuse. Now that I'm here, I feel all gay and girlish, like . . . like I was a virgin again and you were courting! Isn't that just the silliest thing!"

"I think it's sweet and flattering," Spur said. "May I sit down beside you?"

She caught her breath, and nodded.

He sat beside her so their thighs touched and she pulled away, then let the contact resume.

"Oh my!"

He touched her chin and lifted her face so she would look at him.

"Eugenia. Why did you come here?"

She sighed and looked away. He caught her chin and turned her face back to his.

"I . . . I'm not sure. I know I thought all night how it would feel if you . . . if you kissed me!"

"Easy," he said. Spur leaned in and kissed her. She met him halfway and just their lips touched. Her eyes were closed. Spur held the kiss as long as she did. Then they parted and her eyes came open slowly.

"Would you? . . . could we try that again?"

They kissed again and she made soft sounds deep in her throat. This time Spur put his arm round her and drew her close to him, her breasts touching his chest. The kiss was longer and when it ended she snuggled against him. She spoke softly without looking at him.

"I think, Spur McCoy, that I came here to get even with my husband. I know he's had other women. I just wondered . . . I mean . . . Oh, damn!"

He held her; then tenderly put his hand over one of her half exposed breasts.

"Oh, Lordy!" she whispered. Eugenia shivered, then reached to kiss him again. This time when his lips met hers, they were parted and Spur's tongue slid into her mouth and she moaned and he felt her hips move against him.

His hand massaged the soft, whiteness of her breast, then edged under the fabric until he had her whole breast in his hand.

Slowly he eased backward on the bed and brought her with him. She pushed over more until she lay fully on top of him. Her eyes came open and she stared down at him. His hand was still inside her dress top, massaging the warming breast.

"Oh, Lordy!" she said.

Spur lifted up and kissed the side of her breast and he felt her shiver again. Her whole body vibrated for a moment and then she opened her eyes.

"Nobody has ever . . . I mean Kane isn't very romantic. He just thinks about his own . . . needs."

"The man is an idiot," Spur growled. He moved his hand from her breast and found the fasteners on the dress in back and opened it to her waist, then slid the fabric off her shoulders. The dress had a sewn in chemise of some sort and when he pushed the cloth down, it left her bare to the waist.

"I really shouldn't," she whispered, biting her lip. Her wide set brown eyes blinked back the start of tears. He smoothed her long black hair that showered around her bare shoulders now like black rain.

Spur used both hands and fondled her hanging breasts. Until now he had not realized how full they were, like a pair of small melons waiting to be picked. Her eyes glowed as he warmed her breasts. The light pink areolas took on a deeper shade and her small nipples stiffened and stood taller with hot blood surging into them.

Spur reached up and kissed one breast, then licked her nipple and bit it gently.

"Oh, God, but that is marvelous!" she whispered. Then her body jolted in a series of spasms as she climaxed. She fell on him, her breasts crushed against him as she climaxed three times bringing tears of joy to her eyes, and a gasping, desperation to try to pump enough oxygen into her bloodstream to supply her vibrating muscles.

When the spasms passed she lifted up from him and stared down.

"I've never done . . . That's the very first time I've ever done that so soon. You weren't even undressed. I mean . . ." the blush colored her neck and chest red.

Spur chuckled and kissed her other breast, then rolled her beside him on the bed. She began unbuttoning his vest and his shirt at once, and smiled in delight as she found black hair on his chest she could twirl and play with.

"Could we get out of the rest of our clothes?" she asked.

"That sounds interesting," Spur said. She sat up and pulled the dress over her head, then sat there watching him.

She still wore the conventional drawers, knee length underwear that clung tightly to the body, with a draw string at the top and a six inch ruffle of embroidery around the bottom of each leg. A dozen pink bows decorated the white lawn material.

He enjoyed the way the movement made her breasts roll and bounce. He slipped out of his shirt, then kicked off his boots and socks and pulled down his denim pants. This time Spur wore no underwear and she gasped as she saw his genitals spring fully ready from the fabric.

"Oh, Lordy!" She said. "I had no idea . . . ! I mean Kane's is so small compared . . ." She laughed.

He put his hands on her drawers and untied the draw string. Her hand covered hers.

"I'm not ready. Play with me more."

He lay on his back and pulled her down over him, then let her dip one breast into his mouth. He licked it and then sucked all he could into his mouth and chewed tenderly. He switched and then put his hands on her rounded buttocks.

"I could spank you," he said.

She frowned. "Why?"

"You've never been spanked . . . this way?"

She shook her head.

"You'll like it." He began softly at first then harder until she tenderly growled and nipped at him with her teeth.

"That is wonderful! Why didn't somebody tell me before!"

She rolled over and smiled at him. He lowered toward her, his lips kissing her breasts, then moving down to her waist. She gasped as he lifted the edge of her drawers and kissed under it.

Slowly Spur pulled down the loosened drawers, kissing them lower and lower.

When he came to the edge of her pubic hair she held his face.

"That's far enough, for right now. I'll take them off. Damn! I'll rip them off if I have to!"

A moment later she was naked, writhing slowly as she lay beside him.

She leaned over and kissed his lips and watched him when she came away. "I've never wanted to make love before so much in my life! You have just set me on fire!"

"Good. It should always be that way." He nibbled at her lips, then let his hand fondle her breasts and move lower.

"Oh, Lordy!" she said softly as his fingers crept through her protecting "V" of soft fur at her crotch.

Her own hand slid over toward him and rubbed his chest, then moved lower and she gasped as she found his erect penis.

"I don't believe it! I don't see how any man could have one this huge! Beautiful! He is just absolutely amazingly beautiful!"

His hand parted the fur and stroked around her moist center. Eugenia gasped.

"Oh, yes! Darling, yes! Right now. Not another second to waste. We've wasted too much time already. Now! Right now!"

She tugged at him to come over her. He went between her spread legs, her knees were lifted and he bent, then touched her and thrust, came back, and thrust again and she yelped in delight.

"Yes! Inside! Yes! More, more!"

Then it was one short race to the finish line. Eugenia was so worked up that she climaxed the moment he was fully in her and three more times.

Spur worked at his own pace, but soon found he was speeding up to match her movements. He charged, then sprinted and at last he was pounding with a vengeance until he erupted and her feet were locked over his back riding him from below until she squeezed every drop of fluid from him.

He fell on her heavily and she grunted, then smiled, and they both closed their eyes and rested.

Ten minutes later she roused and kissed his cheek.

"Again" she said.

Spur grinned, lifted and began stroking until he felt the juices surging. It was a repeat performance. They both were sweating by then, wetness dripping from Spur's nose and chin onto her face, their bodies glued together with salt tinged perspiration.

They both exploded at the same time. Eugenia screeched in wonder and awe and delight and Spur rumbled until he had driven the last of his seed into her fertile soil.

They slept a half hour this time and when she roused, Spur had sat up and smoked half way down on a thin black cigar.

She snuggled against him, licking his side, looking up.

"Can I snuggle into your pocket and stay with you always?" she asked.

"What would your husband say?"

"He's going to be in prison anyway."

"Probably."

"So can I go with you?"

"No."

She scowled, stuck her tongue out at him. "Just a *No*? No explanation? I'm throwing my body at your feet and you step on me?"

He kissed her forehead. "Not at all, I'm thinking what will be best for you."

"Sure you are. You have just spoiled me for any ordinary man. I'll always compare their lovemaking to yours and it will be lacking."

"Not true. You're just starting to awaken. You'll make any man a better lover now. You know you will be."

"I want to keep you."

"I'm a fiddlefoot. A rover. I'm never in one place more than a week at a time."

"I like to travel."

"I sleep outdoors more than in a bed."

"Oh."

"People keep trying to kill me."

"Oh."

"I never make much money."

"Oh."

"I spend half my travel time on horseback."

"I don't like to ride."

"So?"

"So, maybe I can't go with you," she said, tears wetting her cheeks.

"Maybe so. But you could come back to my room again before I go."

"And stay all night?"

"We'll see."

She cried as she dressed, then clung to him as they walked to the door. She reached up and kissed him again.

"Spur McCoy, no matter what else I do, I'll always love you, always want you." She bit her lip so she couldn't say anything more, turned and went out the doorway into the hall, holding her small shoulders straight and stiff so she would not turn to look back at him.

Spur watched her walk down the hall, then turn toward the front door. She never did look back.

13

Spur dressed slowly, thinking about the sexy and complicated woman called Eugenia Turner. He decided she would not be a problem no matter what happened to her husband. She had decided she must act concerning the counterfeiting and she had. Now she would let the drama run its course and take the consequences even if they meant hardship for her.

McCoy turned his thinking to his next move. He had only two men involved so far in the conspiracy. Something this big must have more people taking part than that. He needed the rest of the participants. There had to be at least one more man in on the plot. Spur did as he so often did, strike at the weak link in the other camp.

It was a little after three that afternoon when Spur walked up to the newspaper office. J. Larson Wintergarden was not there. A note on the door said he was out on business and would return before five that afternoon.

Spur looked through the window, scowled and

thought of going to the Mercantile and harrasssing Joshua Hoffer, but he was saving that for an all day affair. Instead he went to Doc Rawson's office and let the sawbones take a look at his injured flesh.

The old doctor mumbled as he checked Spur's leg.

"Glad to see you've been staying off it, like I told you," he said sarcastically. Doc Rawson shook his head. "Damn fool! Part of it's busted lose again. When you gonna learn?"

"When they plow me under about six feet, I reckon, Doc. Did you know much at my age?"

Rawson chuckled. "Hell no, still can't brag about my smarts. But dang-blasted, McCoy. You could loose that leg."

"You're just trying to scare me, old man. What does my neck look like? You ever make love with a bandage around your neck?"

"So that's what's bothering you." He took off the wrappings and nodded.

"Yep. Yep."

"So what does that mean?"

"Mean, yep, or yes, or some such nonsense."

He used an instrument and picked off dead skin from Spur's neck. "Healing up better than I expected. Figured you'd have a nice furrow across your throat to the day you stop breathing, but don't look like it now."

"Let me look," Spur said.

The doctor found a hand glass and Spur stared at his neck and the ugly red flesh. Some of it had healed, the edges, but the raw open wound was still there.

"Six weeks, son," Doc Rawson said. "Six, maybe seven before you can go without some kind of a bandage on there. Your sex life might have to suffer for a while if'n you can't function with your neck wrapped."

"Didn't say couldn't."

"Yeah, rightly, rightly. Didn't say wouldn't either."

They both laughed.

Doc Rawson went to work then, putting some ointment on Spur's neck and wrapping it up securely. Then he pressed the wound in his leg together again and bandaged it.

When he was done he sat back and motioned for Spur to put on his pants.

"Couple of years you should be good as new, depending on how good that was way back then."

"Better than I remember, Doc."

Spur handed him a five dollar gold piece and waved off any change. "I'll charge it to Uncle Sam anyway, the government has lots of money."

"I don't send them any," Doc said. He frowned slightly and waved. "Get out of here and don't get yourself shot up again."

Spur wandered around the small town, had a cold beer at a saloon and watched some gamblers work the dollar bet table. Then he headed toward the newspaper office.

He arrived about 4:30 and saw the note gone from the door. When he pushed inside he found Wintergarden coming in from the back shop. His hands were black with ink and he wore a green visor.

"Yes sir? Oh, Mr. McCoy, the man who buys newspapers. Am I still in business?" He smiled at the little joke.

Spur did not smile.

"You may be out of business in a few minutes. You printed these on your Isaac Adams, and I want to know everyone who worked with you."

Spur spread out three of the twenty dollar bills on the counter top.

"You'll notice that each bill has the same serial number, the giveaway in counterfeiting."

Wintergarden made a strange little noise in his throat and started to step back, but Spur grabbed him by the shirt front and pulled him against the near side of the counter.

"I don't know what you're saying. I deal in facts and news stories. I'm just a newspaper man."

"Yeah, one with a past. I'd put a year's pay on a bet that you have a record, that you've printed funny money like this before somewhere back East."

"No!"

"Too quick with the denial, little man. You have the only press this side of Chicago that could do this print job. It's extremely well done, a masterful job. First you dig out the engraved plates you printed from and then you tell me who you're working with."

"I tell you I'm just a news man with a small paper that is almost ready to make money. If I can hold on another three or four years this town is going to grow. Railroad might even come through . . ."

Spur let go of him, went around the counter and into the back shop.

"Plates must be back here somewhere."

The back shop was like most of the others he had seen. The job press with a place of honor, stacks of paper and racks with more sheets in it. A hand cranked paper cutter thirty-six inches wide, the big flat bed press where the newspaper was printed, a barrel of ink, and dozens and dozens of small boxes.

Against the wall stood a type cabinet. It was five

feet high and had slots where fonts of type were slid in each in its own type case made of wood. Each case was divided into dozens of small spaces where the individual letters for that size and style of type were "cased."

Depending on the size and style of type, there could be two or three thousand individual metal letters in each drawer.

"Maybe you hid the plates in one of these type drawers." Spur pulled out one of the wooden drawers two feet by three feet and dumped it on the floor.

"Oh, oh, I pied the type," Spur said.

"Stop it! I don't have the plates. They took them with them."

"Then you did print the money, you did the counterfeiting?"

"Only the printing. They watched me carefully. And I only get a hundred dollars a month of the money to spend."

"Why?"

"Does it matter?"

"It does to me. Why?"

"I got in trouble back in Illinois, like you said. Printing again, green ink from some artistic plates that were not good enough."

"How long?"

"Five years, with two months off for good behavior. I ran the prison printing plant. I'm an excellent printer."

"You proved that. Let's go back up front. I want you to write out what you've told me, all of it."

"The others will be furious."

"Won't matter, Wintergarden, they'll be in jail too. Start writing."

Spur read it as he wrote. He used no names except

his own. When it was all down, Spur had him sign it. Then read through it again, and Spur signed and dated it.

"Good, it's all there except the names. Who are the rest of them? I know about Kane Turner. Who else is in on the scheme?"

"I'll tell you as soon as I'm in jail. I don't trust them."

"Fair enough. Nobody says you have to get killed. How many more are there?"

"Just one."

"Fine that makes it easier. Anything you want to take with you to jail? You could be gone for some time, I'd guess fifteen to twenty this time."

Wintergarden shook his head, looked around one last time and opened the front door.

The shot came from outside, blasted twice and pounded Wintergarden backward, falling against Spur and they both went down on the wooden floor in a tangle. By the time Spur jumped up and got to the door, he could see no one with a gun out and no one running away.

There were few people on the street. A man hurried up panting from the run.

"I saw the bastard! He ran around the back of the shop. Wasn't such a big guy, but I was too far away to see who he was."

Spur sprinted in the direction the man pointed. No one was in the alley, there were a dozen other shops and stores on this side of the alley, and six houses on the far side. The killer could have escaped into any one of them.

Back at the print shop, a crowd had gathered. The sheriff elbowed his way through and checked Wintergarden.

"Dead," he said.

A flurry of talk went through the crowd. Spur took the sheriff in the back part of the print shop and told him what happened.

Sheriff Sloan nodded. "This the real reason you came to town?"

"Right, and it's not ready to end here. I need another day or two. When I find the man who killed Wintergarden there, I'll have the other man I want."

"You're not telling me the whole story, are you, McCoy?"

"Not until I get the other man. For all I know it could be you." He grinned. "Sheriff, you'll get the arrest and the credit for wrapping this up, just as soon as it's done."

Sheriff Sloan's hand hovered over his pistol. "I could take you in and lock you up until you talk."

"Could, but won't."

"Why?"

"Because I'm a lawman, too, and you've never drawn on another lawman, have you, Sheriff?" Spur's stare was cold, hard.

"Can't say as I have. Guess I won't this time, either." He grinned and relaxed his hand over the gun. "But make it quick as you can. Folks around here like their killings solved fast."

Spur left the room and worked through the crowd. The town's barber and undertaker was officiating as two men carried the body down the block to the undertaking parlor.

By the time Spur got to the law office of Kane Turner, the door was closed and locked. It was a little after 5:30. He asked two people on the street before one knew where the Turners lived. It was only three blocks away.

When Spur came to the house he saw three

330 / Dirk Fletcher

buggies drawn up to the side of the street in front of
the residence.

Lights glowed all over the three story wooden
structure and he could hear the music of a piano.
Spur marched up the sidewalk and rang a twist bell.

Kane Turner came to the door, saw Spur and lifted
his eyebrows in surprise.

"Mr. McCoy? This is a surprise. Are you in a
hurry to find out what I did today about your
building."

"Not really. I'm more interested in retaining you
in a personal matter. I was almost a witness to a
shooting tonight. The sheriff was not friendly. If I
am charged with anything, will you represent me in
court?"

"Of course! A killing. I hadn't heard. We've had
this dinner planned for weeks and I came home early
to help Eugenia and the cook and to greet the
guests. They came about 4:30." He paused. "Do you
know who was killed?"

"A man by the name of Wintergarden, I understand, the newspaper man."

Spur saw Turner's eyes close into a squint, his
mouth came open in surprise, then he recovered.

"Yes, I know him, good printer, fair news man.
But he's dead now, you say?"

"I'm afraid so. Well, I'll let you get back to your
guests. Just wanted to be sure you were my lawyer
in case I need one."

"Of course, and thanks."

They nodded and Spur walked down the steps to
the sidewalk and out to the dirt street. He kept
going for half a block to the end, then doublebacked
and hurried down an alley so he could see both the
front and rear entrances to the big Turner house.

The lawyer could not have shot Wintergarden. He

was truly shocked at the news. He had five or six witnesses for the time of the killing. But Turner would have an idea who might have killed the printer. THEIR printer!

Spur did not think it would be a long wait. Turner would be as anxious as Spur was to learn for sure who had pulled the trigger twice.

The Secret Service Agent leaned against a tree in the alley and waited. It was fully dark now. Spur edged around the tree so he could see better.

Just then the rear door of the Turner place opened quietly, a figure slipped out and walked quickly down the alley toward where Spur hid.

14

The Secret Service Agent edged around the big tree he had been hiding behind as the figure of a man walked toward him down the alley, then past.

The man was Kane Turner, no mistake.

When the black shadow on black alley moved close to the street, Spur followed him. It was a simple task, not once did Turner look back to see if anyone were behind him.

He walked quickly to the end of the next block, then out a lane that had little suggestion that any official street work had ever been done on it. Only two houses were on the track. They sat back from the other residences, as if to say by positioning that they were superior.

From a quick look at the size and spread of the places, they were probably the biggest and best homes in Twin Falls. Turner went to the front door, knocked and waited. A few moments later the door opened and he vanished inside.

Spur found a good place to sit down and waited.

The Big Dipper made a two hour move around the North star and Spur decided he had watched long enough. Whatever was going on had not turned violent but didn't seem to be ending quickly, either.

McCoy went back to his hotel, found his room unoccupied, washed up in the heavy china bowl with the tepid water, and fell on the bed naked to try to sleep. The weather had turned warm and the nights had not cooled down that much.

In the morning, McCoy was up at dawn as usual, shaved, washed off his upper body and put on a clean shirt. He would have to hunt up a laundry if he were in town much longer. He checked his carpetbag and decided now was the time. Spur chuckled at the heroic image he made stuffing dirty laundry into the pillow case from the bed. Not at all what he had in mind when he signed up for this glorious life as a Secret Service Agent.

The clerk told him where he could get his laundry done. It was a combination dry goods store and laundry just down the block. At the counter where he left his laundry a wide eyed girl with a big grin winked at him.

"Hi, new in town I bet, and not married or you wouldn't bring us your dirty socks, right?" She had deep green eyes, a turned up nose and her peasant white blouse clung to large, firm breasts.

"Caught me. Just don't starch my socks."

She laughed and bent over to look in the sack. It let her blouse fall forward and Spur found himself staring straight down the open blouse at her breasts that swung and swayed under the blouse with nothing else covering them.

She glanced up at him without moving.

"See anything you like," she asked softly.

"I see two beauties I like," he said so no one else could hear.

She leaned back so the blouse covered her again. "The laundry will cost you sixty-five cents. Those other things you like are three dollars—but you get dinner and drinks at my place. How about tonight?"

"Sorry, I have to see a lady about her pet bird."

The girl laughed. "You talk crazy. I've got a wild bird, you want to see her dance?"

"Next time, pretty lady. When will my socks be starched and ready to pick up?"

"This afternoon, about 4:30 if you're in a rush. Or at my place at 6:30 if you're in no hurry."

"Right, 4:30. I'll be here."

"Damn, I could come down to two dollars."

"Never cut your prices, little darling, it's bad for business." Spur patted her shoulder and went out into the sunshine.

It was going to be hot again today.

A dust devil three feet wide spun its corkscrew journey across the street.

A woman's sunbonnet went sailing down the boardwalk.

Spur moved out toward the big house on the lane just north of most of the town. When he was within sight of it, he saw a woman watering scraggly flowers in her front yard.

"Beg your pardon, Ma'am," Spur said.

She turned, frowning. She was about thirty, plain, wearing a simple print dress that covered her chin to wrist and dragged in the dust.

"I ain't buying nothing more. After I got those hair brushes my Charley fairly threw me out of the house. He said . . ." She stopped. "Oh, you're not the same drummer."

"No Ma'am. Just wanted to know who lives in

that first house down there, the big one on the lane?"

"Everybody knows that, so you must be a stranger. You mean them folks any harm?"

"No, Ma'am. I was just wondering if the house was for sale?"

"Don't rightly know. Might ask at the Mercantile, the Hoffer Mercantile. He owns it. Lives in the house. But he don't treat his wife right. I see the poor thing crying behind that big window just lots of times."

"Yes, Ma'am. I feel like crying sometimes myself." He watched her look up, surprised. He touched the brim of his low crowned brown hat with the silver pesos around it, and walked back toward town.

Hoffer! The man could be hanged only once. If he tied in with the counterfeiters, he must be the most important one, or the only other one. He could be the engraver. Or the plates could have been produced elsewhere and brought here. No, engravers were artists, but they were also vain and selfish.

If Hoffer made the plates, he would not let them out of his sight, not even when they were being used to print the bogus money. The engraver must come from right here in town. Chances are it was Hoffer.

On his way back to Hoffer's store, Spur saw that the newspaper office was closed and padlocked. There was a notice on the door that anyone who had any claim against H. Larson Wintergarden or his newspaper, should file his claim with the sheriff's office within ten days.

Spur read the notice again. That could mean there were no known relatives, and that the county had taken charge of the property.

He continued to the Mercantile and walked in the

front door. This time he made no effort to avoid the small, fat man who worked behind the counter. Hoffer looked up as Spur stood across the counter from him.

The merchant's small green eyes under the thinning brown hair, stared at the Agent.

"Yes sir. How may I help you?"

The nervous tick over Hoffer's right eye pulsated once, then remained inactive.

Spur nodded. "Yes, it had to be you."

"What? I don't understand."

"Of course you do, Hoffer. I was standing beside Wintergarden when you shot him. I saw you through the window, then I saw you outside running down the alley. Not hard to miss that limp-legged way you run."

"You're saying that I shot . . . Ridiculous, simply ridiculous. I'm a busy man and don't have time for wild stories. If you'll kindly remove yourself from the premises . . . "

Spur put one big hand around the merchant's throat from the front and squeezed both sides.

"I could kill you this way in about three minutes, Hoffer. Cuts off all the blood supply to the brain. Almost like being hung. Now think again about the shooting. I saw you, how can you deny it?"

Hoffer's face grew redder as the seconds ticked by. Before he passed out, Spur let up on the pressure, and moved his big hand.

"Oh, God . . . oh, God!" Hoffer's voice came out soft, garbled. A minute later he could speak normally.

"You get out of here! I've got a shotgun in back of the counter, and I'll shoot you down in a minute and never be sorry!"

"You probably never are sorry, Hoffer. You shot

Wintergarden, didn't you?"

"Of course not. I don't care what he prints in his silly little newspaper. Nobody reads it anyway."

"I read it, Hoffer, and it tells me a lot about you."

Hoffer stared at him, still massaging his sore throat.

"Hoffer, I'd say you spent three to five years in Midvale Federal prison for forgery. That come close?"

"Absolutely not! I am not a convict, I've never been in prison."

"I can get the records. Changed your name, of course, but I can find it. Doesn't matter that much. It wasn't what Wintergarden printed in his paper that you objected to, it was what he talked to me about the day before he was killed."

"Lies, all lies! I don't have to put up with this."

"Are you going to run away, again, Hoffer? You did last time. A new state, a new name, and some of the old money to get a new start. Then the old itch comes back. Hard to get rid of completely, isn't it?"

"What the hell are you talking about?"

"Bringing in that Isaac Adams press was the first mistake. It's the first thing we watch for."

Hoffer began looking around, his eyes darting to the counter top.

"Don't reach for that shotgun or you'll be a dead man before you hit the floor!"

Hoffer stared at him blankly.

Spur took two twenty dollar bills from his pocket and laid them on the counter top.

"Notice the serial numbers on both bills, Mr. Hoffer. You'll see they are exactly the same. We can't expect you to stop the press and engrave a new number for every bill, can we?"

Hoffer slumped on the counter.

Spur shook his head. "Only a matter of time, Hoffer. I find those plates here in your store, you are a dead man. You thought Wintergarden was going to talk, that's why you shot him. Now you're worried about Kane Turner blasting you when you walk out the door tonight. Could happen. You two on best of terms, I hope."

Hoffer glared at Spur. "If you have any evidence, you just go ahead and arrest me. Otherwise you get out of my store!" Hoffer got back some of his courage. "You had proof you wouldn't be jawboning me this way. Yeah, you're fishing!"

Spur reached up and took the neckerchief down from where it had been covering his bandaged neck. He removed his hat and stared at Hoffer.

"Ever seen me before, Hoffer?"

"Course not, you're a stranger in . . ."

He squinted his green eyes and looked at Spur's neck.

"What happened to your neck?"

"Bad burn, a rope burn. I was the guest of honor at a lynching one morning out east of town. Remember it, Hoffer?"

"My God! NO! It can't be. You was dead! Damn eyes bulged out, and you was hanging there." He took two steps back until he hit the wall. "Now, look here. That lynching was Gabe Young's idea. You was there. He had the gun. He had ALL OF US under his gun. Me and that ranch kid, Boots, we couldn't do nothing!"

You *helped him* you bastard. You jabbed your knife into my horse and made her race out from under me. *You were my hangman!*"

Hoffer was shaking now. Spittle drooled down the

side of his chin. His eyes were wild. He kept looking at the place under the counter where the shotgun must be.

"Hoffer, think back. Young didn't have you under his gun. You were enjoying yourself, laughing, teasing Boots. Hell, you said you enjoy a good hanging."

"No . . . no!"

"Yes, yes, Hoffer! You hung me, you bastard!"

"Get Gabe Young! He done it. Gabe's fault."

"You can tell him that, Hoffer, next time you two talk in hell. I hung Gabe in Boise a few days ago. He was robbing a bank at the time. Might say I killed two snakes with the same rope."

Hoffer mumbled something and leaned against the wall, then slid down it slowly until he slumped to a sitting position on the floor.

"All Gabe's idea! All Gabe's . . ."

"Ever wonder what it feels like to be hung, Hoffer? You should know because one of these days you're going to find out in person. Just having that noose lower over your head is the worst part, because it's the start of the end of your life. The rope is over the limb and tied off tight, the rope's been tested, no way it's going to slip or break. And there you are staring at the last few seconds of your *entire life!*"

"No! No more. Don't tell me."

"Afraid, Hoffer? Good. Sweat you bastard! Every day and every night you're going to be thinking about being hung, and knowing that I'm out there waiting for exactly the right time. Yeah, Hoffer, you're right. I'm a lawman, a federal lawman, and I believe in the law and justice. But this time it's Spur McCoy's law, and Spur McCoy's justice, because it was Spur McCoy's neck that got stretched by your rope!" Spur watched him on the floor. He had laid down now and curled into a ball as tight as he could. The fetal position, he was trying to go back to his mother's womb for protection.

"Leaves you with an interesting decision to make, Hoffer. You can go to the sheriff and admit that you murdered H.L. Wintergarden. That way you'll have the sheriff's protection when he jails you. After that all you have to do is try to beat the murder charge. If you do, I'll still be around to stretch your neck with a stout rope. Of course, if they convict you of murder, the sheriff will get the honor of dropping the trap on you up there on the scaffold."

Spur pushed his toe into the balled up little merchant.

"Make up your mind you lynching little sonofabitch! You don't have much longer." Spur turned and walked out of the store.

15

By noon that day, Spur McCoy was in a smattering of brush a quarter of a mile behind the Boots Dallman ranch. He had checked at the Box B spread and the ramrod said Boots had gone home the day before. He looked as slick as a year old orphaned heifer.

Spur pulled out a pair of battered but still workable ex-army binoculars and studied the small farm-ranch layout. A woman came out of the back door of the house, shook a dust mop, stared at the vegetable garden down by the creek, and retreated into the shade of the structure.

Ten minutes later a man came out. He had a small limp as he moved to the barn. He was as tall as a new-split rail and blond—Boots Dallman for sure.

Spur waited until he was in the barn, then went along the small line of brush next to the creek that swept within twenty yards of the back of the barn. With the building between him and the house, Spur walked to the unpainted excuse for a barn and slid in

344 / Dirk Fletcher

a back door. He carried a coil of new, half inch rope. On one end hung a hangman's noose with thirteen wraps.

Dallman was pitching hay into a stall with two milk cows waiting.

Spur's Colt .45 came in his hand and as he walked up he pulled the hammer back.

The clicking of the metal on metal made a deadly sound in the quietness of the barn. Dallman froze when he heard the sound and turned slowly, his hands still on the four-tined pitchfork.

"Put the fork down easy like," Spur said.

Dallman looked at him with hollow eyes, nodded, then dropped the haying tool that could also be a deadly weapon.

"Figured you'd come when I wasn't alooking. McCoy, wasn't it?" Dallman's eyes were bloodshot, sagging black half circles showed beneath his lids. His hands plucked at each other as if they were finding lice.

"A man should remember the name of everyone he lynches, Dallman. How has it been these past couple of days knowing that at any time you might turn around and see me holding a noose made from a sturdy half inch hemp rope?"

"It's been pure hell, McCoy. I ain't slept for three nights running now. Better I just keep working so things will be easier for Martha when I'm . . . after I . . ."

"After you're hung and dead and buried. No sense putting it off any longer. Get one horse and bring it around back. I'll have you in my sights all the time. Just put the bridle on it. Dallman, I'm good with this .45."

Boots watched him with furious eyes, yet there was no violence in the man. Slowly he nodded.

"Time for me to say goodbye to my family?"

"Did you give me time for that, Dallman?"

"Reckon we didn't."

"You remember that much. Get moving, Dallman. We'll go out from the back of the barn so Martha won't get curious, won't unlimber a Sharps at us. I've seen some Western women who were damn fine shots."

"Martha don't like guns." Dallman stared at Spur, then went down the alley of the barn to the far stalls, put a bridle on a horse and led it to the back door.

He looked at Spur. "You ready?"

"Damn right. I got hung once, now it's your turn."

They walked out the back door of the barn. Spur did not bother to close it. They went across the field two hundred yards to a scraggly maple tree that had a solid limb about the right height.

Spur threw the noose over the overhanging limb on the first try, raised it ten feet off the ground and belayed the end of the rope around the base of the maple tree and tied it off tightly.

"Sit down over there and wait," he told Boots.

Spur jumped on the back of the saddleless horse, caught the noose and held the rope above the big slip knot. He put his weight on it and hung there by his hands a moment to be sure it would not slip.

Boots looked up.

"Not even a Murphy's knot?"

"You know damn well it isn't, Boots. You only get one chance when you kill a man, or when you try damn hard and miss like you did. Then you pay the price."

"Don't you think I've thought of that for the past few days! I've been in a living hell! Almost glad that it will be over. Martha ain't been too happy with me neither. I was stone dead drunk walking those two days with the posse but I didn't know what the hell I was doing. Told you that. Told you I get drunk about twice a year. Martha understands!"

"I didn't understand, Boots! Not when that rope seared my neck and cut off my air and damn near broke my neck! I didn't understand it when I passed out and didn't know a fucking thing until Sheriff Sloan cut me down and slapped me awake. Even then I thought I was dead! I sure as hell didn't understand!"

Spur dropped off the rope and went to the tree.

"Just to make damn sure this thing holds. Hate like hell to bungle it as bad as you guys did and have to shoot you." Spur looked at the rope where it was tied behind the tree. He paused a minute, then came back.

"Might as well get it over with. Get up on the horse, Boots, then put the noose around your neck and cinch it up."

"I got to hang myself?"

"Almost. I'll help on the tough parts."

Boots jumped on the horse, moved her under the noose and pulled it down so his head would go through the opening. He glared at Spur, then shrugged.

"Tell . . . Tell Martha I'm damn sorry it ended this way. I tried. Tried like hell. Just one stupid mistake . . ." He wiped away wetness from his eyes. "Tell her I love her and the kids."

Spur nodded.

"Guess it's time, Boots. You're going to find out what it feels like to be hung. What is it the sheriff always says, 'May God have mercy on your soul.' "

Spur tied Boots' hands behind his back, then looked up at the haggard man.

"Remember, Boots, you earned this," Spur said. He whacked his flat hand against the rump of the mare and she bolted forward.

Without the saddle to hold him, Boots skidded off the hind quarters of the mare at once, the rope tightened and he fell a foot before it took up the slack. Boots screamed and all the anguish and anger and shame and fury of what he done poured out.

Then the rope gave way behind the tree and it snaked across the limb. Boots Dallman fell three feet to the ground. His boots hit and he buckled forward, skidding in the dust.

Spur squatted down beside the cowboy-farmer who lay in the dust under the maple tree. His face was wet with tears. Spur cut the rawhide that held his hands together and Boots sat up. His eyes were still closed.

"Dear God, I hit the ground, I can't be dead!"

"Not unless dropping three feet is going to kill your boots," Spur said. "You're as alive as you ever were. Maybe a little smarter now."

Boots wiped the tears away and opened his eyes, staring at Spur with only a slight frown.

"Why?"

"I believed you. I believed what the sheriff said about you. Remembering back, I couldn't remember what you did during my own hanging. You did nothing. You didn't even hold their coats, but at least you didn't help the bastards."

"But I didn't try to stop them."

"The law doesn't say you have to be a hero, or be a brave man."

"Gabe Young?"

"I hanged him, in the bank in Boise. He and four others were robbing it late one night."

"Josh Hoffer?"

"I still have plans for him."

"I'd rather not know."

"How did you like being almost hung, Boots?"

"Terror. Stark, total, unrelenting, massive, hellish terror." He looked at Spur. "You know that better than I do. I don't blame you, McCoy. I'd want to do the same thing if I had been in your place. Know one thing for damned certain. I'm never going to touch another drop of booze for as long as I live!"

"With your capacity, that sounds like a good idea," Spur said.

They both saw her at the same time. Martha Dallman walked across the field toward them. They waited, Spur squatting, Boots sitting in the dust, the noose still around his neck.

"You cut the rope when you went over to check?"

"True. All but one tiny strand that I knew wouldn't hold your weight. I did want to scare the shit out of you."

"Damned well did that."

Martha came up to them and looked at both.

"I still have a husband, good."

Boots pulled the noose open and took it off his head. He threw it at the tree.

"Mr. McCoy, Boots told me all about it. I know the whole story. I saw most of what happened here from the barn. Got curious why Boots was gone so long. Want to tell you that I had the rifle, but I didn't shoot." She laughed softly. "But that was only because I was afraid I might hit my husband."

"Yes, Ma'am," Spur said. He was uneasy. The lesson was learned. He wanted to move back to town.

"Come down to the house, both of you. There's something I have to do."

"Mrs. Dallman, I better get on back to town."

"This is something that needs to be done. It must be accomplished now, Mr. McCoy. Long overdue. I hope you don't mind."

"Yes, Ma'am."

They walked toward the barn. The horse was a quarter of a mile down the valley where she had run, but she would be back for oats when it got dark. Spur walked slightly behind the other two, but they did not talk. No one said a word until they stepped into the farmhouse kitchen.

It was neat, clean and a pot of coffee simmered on a wood burning cookstove.

Martha Dallman poured a cup of coffee and took it to her husband.

"Boots, I want you to sit right there at the table and not say a word. No matter what happens you say a single word and I'll divorce you and take the kids and go back to Illinois. You understand Bobby Lee Dallman?"

His eyes widened as she used his given names. He nodded.

She turned and poured a second cup of coffee and handed this one to Spur who stood at one side.

He sipped at it and was about to say something when she spoke again.

"Mr. McCoy, Boots does get a wild streak now and again and thinks he needs a night in town. He goes in, gets liquored up and then jumps one of them fancy women in a saloon. Last time I warned him. I told him one more time and I was going to get me a lover and do it and tell him about it.

"That was before I knew about him going on that posse that turned into the lynching party. Now I figure it's time to pay back Boots Dallman."

Martha wore a green blouse that buttoned to the throat and a long green skirt that covered her ankles. Now she smiled at Spur and began unbuttoning her blouse.

"I hear some men think it's torture to watch while someone else makes love to their wife. I'm sure Boots thinks so. Mr. McCoy could you do me the honor of fucking me right now while Boots watches? It would be like a double payment to him and I would be highly thankful."

"No, I'm afraid not. I evened the score with Boots. He learned his lesson." Spur watched as her blouse came open to reveal surging breasts that had large brown areolas and pink tipped nipples that had flared and surged to erection.

She dropped her blouse on the floor and walked toward him.

"Once or twice or three times, Spur. Whatever you like. Wherever you want to put it. I'm a farm girl, we learn about sex early from watching the animals, dogs first."

Boots groaned and looked away.

"Dallman, you get your eyes looking this way again!" Martha bellowed. ".You watch, damnit, like I told you to!"

She stood directly in front of Spur, so close her nipples almost touched his chest.

"This isn't necessary, Mrs. Dallman. He promised me he's never going to drink again. I'm sure you can keep him home. You're a beautiful woman, and obviously can satisfy a man . . . ."

Her hand reached down and began massaging his crotch, then the long lump that appeared by magic behind the fly of his denim pants.

"My, my, for saying no, you sure didn't instruct your big boy here not to get ready for action."

"Mrs. Dallman, this isn't necessary."

"You think I'm ugly."

"No, not at all."

"You think my titties are too small."

"They are beautiful."

"Then show me."

She unbuttoned his fly, loosened his belt and tried to pull down his pants. He stopped her.

In one quick move she loosened her skirt. It fell to the floor and just as fast she pulled down soft white underwear and stood in front of him naked. Her legs were slender and long, ending in a bush of brown hair. Her hips were full, waist narrowed and then her breasts surged out.

She caught his hand and knelt on the floor, tugging Spur with her. Then she lay on her back, spread her legs and pulled him down on top of her.

She had his pants pushed down now and pulled his turgid penis from white underpants.

"Yes, big boy, I knew you would be a huge one. Look, Boots, look what a fantastic prick McCoy has!"

Boots groaned where he sat with his coffee.

They lay on the bare wooden floor.

"It is what he needs," Martha said softly. "One last humiliation and I can cure him of going into town and getting wild drunk. Now is the time."

"This is strange, Martha. He's watching!"

"He better be!" She lifted her knees and pulled him forward. He felt his lance touch the wetness that was waiting for him.

"Hell, why not?" Spur said softly, then massaged her breasts. He saw her smile, then he eased forward and when he was inside rammed hard until he jolted forward sliding into her all the way to his pelvic bones.

She moaned softly in acceptance.

"Beautiful," she whispered in his ear. "Just marvelous. I knew you would be a good fucker. I need to talk dirty when I'm getting poked. I work better that way."

Her hips began to grind under him and set up a rhythm and soon Spur was moving to her tune. He bent and chewed on her breasts still large even though they had flattened as she lay on her back. Her legs came around his back, then lifted again and lay on his shoulders. She was almost standing on her shoulders and Spur gunned into her.

"Yes!" she said, then she climaxed. Her body shook and she wailed. A moment later he did the same thing. After fifteen of the same soft climaxes, she screamed at the top of her lungs and her hips rose to smash into his five times, then she fainted.

Spur looked at Boots.

"Don't worry. She does that when it's very good for her. She will be all right in a minute or two."

Spur stopped thrusting, then she came to and her hips pounded his and he responded and climaxed almost at once. She pushed him up and off her, gathered up her clothes and hurried into the other room.

Spur shook his head, pulled up his pants and buttoned his fly. He had not even taken off his clothes.

Martha was back a moment later, dressed and combing her soft brown hair.

"Mr. McCoy, I don't imagine you'll be around town much longer, but if you are, this never happened. Only Boots is to remember it. And if he gets a wild hair up his ass and wants to go to town to try out a new bimbo, he will be reminded what I will do if he does. And I'll make him watch me fucking one of our neighbors."

She smiled. "Between us, I think we've taught Mr. Boots Dallman two lessons in one day."

Spur grinned. "You very well may be right. I'll be happy if he never lynches anyone again."

"You can be damn sure of that!" Boots said. "I thought I was going to die out there today. That I'll remember for the rest of my life. It's not much fun facing what I did today." He looked at his wife, then reached out and petted her breasts through the green blouse.

"As for you, I'll save all my fucking for you. Twice a week, at least."

"Hey, every night if you want. I'm here and ready."

Spur saw Boots' hand vanish inside her blouse and saw the light sparkle in her eyes. Spur faded out the door. For Boots, one of the worst days in his life was going to start getting a lot better quickly.

Spur walked back to his horse, mounted and rode away. He took one last look at Boots Dallman's ranch and farm and wished him well.

16

On his way into town, Spur rode past the laundry.
He grinned and moved up to the hitching rail and
tied his mare, then went inside. At first he thought
the place was empty.

"Just about to close up," a voice called. "State
your business." It was a woman.

"Came to pick up some laundry," Spur called.

A fluff of brown hair showed from behind a stack
of boxes, then deep green eyes peered out.

"Oh, hi!" the owner of the voice came out from the
stack of boxes and grinned. It was the same girl who
had taken in his laundry that morning. "Decided to
come back after all?"

"Figures as how. My laundry ready?"

"Almost. I'll finish it, only be a minute. Would
you mind snapping that spring night lock and
throwing the bolt for me so nobody else will come?
We start so early in the morning we usually close
early as well."

Spur locked the door and slid the bolt home, then

stood at the counter waiting.

"Could you give me a hand?" the girl asked. "Right back here."

Spur grinned and went around the end of the counter and through the baskets and trays to where the voice came from.

She stood at a work table, and had just tied up a bundle of wash in white paper. She knotted the string, snapped it in half, then handed the package to him.

Her eyes widened as he took it, brushing his hand against hers.

"Oh, say, I was wondering . . ." She frowned, looked away, then sighed and looked back. "Oh, forget it."

Spur let a small smile slide onto his face. "What were you wondering? I'm in no big hurry. What's bothering you?"

She turned back, eyes snapping, a dimple on her right cheek. She brushed at long brown hair that had straggled over one eye.

"Well, I was wondering if you could give me some advice. You're a stranger but I feel I could trust you."

"Advice is cheap."

"But I need some—please?" She reached out and touched his arm, then drew her hand back quickly.

"About this morning, that three dollars and dinner. That was just talk. I was feeling all squirmy and hot and I just said things I shouldn't."

"I understand."

She motioned with one hand. "Come back here so we can talk."

They moved through the back part of the store to a sectioned-off area that were apparently living quarters. Two rooms were furnished, a bedroom and small kitchen. A window looked out on the alley.

"Home," she said simply. "Oh—I'm Sue, and I'm eighteen and I'm just all mixed up."

"I'm Spur McCoy," he said.

She waved him into a straight-backed chair near a small table and she sat in a second chair.

"I tell everyone I'm twenty-one and an orphan. Not true. I got folks. They live in Portland, but I ran away. Was that wrong?"

Spur watched her. She was serious. "It just depends on why you ran away, and what you've done since. Why did you leave your parents' home?"

"I was sixteen, and my daddy drank a lot, and Momma was sickly, she had the fever. Days at a time she barely woke up. So I had to do the chores and cooking. Daddy liked to hug me, and one day he hugged and hugged and then his hips started pushing and pumping against mine. He was *doing* it. He stops and tells me to lay down on my bed and lifts up my skirt and then he undresses me.

"I was so scared I couldn't even talk. When I was all bare he made me undress him, and I was trembling and scared and excited. I'd never seen a man's . . . thing . . . before. It was so big!

"Then he was naked and he grabbed it with his hand and began pumping back and forth with one hand and rubbing my breasts with the other. I was still scared but it felt kind of good, all warm and wanting him to rub and rub. Then he just spurted all over me and he grunted and grabbed his clothes and left.

"The next night he came in and did the same thing. About a week later he started playing with me and pushing his finger into me, and then in another week, he was doing it, right inside me.

"I tried to make him stop, 'cause I knew it was

bad. But he wouldn't stop. I locked my door and he broke it down. He made me do terrible things to him and for him. I decided I could either kill him or run away. I didn't know how to kill him, so I took all the money I could find in his wallet one night when he was drunk, and got a stage ticket to Boise, and then came down here."

She looked up at him, her big green eyes still serious. "I been here almost two years working in this laundry, and now the owner lets me stay in back here and watch the place. Did I do wrong running away?"

"No, Sue, of course not. Your father was the wrong one."

"Yeah, I thought of that. But somehow it never mattered much to me when he did it to me. I didn't mind. I finally learned to get a little excited myself. The advice I want is this. Since I don't mind it, should I be a fancy woman in a saloon and make six or eight dollars a night? That's a lot of money, maybe two hundred dollars a month! I get fifteen dollars a month and my room here."

"Well, Sue, that's a decision you'll have to make. Is there anything else you think you might like doing? Like teaching school or getting married?"

She laughed. "Oh, yes, I wanted to get married. But that will just kind of happen. I don't talk or write good enough to teach school."

"Sue, the best advice I can give you is that you should do exactly what you want to do. Life is short, in spite of what you might think at eighteen. So don't waste life, live it. Do what you want to do— and of course be prepared for any consequences."

"Like fancy women when they get diseases and pregnant and things like that?"

"Yes, and they sometimes get beat up, and every now and then one of the whores get killed."

"Heaven protect us!" She watched him a minute. "Yes, thank you, I have decided." She stood and moved to the stove, making a fire. "Now, I promised you supper, so I had better make you something to eat. How about some fried potatoes and onions mixed up with some chopped up bacon? My daddy always liked that."

Spur said that would be fine and watched her work over the small sink and the stove. She chattered on, about Portland, about how much it rained, how you could count on rain every single day during winter.

"Then if it didn't rain, you could run and sing and jump and be so happy because it wasn't raining! But I really liked Portland. Maybe I'll go back there sometime after daddy dies. He's getting old. I bet he's over forty-five now!"

The fried potatoes were delightful. She served them with biscuits and homemade jam and hot coffee and some fresh peas.

"Best meal I've had in a week," Spur said.

She smiled and poured him more coffee, then sat and stared at him.

"You are the most handsome man that I've ever cooked supper for," she said. It was an honest, straight statement. "I guess you're about the prettiest man I've ever seen!" Sue came and stood in front of where he sat. "You have helped me make up my mind. I am going to try to better myself. I got past the eighth grade, but not much farther. If I work on my numbers, I bet I could be a clerk in one of the mercantiles. That would be a step up. Hoffer's has all that nice household merchandise. But the women don't like to go in there and have him wait on them. They think he's weird. Maybe I could work for him."

As she talked she leaned forward, her white peasant blouse billowed forward as it had in the store.

"I also believe in paying my debts. You helped me, now I will give you the only thing I have you might want."

Spur looked down her blouse at her big breasts.

"Sue, you don't have to do this."

"I know, but I want to. I don't jump in bed with just any man I see." She caught the bottom of the blouse and slid it off over her head.

Her breasts jiggled from the motion and Spur sucked in his breath. Twin peaks thrust out at him, the nipples extended by hot, pulsating blood. The large pink areolas over cream white flesh were begging to be kissed.

"Mr. McCoy," she said, her eyes half closed. "I would be ever so grateful if you would kiss me now."

He leaned forward and kissed her soft lips. Her arms went around him and her breasts crushed against him. Her tongue darted into his mouth at once and he could feel her hips thrusting against his.

She let the kiss last a long time, then leaned back and looked up at him.

"Everytime I kiss someone I think it gets better and better. Why is that, Mr. McCoy?"

"Because you only kiss when you're sexually excited, and that increases your excitement, and mine, and it seems like you want those feelings to go on forever and ever."

Her face brightened. "Yes!" Then she kissed him again. Her slender body pressed against him from knee to chest now and he had to suck in a quick breath. He was surprised by the heat of her body through the cloth.

When the second kiss ended, she caught his hand and moved it to her breasts.

"Rub them, pet them for me," she whispered, an urgency in her voice he had not heard before.

His hand massaged one mound, then the other, and her breathing became a panting, her mouth opened and her eyes closed and her hands massaged his back and then his chest. Slowly she opened the buttons on his shirt and one hand snaked inside, rubbing his chest, toying with his chest hair.

"I'm going to fall over unless we lay down somewhere!" she said. She took his hand and led him into the small bedroom with its single bed covered by a quilted comforter done in the double wedding ring design.

She sat on the edge of the bed and motioned him to sit beside her.

She stared into his eyes, her deep green orbs now serious and determined.

"I am not going to become a whore, and I won't even joke about it anymore, the way I did to you. I promise never, never again to let anyone see my titties like I did today, and I'll always wear a chemise and a wrapper so they won't look so big. There, that will be a good start."

"I should think so," Spur said. He reached down and kissed her. She was as eager and enthused as ever, and slowly pushed him down on his back so she could lie on top of him.

Spur realized it had been weeks since he had taken on two different women the same day. Mentally he shrugged; he took life as it came to him, there was no sense fighting it.

She took his shirt off, then his boots, and then her

own long skirt. She had on only knee-length drawers. Her breasts bounded and jolted around, to Spur's immense delight.

When she pulled down his pants and his underwear, Sue gasped. His staff was at full erection and ready to perform.

"Golly whee!" Sue said. "Golly whee! I've never seen anything like that before. It's huge!"

"The better to love you," Spur said and she let him unfasten the drawstring on the drawers and pull them down.

She stopped him and pushed him back on the bed and sat on his stomach, then lowered her breasts to his mouth. She smiled at the look of satisfaction on his face.

"I thought you would like to chew on me. Men just seem to enjoy it. I climaxed the first time. Now I'm a little slower. Oh, I might yell if I really get excited, don't be surprised."

For the next fifteen minutes, several things she did surprised him, but he had some new ideas for her as well, and she kissed him one last time, then nodded.

"Yes, please, Mr. Spur McCoy, I really wish that you would fuck me now, fast and hard before I just explode!"

The second time she insisted they do it standing up. She leaned against the wall and locked her legs behind his back. To Spur's pleasure it worked delightfully well. They laughed and the second time Sue cried as she climaxed, and then they rested side by side on the bed.

She touched his shoulder and looked at her.

"I am going to start dressing better, and I'm going to try to get a better job. Yes, I definitely do want to get married and have babies. Three, I guess, two boys and a girl. That would be about right." She rolled over and held her chin in her hands and stared at him, her fingers twirling the hairs on his chest.

"You want to marry me? We're good fucking together."

Spur chuckled. "I'm afraid I'm a traveling man. I'll be gone from here in two or three days."

"Oh. You don't like me."

He kissed her nose, then her cheek, then her lips. "I *do* like you. You are a wonderful, bouncy, smart, ambitious girl. But I have to move on." He looked at his watch. It was almost six-thirty. He had another job to do before the night was over. He had to get the principals in the counterfeiting game to show their hand.

17

The time was nearly four P.M. when Spur rode back into town and tied his horse in back of the hotel. He went up to his room for some supplies. The drama was nearing an end and he might have to leave town quickly. He took his Spencer repeating rifle and an extra box of rounds, along with two loaded tubes and put them in the boot on the saddle.

In his saddlebags he put an extra shirt and a pair of jeans, then packed in some store bought jerky and dried fruit. He put the horse in the small hotel stable behind the hotel and knew it would be safe there.

He washed up, changed his shirt and put on a clean neckerchief to keep his throat bandage clean. He could turn his head anyway he wanted to now with little pain. It must be healing. His leg gave him no trouble at all now.

Spur checked his boots. The heel on one was loose. He dug out the spare pair of boots he had picked up in Denver. They had a feature built into the heel that had fascinated him. On the right boot, there was a small trigger in the hollow just in front of the heel. By pushing the button, a two inch knife slid out from the side of the heel leather. He had sharpened it to razor proportions.

Spur tried the device, then pressed the button again and carefully pushed the blade back until it locked. It could come in handy sometime. He put on the new boots and was ready to go.

Spur walked out of the hotel with his .45 riding low on his right hip, crossed the street and angled for the second floor office of lawyer Kane Turner. It was time to tighten up the set screws and let Turner know he was under suspicion.

McCoy went in without knocking and found Kane working on some papers on his desk. He looked up, his brow creasing with a frown. Hoffer probably had talked with Kane, telling him that Spur was on to them, or at least knew about Hoffer and the printer.

"Yes, Mr. McCoy. I haven't heard a thing from the sheriff about that shooting. I'd guess you won't be charged. Hell, you were a witness not a suspect."

"Never can tell in a strange town, Mr. Turner. I'm glad to hear the news. Trouble is, now I have a new problem."

Kane stood. Spur saw no weapon, but he could have a hideout somewhere within reaching distance.

"Yeah, counselor, seems like somebody pawned off some bogus money on me. Look at this." Spur tossed an envelope on the lawyer's desk. It held three new, virgin, unfolded twenty dollar bills. They were from the counterfeit supply Turner's wife had given to Spur.

"Look good to me. Bank gets new bills from time to time. What's wrong with them?"

"You know what's wrong, Turner. You've been

watching the work on the plates and the press for the last two or three months. All the serial numbers are identical. It's the first thing to check for on a batch of counterfeit bills."

Kane never looked at the money.

"And you're saying I had something to do with this counterfeiting?"

"Damn right, Kane, you, the artist and engraving man, Hoffer, and the printer Wintergarden who Hoffer shot dead. Last night you went to see Hoffer just after I told you about the killing. You wanted to be sure Hoffer had done it."

Kane smiled. "Afraid you'll need more evidence than that to make it stand up in our circuit rider courtroom, Mr. McCoy. Proof is what the judge looks for."

"I've got a million dollars worth of proof," McCoy said. He drew his .45 so quickly that Kane could only stare at it.

"There is no need for firearms, I'm a peaceful man, and I uphold the law."

"The ones you want to," Spur said.

"I can prove I had nothing to do with those counterfeit bills. I have a document in my desk drawer."

"Get it."

Kane bent toward the drawer, then drew a derringer from his inner coat pocket and fired a shot blindly toward Spur. If it had been bird shot it could have blinded Spur. As it was the solid lead slug from the .45 derringer slammed past Spur's left ear, buzzing as it flew past and stuck in the plastered walls.

Spur lunged away and fired, digging a .45 round into Kane's right shoulder before he could get off a second shot. The small weapon fell from Kane's hand as he jolted backward against the wall. His left hand held his bleeding shoulder.

"If you get in the first shot, never miss. Think about that when you're in prison on counterfeiting charges."

"Get me to Doc Rawson! I'll bleed to death."

"Good, save the county and state some money. You show me where you hid the engraved plates for those twenty dollar bills and I'll carry you to the Doc's office."

"I don't know what you're talking about."

"Then why did you try to kill me just now?"

"You were threatening me with a gun. I have a right to defend myself with deadly force."

"True." Spur searched the man, found no other weapon and pushed him into a chair. "Stay there until I finish tearing this place apart."

"Why?"

"I figure you have something near a half million dollars around here somewhere in twenties. Want to tell me where you hid them?"

"Ridiculous!" Kane said, but his frown deepened. He used his handkerchief to push inside his shirt to try to slow down the bleeding.

Spur jerked open drawers, dumped out two on the desk top. When he pulled out the wide drawer in the center of the desk, it stuck. Underneath it he found a box fastened to the bottom of the drawer. In the box were stacks of twenty dollar bills. There were ten packets.

"Twenty thousand dollars worth," Spur said. "That's a start, now where is the rest?"

"Bastard! I'm still bleeding!"

"So suffer a little." Spur kept looking. In a locked file which he broke open he found trust deeds and legal descriptions and property deeds to town property. Most were dated within a two month period. He guessed the property had been purchased somehow with the bogus money, so the sales were invalid. He set them aside, and went back to dumping drawers.

No more money.

Spur moved to the small storage closet. Three boxes on a shelf were marked, "Old records 1872." One of the boxes looked newer than the others and had been marked with a different kind of pen making a wide line. He pulled the box off the shelf and opened it. The box was full of packets of twenty dollar bills, all with identical serial numbers.

"Don't know a thing about this either, I'd guess," Spur said looking up at Kane Turner.

The lawyer scowled. "Get me a doctor!"

"The doctors in prison aren't much good, but you have a month or two in jail here before you head to a federal lockup. You might even live."

"I don't know a thing about any counterfeiting," Turner said. "I do keep records for some of my clients. Somebody else put those there. Planted them on me to get me in trouble. It's all circumstantial. You have no proof that I did anything wrong. And you shot me. I'll charge you with attempted murder."

"You're a dreamer, Kane."

Spur heard something behind him and whirled, but there wasn't time. A .44 roared behind him and he felt the pain as a bullet grazed his left shoulder as he went down to one knee. He had no chance for a shot. He couldn't even see his attacker.

"Sloppy, McCoy, damned sloppy police work," a voice said behind him. "You want to live more than a few seconds, ease your hogsleg onto the floor and lay down flat on your belly."

Spur had no choice. He did as he was told. It had to be Hoffer. Sounded lilke his voice. Spur turned and looked.

"Good evening, Mr. McCoy," Hoffer said, the .44 six-gun aimed at Spur's head. "Nice that you could come along on our little trip."

"Josh, get me to a doctor. I'm bleeding like a stuck hog."

"Yes indeed, Kane, right soon. Get your half of the twenties first and wrap them for traveling."

"Travel . . ."

"Right. We can't stay here anymore. McCoy here has probably been working with the sheriff. We've got too much to lose."

Kane helped as they wrapped the box of money with twine, then Turner held the gun on McCoy as they went down to the street by the back stairs. Hoffer put the big box into the back of a surrey beside another one the same size.

"Only rig I've ever seen worth a million dollars," Hoffer said. "Come on, Kane, smile damnit! We're getting out of here clean and taking our little witness along."

"First the doctor!" Turner shrieked.

"Yes, Yes." Hoffer took rawhide from his pocket and tied Spur's wrists together in front of his chest, then ordered him into the rear seat of the surrey.

They drove to Doc Rawson's office. Turner went in by himself and Hoffer watched Spur.

"Never work," Spur said.

"I've got plans," Hoffer said. "I don't like to be pushed around, by anybody. You made a mistake there. I've been working it all out."

"Everybody will be watching for those bogus bills now, in all the states and territories."

Hoffer mopped his brow with a kerchief. "Not rightly possible, because nobody will know about them. You ain't gonna tell nobody nothing about them."

"Only one way to make that work."

"Right, you guessed it, big man. Only this time I make sure the damn hangman's knot is tied right. Got a couple of old timers to make it for me, to tie it right. Guess where the rope is, McCoy, you damned fool? You think I was gonna sit by and let you come in here and threaten me like that? Not a chance."

"You kill me and there'll be twenty federal lawmen in here within two weeks."

"Fine, we won't be anywhere around. They won't never find us, not in a million years." Hoffer chuckled and the nervous tick over his right eye began pulsating again. "Might say we have a million reasons they won't find us." He laughed again.

Spur tried to get the rawhide undone. Hoffer had tied him the right way, one strand and strong knots, no chance to stretch the rawhide. At least his feet were free. He leaned against the boxes holding the counterfeit. He'd never had a million dollar pillow before.

Spur also had to make certain, somehow, that he didn't have a pair of millionaires as his executioner and grave digger.

It was nearly a half hour later when Kane Turner came out of the doctor's office. He carried his jacket and his shirt sleeve was empty, his arm in a sling across his chest.

Turner got into the rig and Hoffer drove away.

"Looks like you'll live," Hoffer said.

"Cut up my shoulder bad. Doc said I shouldn't

even move it for two weeks."

"He always says that. Makes the old fart feel important."

"What now?"

"We go past your place so you can pack a bag of traveling clothes. I got everything I need."

"What about him?" Turner said pointing at Spur.

"Hell, he ain't gonna need much, and he won't eat nothing at all." Hoffer laughed. "I owe that bastard one for threatening me yesterday. Now let's get to your place. Don't bother with your old woman. Just pack some clothes and a couple of six-guns if you got them, and let's get moving."

Spur McCoy narrowed his eyes a little as he considered his situation. Hoffer wanted to hang him, and this time he was sure the fat little man would do it right with a few .44 slugs to make certain. Hoffer wouldn't let him live through the night, that was certain.

Spur had to figure some way to get free and get the jump on Hoffer, before they stopped the rig for the execution if possible.

Damn, getting hung once was plenty. Spur had no desire to be the guest of honor at another hanging.

18

At the Turner house, Hoffer grabbed the lawyer's sleeve before he stepped down.

"I'll give you five minutes, no more. If you're not here in five minutes I'm leaving. Make sure you're here." Hoffer took out a gold watch, popped open the face and read the time. In five minutes it would be dusk. Spur watched Turner go up to his back door and inside. They sat parked in the alley waiting.

Hoffer turned and watched Spur.

"Hear you're some kind of a lawman. Tough turnips! Just one less lawman to worry about. I ain't never been too fond of your type anyway. This is just frosting on the cake for me." He laughed softly and Spur saw his small, close set green eyes darken.

"Damn! but I am gonna enjoy hanging you again. Not many men can brag that they've personally hung the same man twice! Yes sir, I'll have a story to tell!"

Hoffer checked his watch, then put it away.

"Hurry up, lawyer! I ain't got all night to sit here and wait for you. Fact is, if I left now, I'd be twice as rich. A damn fine idea to consider!"

Spur looked down at his boots—and remembered, he had on the new pair, the ones with the knife in the heel! Now he watched the sky darken. When it was dark enough he could pull his right leg up and push the trigger, then it would be a matter of seconds before his hands would be free!

Before he could build a plan, Turner came out the back door, ran to the buggy and pushed a large carpetbag in back next to the boxes of money and beside Spur.

"Let's go!" Turner said.

The whip cracked over the back of the black mare and she stepped out smartly.

Spur knew he would have a better chance if he could get free before they left town. The problem was it wasn't quite dark enough yet, and when he tried to move his right boot, he found his foot wedged under the carpetbag.

"Boise?" Turner asked, "then on to San Francisco. What do you think of that plan? We could pass plenty of the twenties in Frisco."

"Might be worth considering. First we have our necktie party. I want you to watch Spur so he don't get feisty back there. Be a damn shame to have to shoot him and miss a hanging."

Spur could see Turner shaking his head. "I don't know if it's such a good idea to kill a lawman, especially a United States lawman. They are going to do a search." Turner shifted his position so he could see Spur.

"So what? We'll be out of the state by the time they know about it." Hoffer turned and grinned at

Spur. "How does it feel to hear us talking about killing your ass?"

"Like listening to a pair of crazy men talking," Spur said.

Hoffer slammed the handle of the buggy whip at Spur, but only grazed him on the shoulder. It was the same one where the derringer bullet had left a bloody crease. Spur grimaced and settled lower in the back seat of the surrey.

Five minutes later it was fully dark, but they had left the last houses at the edge of town as well. They were heading west along the river road, downstream toward Boise. That was a hundred and forty-five mile ride. Spur knew he would never last that long.

For an hour they drove along. Turner kept looking over the back seat at Spur, and even in the dark he was so close he could tell if Spur tried to cut free his hands. Spur knew he had to wait.

They came to occasional trees along the road, and once the stage trail dipped closer to the river and went through a heavy patch of woods, but Hoffer kept shaking his head. "We got to find exactly the right limb for this sucker to swing from."

Turner appeared to be tiring of his turned position, and gradually he edged back more forward. Soon his back was to Spur and it was time!

Spur edged his leg out from under the carpetbag and with his left hand pulled his right boot up on his left leg. He watched the two in the front seat but they were talking softly about something. He pushed the small trigger in front of the boot heel and saw the glint of the blade. Carefully he placed his bound wrists next to the blade, adjusted, then moved them again until the blade touched the rawhide.

Then he sawed back and forth with his wrists.

The blade bit into his flesh and he could feel the warm blood dripping. He looked again in the dimness of the bad light and adjusted his wrists and sawed again.

Hoffer turned and looked at Spur.

"You care what kind of a tree I use to hang you from, McCoy?" Hoffer laughed. "Be poetic if it was another oak tree, but we'll probably have to settle for a maple, or maybe even a pine or a fir. Going to get farther away from town, so just rest yourself. You try anything funny and you get gut shot. That way you'll live for an hour or so and we can still hang you!" Hoffer laughed again and whacked the reins against the mare who picked up the pace a little.

Spur had not moved while Hoffer talked to him. Now he tried again, slicing harder, faster with the razor sharp blade. He felt one strand part, then the second and his hands came apart. He pushed the blade back in place.

Cautiously and with no sound he opened the carpetbag, hoping against hope that Turner had put an extra six gun in it. His hands explored the bag silently, no gun.

He took out a heavy wool sweater and considered it. It was the pullover type and would work for one. He checked the surrey. It was the open kind with a roof but no side curtains of any kind. The buggy whip rode in its holder fastened on the left side of the driver's seat for easy access by the driver.

It also was within easy reach for Spur. He held the sweater in his lap with the opening spread and waited. Then he reached carefully forward and lifted the whip out of its holder without a sound.

He was ready. Spur put the whip across his lap, picked up the sweater and in one swift movement, leaned over the front seat, jerked the open part of the sweater downward over Kane Turner's head and at the same time, pushed him so he toppled out of the open side of the surrey.

Without a wasted move Spur grabbed the thin leather end of the buggy whip, threw it around Hoffer's head, then pulled both ends backward sharply choking the killer with his own whip.

Turner screamed as he fell out of the surrey in his blinded condition and hit the roadway hard.

Spur shouted at the horse to giddap and at the same time pulled the leather whip tighter and tighter around Hoffer's neck.

Then Hoffer did something Spur had not anticipated. He surged backwards, both hands over his head, grasping, clawing for Spur's face or head. One of his hands caught Spur's bandage around his throat and he yanked forward, half tearing the bandage away, sending waves of pain through Spur. In his agony Spur dropped the whip, tore Hoffer's hands from his neck, and jumped out of the rig.

He hit on the rutted dirt of the trail, rolled once and sprang to his feet, running at right angles to the roadway and the surrey. Here they were a mile from the river, but each valley held scatterings of pine, fir and heavy underbrush.

Spur charged for the dark shapes of the trees maybe two hundred yards ahead. He heard Hoffer shouting behind him. A pistol cracked twice, but Hoffer had no idea which direction Spur had run in the solid darkness. The shots went wild.

McCoy kept running. He heard the men talking behind him. Hoffer screaming that of course they had to find him. He would expose their whole scheme. Everything was ruined if Spur got away.

Spur stopped running and listened. They stopped

shouting but some of the words still came through.

They would stop there for the night, and find him in the morning. Take turns sleeping in the rig. No fire, that would bring him back.

Yes, they would keep their guns ready!

Spur sat on the ground and took stock. He felt the bandage and did what he could to get it back in position to cover his aching throat. Doc Rawson would be furious. Still it was better than testing another hangman's noose.

He looked back and could hear sounds as the pair began getting ready to spend the night. The horse was unhitched. Spur grinned. That was their first mistake.

Neither of them seemed to be an outdoorsman. Both had spent most of their time indoors, in court or in a store. He would have the advantage here.

What he needed was a gun. Could he slip up on them, knock out or kill the one awake silently, and get his gun?

The odds were not on his side.

If he tried and failed, he was a dead man.

Another idea was needed. Spur continued to the woods. He had checked his pockets and found nothing useful, not even a pen knife. He had no sheath knife on his belt. The only blade he had was on his boot. He sat down and triggered it into place, then tried to detach it. He could not see well enough to figure it out. Spur found a double fist sized rock, put his heel on the ground and broke the blade off his boot. It was an inch and a half long, but sharp.

An hour later, Spur had made two spears, not very straight, but sharpened to needle points. He spent another two hours scouting a good spot to ambush the pair. They would move together to protect each other.

A pit would be good if he had a shovel.

His Spencer repeating rifle would be better.

Spur quit dreaming.

They were about ten miles from town. He could start walking now and get to Twin Falls by morning. But only if one of them had gone down the trail toward town to watch for him. Both men could shoot. He would be dead a mile down the road.

The second obvious solution was to disable the horse and put the men on foot. That way he would have the advantage.

Or disable the surrey.

Well before dawn, Spur decided the horse had to be put down. He had made four more spears. The best was six feet long and sharp as a pencil point. He went back to the stage road and left a trail in the dust that even Hoffer should be able to follow. It went back toward town.

After a quarter of a mile the stage road went through an arm of the wooded area. Trees and brush grew close on both sides. Spur spent another hour dragging logs and brush and downed limbs into the middle of the road to make a barricade. It was just around a corner so the driver would have no chance to see it before he had to stop.

Spur picked his attack point carefully, then screened it from the roadway with more broken brush so neither man on the rig could see him until it was too late.

Spur sat against a tree then and went to sleep. Each time he slept four or five minutes he would fall away from the tree and wake up.

He stayed awake the last time he came to and found the sun just coming up.

McCoy checked his spears and his retreat plan, then climbed a friendly fir tree and looked down the trail toward Boise.

He saw one man on the stage road, and it was obvious that he had found Spur's tracks. Soon the surrey joined him and both men rode toward the trap.

Spur went down the tree, positioned himself behind his blind and waited.

He could hear the jingle of the harness and the singletree long before he saw the surrey. The sounds came closer and then the rig came around the bend in the trail.

Spur had positioned himself at the point where the rig probably would stop after Hoffer saw the brush pile. The horse was just across from him now.

Spur leaped out of the blind, with the six foot long and inch and a half diameter spear poised and ran forward with it like a lance, and point aimed directly at the mare's heaving side.

Hoffer saw him and shouted. Turner swept around with his pistol, but hit the roof supports and swore. Hoffer tried to get his six-gun up, but he was too late.

Spur lunged forward with the spear, driving it all the way through the animal, smashing one rib, separating another on the far side, tearing through vital organs.

The Secret Agent darted around the front of the horse and bolted into the deep brush five feet away on the far side of the roadway. Hoffer got off one shot that went high. Turner never did fire. He had banged his wounded shoulder and screamed in agony.

Once outside the covering trees, Spur stopped and peered back at the horse. The mare screamed in mortal pain and he heard her going down, thrashing on the ground in the harness and the traces. She screamed again, a nerve jangling sound, but it cut off suddenly with the report of a pistol shot.

Then all was quiet.

"Now, you sons of bitches, I'm coming to get you," Spur said quietly.

Spur found a point where he could watch the pair of tenderfoots as he peered around a fir tree so they could not see him. They opened the boxes of money and held it, threw it down and stormed around. He could not hear what they said. They found a small shovel on the surrey and tried to bury the money. Both gave up long before they had a hole deep enough.

At last they stuffed their carpetbags with as many of the stacks of bills as they could carry and began walking down the stage road toward Boise.

As he waited, Spur had worked on constructing a bow. He had found a flexible piece of maple and tried it. Not the best, but with the laces from his boot he had a serviceable bowstring. Then he found willow and cut some arrows that would be enough to scare the pair. He had to drive them away from the stage road, and any chance of them catching the stage heading for Boise.

Spur cut back to the stage road three miles ahead. He was forward of the heavily loaded pair. He found his spot. The road followed a narrow valley that passed near a sharp cliff. Spur went to the top of the sixty foot dropoff and gathered a dozen, fifty pound boulders. Then he sat down and sharpened six more arrows and waited. He had no feathers or any way to attach them. The rocks might be more effective.

A half hour later he spotted the counterfeiting pair coming along the road. They were moving slow, dragging along, the paper money much heavier now than when they had packed it in the carpetbags.

They found the cut and moved at once to the shady side, right under where Spur lay above.

He readied four of the boulders, placing them on the brink of the cliff, then pushed them over as quickly as he could. All four thundered down, hitting the cliff, knocking loose more rocks and sand. Hoffer heard them coming and darted out of the way.

Turner was slower. He lifted up, tried to push with his shot up arm and it folded. One of the fifty pound rocks caught him squarely on the left knee and smashed it, dropping him to the ground where a dozen other smaller rocks hit him as they raced past.

Turner screamed at Hoffer to help him. Hoffer looked up at the cliff and shook his head.

"Only one way you can help me now, asshole," he said. "That is not to slow me down." Hoffer ran back toward Turner, then looked up and saw two more rocks coming. Hoffer stood and aimed carefully with his pistol. He fired four times. Three of the rounds hit Kane Turner in the chest, slashing through his heart and lungs, killing him instantly.

"Now it's all mine!" Hoffer screamed. "I'm a millionaire!"

Spur shot one arrow at him. It went straight for a ways, then slanted to the left and tumbled to the ground. Spur knew he would have to do a lot more work on the arrows so they would function without feathers. He needed to lighten the tails because he could not make the points heavier.

Hoffer put two shots into the top of the cliff and reloaded.

"You're a dead man, Spur McCoy. You just don't know it yet. I'm no tenderfoot out here, and remember I have the guns. He ran forward toward Turner's body, but turned back. Spur kept dropping more rocks at the right time to keep Hoffer away. Turner must have a weapon! Spur wanted it.

After ten minutes, Hoffer shot twice more at Spur, then threw out half of the stacks of bills, and began to run down the stage road toward Boise. Now it looked like he would take the stage no matter which way it was headed.

When Spur was sure Hoffer was gone, he worked around to the side of the cliff and went down. He checked Turner's body and found a well worn .44, a holster and a gunbelt with another twenty rounds. Spur stripped the gun belt off the dead man, went through his pockets and found a pen knife, but little else of value. He strapped the gun belt on, discarding his useless one with the .45 rounds in it.

"Now, Hoffer, the odds are evened up just a little bit. I'm coming to nail your carcass, and then hang you!"

19

His big fist hefted the six-gun, slid it into leather, then pulled it out and aimed. He did that five times, each time getting a little faster, more familiar with the new weapon.

The iron had a different feel to it, a different balance than the Colt .45 Spur usually carried— but any hogleg in a storm.

He took one more look at Kane Turner, then jogged in the general direction Josh Hoffer had taken. He left the road that made only a scratch on the surface of the bold Idaho land, and worked his way up to an open spot. From the height he could see three miles in both directions along the stage road.

Far to the right, heading west, he saw a solitary figure moving steadily along the road. Hoffer.

Walking. How far would he go before he elected to wait for the stage?

Spur looked to the west. At the far end of his view of the road he saw a thin trail of dust rising into the sky. He waited a moment more and knew the rig was coming toward him.

The stage from Boise heading for Twin Falls!

Without consciously making the decision, Spur ran downhill. He moved at an angle to cut off Hoffer before the stage arrived. Could he do it?

Spur slowed his charge down the hill, held onto the flapping holster and resumed his Indian trot. A Mescalero Apache had taught him the technique one summer. The idea was that a man alone in the mountains or desert could outrun a man or a horse if he knows how.

Spur learned how. The gait was faster than walking, but was not an actual run, more of a trot, with one foot barely leaving the ground before the other one touched. The Apaches could set a pace at six to eight miles an hour, and keep it up for ten hours straight.

Spur knew he could get the two miles to the stage road, but he wasn't sure where Hoffer would be. He couldn't have seen the stage coming yet. Spur changed his angle so he moved slightly west, which would put him between Hoffer and the stage. He had another idea that just might work, no matter where Hoffer was hiding.

The first mile went easily, with Spur breaking a sweat after the first ten minutes. He was closer now, and could not see the spiral of dust over the slight rise in the stage road. For that he was thankful because Hoffer couldn't see it either.

He ran, sticking as close to six miles an hour as he could, and when he looked up at the stage trail the next time, he saw the dust, and a black dot moving toward him.

Five minutes later he came to the road and checked to the east, but Hoffer was not in sight.

There was no chance that Hoffer was west of Spur, so the plan would work.

He dragged the remains of a downed fir tree across the trail. The tree was only four inches in diameter and twenty feet tall. It would not even slow down a charging stage coach. And Spur intended for it to be charging. He picked his spot near a pair of man-sized boulders, and checked the six-gun. It held four rounds. He put two more in and let the hammer down carefully.

Spur stayed out of sight as the coach came closer. Then as the rig rolled within fifty yards, it started to slow when it saw the tree across the main track. There was plenty of room on either side to drive around it in this flat, open country.

About the time the driver decided to go around the tree, Spur jumped up and charged the stage, his six-gun out. He fired two shots in the air, and when the driver looked in his direction, fired twice more well in front of the horses. The driver hunkered down and slapped the reins on the team of six, urging them faster. A pistol cracked out the side window of the coach and Spur dove for the dirt.

He fired his last two rounds as the coach whipped past him in a swirl of dust. Spur dumped out the brass, loaded three more and fired them into the air as the coach raced away.

The Secret Service Agent grinned at the vanishing coach. The driver would be spooked enough that he wouldn't even slow down no matter who was standing beside the road trying to stop him for a ride. And what a story he would have to tell when he got to Twin Falls!

Spur walked toward Twin Falls for half a mile to a patch of woods, found himself a good observation point and settled down to wait. Hoffer would be coming along soon, he had no other choice of a place to go. The next stage would be heading for Boise, but it might not come for several hours.

An hour later Spur still waited. He decided if Hoffer didn't show up in another hour, Spur would start back-tracking him.

Josh Hoffer did not come. Spur stared down the stage road as far as he could see. There was no sign of anyone.

Spur sighed and began walking back toward where Josh Hoffer had last been seen, not much more than a half mile. When Spur came to the spot along the roadway he could see Hoffer's tracks, then where his footprints had crossed the new prints made by the horses and stage.

Spur looked up. The counterfeiter's tracks headed for a small grove of trees at the side of a ravine a quarter of a mile away. Hoffer was looking for some shade; he was not used to the burning sun and the outdoors.

A half hour later Spur edged into the trees from the side, moved cautiously toward the point nearest the stage road, and scanned the wooded area carefully.

He could not see Hoffer. Without making a sound, Spur moved up to the edge of the woods until he had checked behind every tree. Hoffer was not hiding there.

Spur creased his brow, slapped his hat against his leg to dislodge some of the dust, and went back to the open area. It took him three crossings before he found Hoffer's tracks. The tenderfoot had angled around the woods and moved into the mouth of the small canyon.

Spur eyed the area. It could be a trap with Hoffer just inside the opening of the rock sided ravine, waiting for Spur to fall into the snare. McCoy followed the tracks another hundred yards until he was sure they led into the ravine, then ran to one side and came up at the edge of the opening.

The gully was maybe fifty yards wide at the mouth, held a dry stream bed and a few spots of brush, but no real trees. The soil was sandy and rocky here and the arroyo angled into the low range of hills, bent sharply to the left and continued.

There was no ambush point near the opening. Spur walked across the entrance slowly, scanning the ground, and soon came up with the counterfeiter's bootprints. They led directly up the center of the little canyon.

Spur eyed the area critically. There was shade higher in the canyon, and there well could be a spring that fed the trees. Hoffer must be out of water and be hunting a drink. Spur could think of no other reason the fugitive would leave the stage road and wander back in the hills.

There was nothing to do but dig him out. Spur eyed the iron he carried and wished he knew more about it. But the twenty rounds he had for the .44 did not give him the luxury of sighting in the weapon.

The big U.S. Secret Service agent pushed the iron back in its leather home and watched the ground as he tracked Hoffer into the canyon. Here and there, sheet rock slanted down toward the creek, but another fifty yards ahead the ground was soft again and Spur picked up the tracks.

He had moved less than a quarter of a mile when he came to the bend and decided a small recon was in order. He should have a point man to send out, but this was a long time after the war. He peered over a boulder into this part of the canyon. It was much narrower, less than fifty feet now of level ground between slabs of basalt and granite that slanted upward.

Above, a cloud skittered over the sun, blocking it out for a moment. Spur looked up and saw a row of thunderheads building. They could mean refreshing rain, a thunderstorm, possibly lightning as well.

He went back to the matter at hand. There were some slabs of rock ahead where Hoffer could be hiding. He saw no blush of new green that might show where a spring seeped from the ground, though there should be a spring somewhere in there.

Spur saw a dove fly up from a perch ahead, but there was no more activity. The bird probably had not been flushed up by Hoffer.

Where *was* the bastard?

Spur checked the next cover, several yards up the gentle incline of the canyon and on the left side. It would be his emergency objective.

Hoffer was still going up the valley. Halfway to the boulder, Spur found a twenty dollar bill, one of the counterfeits. Spur put it in his pocket and kept moving. The length of Hoffer's stride was shorter now and the toes were dragging dirt with each step.

Hoffer was getting tired. How much farther could he go?

When Spur got to the boulder, he paused. The canyon went straight ahead for what looked like a mile, moving up the mountain gradually and narrowing slightly. Hoffer could be anywhere up there. Trees dotted the sides of the canyon now, and ahead the entire floor and sides were carpeted with evergreens.

Spur tried to put himself in Hoffer's place. Why had he come up here except for water and shade? There was no good reason. It was getting hotter, and so far no water. Hoffer might be lost, disoriented and simply going the wrong way. Possible. He might even have lost his mind.

McCoy scanned the area ahead. There was no sign of another human being. If Hoffer continued in this direction he would have a two hundred mile walk before he found a house or a settlement.

The merchant had to be out of his mind. Spur stood and found the tracks and moved forward again. He had picked out an emergency shelter twenty yards forward, but kept his glance mostly on the tracks.

The toes were digging short trails now with each step, dragging in the dirt before lifting out on every move. It was the sign of a man almost at the end of his endurance.

Far off to the west, Spur heard a roll of thunder. The storm was coming.

He concentrated on the prints. There was no walking stick or crutch or cane. Hoffer should be good for another mile before he collapsed.

The shot came as a surprise to Spur. He heard the report and almost at once a round whistled past his head. Spur dove into the dirt and rolled, came to his feet and sprinted ten yards left to his boulder for cover. One round whined off the granite upthrust and Spur ducked lower.

"McCoy, you asshole! Why don't you leave me alone?"

It was Hoffer's voice, strained, scratchy, but lucid.

"Hoffer—out for a nice little walk? Looks like you're getting tired. How about a drink from my canteen?"

Another slug slammed off the rock that protected Spur.

"I'll take your whole canteen just as soon as I ventilate your body with lead!"

"You're not much better shooting a man than you are at hanging him, Hoffer."

Three more shots hit the big boulder. Spur grinned. He wondered how many cartridges the man had.

"Come get me, you damned lawman!"

"No hurry," Spur said. "Figure to wait a while. I got water and grub, wait until you get so thirsty that you can't even spit."

Two more shots churned the air just over the top of the boulder.

Spur looked around the far side. There was more cover ten yards ahead. He could waste two shots and get that far in one rush. He watched the rocks ahead and to the right and soon saw a hat poke up, then two eyes and a sixgun.

"Gotcha!" Spur said softly. He pulled his feet under him, crouching, ready to spring forward. The hat came a little higher and Spur sent one round at it, then jolted forward and fired one more shot before he slid behind the new location and waited.

"Moved, I'd wager," Hoffer said. "Not that it matters, but you were right about prison. I did six years hard time in New York, got out, dug up fifty thousand dollars I had hidden and began passing it until I had ten thousand good dollars. Then I came West and opened up my store, or rather bought in and then married the rest of it." He laughed. "Hell, that's a better way than printing money—marry it! Of course it can be a little hard on the nerves."

"So why did you try counterfeiting again?"

"It's like a fever. I got a plate and my tools, and once I got started it's like painting a picture. You have to finish it. I'm good. One of the best alive. Always have been. I'm an artist."

"You're a killer. You shot down both your partners."

"I didn't need them anymore. Partners become a liability. Nothing personal, just business."

Spur used two more rounds as he rushed forward again. He reloaded his revolver as he lay behind a smaller boulder. He had sixteen rounds left. He had to remember that.

"I'm going to take you in, Hoffer."

"Not a chance. I'll save my last round for my own brain if it comes to that. I figured I'd get you up here away from the stage, kill you and then walk out and catch the stage no matter which way it was going. With you dead it wouldn't matter. And I'd have almost a million dollars, all my own!"

"But first you have to kill me, Hoffer." Spur stood up suddenly. "Over here, Hoffer!" he shouted, paused a moment then dropped behind the rock.

Six shots came in rapid order, over and around and into the rock, but none of them hit Spur. He checked the rounds in his belt loops again, and stared in disbelief. The ammunition was all for a .45 weapon. He had taken four from the near end and they were .44 and fit, but there was only one more .44 round. He was suddenly down to six rounds, not sixteen!

Lightning zig-zagged through the darkening sky to the west, and in seconds the rumbling thunder rolled over them.

"You're going to get wet," Spur shouted.

"*You're* going to get dead!"

Spur saw the intensity of the rain as it battered the ridge just to the west, moving toward them. A dozen more lightning bolts stabbed the earth and Spur looked at the sides of the canyon. Too steep to climb, but there were a few spots where he could get up part way. He watched the rain up the canyon and knew it was a cloudburst. He fired one shot at Hoffer's rock, retreated ten yards and slanted twenty more up the side of the ravine.

The higher ground seemed like a good idea, a damn good plan!

Hoffer tried to move, but Spur pinned him down with another shot. (He was down to four, but Hoffer didn't know that.) Spur made one more dash up the slope and threw himself into the dirt behind a boulder and a pine tree just as three shots jolted the foot thick pine.

"Good shooting," Spur called.

A moment later the rain hit them, light at first, then a downpour. Spur spent one more round sending it just over Hoffer's rock. Hoffer edged over the rock and then dropped down. Spur had to fire again; he did, hitting the rock. Two rounds left.

Before Hoffer could try to move, Spur heard it. At first it was a soft rumble that he thought was thunder, then it turned harsher and a moment later was a driving roar. He looked above, up the side of the canyon wall. There was no other safe spot. Spur guessed he was forty feet above the bottom of the gully and he had a rooted tree to hang onto.

"What the hell is that thunder when there ain't no lightning?" Hoffer screeched over the sound of the rain.

Spur didn't tell him. Once before he had been caught in a ravine during a thunderstorm and had nearly drowned as he learned his lesson.

The roar became louder and as Spur looked through the rain he could see the growing wall of water a half mile away, racing, roaring and crashing down the water course. His only hope was that by the time it reached him, it would have spread out enough to pass below his forty foot elevation.

Spur put one more round into the soft soil behind the rock where Hoffer crouched.

One shot left.

"Like the rain, Hoffer?"

"Wet as hell. Why don't the two of us call a truce until it stops?"

"No truces and no prisoners, that's my new motto, Hoffer."

The gunman below fired three times, and a chip of bark from the pine tree tore into Spur's cheek. Blood ran down his face. He wiped it away and looked at the raging waters.

"That noise!" Hoffer shouted. "A damn flood is coming down this gully. We got to get out of here!" Hoffer ended on a scream of terror.

"You move a foot away from that rock and I'll cut you in half with six .44 slugs!" Spur bellowed. "Just give me the chance, killer!"

Hoffer edged over the rock, then dropped down. He stood up once, then dropped just as Spur sent a round through the space he had been in a fraction of a second before.

Spur checked the gun belt again. Damn! He was out of ammunition!

The roar increased; he could barely shout over it.

"Give me another chance, Hoffer. It's a nice, clean way to die!"

Hoffer snarled four rounds at Spur, then hunkered down out of sight.

Spur watched the water. He could climb maybe ten feet up the pine tree if he had to. Lower limbs had died and broken off, leaving sturdy spike-like hand and foot holds up the trunk.

The water was less than a hundred yards away. Spur watched it and Hoffer's rock. The little man had not moved.

The water crashed and smashed through the bottom of the canyon. It must be moving faster than a horse could gallop—twenty, maybe twenty-five miles an hour! As fast as a railroad train!

Spur looked out and saw that he was almost level with the top of the flood waters. Logs boiled and churned in the flood, trees popping to the surface.

Below he could see large boulders roll. Then the upper part of the water overwhelmed them as it surged lower, seeking its level.

When the water was twenty yards away, Hoffer must have seen it clearly.

"NOOOO!" he screeched, jumped up and fired once at Spur, then hobbled downstream. His right leg had been injured, and he dragged it as he tried to run.

The water came surging almost on top of them then, and Spur scrambled up the tree, hoping the tree roots and rocks on the side of the canyon wall would hold.

20

Spur watched the water surge against his tree. It was three feet below his boots. He looked down at Hoffer.

The fat little man was running now, his hurt leg forgotten as he charged down the slight incline. But the water charged faster. A surge of foamy water teased his feet and he slipped. Then the thirty-foot high thundering mountain of water billowed over him, sucking him into its center, crashing down on top of him and churning him into the middle of a vast maelstrom of angry water, plunging tree trunks, brush and limbs from the timbered slopes above.

Spur watched downstream as far as he could see, but there was no sign of Josh Hoffer.

Spur looked to the west, sunshine gleaming on the wet mountains.

The rain slackened, then misted and at last stopped.

He could see the water dropping lower and lower

below him. Five minutes later, the water was low
enough so Spur could climb back down to the base of
the pine. A slippery coating of mud clung to the
sides of the canyon. When he went down it, he would
be on a greased slide.

After another twenty minutes the sun broke
through overhead as the storm slashed on toward
the east.

It was over an hour before the water had drained
away. Now there was only a small stream in the
center of the canyon. Spur began to move down the
wall. There was no way to climb up. He lost his
footing and skidded, dropped to a sitting position
and slid down the side to a big rock that stopped
him.

He stood, wiped some of the mud off his pants and
picked his way cautiously the last twenty feet to the
bottom of the canyon.

Mud, branches and a log now and then clogged the
small valley. He made his way lower. As he went, he
watched for any sign of the body.

There was no chance that Hoffer could have survived such an onslaught. If he had lived long enough
without oxygen to get to the surface, the flotsom
and current would have torn his body apart.

Spur spent another hour moving down the gully,
watching everywhere that a body might be lodged,
but found nothing. By the time he came out of the
mouth of the canyon into the valley itself, he was
wondering if he could ever prove that Josh Hoffer
had been drowned in the flash flood. The sheriff
would be extremely interested in such proof.

Spur checked the mouth of the gully again,
crawled over a muddy pile of trees and branches,
then gave up.

He sat on a dry spot and let the sun dry the water out of his clothes.

The stage coach driver would report the shots, and he surely would see the dead man alongside the stage road. That he would report to the sheriff. When the rig came to the dead horse and the surrey, the driver would have to stop it and move the horse, or at least the brush Spur had piled up to stop the surrey. When he did that, he would find the boxes almost filled with twenty dollar bills. The passengers would go wild. So might the driver.

But if Spur knew the character of these stage coach drivers, he would gather the money and turn it over to the sheriff, which meant the sheriff should have known about the money and the dead man about two hours after the coach passed here. It would take another two hours for the sheriff and a posse to ride to the scene.

Spur stood and angled for the stage road. He would walk back to the surrey and wait for the sheriff. Hopefully the posse would bring along an extra horse. Then he could have some help in searching for Hoffer's body.

By the time Spur stumbled into the shade where the surrey and dead horse were, he was too tired to wonder how far he had walked. Only two or three miles, but he was dead tired. He looked down the road toward town and saw that the brush had been pulled out of the roadway, but he could see no one coming. It could be a while.

Spur stretched out in the shade and went to sleep.

The first thing Spur heard when he awoke was the cocking of a six-gun. He didn't move. A boot lowered slowly but firmly on his right hand that lay by his side.

"I got a live one over here, Sheriff!" the man over Spur called.

"Look, I . . ."

"Not another word until the sheriff gets here!" the man said with a touch of anger. "Right over here, Sheriff."

Spur could hear men moving over the ground, then a soft chuckle.

"Okay, Lon, you can ease off. He's one of the good guys."

"Huh?"

"He's not the killer we're looking for."

"Oh."

The boot moved.

"You can sit up now, McCoy, without getting your head blown off."

Spur came to a sitting position slowly and saw Sheriff Sloan holding a Henry repeating rifle.

"Looks like you took a mudbath. That before or after you shot Turner?"

"After Joshua Hoffer shot him. Way after. You get the counterfeit back?"

"From the stage?"

"Right."

"Two packages. Had to search the passengers. Found another two thousand dollars. I think we have it all."

"There's more out along the trail somewhere. Hope you can spare a man or two to help me look for it."

"Possible."

"You wouldn't have a spare horse, would you? I got a free ride in the surrey with my hands tied and a gun aimed at my midsection. Hoffer wanted to hang me again!"

"Looks like he didn't quite make it. Where *is* Hoffer? Or is that too delicate a question?"

"I want to find him as bad as you do, Sheriff. Last time I saw him a flash flood about thirty feet high was crashing down on top of him in a gully up the road."

"But it missed you. You didn't happen to hang the Jasper first, did you? Then dump him in the flood?"

"If he's got a neck left, you can check for rope burns. You found Turner. I got lucky with a boulder from the cliff and busted up his leg. Hoffer didn't want to wait for Turner, so he killed him."

"Eye witness?"

"Right."

The sheriff shifted his stance, looked at Spur, then his hand brushed past his six-gun.

"Those are two of the leading citizens of our town. Hoffer wasn't by any chance just along for the ride, was he?"

Spur grinned. "Hell no. He was the brains, the third man, the engraver, in this counterfeiting scheme. I figure that was one reason he wanted me hanged out there at the Ned Bailey place when we first met."

"And you say Hoffer is dead in the gully somewhere?"

"Probably under some brush, or hung up on a log or a rock and covered up by a foot of silt. Still wish I had the chance to hang him. He went too easy, too fast."

"Dead is dead."

Spur grunted. "You got a horse for me? I'll show you where if you want to check it out. I could also use your canteen."

An hour later five men began picking their way through the outfall of the death canyon. Hoffer was there somewhere; all they had to do was uncover him.

It was almost dusk when one of the horses shied away and backed up from a pile of brush. Hoffer was under it. The men dug him out and Sheriff Sloan washed off his neck with water from his canteen.

"Neck is broken," the sheriff said. "But no rope marks." He looked at Spur. "I'm glad about that. Now let's get the rest of that money found before dark and get things moving."

The men cleaned up the area near the surrey and hitched one of the extra horses they had trailed in the traces. They loaded Turner's body in and found a dozen packets of money on the body. Spur threw the cash in a gunny sack. Turner's carpetbag was half full of the packets of bills. The men in the posse looked at the cash and couldn't believe it. Spur showed them the serial numbers—all the same, all counterfeit.

Where the two counterfeiters had lightened their luggage of packets of bills, the men picked up another hundred thousand dollars' worth.

Then the real search began along both sides of the trail as they tried to find where Hoffer had hidden his carpetbag with the rest of the fake money.

Spur offered the man who found the bag a double eagle gold piece. Interest picked up. Twenty dollars was a month's wages for lots of men around Twin Falls.

An out-of-work cowboy found the bag behind some heavy brush fifty feet off the stage road. Spur handed him the twenty dollar gold piece as the rest cheered.

They had carried Hoffer's body back to the surrey and they now loaded the merchant's remains in the back seat and got the small party under way. They had a mount for Spur. He talked with the sheriff, then rode out ahead with two other men and hurried back toward Twin Falls. It was almost eight o'clock when they arrived.

Spur had a long, hot bath, then the best steak in the dining room. He had just finished eating when Sheriff Sloan pulled up a chair and stared hard at him.

"You wrapped up here?"

"Not quite."

"If you're thinking about young Boots Dallman, don't. I went back over my memory, and I can't remember a single thing he did to help the lynchers. He didn't even hold their horses."

"He was too drunk to know what was going on," Spur said.

"Then why not leave him alone?"

"Boots? Wouldn't think of hurting him. Fact is, I had a nice lóng chat with him and his wife just a couple of days ago."

"That so? And you didn't hang him?"

"Not a chance. Seems like a solid citizen. He even swore on his mother's grave and in front of his wife that he was giving up booze and wild women."

The sheriff looked relieved. "Sounds like you scared the shit out of him."

Spur laughed. "You might say that."

"Then you are through here?"

"Not quite. You and I still have to find the engraved plates those bills were printed from."

"Hoffer's Mercantile?"

" 'Pears as how. You free for the evening?"

An hour later they were still hunting. Mrs. Hoffer watched them critically, making them put back every box they opened, and keep the store in order.

"I want to open up in the morning, and goodness knows I can't with things spread all around!"

She knew nothing of the counterfeiting though she had been married to Hoffer for three years. Her ex-husband had started the Mercantile twenty years ago and built it into a thriving business before he died in the smallpox epidemic of sixty-eight.

"I ran it before, I can run it again," she told the sheriff calmly when he informed her of Hoffer's death. She knew nothing of his former life, nothing at all.

"Where in hell would *you* hide two engraving plates?" Spur asked the sheriff.

"Somewhere no one would think to look. Like in a framed picture on the wall?"

They checked the four hanging pictures, but none contained the plates.

Mrs. Hoffer suggested the cracker barrel, but the wooden barrel did not harbor the plates.

Spur next looked at the bean bin. It was a wooden affair that held about twenty gallons and was nearly full of white navy beans.

He pushed his hand into the bin and found nothing.

Mrs. Hoffer came up clucking, "No, no! We'll take them out with a scoop into a flour sack. We keep things as clean as we can around here. Notice the covers over the beans and flour and crackers?"

She scooped and Spur held the sack. Halfway down in the bean bin, they found the plates, carefully wrapped in heavy waxed paper.

Spur took them out, broke each one in half over his knee then stared at them.

"Beautiful work," Spur said. "The man was an artist."

Mrs. Hoffer snorted. "He was also a criminal and

a murderer. You say he killed poor Mr. Winter-garden, too?"

The sheriff said Hoffer had admitted to shooting Wintergarden. He thanked Mrs. Hoffer and Spur re-wrapped the plates in the waxed paper.

"Now, Sheriff, I'm starting to finish my work. Next on my agenda is a thin cheroot and a long, peaceful night's sleep."

"The counterfeit bills—what should we do with them?"

"Tomorrow we'll have a bonfire. We'll need wit-nesses. We'll burn them in a fireplace or a stove so we can control it. Tonight, keep the boxes in one of your cells. I have another two thousand dollars' worth I'll donate to the fire tomorrow."

They stood there a minute remembering.

"Oh, did you tell the widow Turner about her loss?"

"Yes, this afternoon when the stage came in. The driver checked the body and found identification on it. So I told her. Strange, she didn't seem very upset. I'd guess the widow Turner will not have a long period of mourning."

Spur thanked the sheriff and went back to his hotel room. The door was locked. Good. He was feeling the effects of almost no sleep the night before and the long walk. A visitor right now would not be welcome.

He stepped inside his door, locked it and moved to the dresser where he struck a match and lit the lamp.

A woman laughed softly behind him. He turned, holding the lamp, and saw Eugenia Turner sitting on the bed. Beside her was Sue, the girl from the laundry. Both were bare to the waist, and Eugenia had her arms around the younger girl.

"Well, it's about time you got back," Eugenia said sweetly. "We got tired of waiting for you, so we decided to start without you."

"Hello, Mr. McCoy," the younger girl said. "I thought it might be nice to come visiting and see if you can help me get a better job. I hope you don't mind." She stretched, and her naked breasts surged forward and danced a highland fling.

She put her hands down and cupped both her breasts. "My titties have been just waiting for you to come!"

"Isn't she a delight!" Eugenia said. "She's so young and unspoiled and eager to please. At first I resented her waiting here for you when I came in. Then we began to talk and we decided you had more than enough for both of us, and we're both understanding, so we decided to share you!"

The women stood and undressed Spur slowly, stripping off his clothes, giggling and feeling his muscles and remarking how strong he was and how well built.

Sue drew the honor of pulling down his underwear and when his penis popped out stiff and sturdy, she squealed and knelt down, took half of it in her mouth and began sucking.

"Darling, you have to take your turn," Eugenia said, pushing Sue away. They urged Spur back on the bed and then eagerly stripped off the rest of their clothes. At once each began ministering to him.

Sue hovered over him, then lowered one big breast into his mouth. Spur caught it, chewed and licked it and purred.

"I think I'm in heaven and the angels have just arrived," he said.

As he said it, Eugenia kissed the tip of his manhood and then took the whole shaft in her mouth. Spur almost climaxed.

He controlled himself and soon had the tables reversed, with the women sitting on the bed as he sampled the four hanging tits. Sue's were large, with a little sag from their bulk and large pink areolas topped by blushing pink nipples that grew and quivered when he licked them.

Spur concentrated on the younger girl a moment, his mouth on her breasts, one hand exploring between her legs, and she suddenly screamed. Her whole body went rigid and she fell backwards on the bed and jolted through the most intense climax Spur had ever seen in a woman.

Eugenia slid back on the bed, her eyes wide, one hand covering her mouth.

It was over in twenty seconds, and Sue sat up and wiped sweat off her forehead.

"Damn! That was fine!" she said. "I win the prize, I beat everybody."

They all laughed.

"What we need is some wine and cheese," Spur said.

Eugenia pointed to two paper sacks near the door. "That comes later," she said. "Fuck first, food second."

The strain of the past two days seeped out of Spur as he rolled over on Eugenia, spread her legs and without any preliminaries, drove his tool deeply into her.

She whimpered for a minute, then swore at him and her hips began a pounding against him that he had to rush to keep up with.

Sue sat naked beside them, observing them with interest.

"Watch and learn," Sue said as the naked bodies

rocked together in perfect rhythm to the explosion that sent them both into temporary oblivion. They had both climaxed at nearly the same time.

"Hell, I'm going to see what we have to eat," Sue said then. She opened the sacks and spread the food out on the dresser top beside the lamp. There was another lamp in the closet and she got it out, lit it and put it on the wash stand.

Spur and Eugenia joined her a few minutes later.

"We have two kinds of wine, and three kinds of crackers and two kinds of cheese," Eugenia said.

Spur sampled both kinds of wine and the cheese, sitting on the room's only chair, a straight-back wooden one. Sue came over, bent for him to kiss her breasts, then pushed his legs apart and quickly brought him to erection with her mouth from where she knelt in front of him.

"My turn," she said. "Don't move. I want you right there." She edged forward, straddled his spread legs, and then positioned herself over his lance. Holding it, she lowered herself on the stiff tool.

Spur growled and she moaned softly as flesh penetrated flesh until they were joined pelvis against pelvis.

"Now *that* is wild fucking!" Sue said. She lifted up and dropped down and lifted and dropped. Each time his penis slid across her clit it brought a shriek of delight from her.

"Yes, yes! More, more!" she said. She took his hands and put them on her breasts, then gyrated and bounced until she climaxed again. This time she fell forward on Spur and he held her as she went rigid again, as spasm after spasm shook her body and left her weak and drained.

Spur lifted her off and lay her on the bed. He still

had an erection. Eugenia bent over him.

"Poor darling, you didn't get your turn." She went down on him with her mouth and gently played with his balls as she mouthed him until he couldn't stand it any more and shot his seed into her willing mouth. She swallowed time after time, and then he sank back on the bed, spent and satisfied.

Later they had more wine and cheese. Before long, the wine was gone, but Eugenia brought out two more bottles. "I wanted to be sure you have plenty," she said.

"I hope you ladies can stay all night," Spur said. They both nodded.

"Good. Wake me up later. I need a nap." He fell on the bed and went to sleep at once.

They woke him up twice during the night, and each time they all sampled each other. By morning all three were so exhausted that they slept until noon.

Spur got up and dressed quietly. Sue looked up once but he kissed her eyes closed and she slept again.

When Spur got to the sheriff's office, he could tell they had been waiting for him. He took out the box of twenties he had brought from his room.

"I think this is the last of them, Sheriff. I suggest you save three of them and mount them in a picture frame under glass as a good example of expert forgery. You can also put one counterfeit under glass for each of the banks in town. Most of them wouldn't know a counterfeit if it had a sign on it!"

They used a woodburning heater in the back room of the office, and spent three hours burning up the fake money.

"Now you can tell your friends that you burned up a million dollars," Spur said to the deputy who helped him. He had the deputy and the sheriff sign a statement that every bill except six being held under display glass had been burned and totally destroyed.

"There probably are a few more around in circulation, Sheriff," Spur said. "Whoever has them will just have to take the loss. You might talk to Mrs. Hoffer. She might stand the loss, or you could take whatever the loss is out of the assets of the newspaper office and equipment. That press is a valuable piece of goods."

They talked a while, then Spur started back to the hotel. He was going to have to think about moving out to Pocatello and then down toward Salt Lake City. He'd wait for the stage; maybe a few days here in Idaho would get his throat healed up. He changed directions and walked to Doc Rawson's office. The medic scowled and scolded him for the rough treatment he had given the rope burn on his neck. The doctor bandaged it and told him to come back in two days.

Spur grinned. Doctor's orders! He had to stay for at least two more days. He hurried to his hotel room, wondering what new delight his two roommates might have thought up.

On the way, he bought a dozen bottles of cold beer, six kinds of cheeses, and a whole sack full of crackers. It wouldn't do to run out of food. Between the three of them, they had plenty of everything else.

BUCKSKIN

The hard-riding,
hard-bitten Adult Western series
that's hotter'n a blazing pistol
and as tough as the men
who tamed the frontier.

#12: RECOIL by Roy LeBeau $2.50US/$2.95CAN
_____2355-5

#11: TRIGGER GUARD by Roy LeBeau
_____2336-9 $2.50US/$2.95CAN

#10: BOLT ACTION by Roy LeBeau
_____2315-6 $2.50US/$2.95CAN

#8: HANGFIRE HILL by Roy LeBeau
_____2271-0 $2.50US/$2.95CAN

#5: GUNSIGHT GAP by Roy LeBeau
_____2189-7 $2.75US/$2.95CAN

SPUR

The wildest, sexiest and most daring
Adult Western series around.
Join Spur McCoy as he fights for
truth, justice and every woman he can
lay his hands on!

_____2608-2 DOUBLE: GOLD TRAIN TRAMP/RED ROCK
              REDHEAD $3.95 US/$4.95 CAN

_____2597-3 SPUR #25: LARAMIE LOVERS
                                 $2.95 US/$3.95 CAN

_____2575-2 SPUR #24: DODGE CITY DOLL
                                 $2.95 US/$3.95 CAN

_____2519-1 SPUR #23: SAN DIEGO SIRENS
                                 $2.95 US/$3.95 CAN

_____2496-9 SPUR #22: DAKOTA DOXY
                                 $2.50 US/$3.25 CAN

_____2475-6 SPUR #21: TEXAS TART
                                 $2.50 US/$3.25 CAN

_____2453-5 SPUR #20: COLORADO CUTIE
                                 $2.50 US/$3.25 CAN

_____2409-8 SPUR #18: MISSOURI MADAM
                                 $2.50 US/$3.25 CAN

LEISURE BOOKS
ATTN: Customer Service Dept.
276 5th Avenue, New York, NY 10001

Please send me the book(s) checked above. I have enclosed $_____
Add $1.25 for shipping and handling for the first book; $ .30 for each book
thereafter. No cash, stamps, or C.O.D.s. All orders shipped within 6 weeks.
Canadian orders please add $1.00 extra postage.

Name _____

Address _____

City_____ State_____ Zip_____

Canadian orders must be paid in U.S. dollars payable through a New York bank-
ing facility.   ☐ Please send a free catalogue.